Terra Tempo

Ice Age Cataclysm!

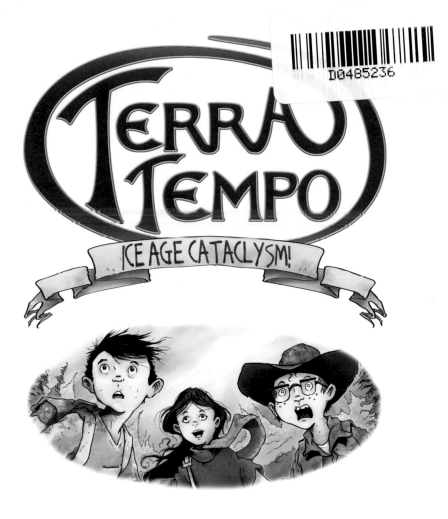

Written by David Shapiro

Illustrated by Christopher Herndon

Color by Erica Melville

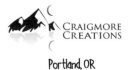

Craigmore Creations

Portland, OR

For The Educators -DRS
For Mom, Dad & Amber -CMH
For Mom, Dad, Rach & Ben -ETM

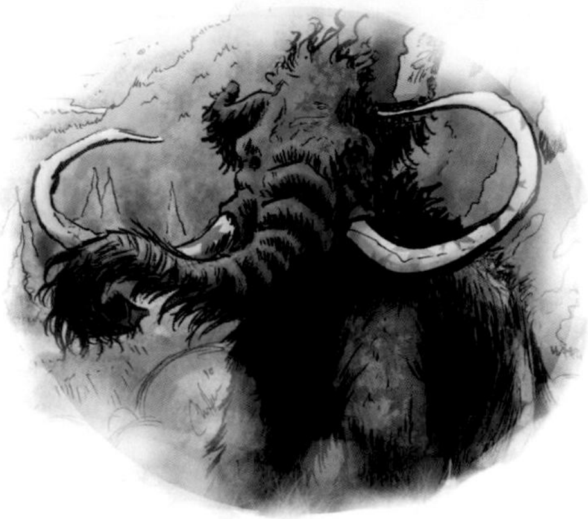

Special Thanks to:
Scott Burns, Mark Buser, Johnny Dwork,
Mary Kole, Greg McDonald, Monica Rollin,
Emily Trinkaus, Michelle Tuffias

Very Special Thanks to Glen Stockton

 First edition October 2010.
Printed in the United States of America
17 16 15 14 13 12 2 3 4 5 6

Library of Congress Catalog Number 2010935557
ISBN-13 978-0-9844422-1-8
ISBN-10 0-9844422-1-9

www.iceagecataclysm.com
www.craigmorecreations.com

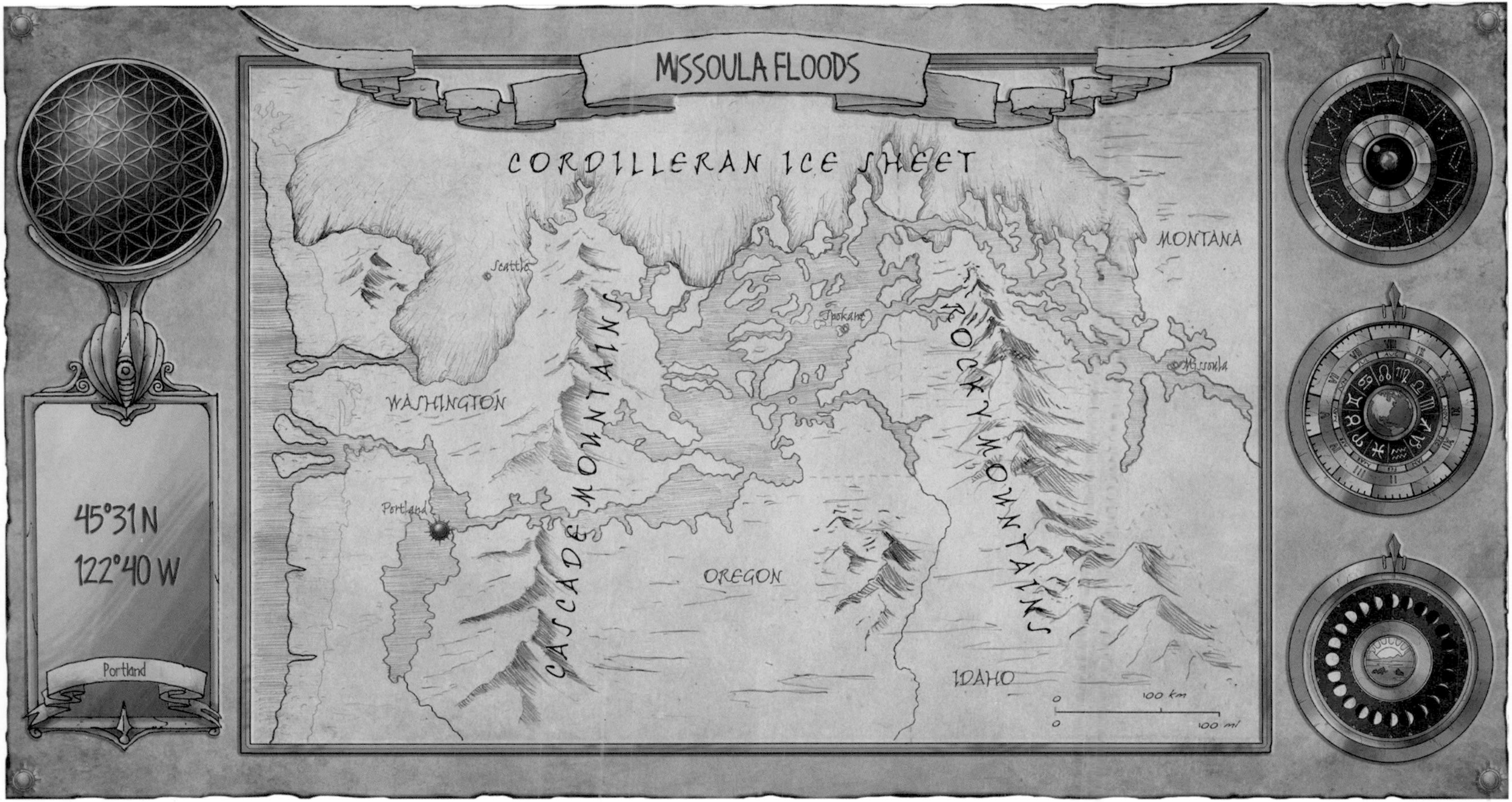
MISSOULA FLOODS
CORDILLERAN ICE SHEET
MONTANA
Seattle
Spokane
Missoula
WASHINGTON
CASCADE MOUNTAINS
ROCKY MOUNTAINS
Portland
OREGON
IDAHO
0
100 km
0
100 mi
45°31 N
122°40 W
Portland

CHAPTER ONE

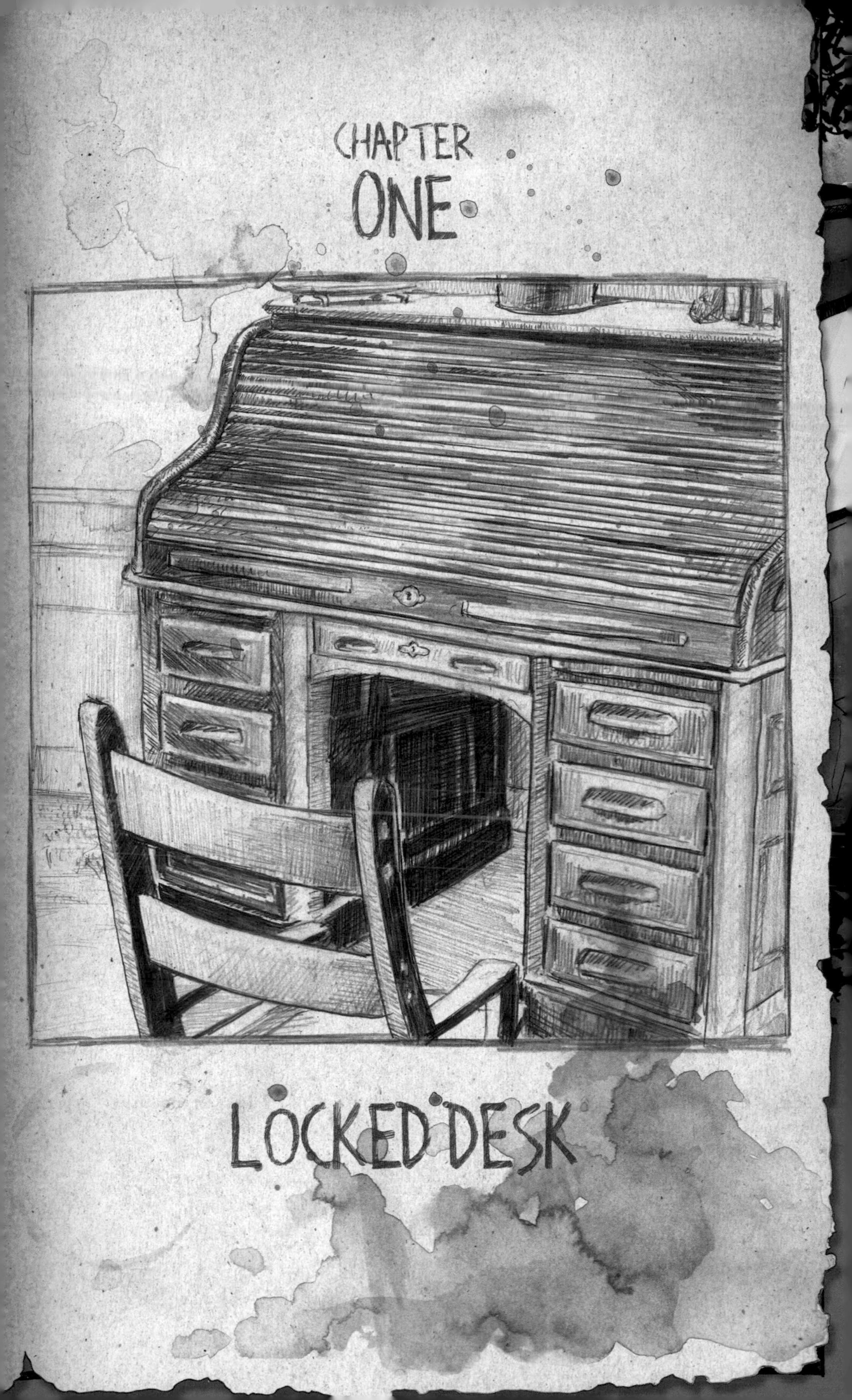

LOCKED DESK

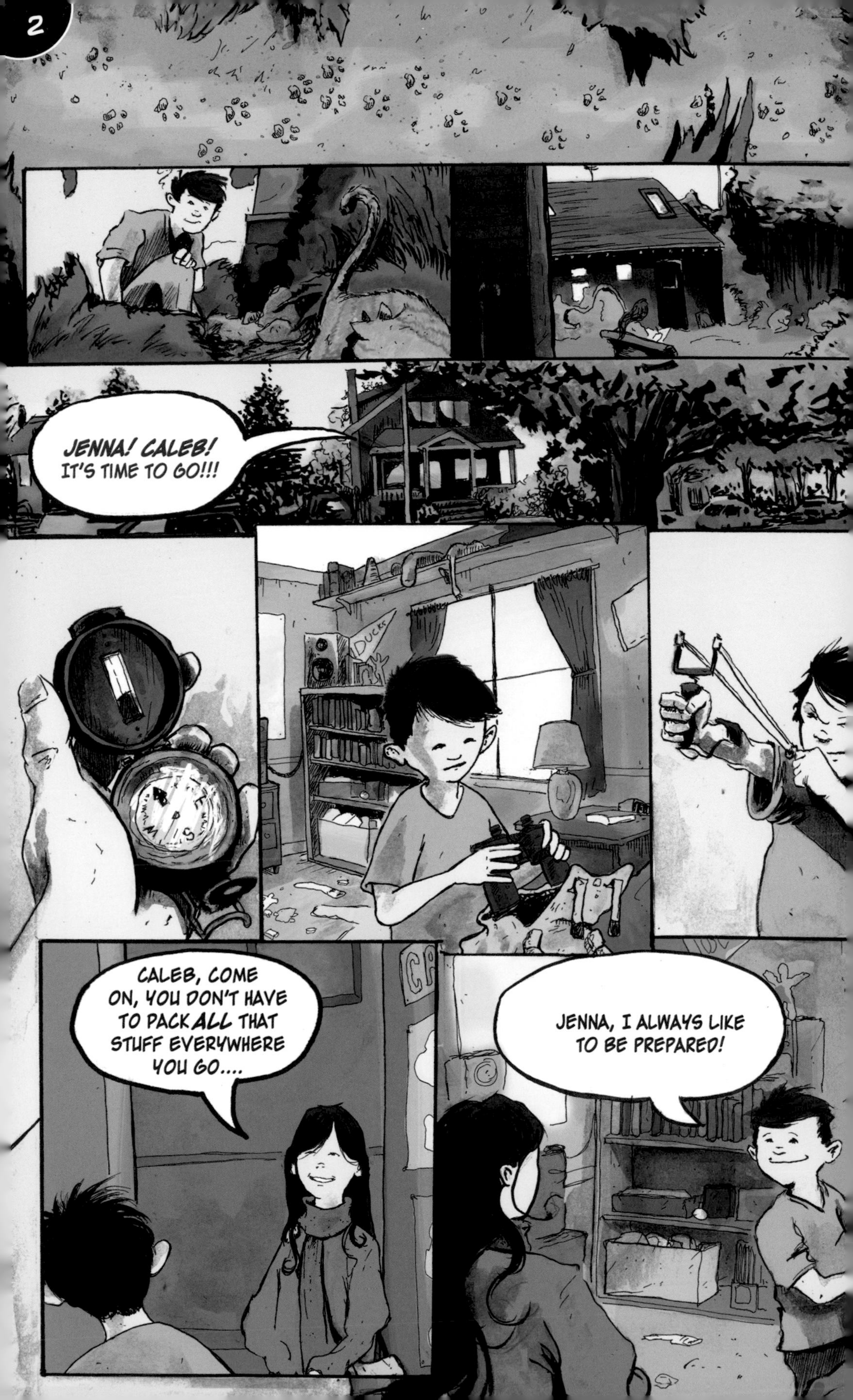
JENNA! CALEB! IT'S TIME TO GO!!!
DUCKS
CALEB, COME ON, YOU DON'T HAVE TO PACK ALL THAT STUFF EVERYWHERE YOU GO....
JENNA, I ALWAYS LIKE TO BE PREPARED!

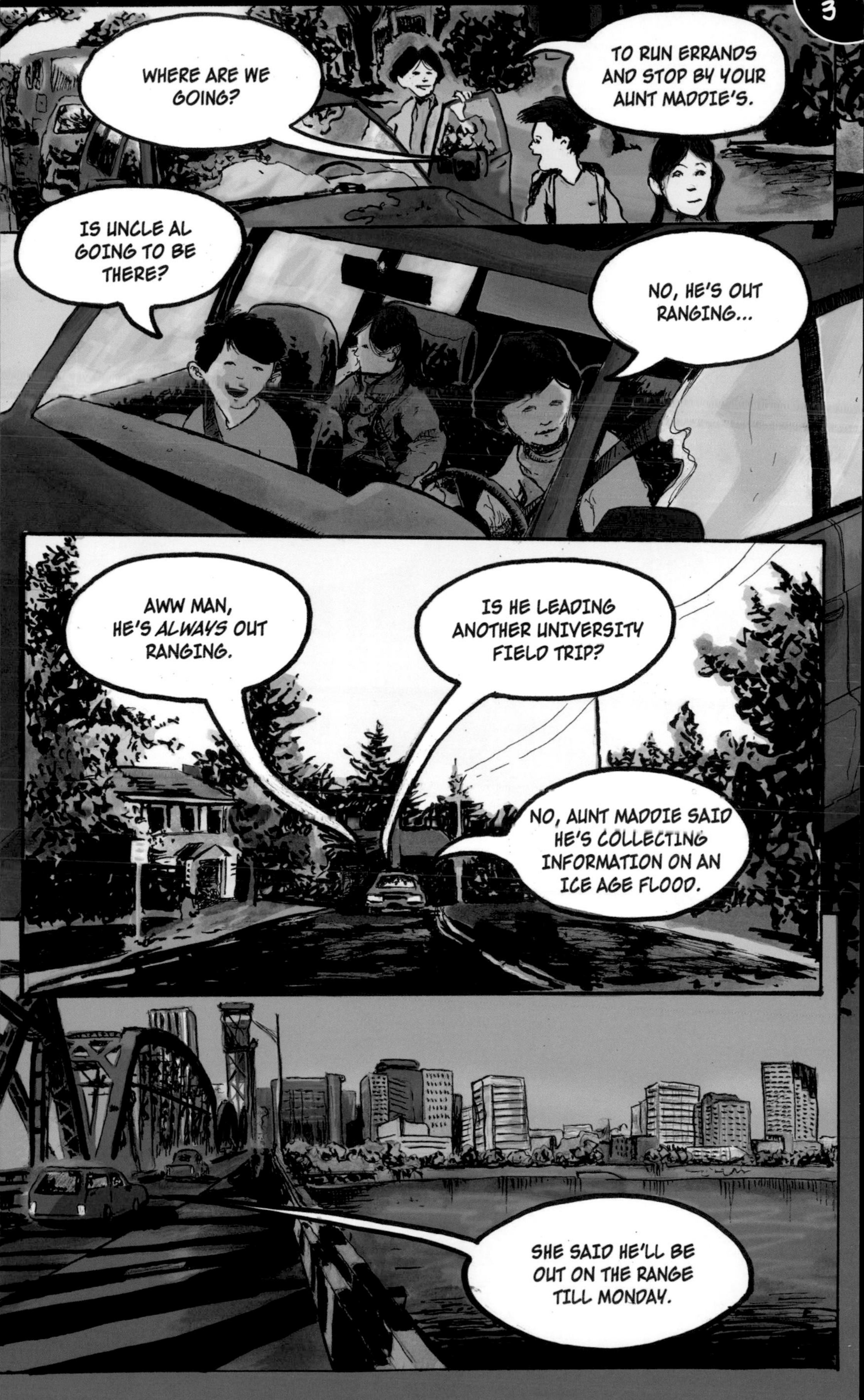
WHERE ARE WE GOING?
TO RUN ERRANDS AND STOP BY YOUR AUNT MADDIE'S.
IS UNCLE AL GOING TO BE THERE?
NO, HE'S OUT RANGING...
AWW MAN, HE'S *ALWAYS* OUT RANGING.
IS HE LEADING ANOTHER UNIVERSITY FIELD TRIP?
NO, AUNT MADDIE SAID HE'S COLLECTING INFORMATION ON AN ICE AGE FLOOD.
SHE SAID HE'LL BE OUT ON THE RANGE TILL MONDAY.

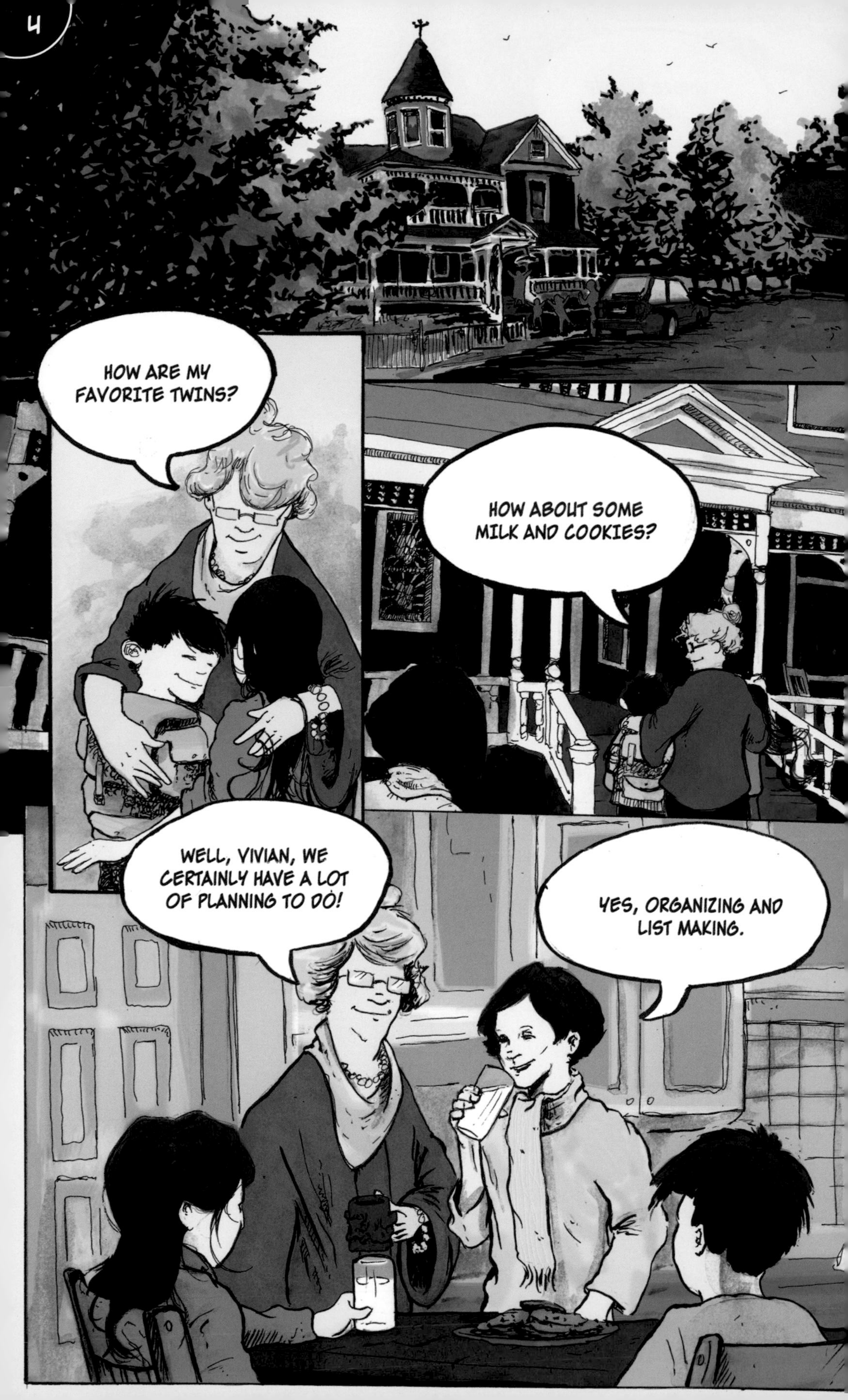
HOW ARE MY FAVORITE TWINS?
HOW ABOUT SOME MILK AND COOKIES?
WELL, VIVIAN, WE CERTAINLY HAVE A LOT OF PLANNING TO DO!
YES, ORGANIZING AND LIST MAKING.

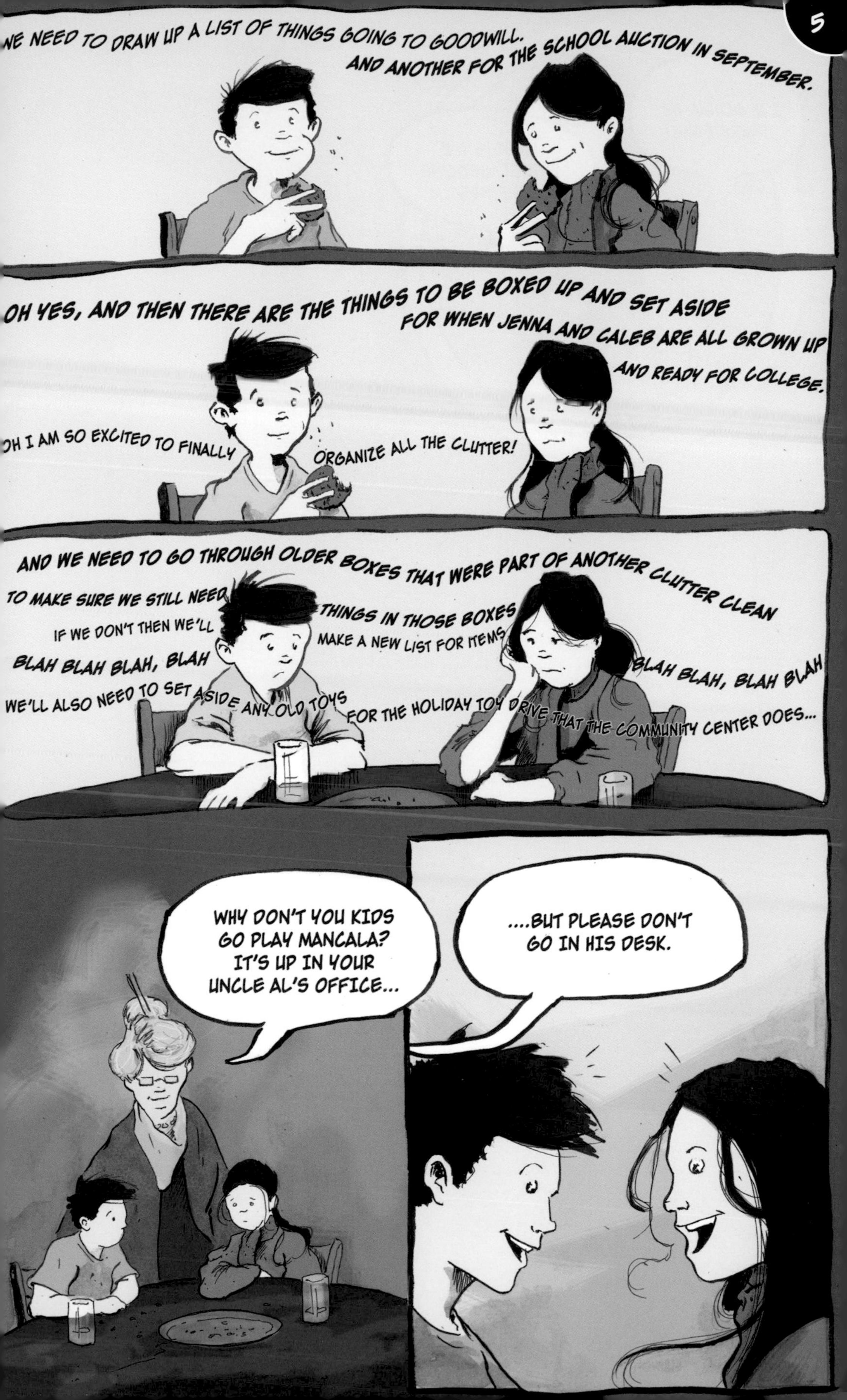
WE NEED TO DRAW UP A LIST OF THINGS GOING TO GOODWILL.
AND ANOTHER FOR THE SCHOOL AUCTION IN SEPTEMBER.
OH YES, AND THEN THERE ARE THE THINGS TO BE BOXED UP AND SET ASIDE
FOR WHEN JENNA AND CALEB ARE ALL GROWN UP
AND READY FOR COLLEGE.
OH I AM SO EXCITED TO FINALLY
ORGANIZE ALL THE CLUTTER!
AND WE NEED TO GO THROUGH OLDER BOXES THAT WERE PART OF ANOTHER CLUTTER CLEAN
TO MAKE SURE WE STILL NEED
THINGS IN THOSE BOXES
IF WE DON'T THEN WE'LL
MAKE A NEW LIST FOR ITEMS
BLAH BLAH BLAH, BLAH
BLAH BLAH, BLAH BLAH
WE'LL ALSO NEED TO SET ASIDE ANY OLD TOYS
FOR THE HOLIDAY TOY DRIVE THAT THE COMMUNITY CENTER DOES...
WHY DON'T YOU KIDS GO PLAY MANCALA? IT'S UP IN YOUR UNCLE AL'S OFFICE...
....BUT PLEASE DON'T GO IN HIS DESK.

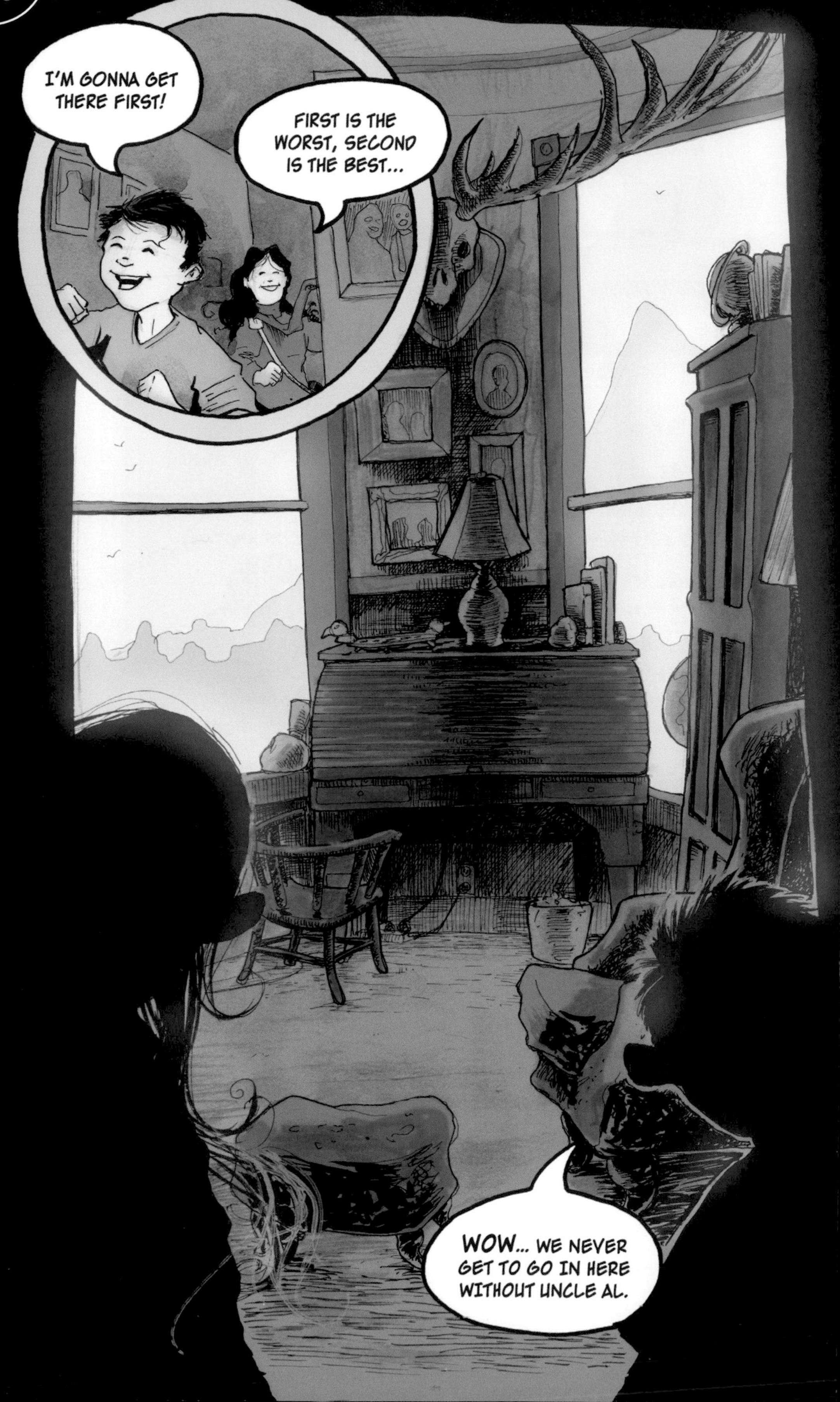
I'M GONNA GET THERE FIRST!
FIRST IS THE WORST, SECOND IS THE BEST...
WOW... WE NEVER GET TO GO IN HERE WITHOUT UNCLE AL.

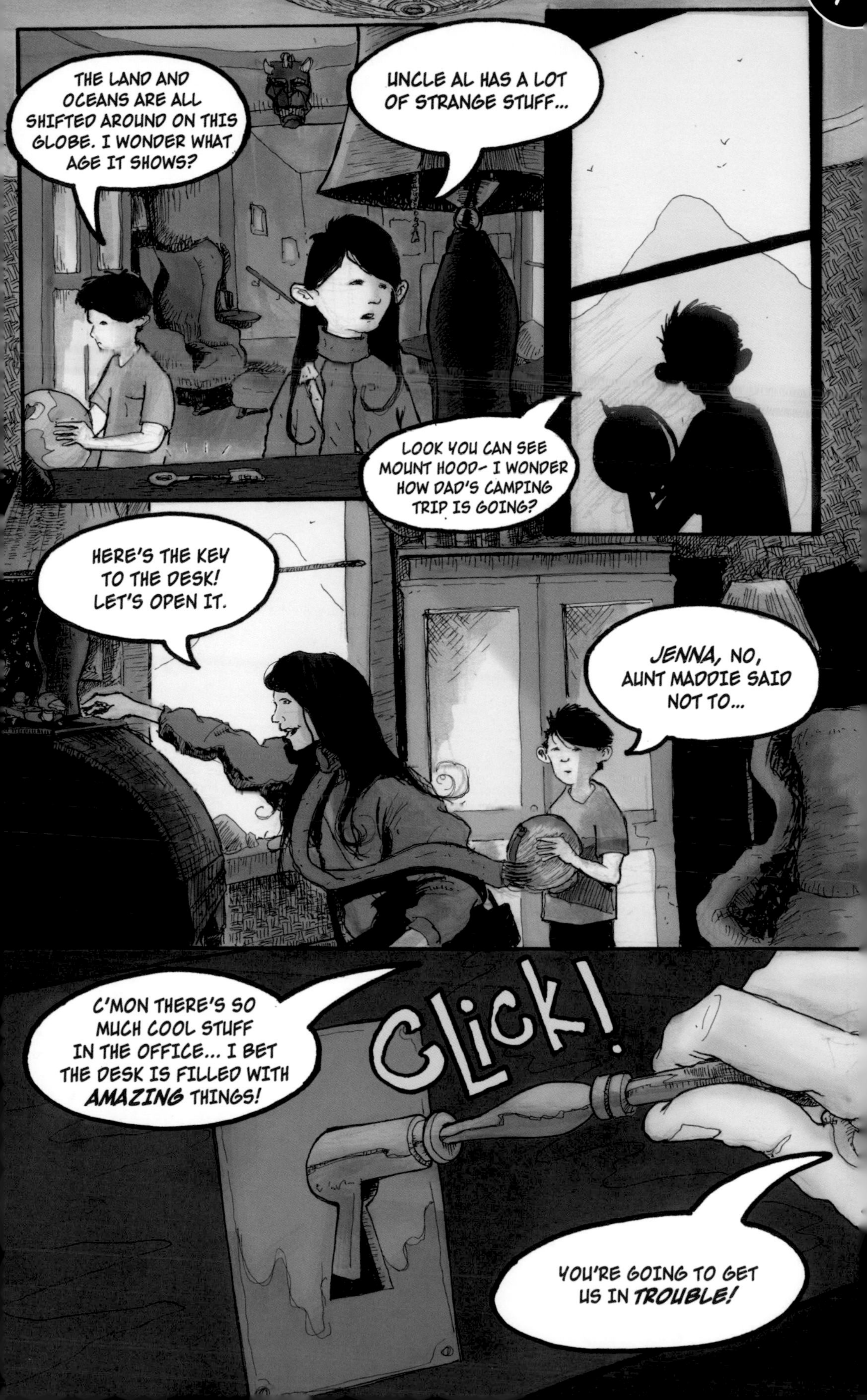
THE LAND AND OCEANS ARE ALL SHIFTED AROUND ON THIS GLOBE. I WONDER WHAT AGE IT SHOWS?
UNCLE AL HAS A LOT OF STRANGE STUFF...
LOOK YOU CAN SEE MOUNT HOOD- I WONDER HOW DAD'S CAMPING TRIP IS GOING?
HERE'S THE KEY TO THE DESK! LET'S OPEN IT.
JENNA, NO, AUNT MADDIE SAID NOT TO...
C'MON THERE'S SO MUCH COOL STUFF IN THE OFFICE... I BET THE DESK IS FILLED WITH AMAZING THINGS!
CLICK!
YOU'RE GOING TO GET US IN TROUBLE!

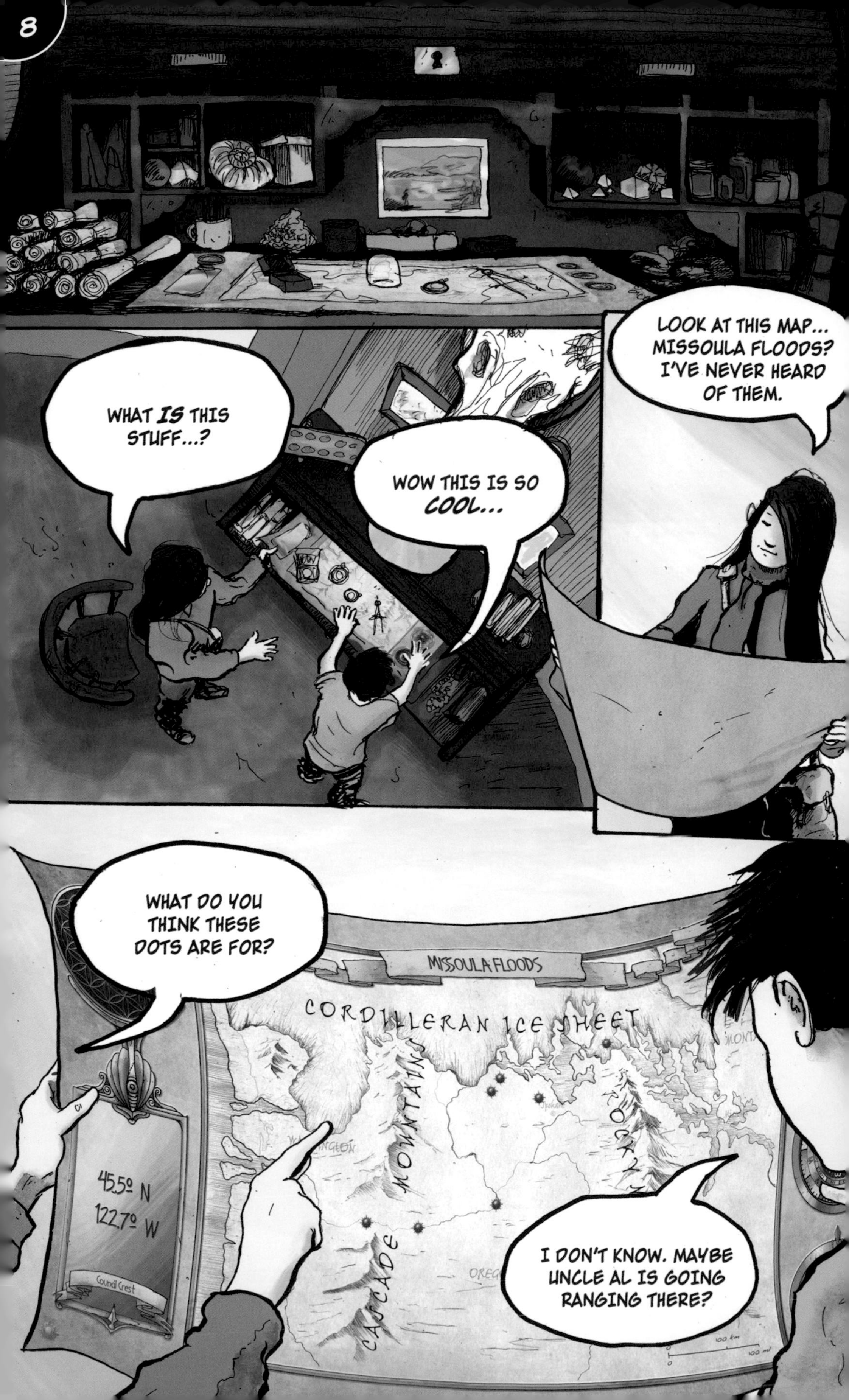
WHAT IS THIS STUFF...?
WOW THIS IS SO COOL...
LOOK AT THIS MAP... MISSOULA FLOODS? I'VE NEVER HEARD OF THEM.
WHAT DO YOU THINK THESE DOTS ARE FOR?
MISSOULA FLOODS
CORDILLERAN ICE SHEET
CASCADE MOUNTAINS
45.5º N
122.7º W
Council Crest
I DON'T KNOW. MAYBE UNCLE AL IS GOING RANGING THERE?

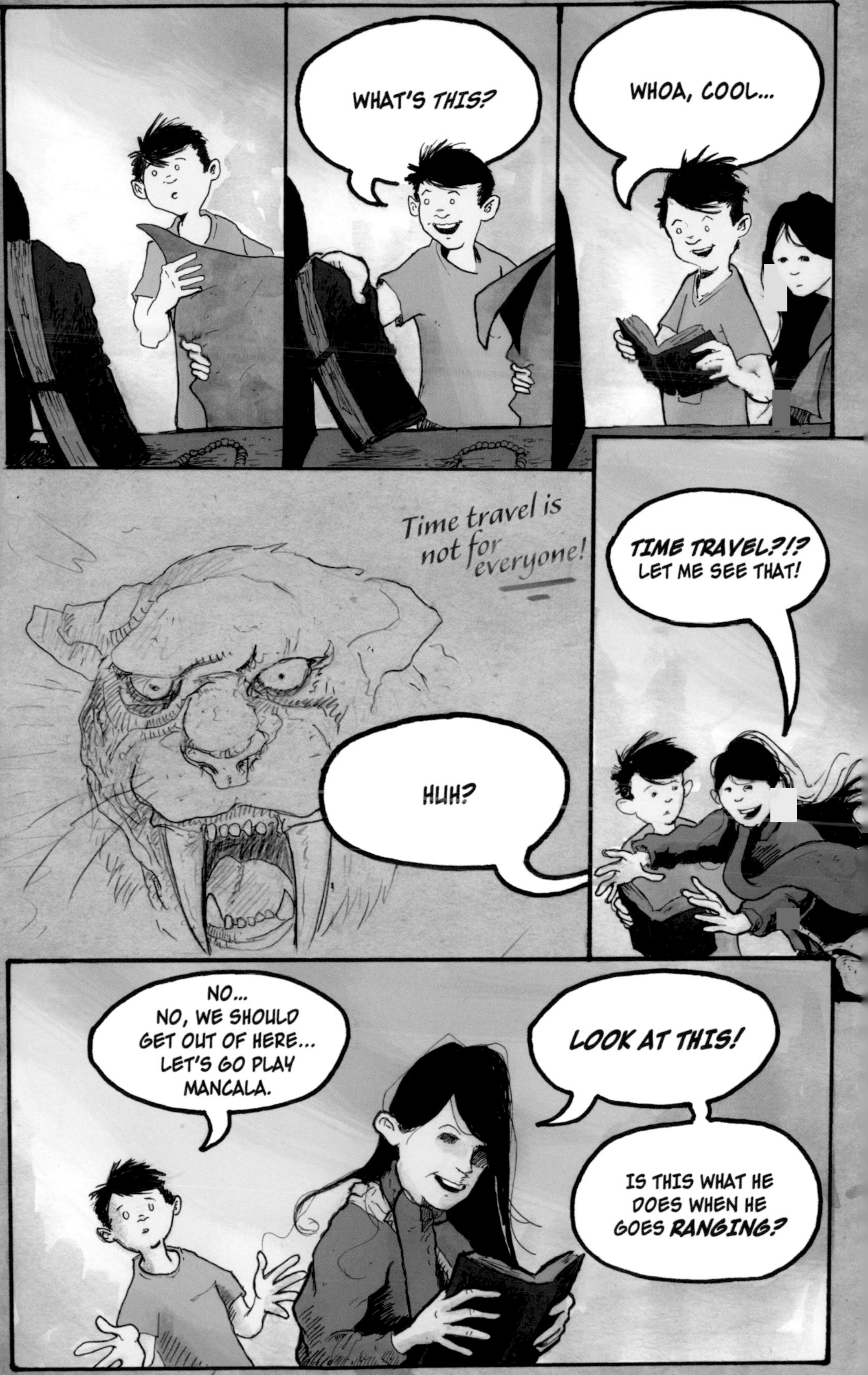
WHAT'S THIS?
WHOA, COOL...
Time travel is not for everyone!
TIME TRAVEL?!? LET ME SEE THAT!
HUH?
NO... NO, WE SHOULD GET OUT OF HERE... LET'S GO PLAY MANCALA.
LOOK AT THIS!
IS THIS WHAT HE DOES WHEN HE GOES RANGING?

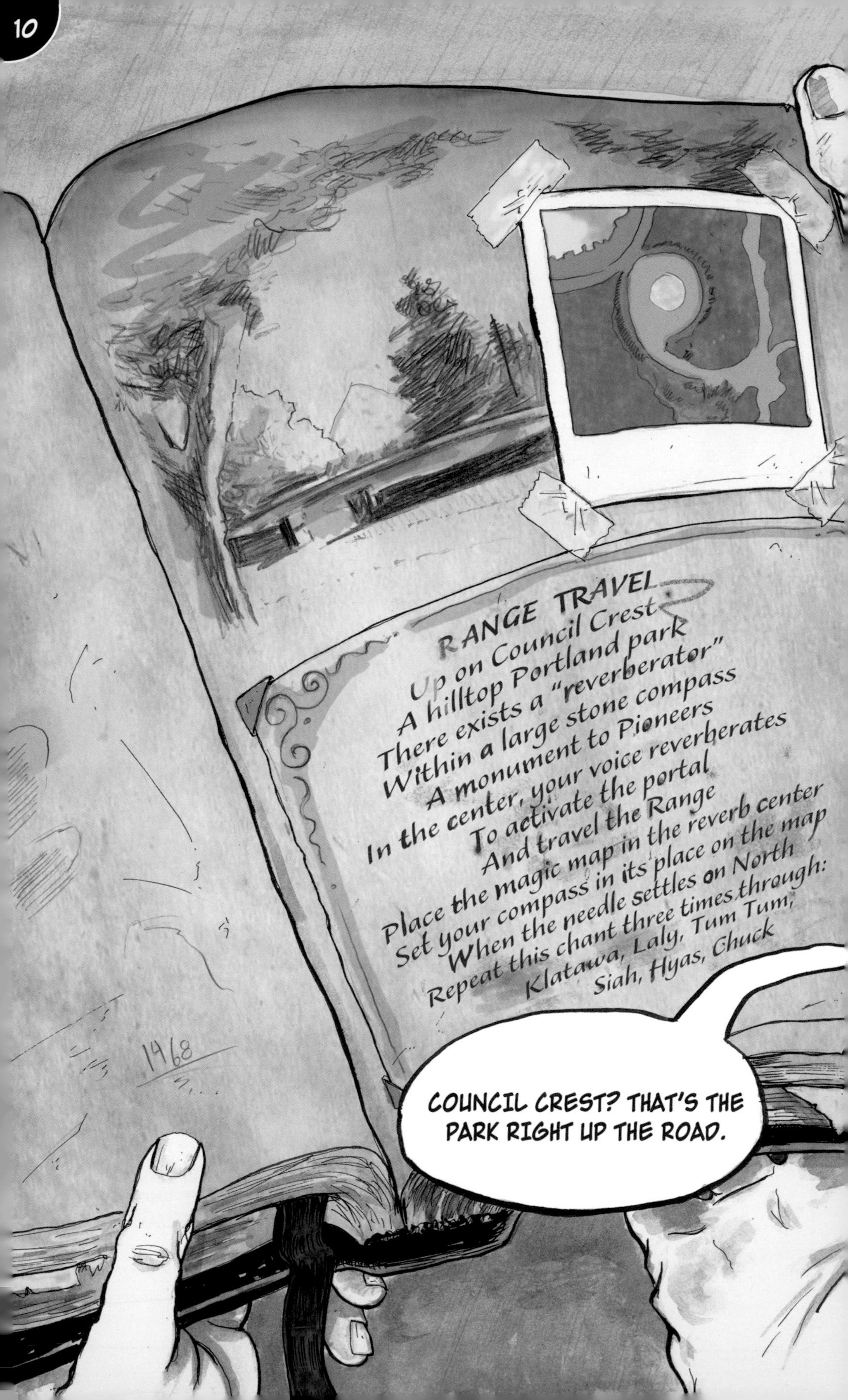
RANGE TRAVEL
Up on Council Crest
A hilltop Portland park
There exists a "reverberator"
Within a large stone compass
A monument to Pioneers
In the center, your voice reverberates
To activate the portal
And travel the Range
Place the magic map in the reverb center
Set your compass in its place on the map
When the needle settles on North
Repeat this chant three times through:
Klatawa, Laly, Tum Tum,
Siah, Hyas, Chuck
1968
COUNCIL CREST? THAT'S THE PARK RIGHT UP THE ROAD.

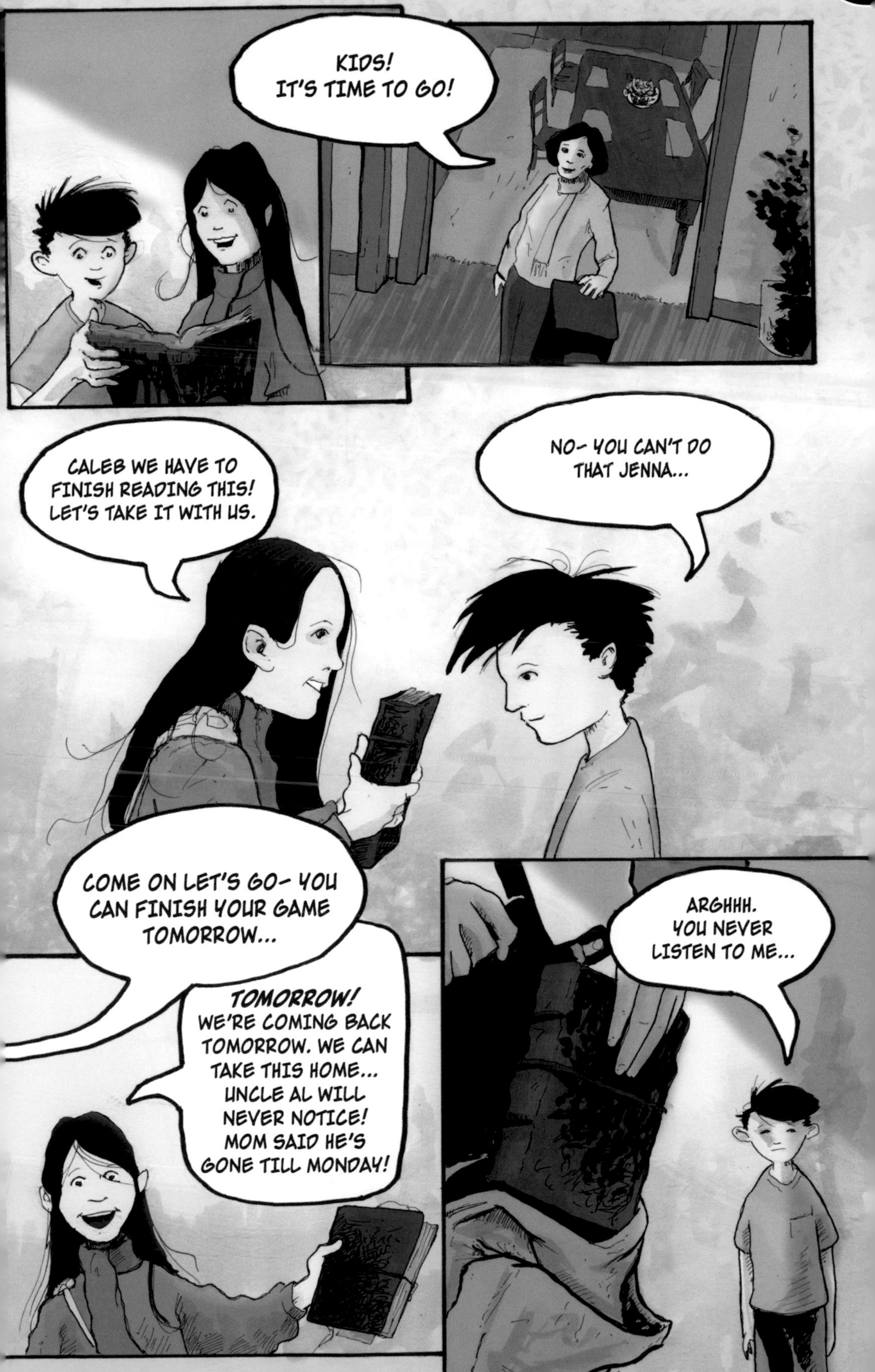
KIDS!
IT'S TIME TO GO!
CALEB WE HAVE TO FINISH READING THIS! LET'S TAKE IT WITH US.
NO- YOU CAN'T DO THAT JENNA...
COME ON LET'S GO- YOU CAN FINISH YOUR GAME TOMORROW...
TOMORROW! WE'RE COMING BACK TOMORROW. WE CAN TAKE THIS HOME... UNCLE AL WILL NEVER NOTICE! MOM SAID HE'S GONE TILL MONDAY!
ARGHHH. YOU NEVER LISTEN TO ME...

JENNA AND CALEB SPEND THE EVENING PORING OVER THE JOURNAL; LEARNING THE CHARTS; STUDYING THE DRAWINGS OF PREHISTORIC BEASTS AND LANDFORMS.

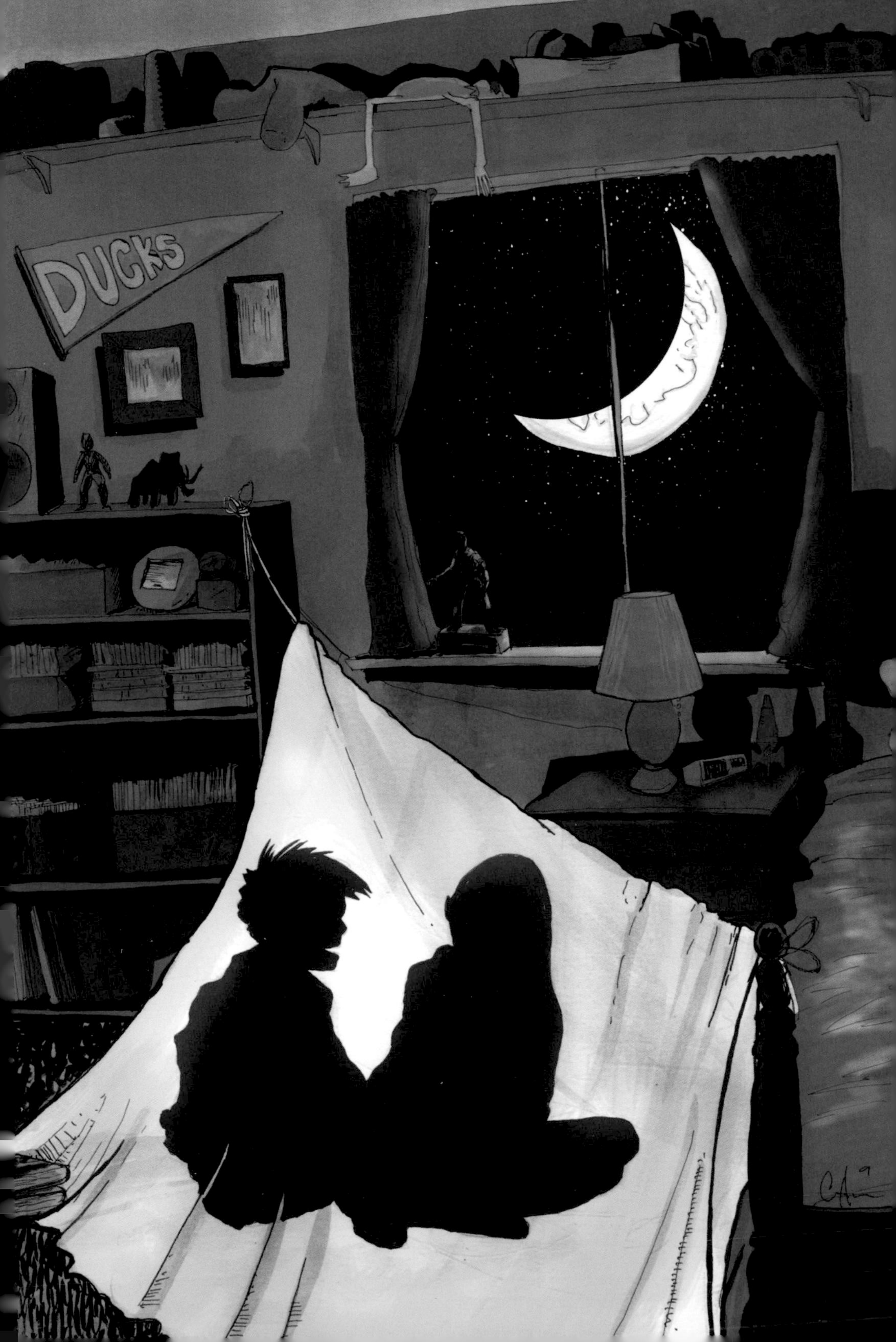
DUCKS

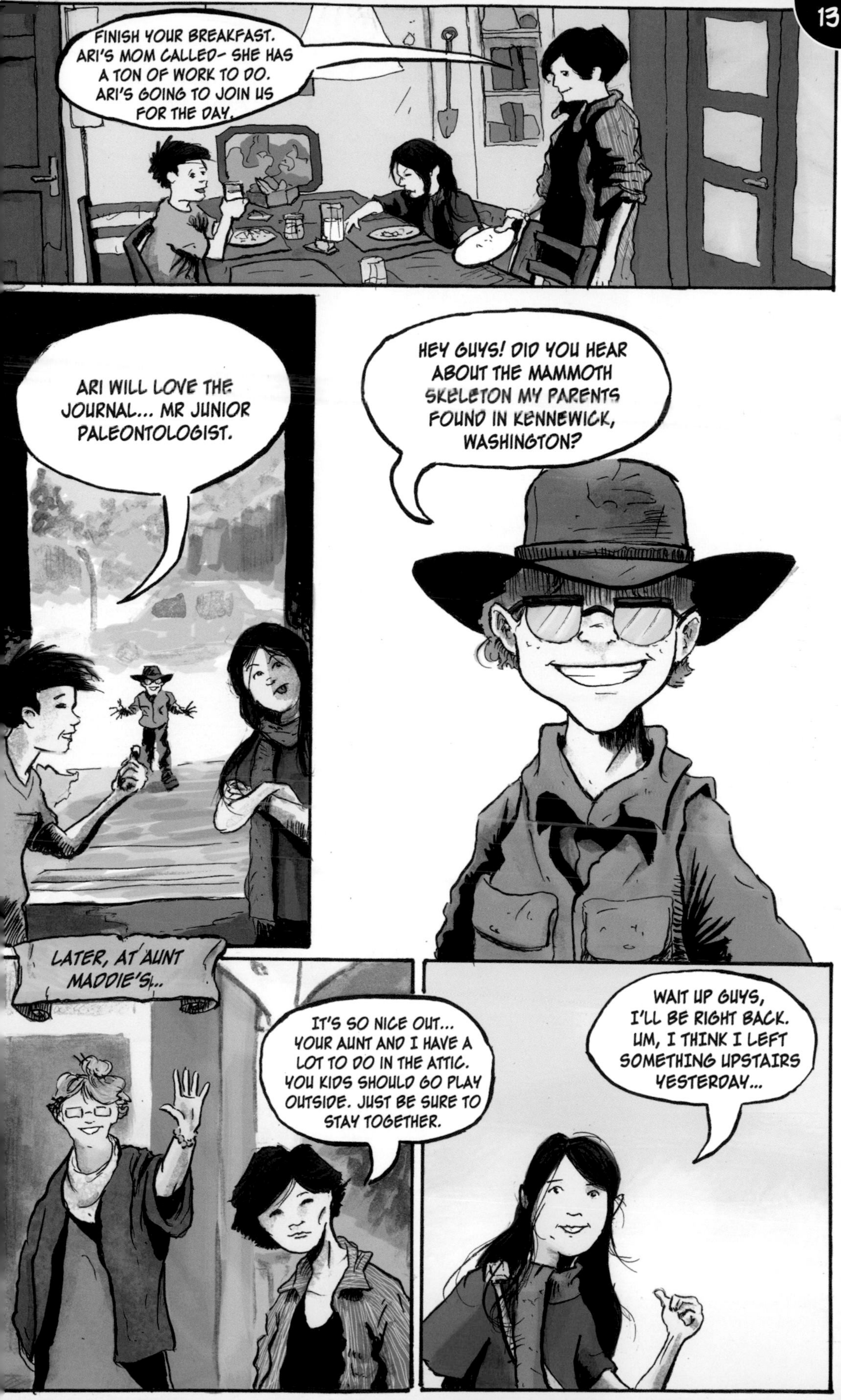
FINISH YOUR BREAKFAST. ARI'S MOM CALLED- SHE HAS A TON OF WORK TO DO. ARI'S GOING TO JOIN US FOR THE DAY.
ARI WILL LOVE THE JOURNAL... MR JUNIOR PALEONTOLOGIST.
HEY GUYS! DID YOU HEAR ABOUT THE MAMMOTH SKELETON MY PARENTS FOUND IN KENNEWICK, WASHINGTON?
LATER, AT AUNT MADDIE'S...
IT'S SO NICE OUT... YOUR AUNT AND I HAVE A LOT TO DO IN THE ATTIC. YOU KIDS SHOULD GO PLAY OUTSIDE. JUST BE SURE TO STAY TOGETHER.
WAIT UP GUYS, I'LL BE RIGHT BACK. UM, I THINK I LEFT SOMETHING UPSTAIRS YESTERDAY...

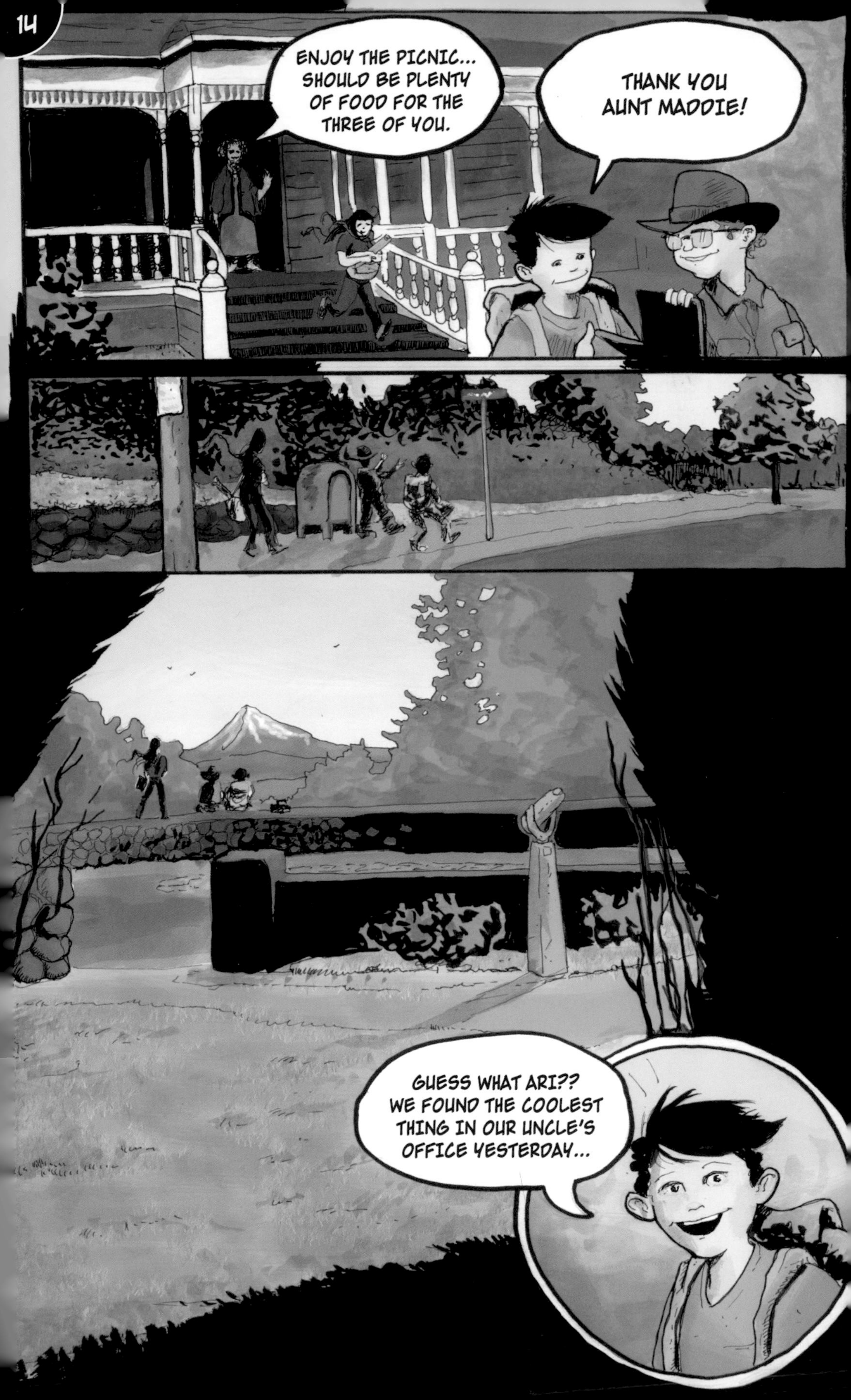
ENJOY THE PICNIC... SHOULD BE PLENTY OF FOOD FOR THE THREE OF YOU.
THANK YOU AUNT MADDIE!
GUESS WHAT ARI?? WE FOUND THE COOLEST THING IN OUR UNCLE'S OFFICE YESTERDAY...

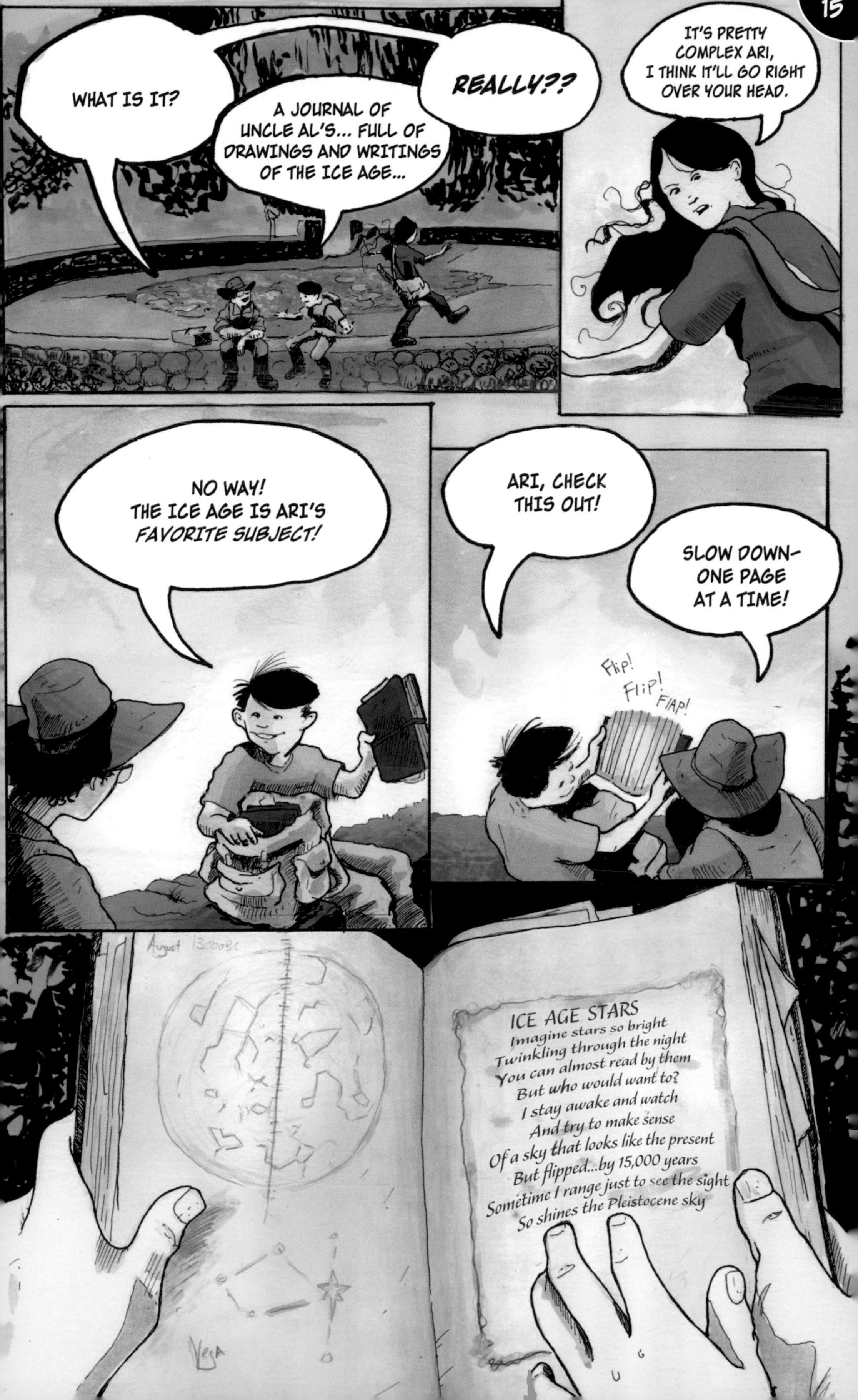
WHAT IS IT?
A JOURNAL OF UNCLE AL'S... FULL OF DRAWINGS AND WRITINGS OF THE ICE AGE...
REALLY??
IT'S PRETTY COMPLEX ARI, I THINK IT'LL GO RIGHT OVER YOUR HEAD.
NO WAY! THE ICE AGE IS ARI'S FAVORITE SUBJECT!
ARI, CHECK THIS OUT!
SLOW DOWN- ONE PAGE AT A TIME!
Flip! Flip! Flap!
August
Vega
ICE AGE STARS
Imagine stars so bright
Twinkling through the night
You can almost read by them
But who would want to?
I stay awake and watch
And try to make sense
Of a sky that looks like the present
But flipped...by 15,000 years
Sometime I range just to see the sight
So shines the Pleistocene sky

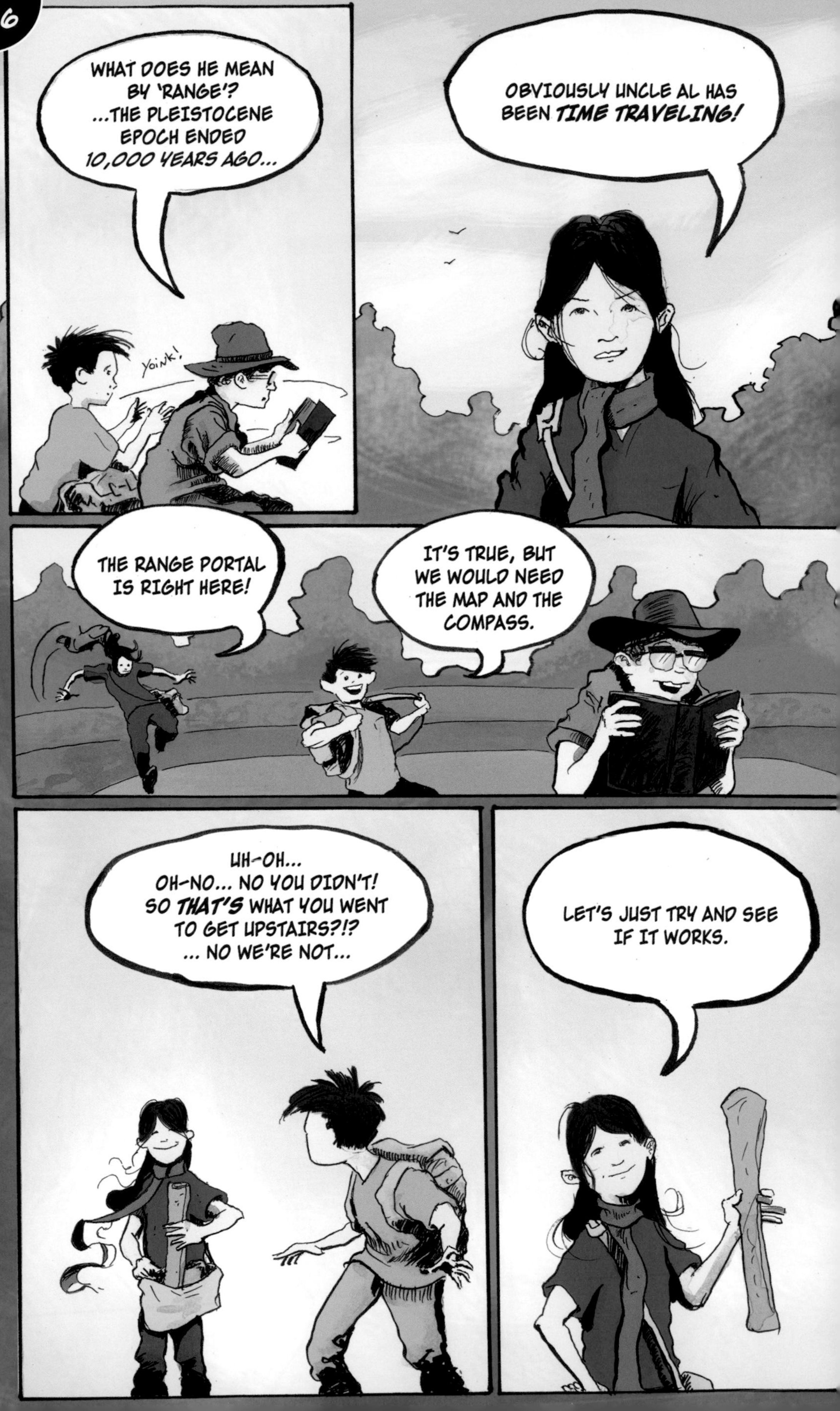
WHAT DOES HE MEAN BY 'RANGE'? ...THE PLEISTOCENE EPOCH ENDED 10,000 YEARS AGO...
YOINK!
OBVIOUSLY UNCLE AL HAS BEEN TIME TRAVELING!
THE RANGE PORTAL IS RIGHT HERE!
IT'S TRUE, BUT WE WOULD NEED THE MAP AND THE COMPASS.
UH-OH... OH-NO... NO YOU DIDN'T! SO THAT'S WHAT YOU WENT TO GET UPSTAIRS?!? ... NO WE'RE NOT...
LET'S JUST TRY AND SEE IF IT WORKS.

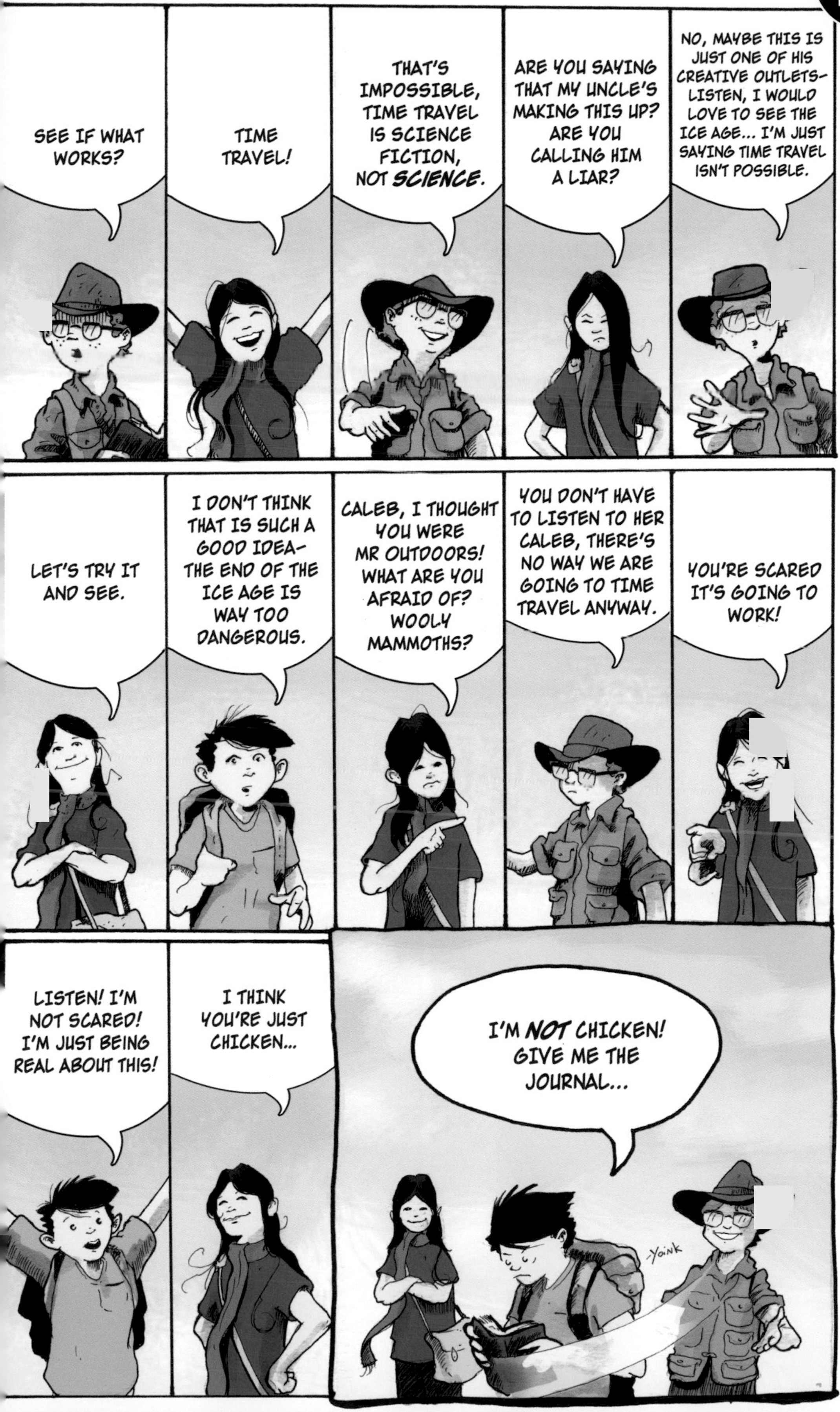
SEE IF WHAT WORKS?
TIME TRAVEL!
THAT'S IMPOSSIBLE, TIME TRAVEL IS SCIENCE FICTION, NOT *SCIENCE*.
ARE YOU SAYING THAT MY UNCLE'S MAKING THIS UP? ARE YOU CALLING HIM A LIAR?
NO, MAYBE THIS IS JUST ONE OF HIS CREATIVE OUTLETS- LISTEN, I WOULD LOVE TO SEE THE ICE AGE... I'M JUST SAYING TIME TRAVEL ISN'T POSSIBLE.
LET'S TRY IT AND SEE.
I DON'T THINK THAT IS SUCH A GOOD IDEA- THE END OF THE ICE AGE IS WAY TOO DANGEROUS.
CALEB, I THOUGHT YOU WERE MR OUTDOORS! WHAT ARE YOU AFRAID OF? WOOLY MAMMOTHS?
YOU DON'T HAVE TO LISTEN TO HER CALEB, THERE'S NO WAY WE ARE GOING TO TIME TRAVEL ANYWAY.
YOU'RE SCARED IT'S GOING TO WORK!
LISTEN! I'M NOT SCARED! I'M JUST BEING REAL ABOUT THIS!
I THINK YOU'RE JUST CHICKEN...
I'M *NOT* CHICKEN! GIVE ME THE JOURNAL...
-Yoink

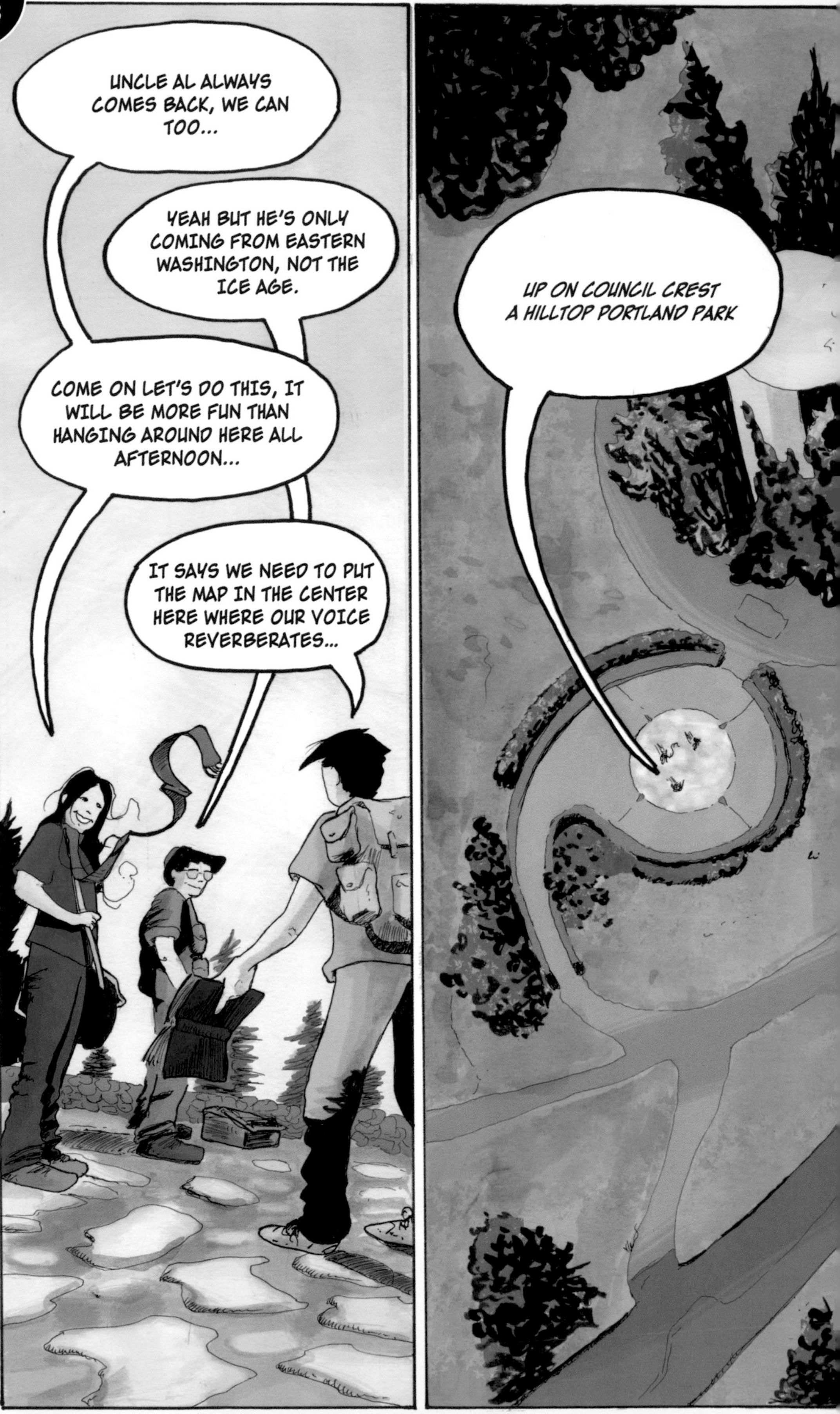
UNCLE AL ALWAYS COMES BACK, WE CAN TOO...
YEAH BUT HE'S ONLY COMING FROM EASTERN WASHINGTON, NOT THE ICE AGE.
COME ON LET'S DO THIS, IT WILL BE MORE FUN THAN HANGING AROUND HERE ALL AFTERNOON...
IT SAYS WE NEED TO PUT THE MAP IN THE CENTER HERE WHERE OUR VOICE REVERBERATES...
UP ON COUNCIL CREST A HILLTOP PORTLAND PARK

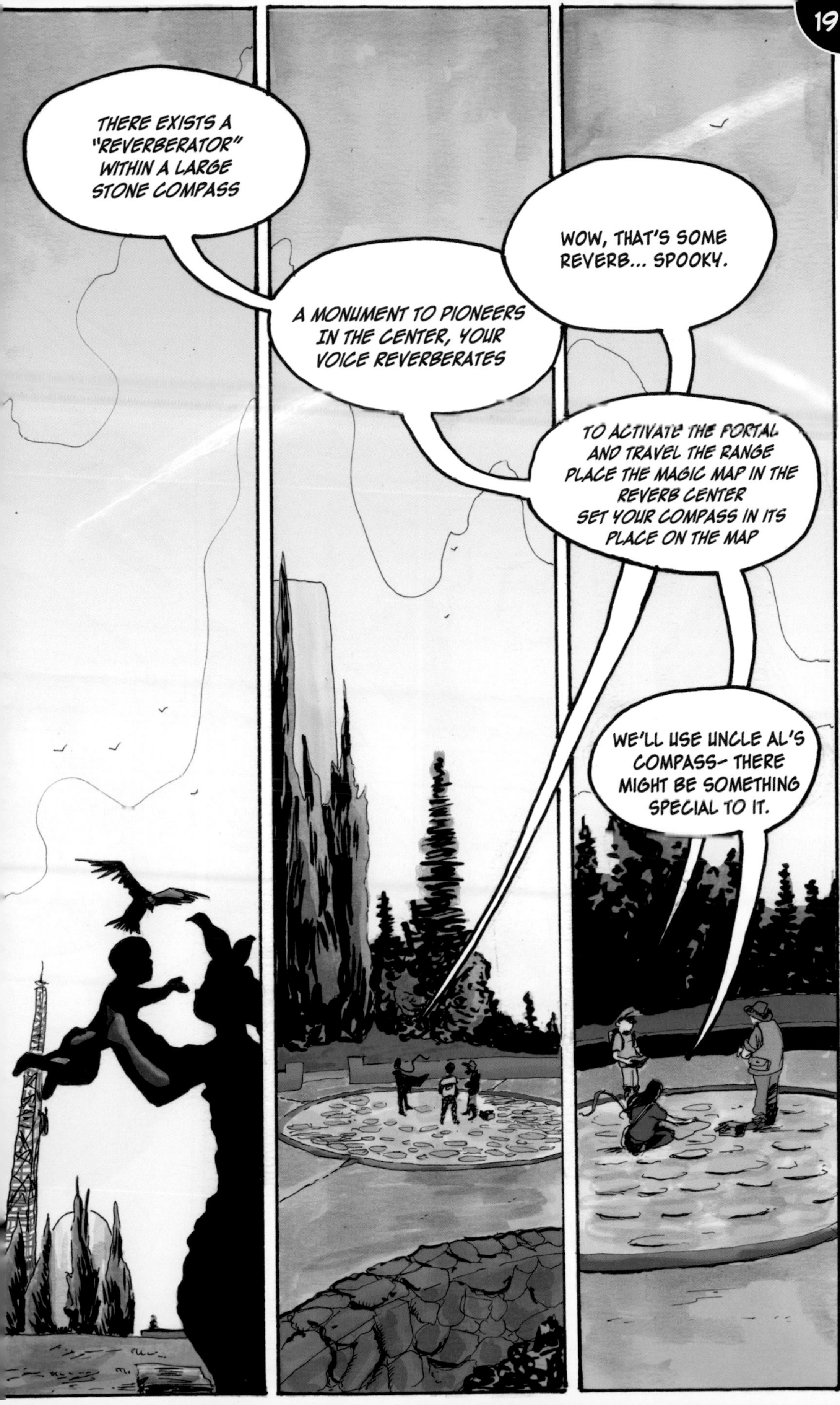
THERE EXISTS A "REVERBERATOR" WITHIN A LARGE STONE COMPASS
A MONUMENT TO PIONEERS IN THE CENTER, YOUR VOICE REVERBERATES
WOW, THAT'S SOME REVERB... SPOOKY.
TO ACTIVATE THE PORTAL AND TRAVEL THE RANGE PLACE THE MAGIC MAP IN THE REVERB CENTER SET YOUR COMPASS IN ITS PLACE ON THE MAP
WE'LL USE UNCLE AL'S COMPASS- THERE MIGHT BE SOMETHING SPECIAL TO IT.

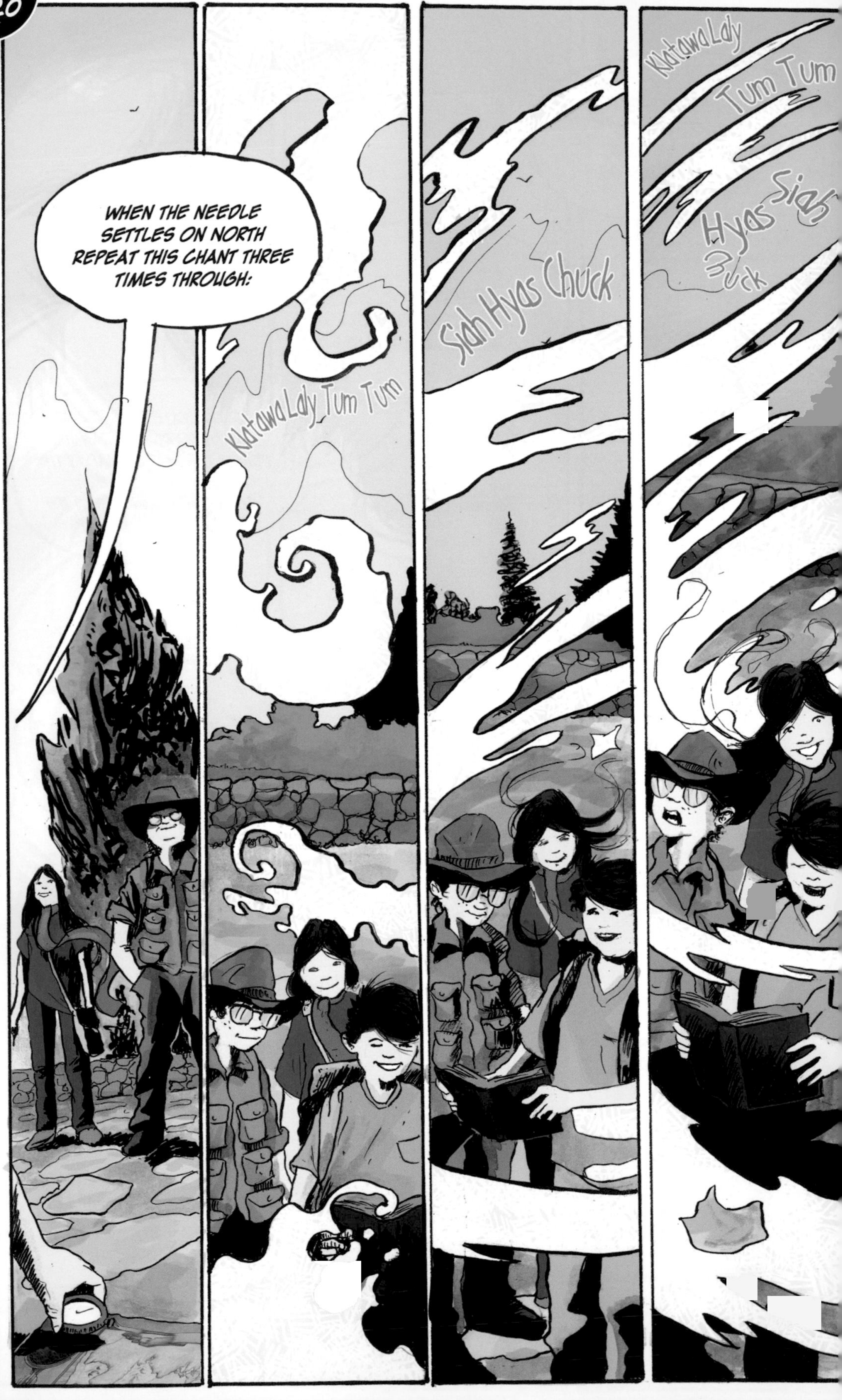
WHEN THE NEEDLE SETTLES ON NORTH REPEAT THIS CHANT THREE TIMES THROUGH:
Klatawa Lady Tum Tum
Siah Hyas Chuck
Klatawa Lady
Tum Tum
Hyas Siah
Chuck

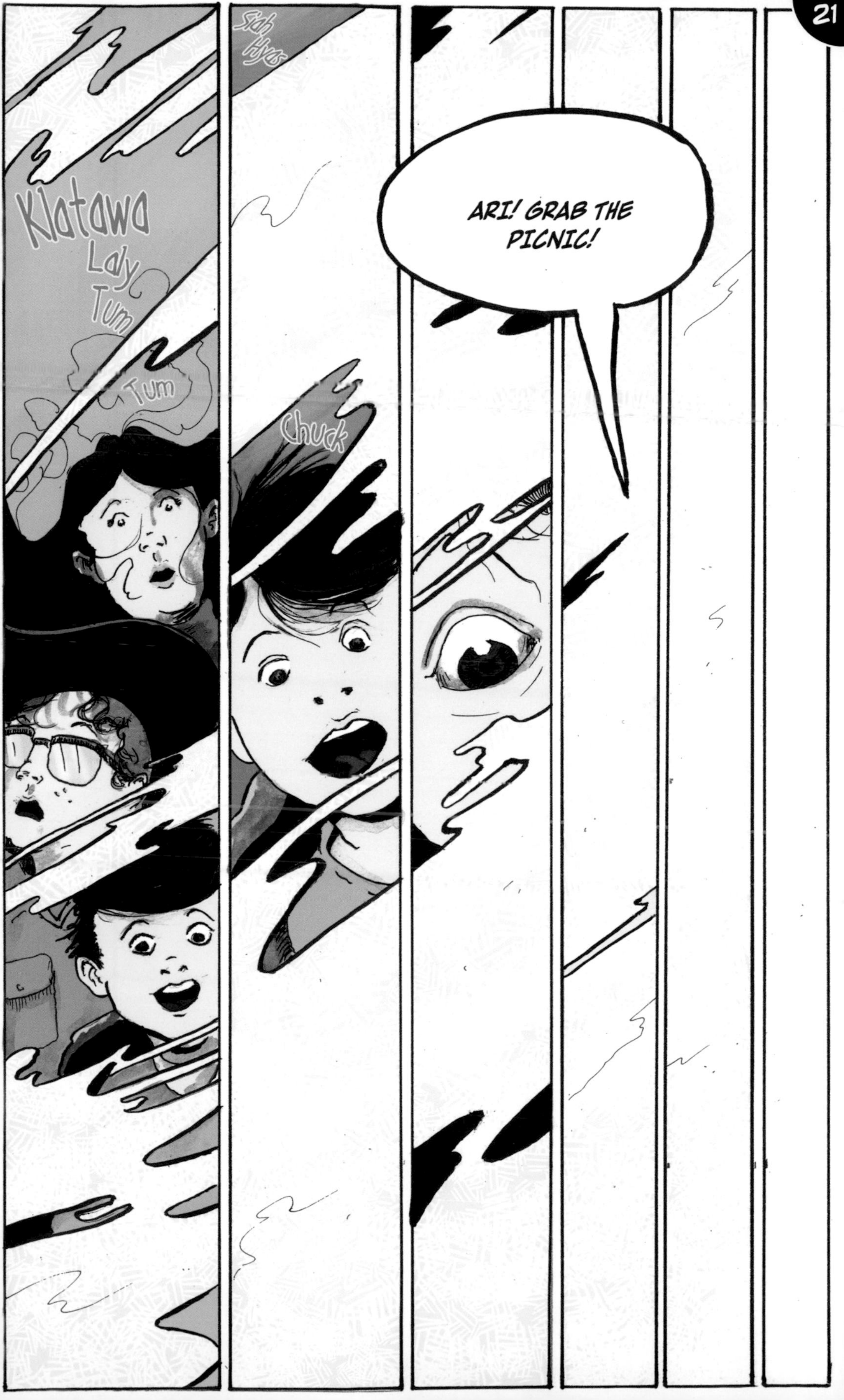
Klatawa
Laly
Tum
Tum
Siah Hyas
Chuck
ARI! GRAB THE PICNIC!

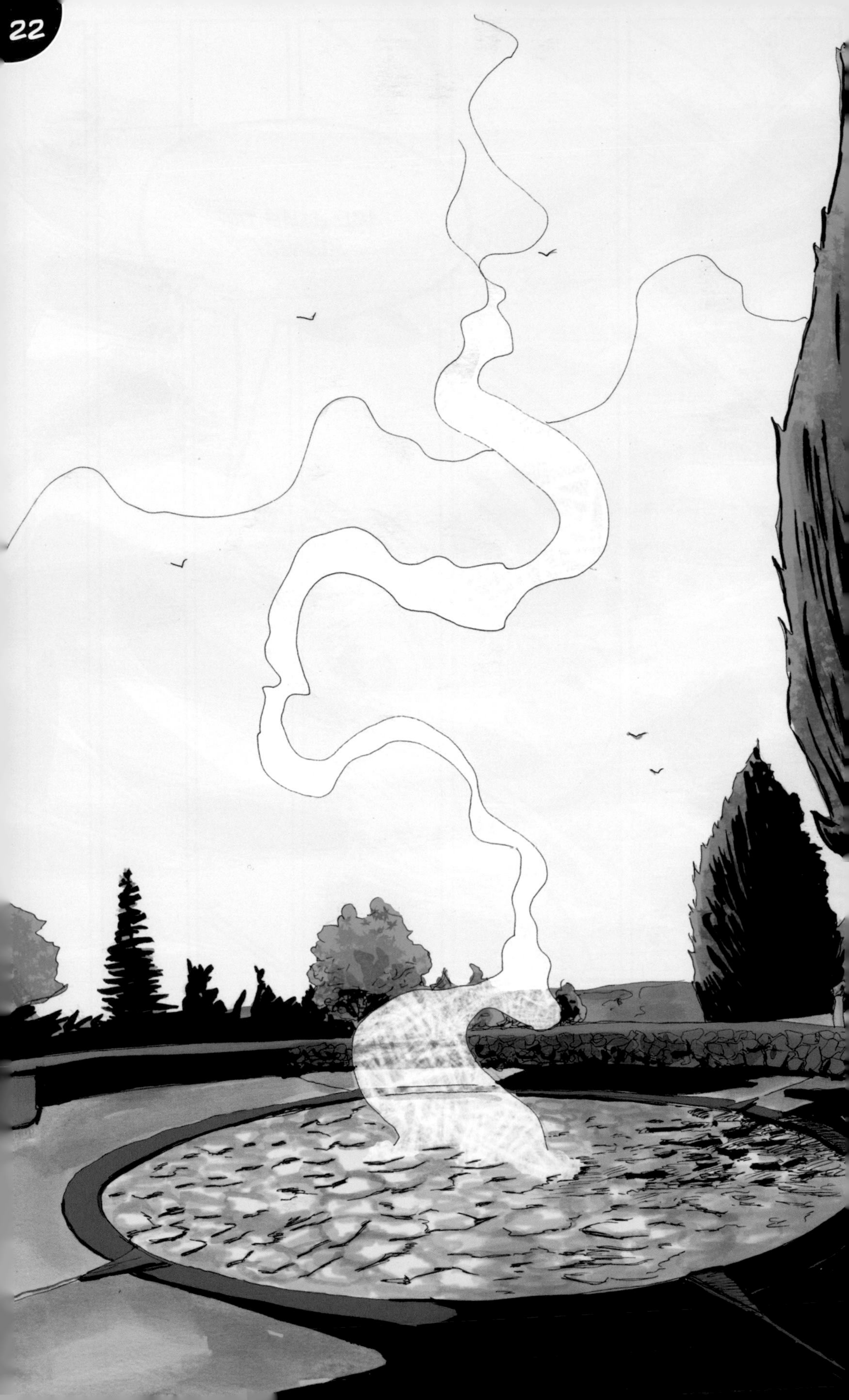

CHAPTER
TWO

THUNDERBIRD

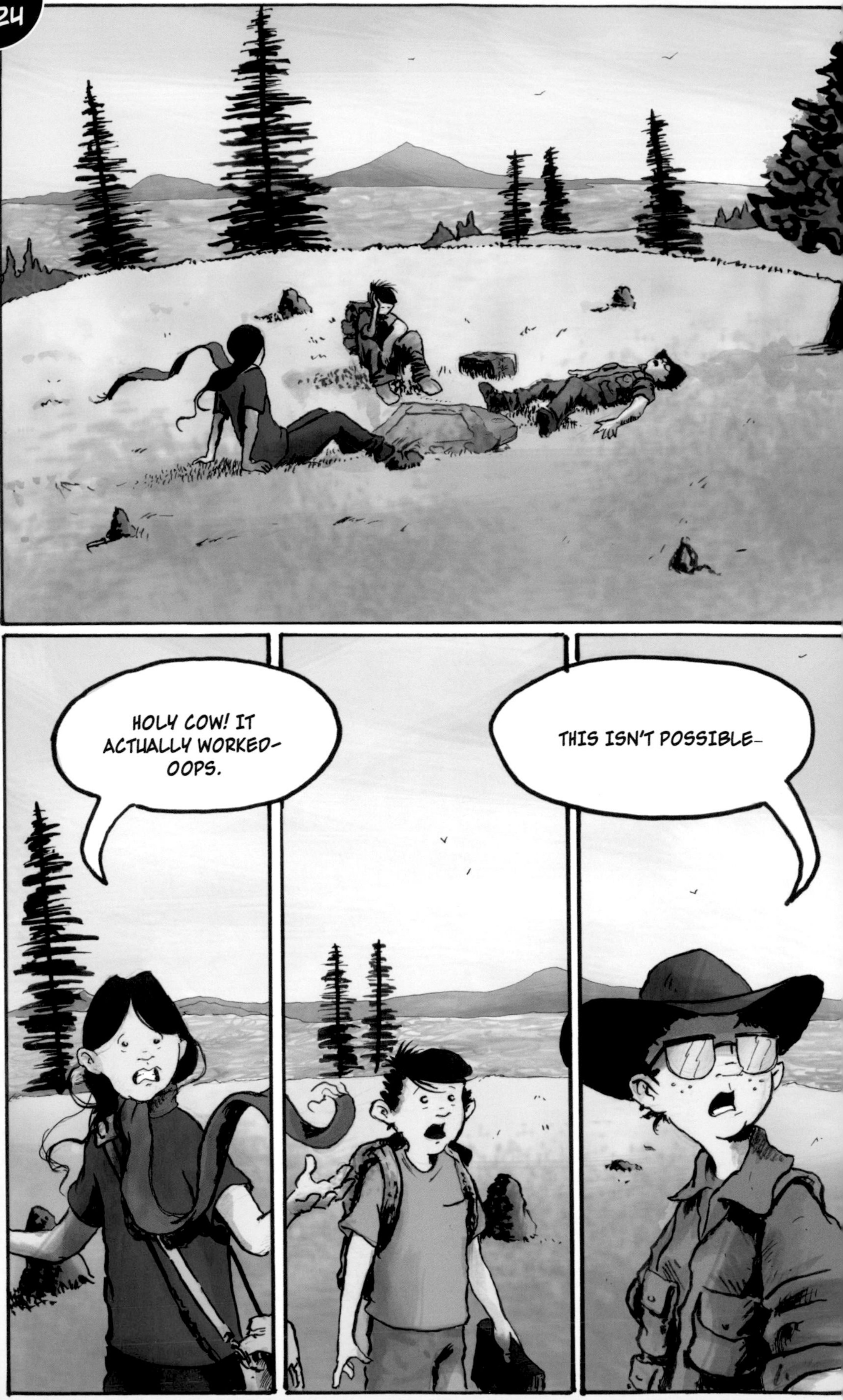
HOLY COW! IT ACTUALLY WORKED- OOPS.
THIS ISN'T POSSIBLE-

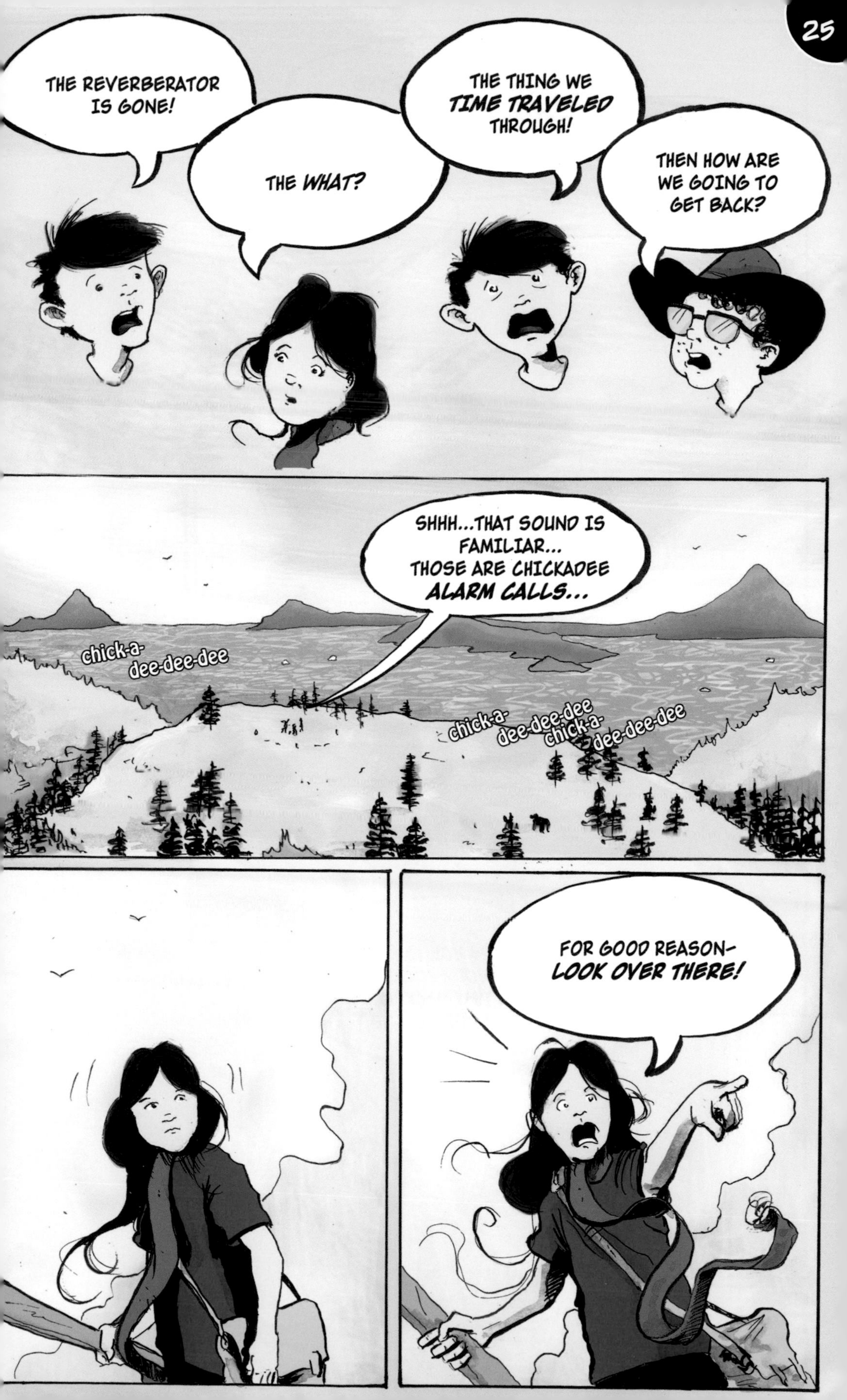
THE REVERBERATOR IS GONE!
THE WHAT?
THE THING WE TIME TRAVELED THROUGH!
THEN HOW ARE WE GOING TO GET BACK?
SHHH...THAT SOUND IS FAMILIAR... THOSE ARE CHICKADEE ALARM CALLS...
chick-a-dee-dee-dee
chick-a-dee-dee-dee
chick-a-dee-dee-dee
FOR GOOD REASON- LOOK OVER THERE!

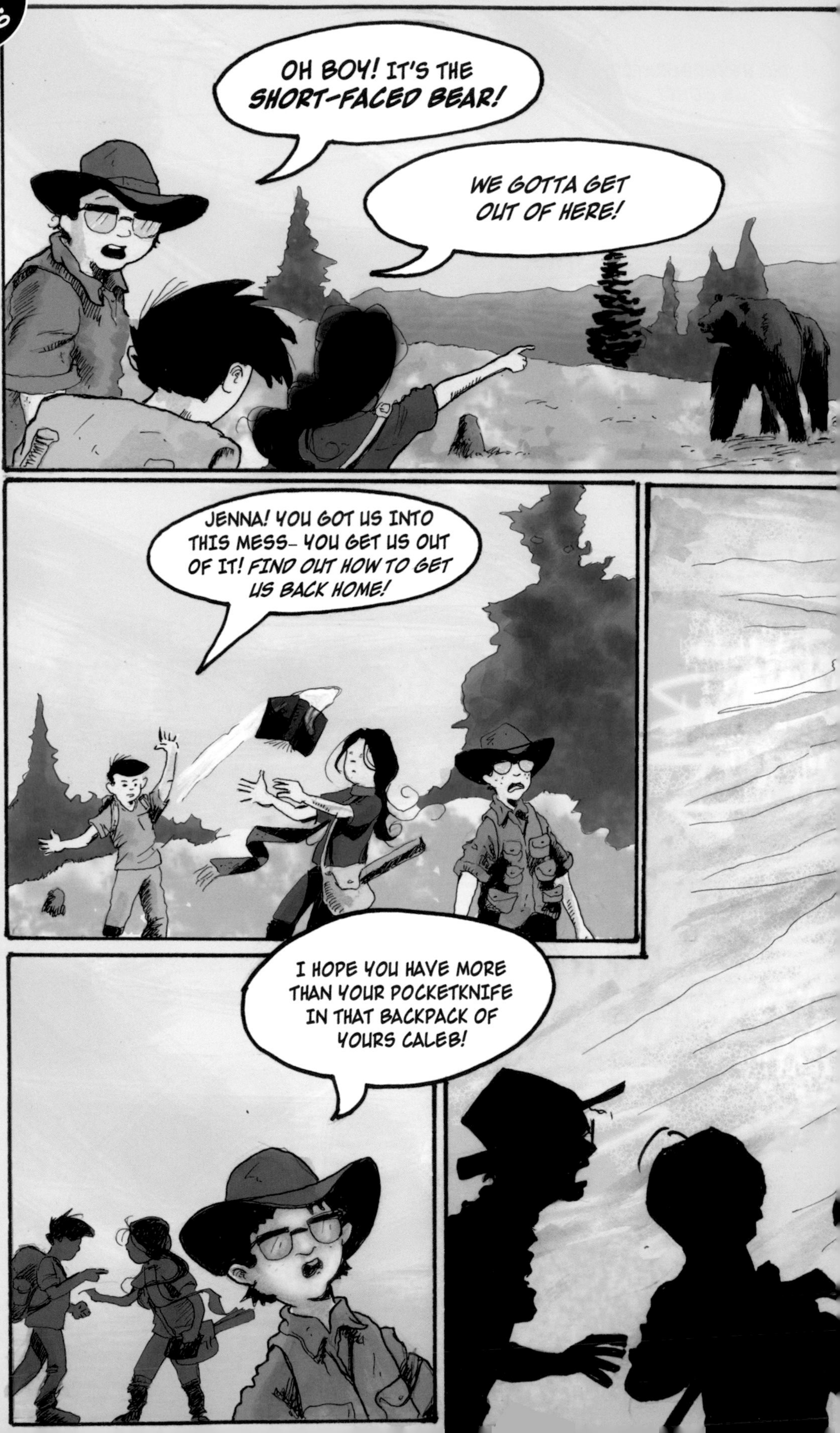
OH BOY! IT'S THE SHORT-FACED BEAR!
WE GOTTA GET OUT OF HERE!
JENNA! YOU GOT US INTO THIS MESS- YOU GET US OUT OF IT! FIND OUT HOW TO GET US BACK HOME!
I HOPE YOU HAVE MORE THAN YOUR POCKETKNIFE IN THAT BACKPACK OF YOURS CALEB!

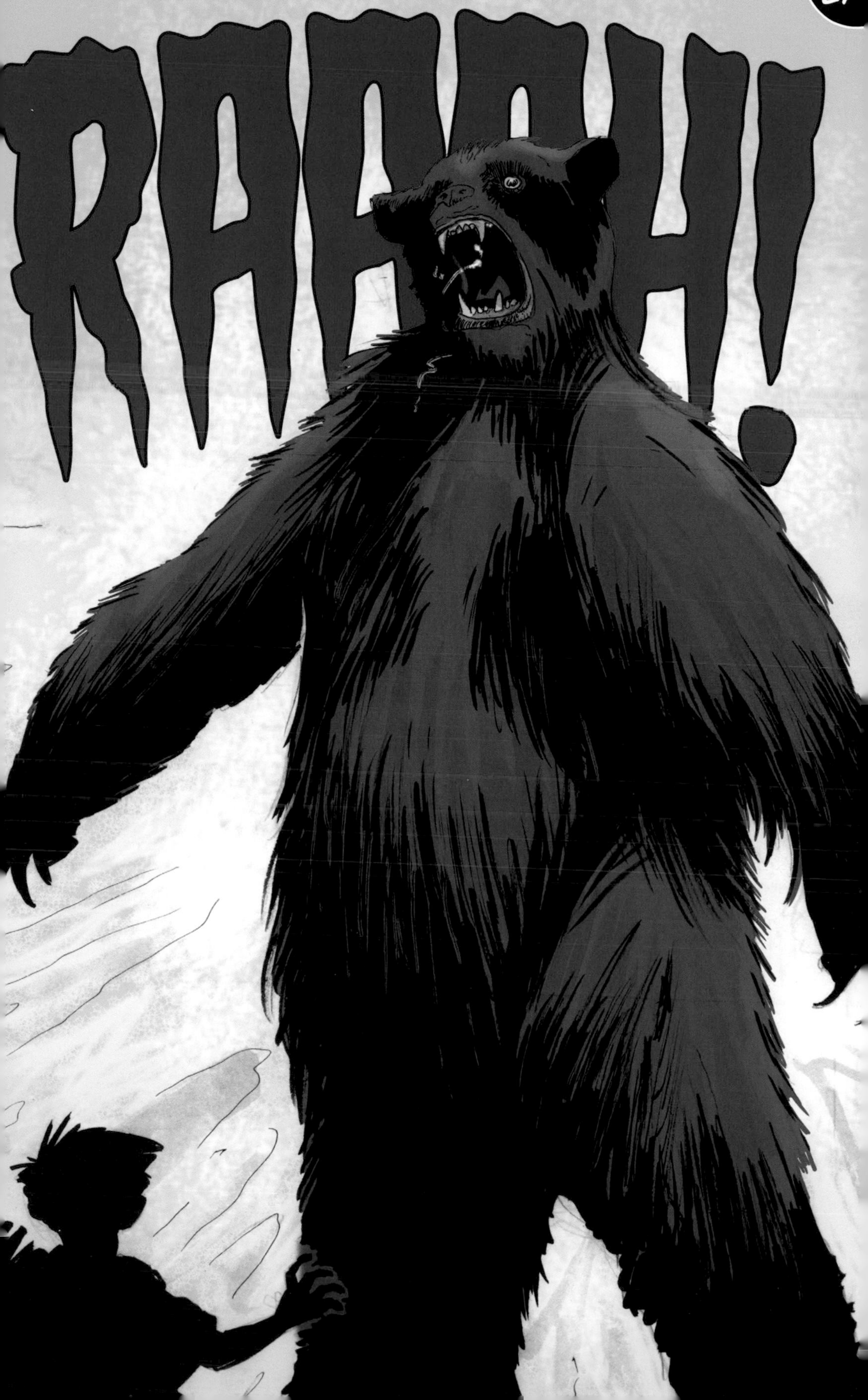
RAAAH!

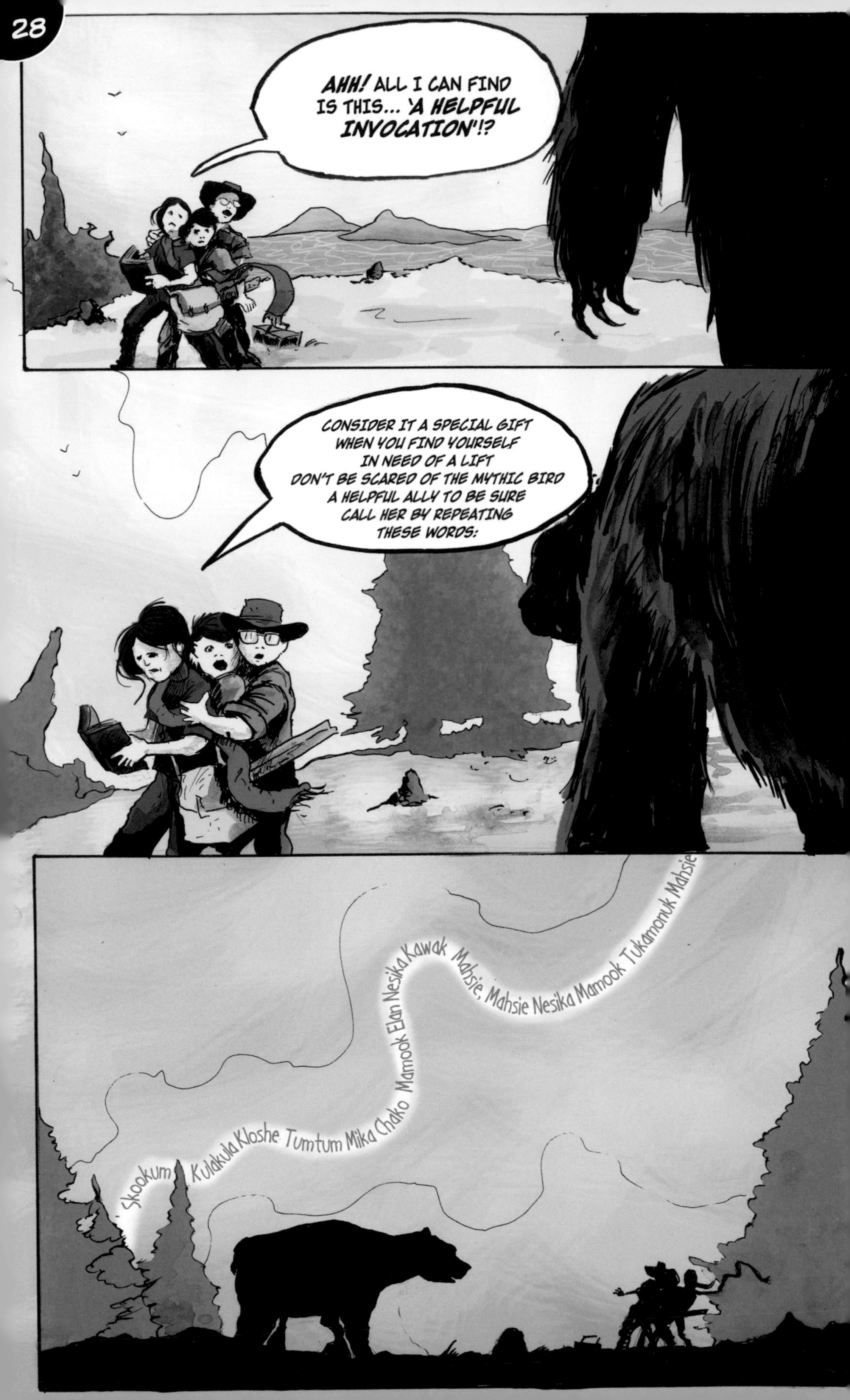
AHH! ALL I CAN FIND IS THIS... 'A HELPFUL INVOCATION'!?
CONSIDER IT A SPECIAL GIFT WHEN YOU FIND YOURSELF IN NEED OF A LIFT DON'T BE SCARED OF THE MYTHIC BIRD A HELPFUL ALLY TO BE SURE CALL HER BY REPEATING THESE WORDS:
Skookum Kulakula Kloshe Tumtum Mika Chako Mamook Elan Nesika Kawak Mahsie, Mahsie Nesika Mamook Tukamonuk Mahsie

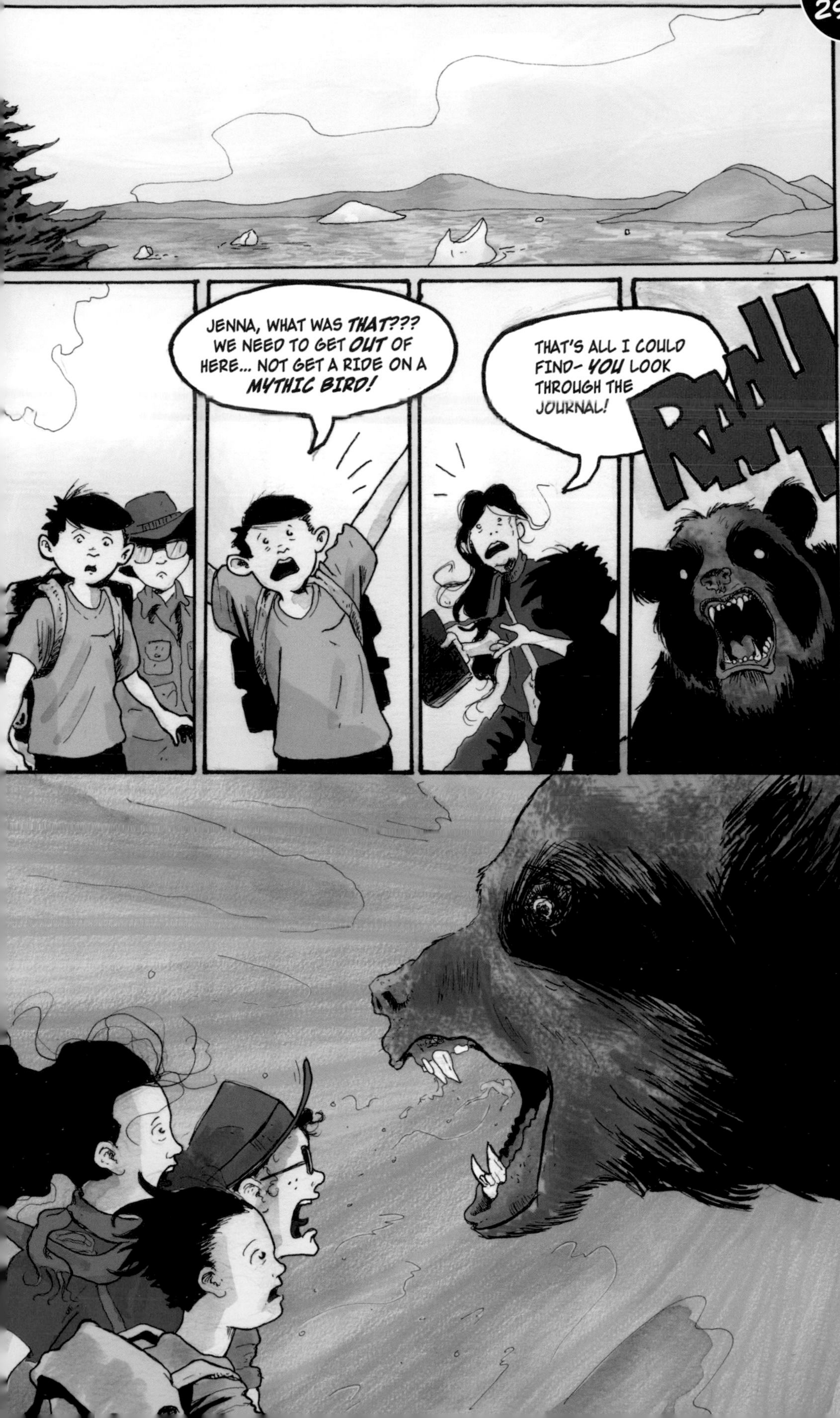
JENNA, WHAT WAS THAT??? WE NEED TO GET OUT OF HERE... NOT GET A RIDE ON A MYTHIC BIRD!
THAT'S ALL I COULD FIND- YOU LOOK THROUGH THE JOURNAL!
RAAH

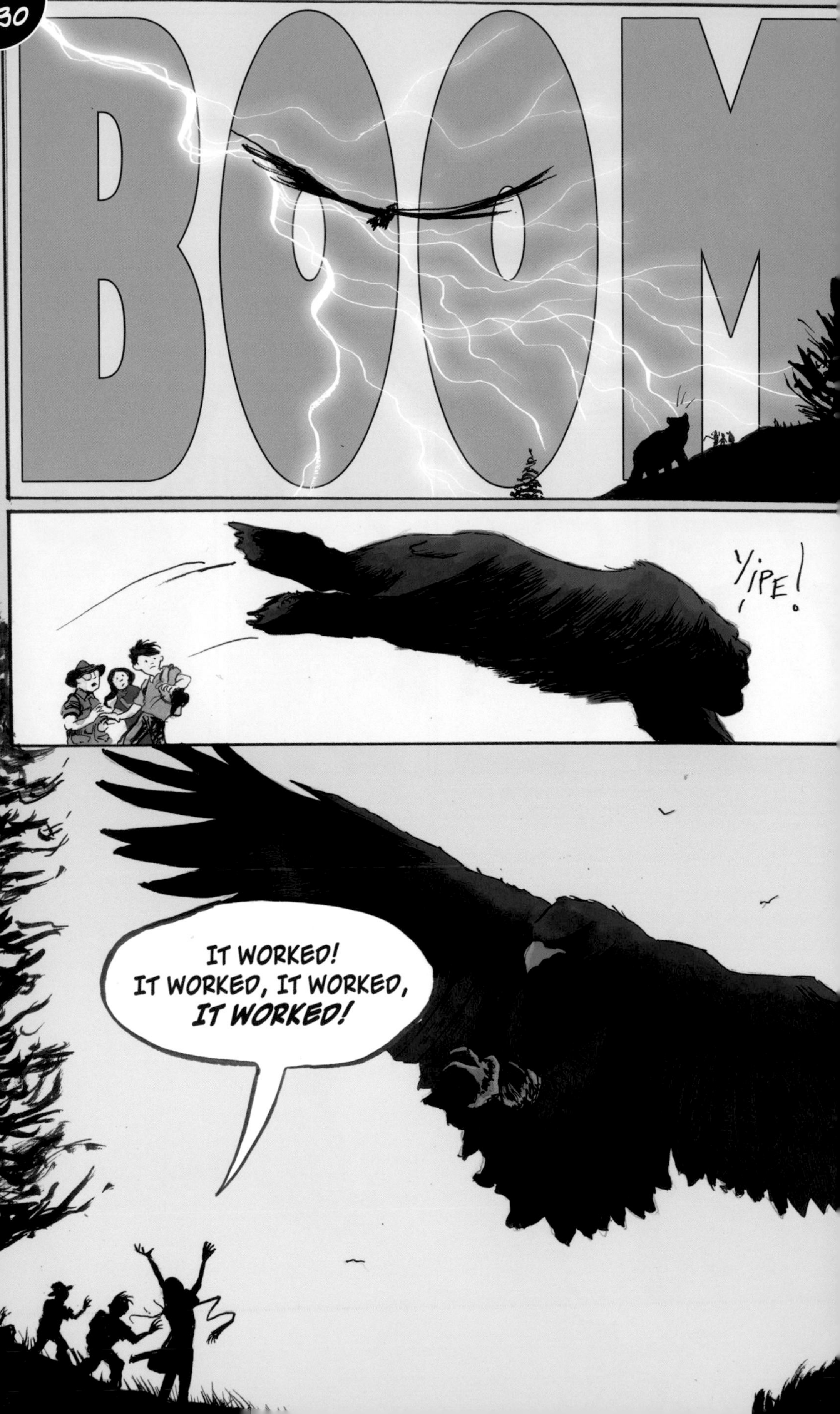
BOOM
YIPE!
IT WORKED!
IT WORKED, IT WORKED,
IT WORKED!

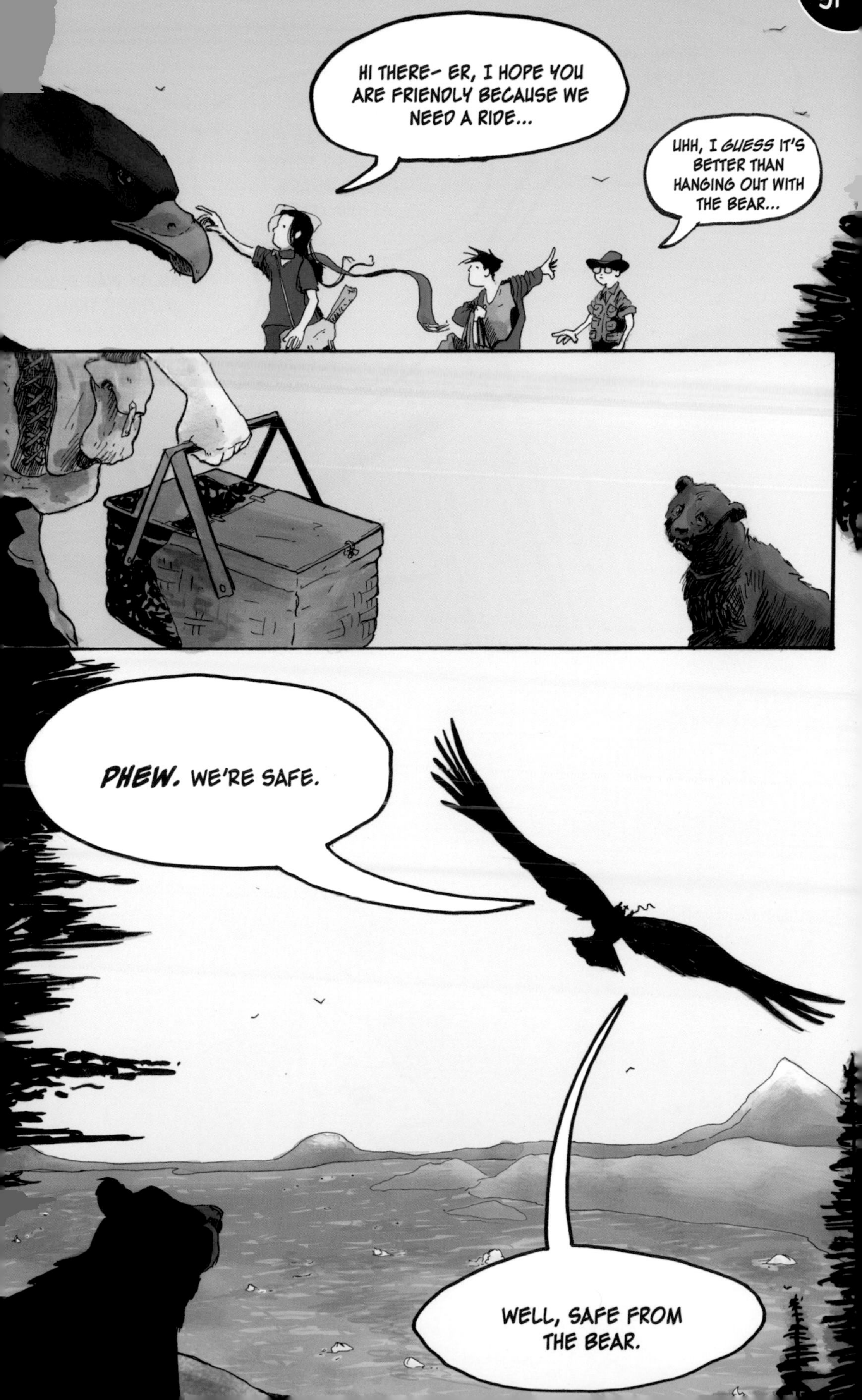
HI THERE- ER, I HOPE YOU ARE FRIENDLY BECAUSE WE NEED A RIDE...
UHH, I *GUESS* IT'S BETTER THAN HANGING OUT WITH THE BEAR...
PHEW. WE'RE SAFE.
WELL, SAFE FROM THE BEAR.

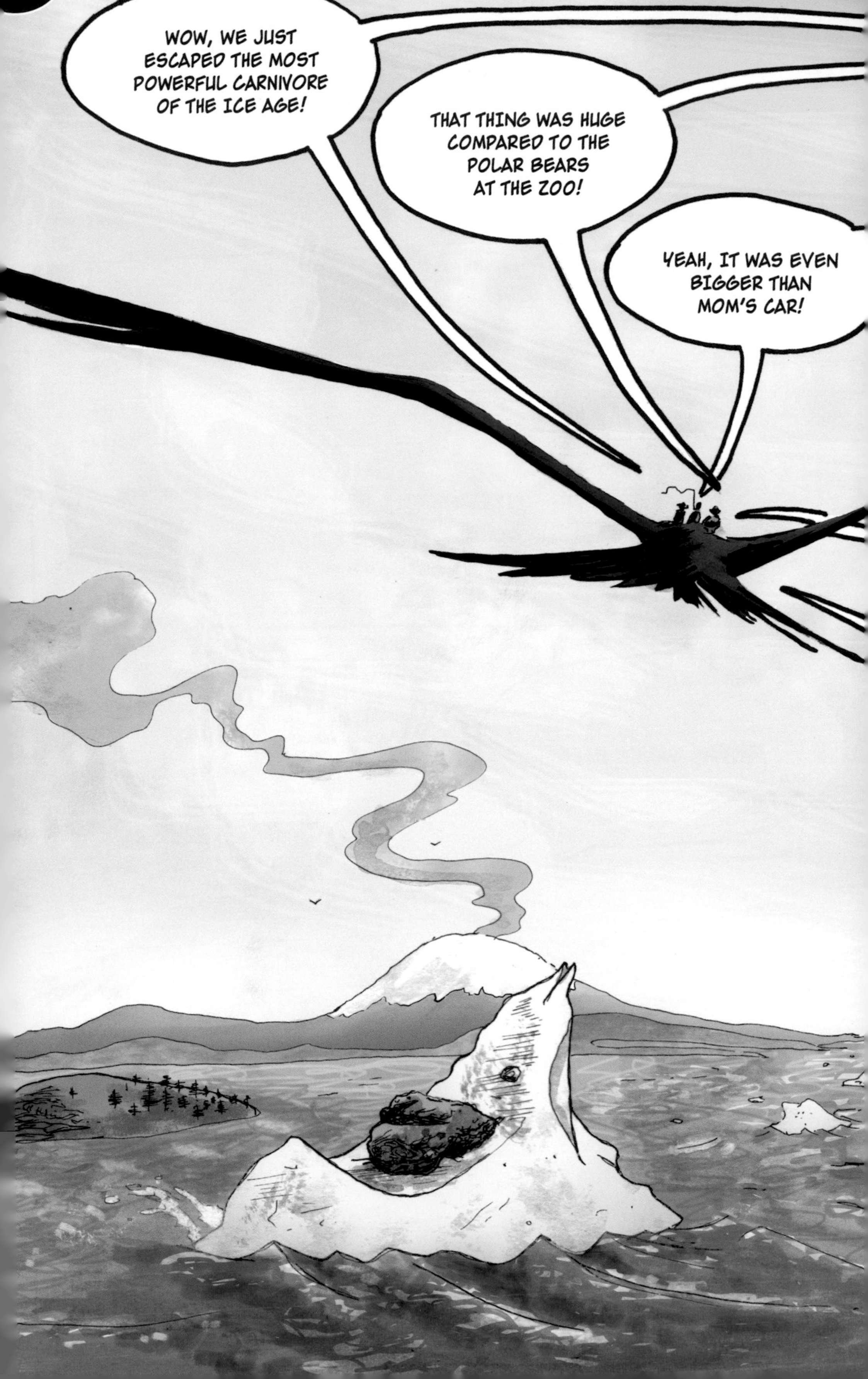
WOW, WE JUST ESCAPED THE MOST POWERFUL CARNIVORE OF THE ICE AGE!
THAT THING WAS HUGE COMPARED TO THE POLAR BEARS AT THE ZOO!
YEAH, IT WAS EVEN BIGGER THAN MOM'S CAR!

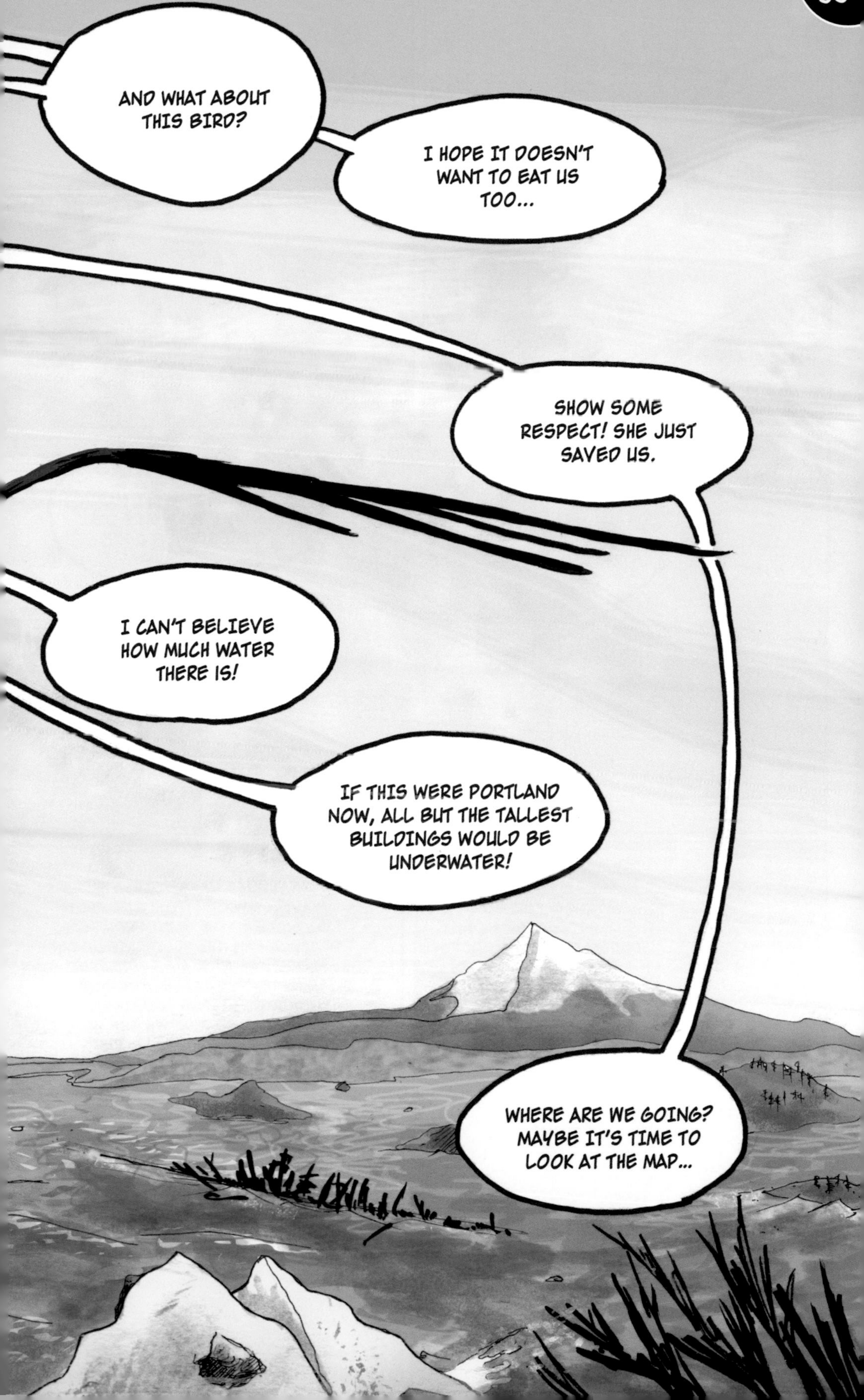
AND WHAT ABOUT THIS BIRD?
I HOPE IT DOESN'T WANT TO EAT US TOO...
SHOW SOME RESPECT! SHE JUST SAVED US.
I CAN'T BELIEVE HOW MUCH WATER THERE IS!
IF THIS WERE PORTLAND NOW, ALL BUT THE TALLEST BUILDINGS WOULD BE UNDERWATER!
WHERE ARE WE GOING? MAYBE IT'S TIME TO LOOK AT THE MAP...

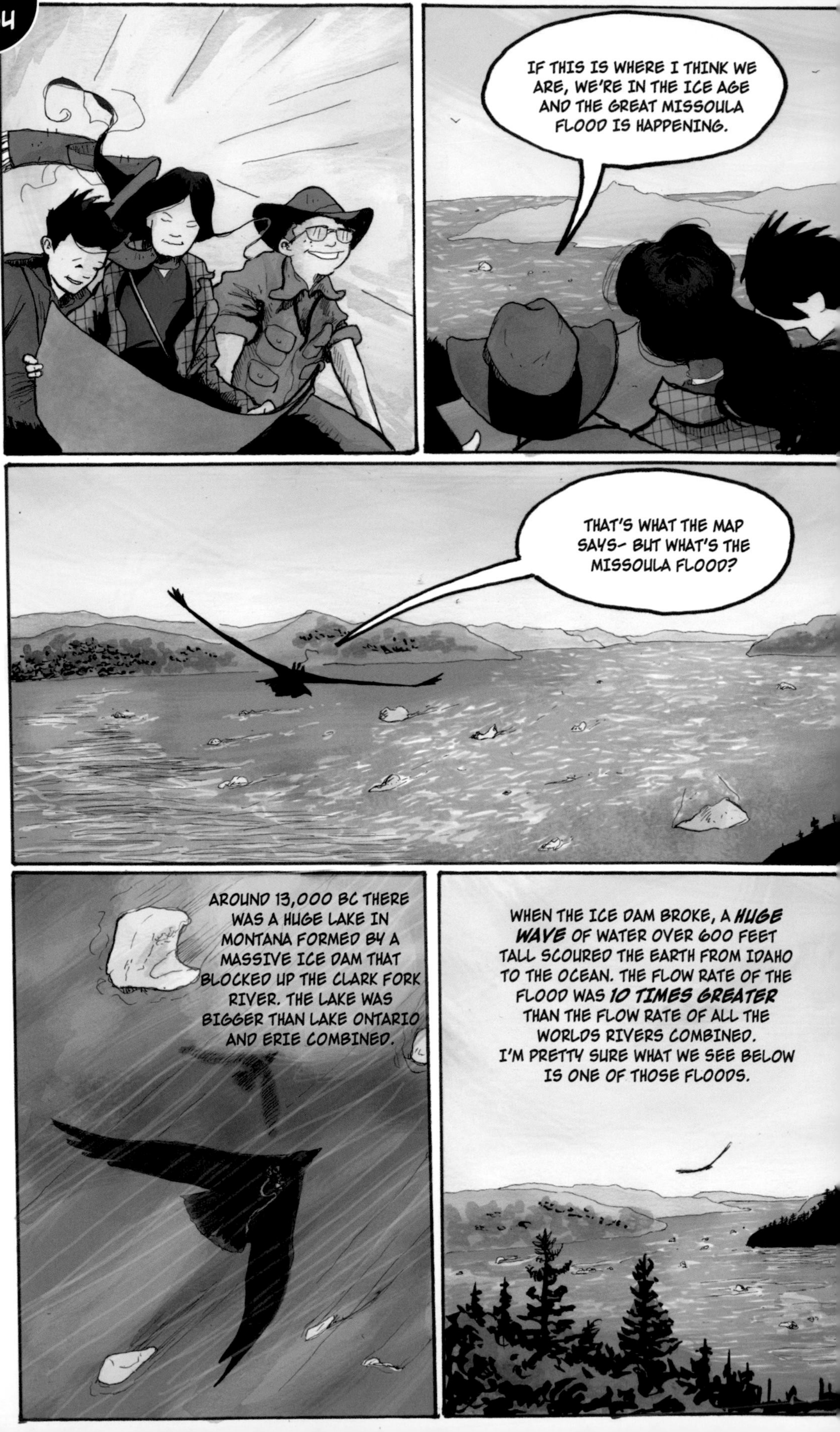
IF THIS IS WHERE I THINK WE ARE, WE'RE IN THE ICE AGE AND THE GREAT MISSOULA FLOOD IS HAPPENING.
THAT'S WHAT THE MAP SAYS- BUT WHAT'S THE MISSOULA FLOOD?
AROUND 13,000 BC THERE WAS A HUGE LAKE IN MONTANA FORMED BY A MASSIVE ICE DAM THAT BLOCKED UP THE CLARK FORK RIVER. THE LAKE WAS BIGGER THAN LAKE ONTARIO AND ERIE COMBINED.
WHEN THE ICE DAM BROKE, A HUGE WAVE OF WATER OVER 600 FEET TALL SCOURED THE EARTH FROM IDAHO TO THE OCEAN. THE FLOW RATE OF THE FLOOD WAS 10 TIMES GREATER THAN THE FLOW RATE OF ALL THE WORLDS RIVERS COMBINED. I'M PRETTY SURE WHAT WE SEE BELOW IS ONE OF THOSE FLOODS.

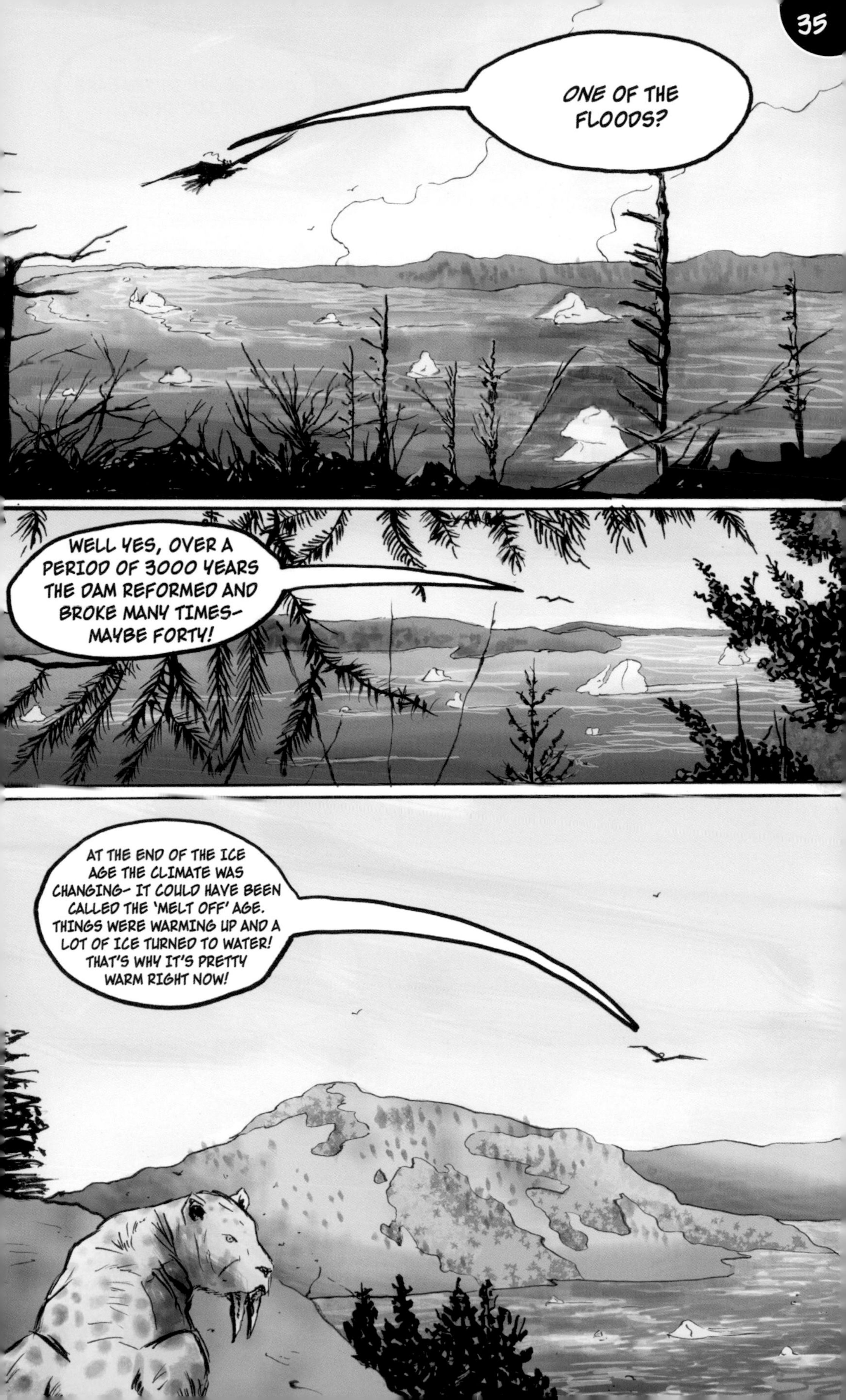
ONE OF THE FLOODS?
WELL YES, OVER A PERIOD OF 3000 YEARS THE DAM REFORMED AND BROKE MANY TIMES- MAYBE FORTY!
AT THE END OF THE ICE AGE THE CLIMATE WAS CHANGING- IT COULD HAVE BEEN CALLED THE 'MELT OFF' AGE. THINGS WERE WARMING UP AND A LOT OF ICE TURNED TO WATER! THAT'S WHY IT'S PRETTY WARM RIGHT NOW!

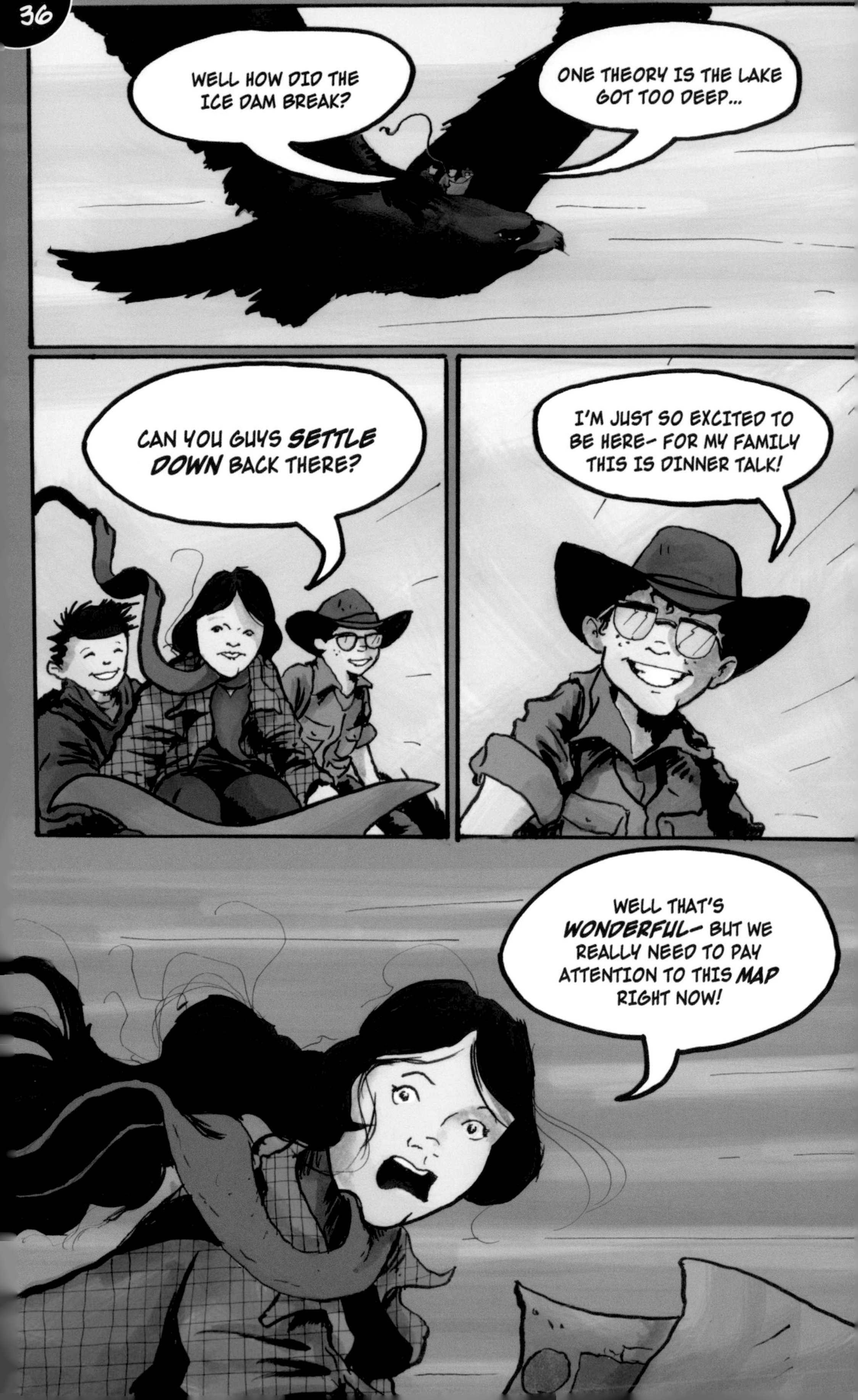
WELL HOW DID THE ICE DAM BREAK?
ONE THEORY IS THE LAKE GOT TOO DEEP...
CAN YOU GUYS SETTLE DOWN BACK THERE?
I'M JUST SO EXCITED TO BE HERE- FOR MY FAMILY THIS IS DINNER TALK!
WELL THAT'S WONDERFUL- BUT WE REALLY NEED TO PAY ATTENTION TO THIS MAP RIGHT NOW!

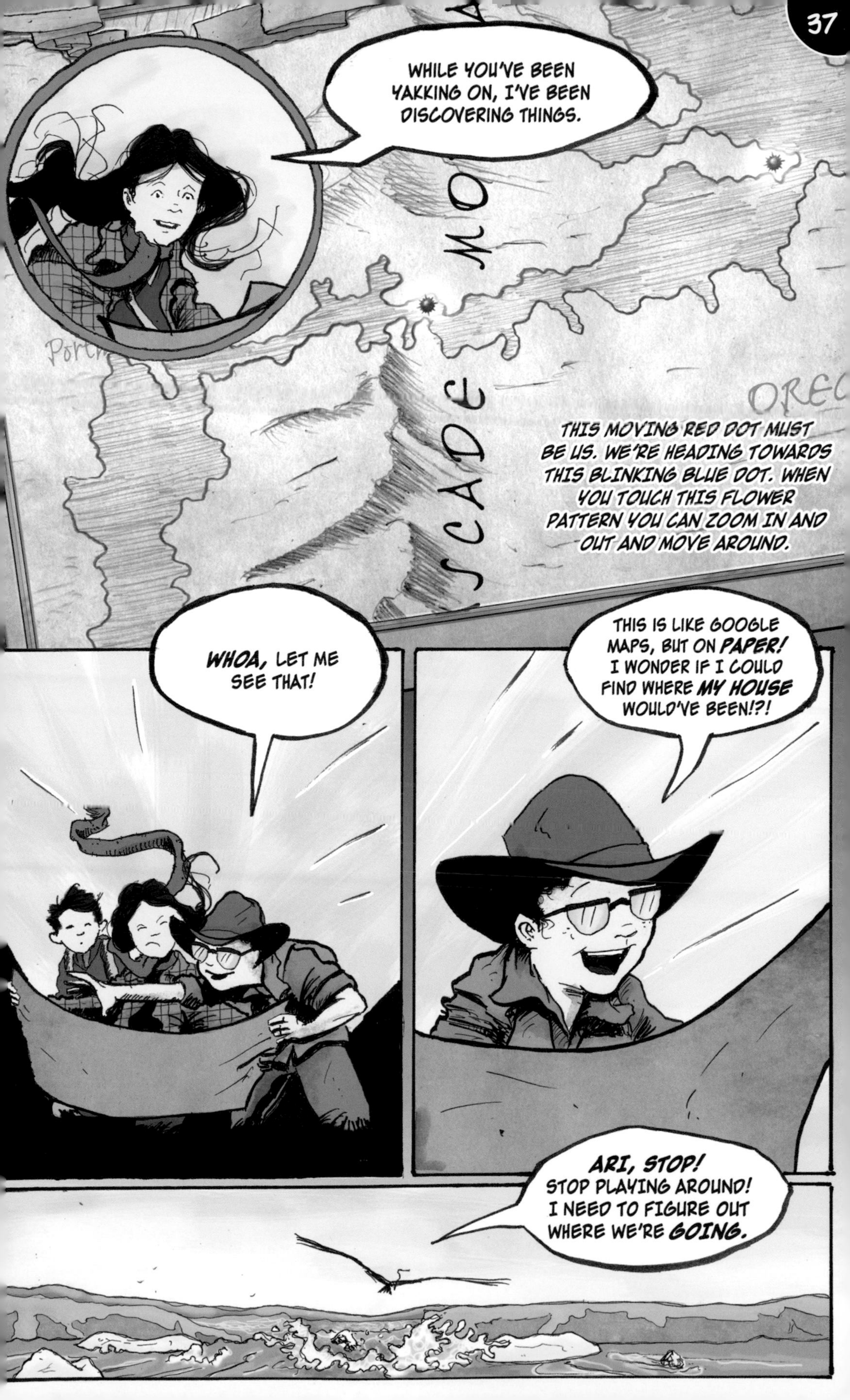
WHILE YOU'VE BEEN YAKKING ON, I'VE BEEN DISCOVERING THINGS.
THIS MOVING RED DOT MUST BE US. WE'RE HEADING TOWARDS THIS BLINKING BLUE DOT. WHEN YOU TOUCH THIS FLOWER PATTERN YOU CAN ZOOM IN AND OUT AND MOVE AROUND.
WHOA, LET ME SEE THAT!
THIS IS LIKE GOOGLE MAPS, BUT ON PAPER! I WONDER IF I COULD FIND WHERE MY HOUSE WOULD'VE BEEN!?!
ARI, STOP! STOP PLAYING AROUND! I NEED TO FIGURE OUT WHERE WE'RE GOING.

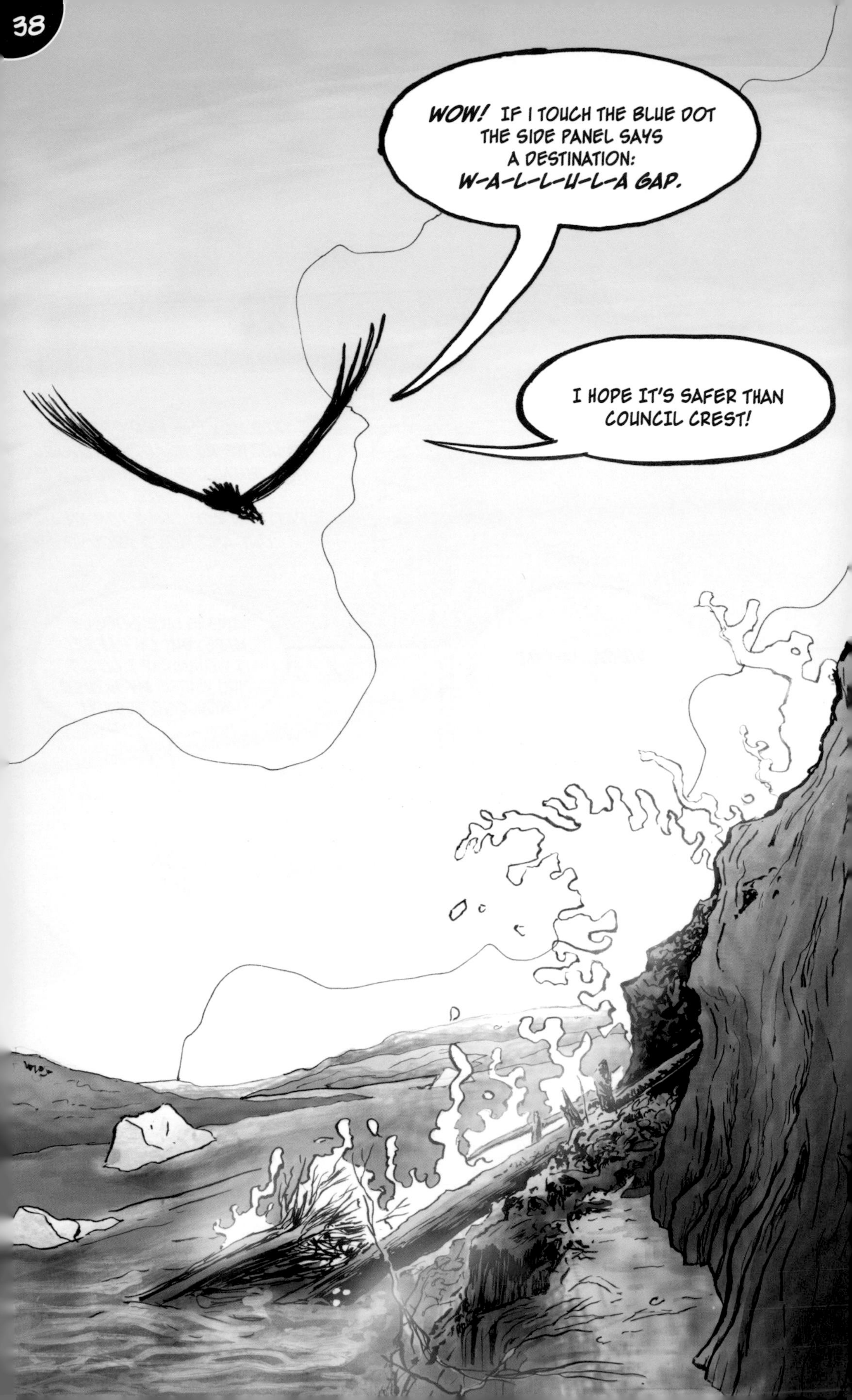
WOW! IF I TOUCH THE BLUE DOT THE SIDE PANEL SAYS A DESTINATION: W-A-L-L-U-L-A GAP.
I HOPE IT'S SAFER THAN COUNCIL CREST!

CHAPTER THREE

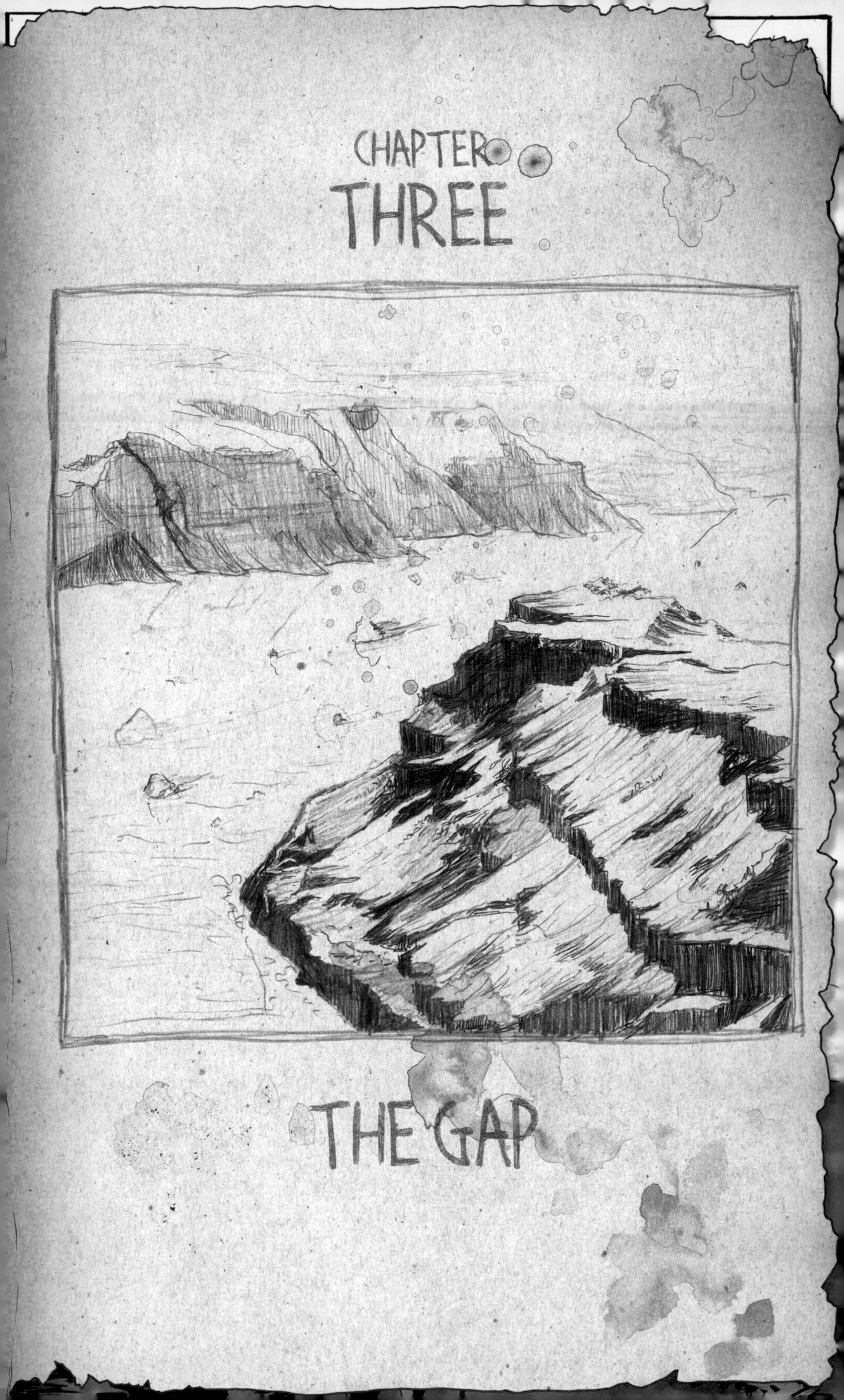

THE GAP

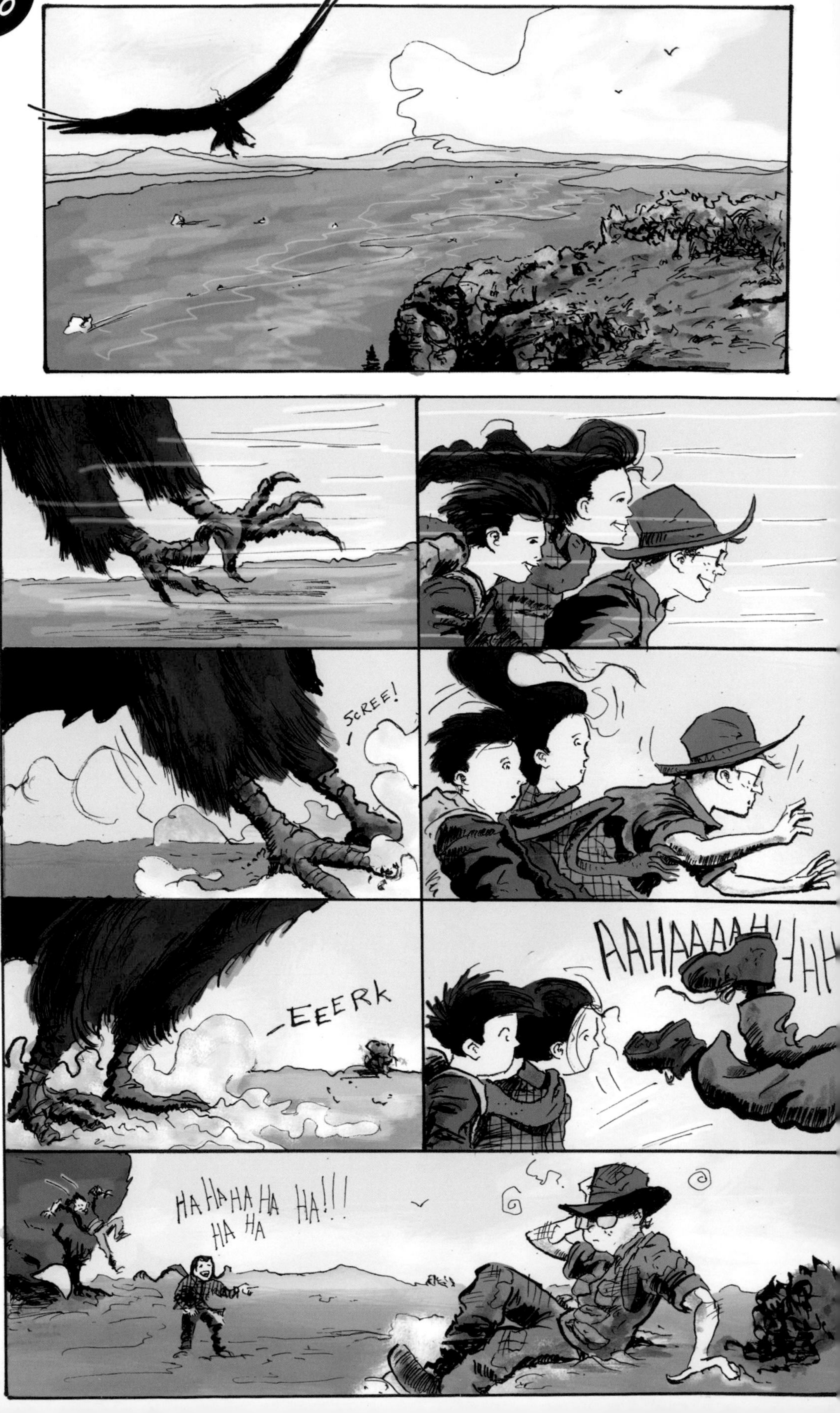
SCREE!
-EEERK
AAHAAAAH'HH
HA HA HA HA HA!!!
HA HA

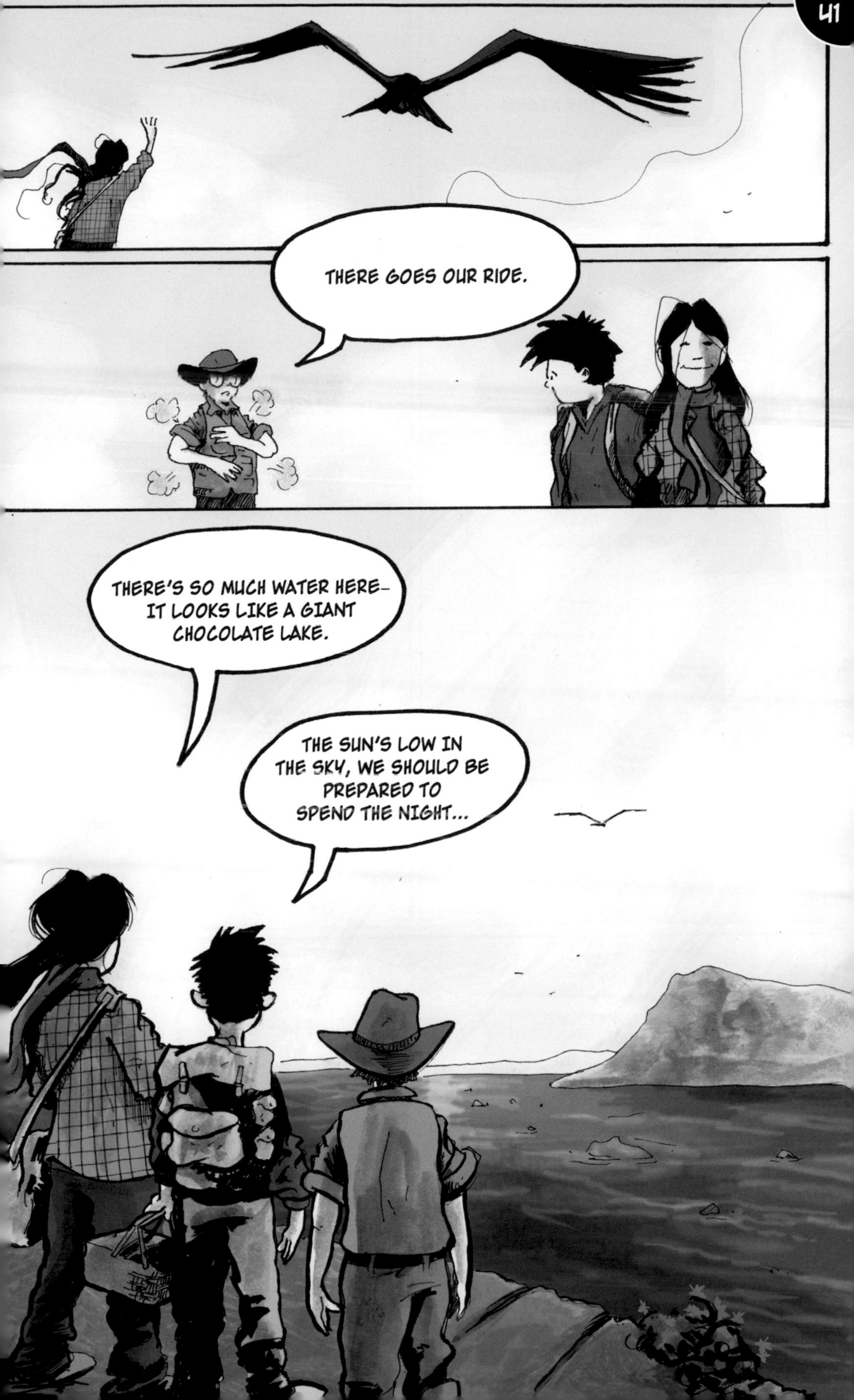
THERE GOES OUR RIDE.
THERE'S SO MUCH WATER HERE– IT LOOKS LIKE A GIANT CHOCOLATE LAKE.
THE SUN'S LOW IN THE SKY, WE SHOULD BE PREPARED TO SPEND THE NIGHT...

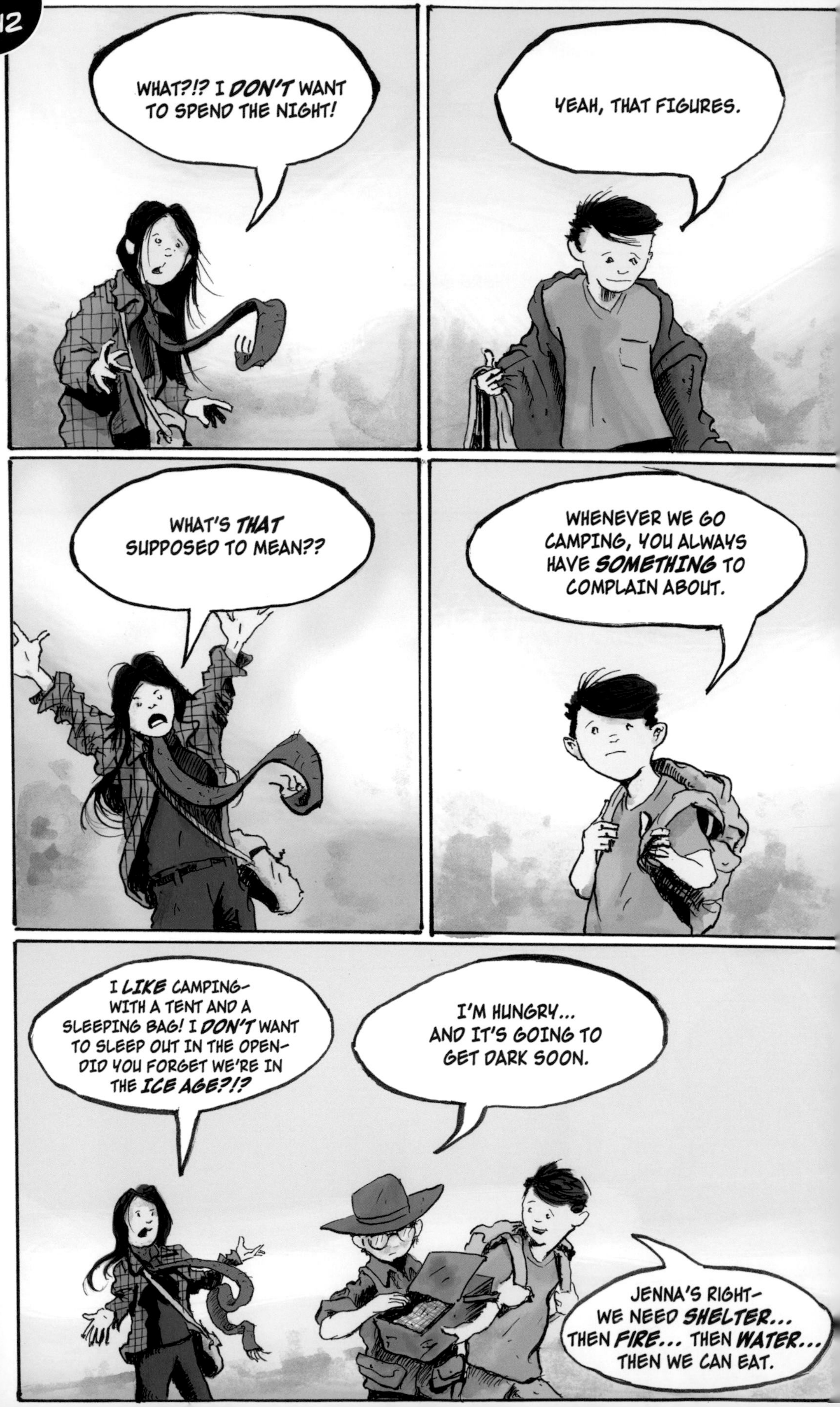
WHAT?!? I DON'T WANT TO SPEND THE NIGHT!
YEAH, THAT FIGURES.
WHAT'S THAT SUPPOSED TO MEAN??
WHENEVER WE GO CAMPING, YOU ALWAYS HAVE SOMETHING TO COMPLAIN ABOUT.
I LIKE CAMPING- WITH A TENT AND A SLEEPING BAG! I DON'T WANT TO SLEEP OUT IN THE OPEN- DID YOU FORGET WE'RE IN THE ICE AGE?!?
I'M HUNGRY... AND IT'S GOING TO GET DARK SOON.
JENNA'S RIGHT- WE NEED SHELTER... THEN FIRE... THEN WATER... THEN WE CAN EAT.

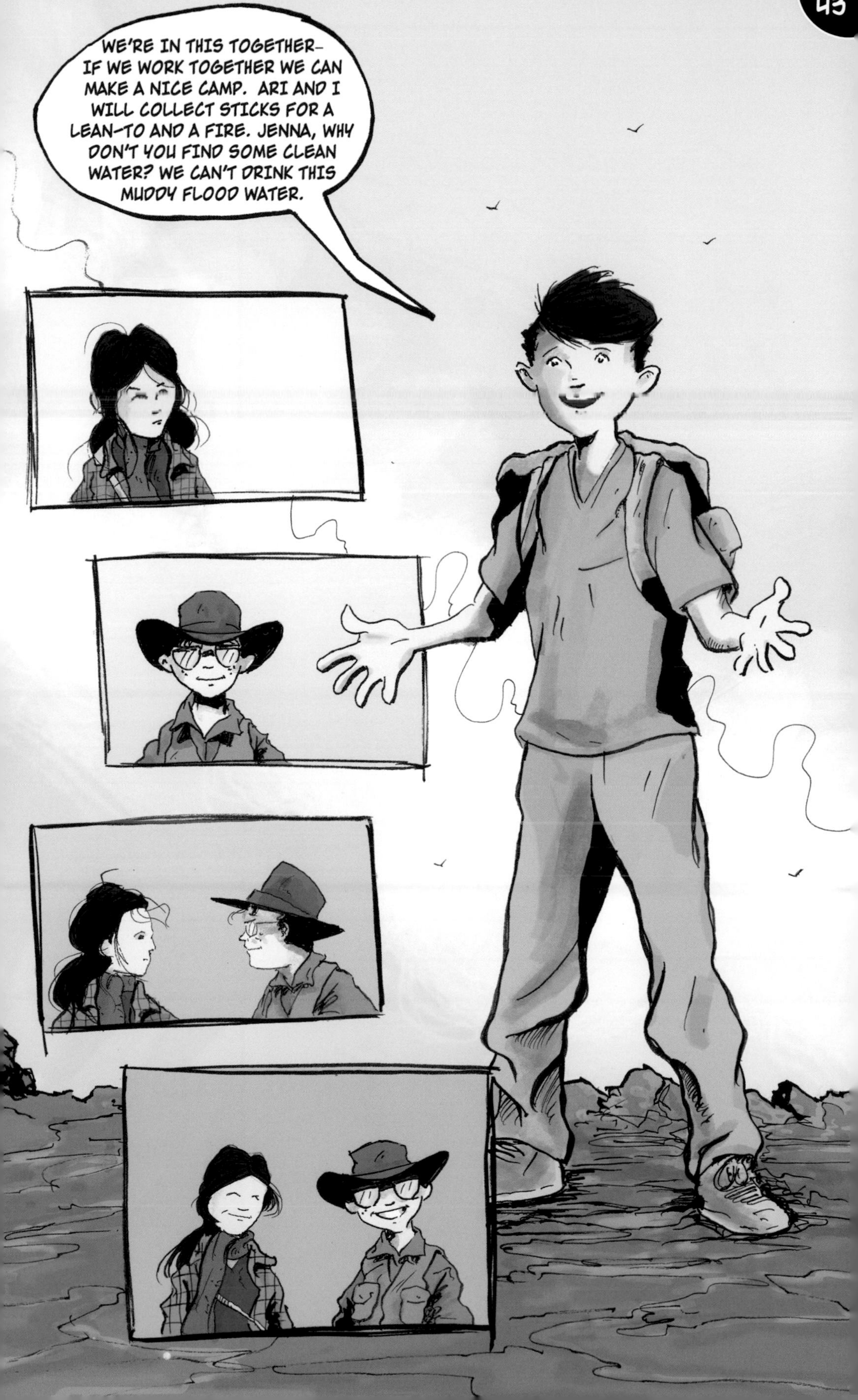
WE'RE IN THIS TOGETHER– IF WE WORK TOGETHER WE CAN MAKE A NICE CAMP. ARI AND I WILL COLLECT STICKS FOR A LEAN-TO AND A FIRE. JENNA, WHY DON'T YOU FIND SOME CLEAN WATER? WE CAN'T DRINK THIS MUDDY FLOOD WATER.

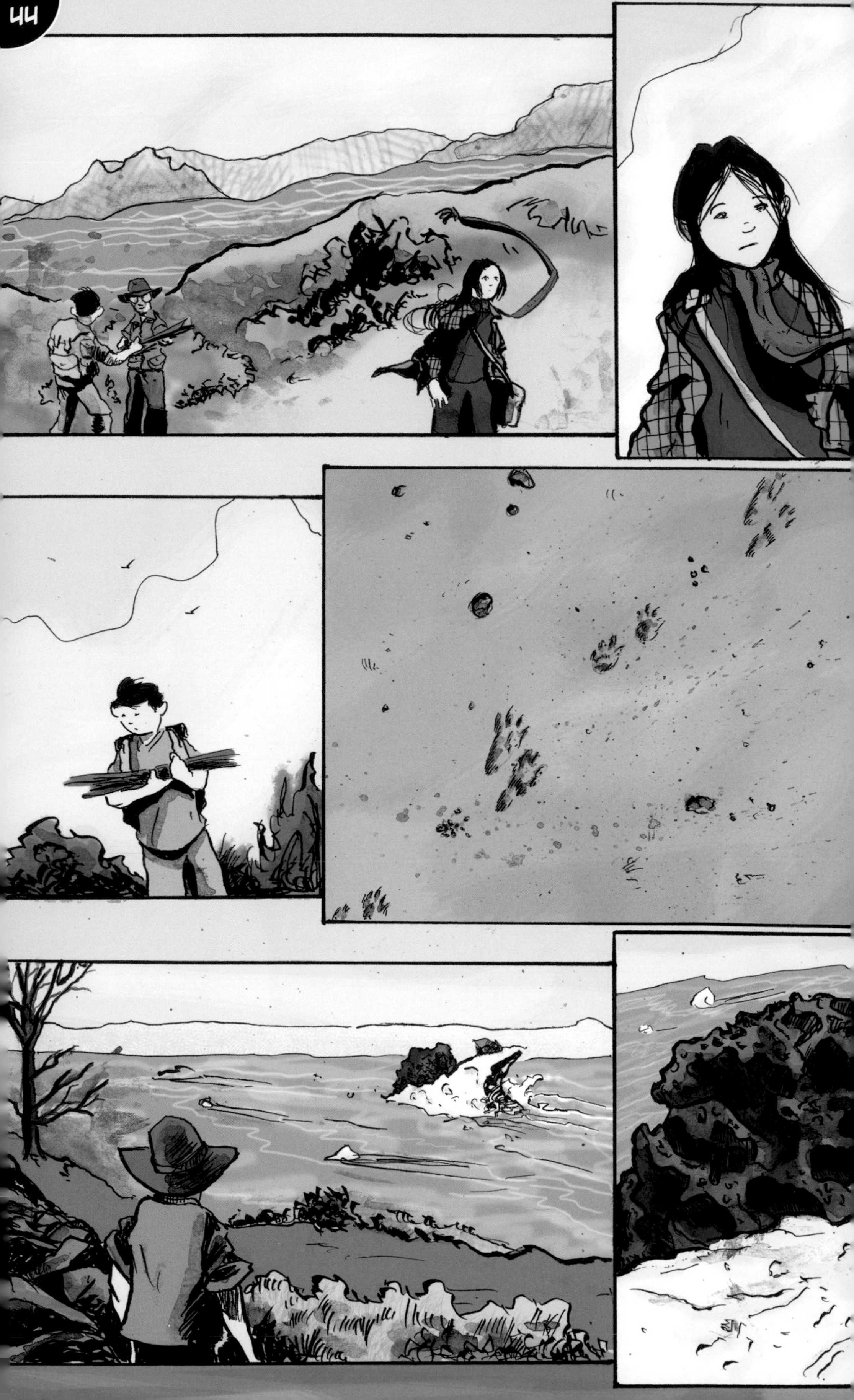

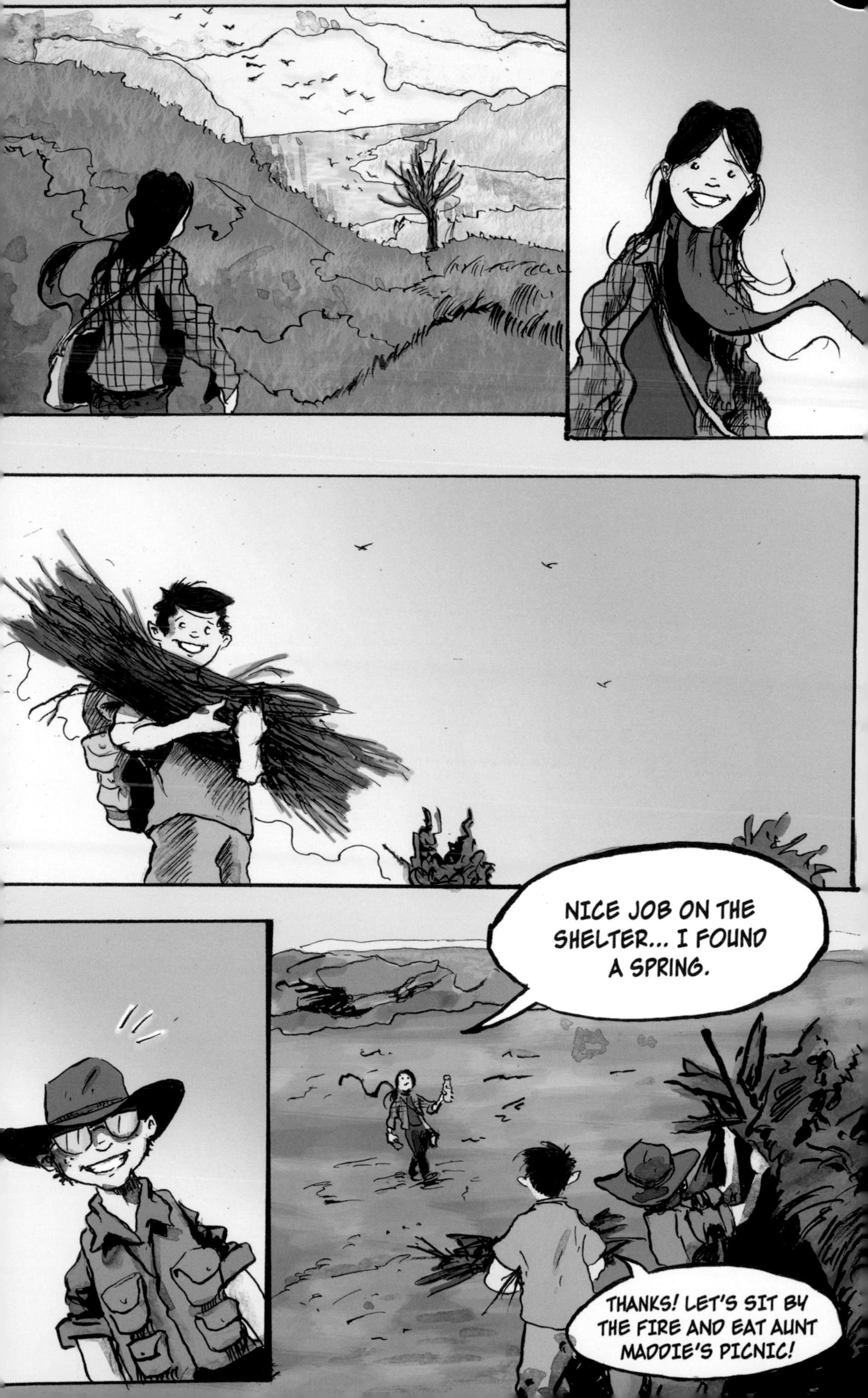
NICE JOB ON THE SHELTER... I FOUND A SPRING.
THANKS! LET'S SIT BY THE FIRE AND EAT AUNT MADDIE'S PICNIC!

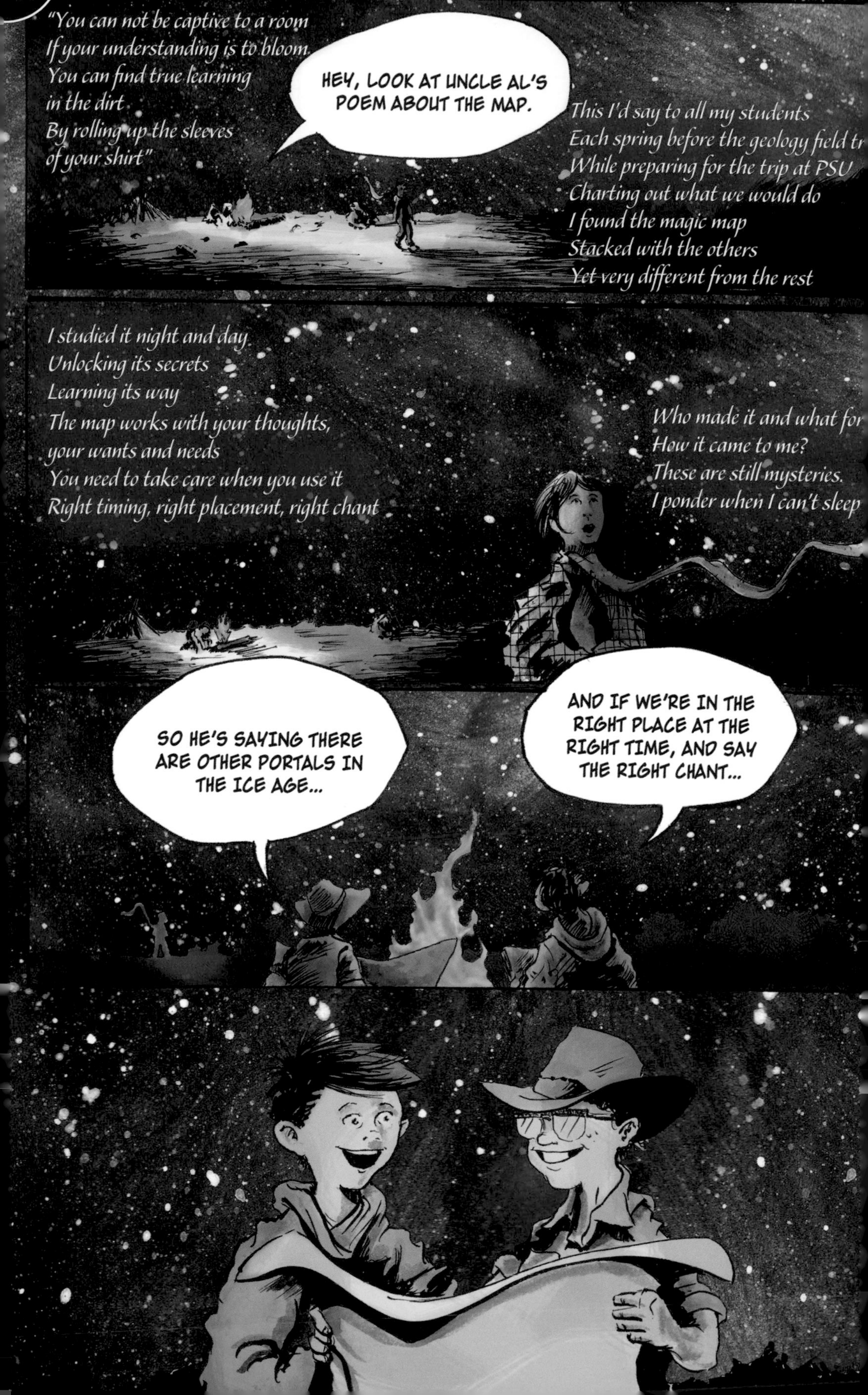
"You can not be captive to a room
If your understanding is to bloom.
You can find true learning
in the dirt
By rolling up the sleeves
of your shirt"
HEY, LOOK AT UNCLE AL'S POEM ABOUT THE MAP.
This I'd say to all my students
Each spring before the geology field tr
While preparing for the trip at PSU
Charting out what we would do
I found the magic map
Stacked with the others
Yet very different from the rest
I studied it night and day
Unlocking its secrets
Learning its way
The map works with your thoughts,
your wants and needs
You need to take care when you use it
Right timing, right placement, right chant
Who made it and what for
How it came to me?
These are still mysteries.
I ponder when I can't sleep
SO HE'S SAYING THERE ARE OTHER PORTALS IN THE ICE AGE...
AND IF WE'RE IN THE RIGHT PLACE AT THE RIGHT TIME, AND SAY THE RIGHT CHANT...

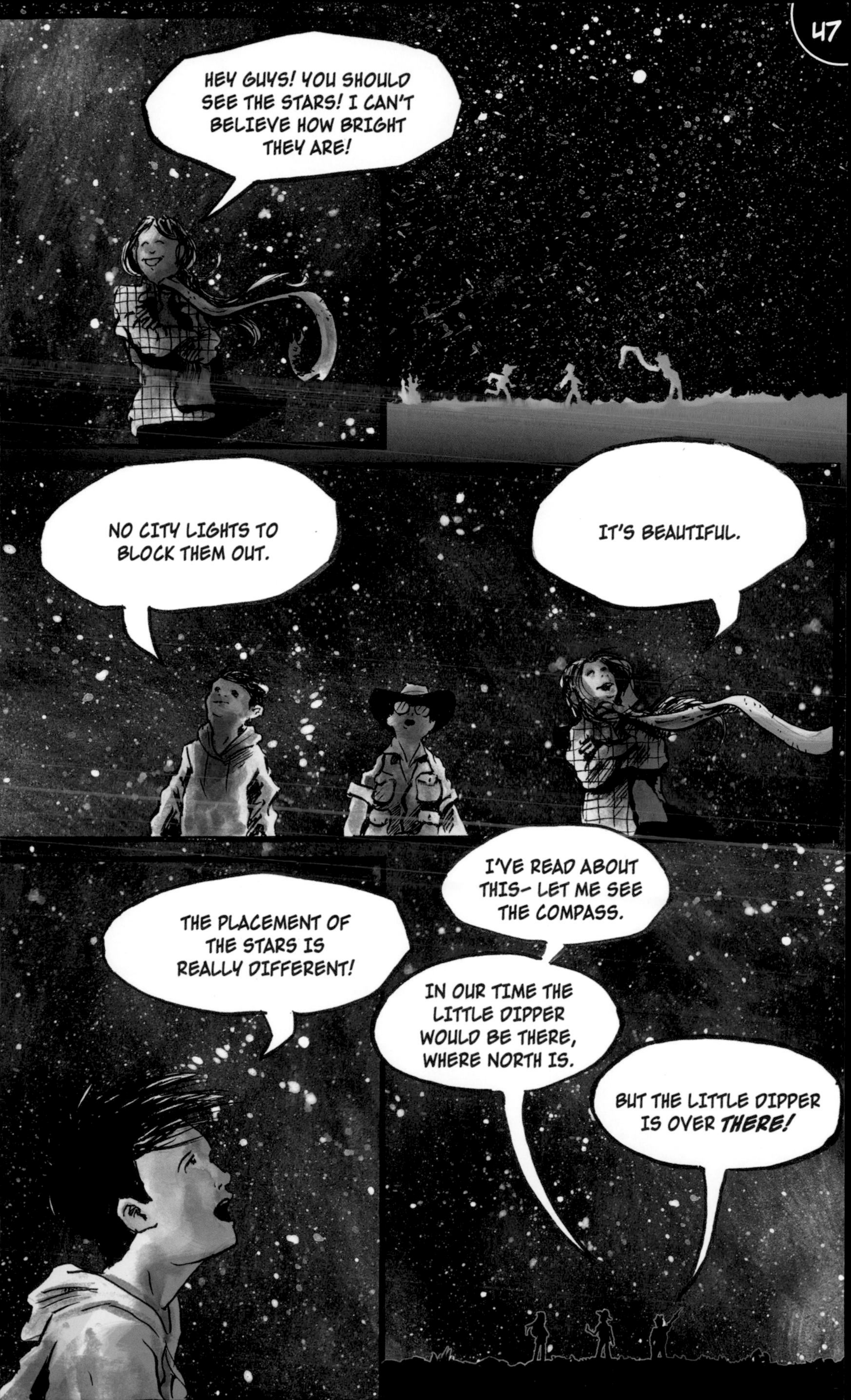
HEY GUYS! YOU SHOULD SEE THE STARS! I CAN'T BELIEVE HOW BRIGHT THEY ARE!
NO CITY LIGHTS TO BLOCK THEM OUT.
IT'S BEAUTIFUL.
THE PLACEMENT OF THE STARS IS REALLY DIFFERENT!
I'VE READ ABOUT THIS- LET ME SEE THE COMPASS.
IN OUR TIME THE LITTLE DIPPER WOULD BE THERE, WHERE NORTH IS.
BUT THE LITTLE DIPPER IS OVER *THERE!*

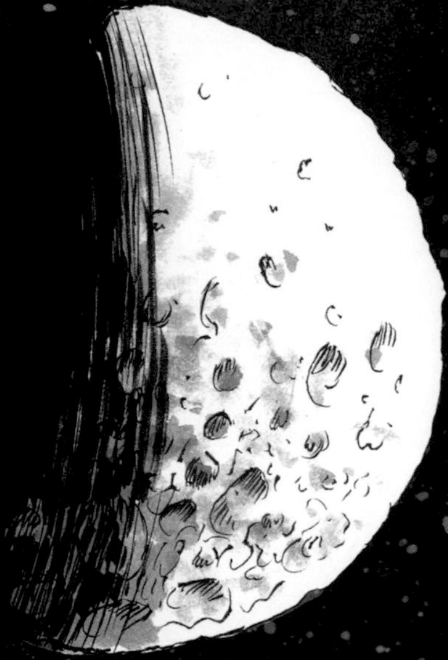

There are three planetary cycles
Every Ranger should know
An understanding of their workings
Will eventually show
That our relative positions
In both time and space
Are always changing, always moving
In a dynamic cosmic race
Moons around planets, planets around the sun
Cause magnetic deviations
With great variations
As pole positions change
So do north stars across the cosmic range

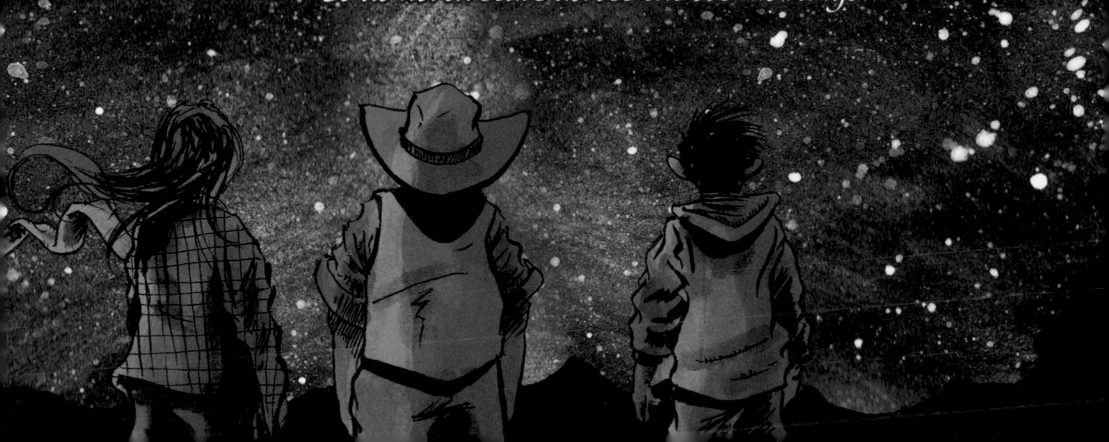

Cycle One:
The 100,000 year cycle
The shape of Earth's orbit
Changes from circular to elliptical
Altering the distance of Earth to Sun
By as much as 12,000,000 miles.
That's quite a sum!

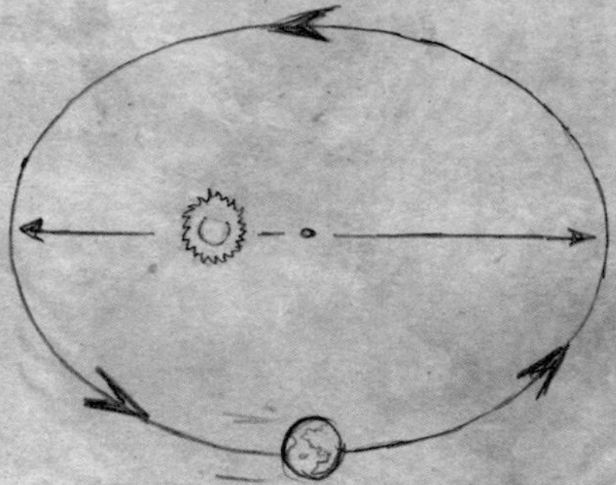

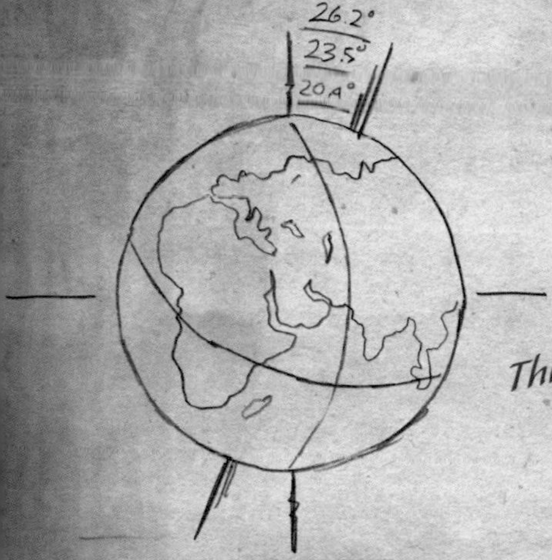
26.2°
23.5°
20.4°

Cycle Two:
Over the course of 42,000 years
The tilt of Earth's axis
Varies from 20.4 to 26.2 degrees
This tilt alters the intensity of the seasons
And changes the view of the stars
from the ground

Cycle Three:
The 26,000 year Zodiac parade
Known as Precession of the Equinox
Happens because Earth's axis
wobbles like a top
The pole star changes
As we move through space
And every 2,150 years
The sun rises in a new sign of the Zodiac
At the spring equinox

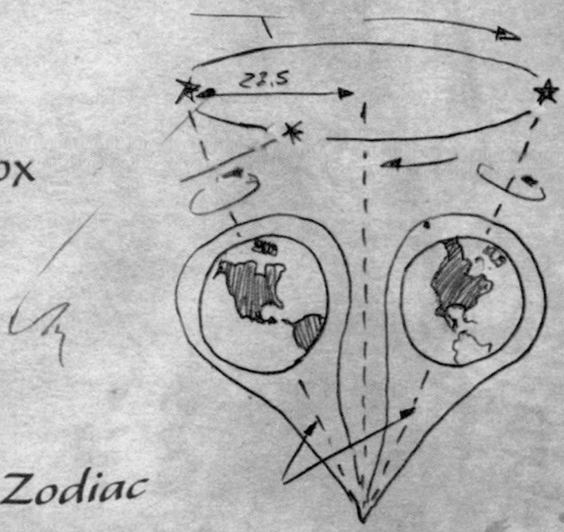
23.5

Milutin Milankovitch was first to chart these cycles
And put the theory together
That Earth has gone through many climate changes
As our relative positions re-arranges
The intensity of the seasons does change
Of solar radiation received
Ice Ages have come and gone and will come again

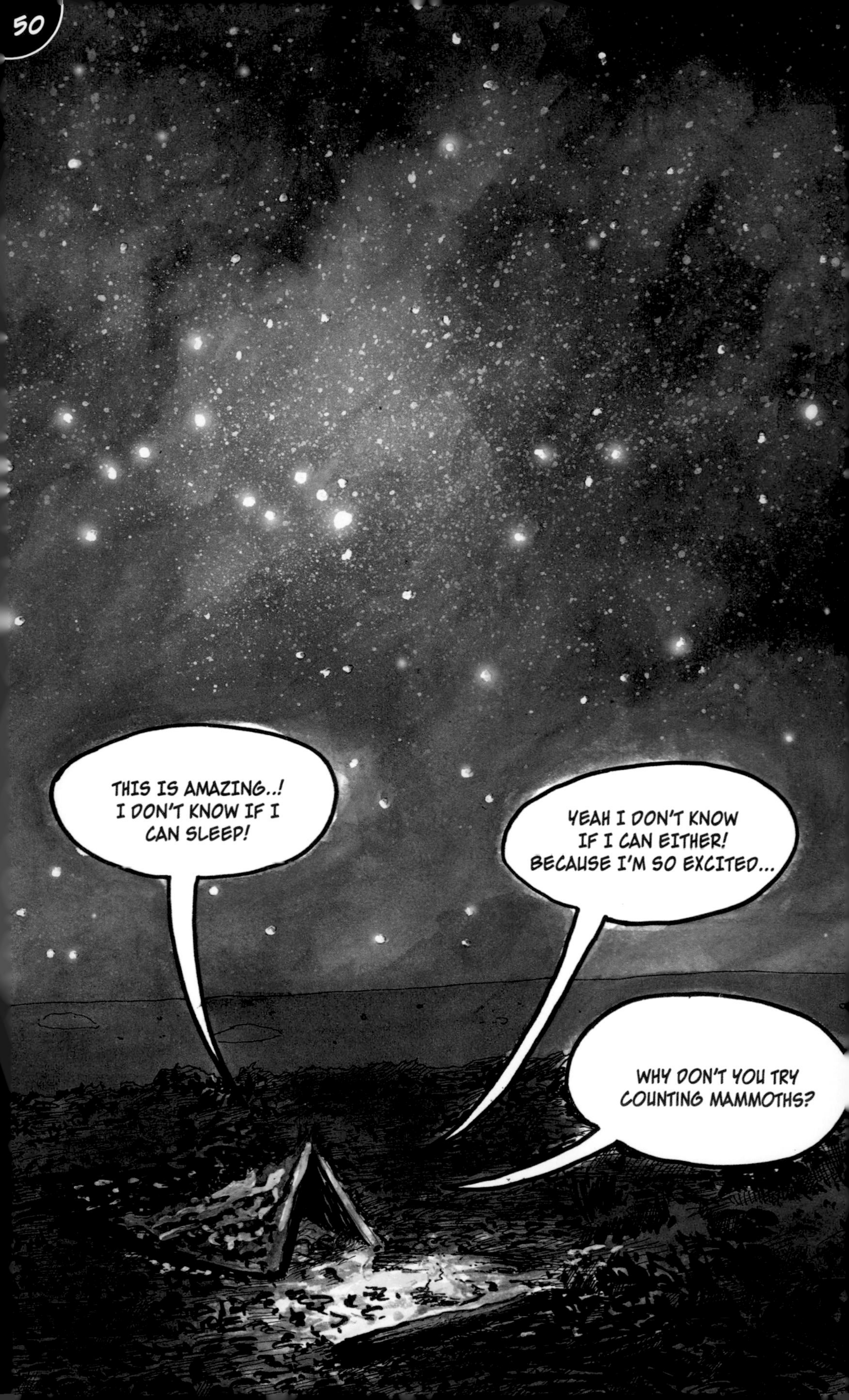
THIS IS AMAZING..! I DON'T KNOW IF I CAN SLEEP!
YEAH I DON'T KNOW IF I CAN EITHER! BECAUSE I'M SO EXCITED...
WHY DON'T YOU TRY COUNTING MAMMOTHS?

CHAPTER FOUR

THERE'S SO MUCH WATER

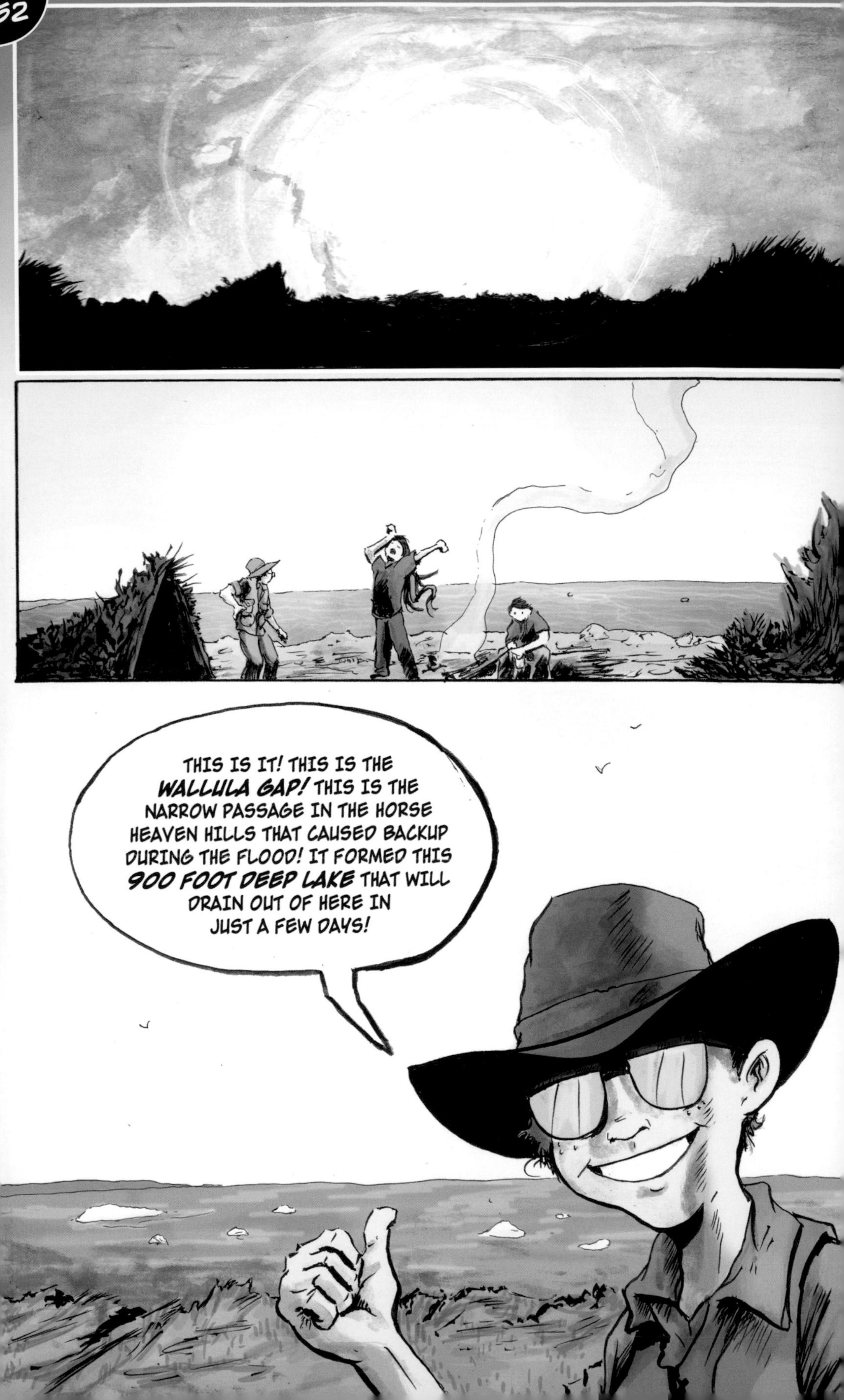
THIS IS IT! THIS IS THE WALLULA GAP! THIS IS THE NARROW PASSAGE IN THE HORSE HEAVEN HILLS THAT CAUSED BACKUP DURING THE FLOOD! IT FORMED THIS 900 FOOT DEEP LAKE THAT WILL DRAIN OUT OF HERE IN JUST A FEW DAYS!

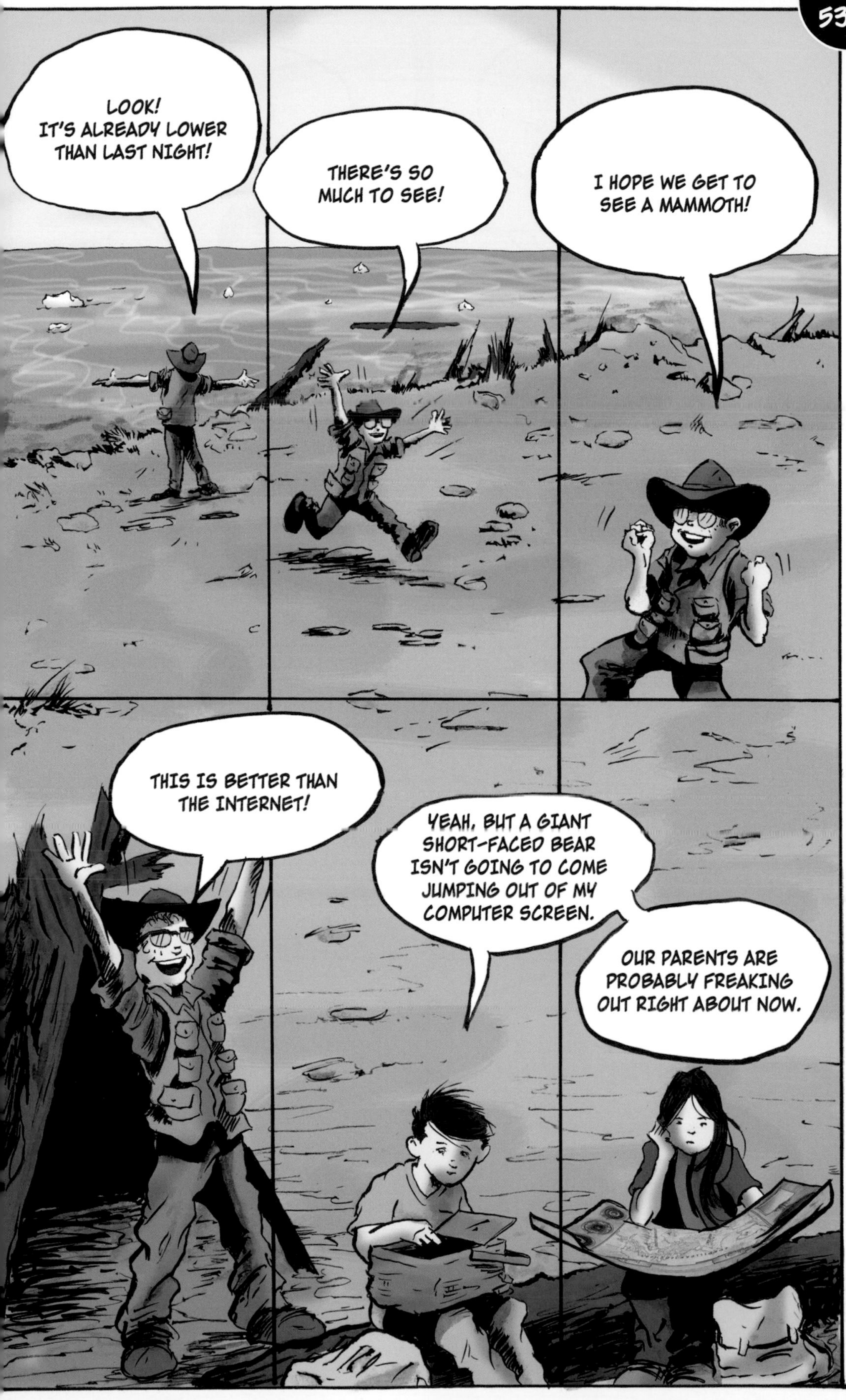
LOOK!
IT'S ALREADY LOWER THAN LAST NIGHT!
THERE'S SO MUCH TO SEE!
I HOPE WE GET TO SEE A MAMMOTH!
THIS IS BETTER THAN THE INTERNET!
YEAH, BUT A GIANT SHORT-FACED BEAR ISN'T GOING TO COME JUMPING OUT OF MY COMPUTER SCREEN.
OUR PARENTS ARE PROBABLY FREAKING OUT RIGHT ABOUT NOW.

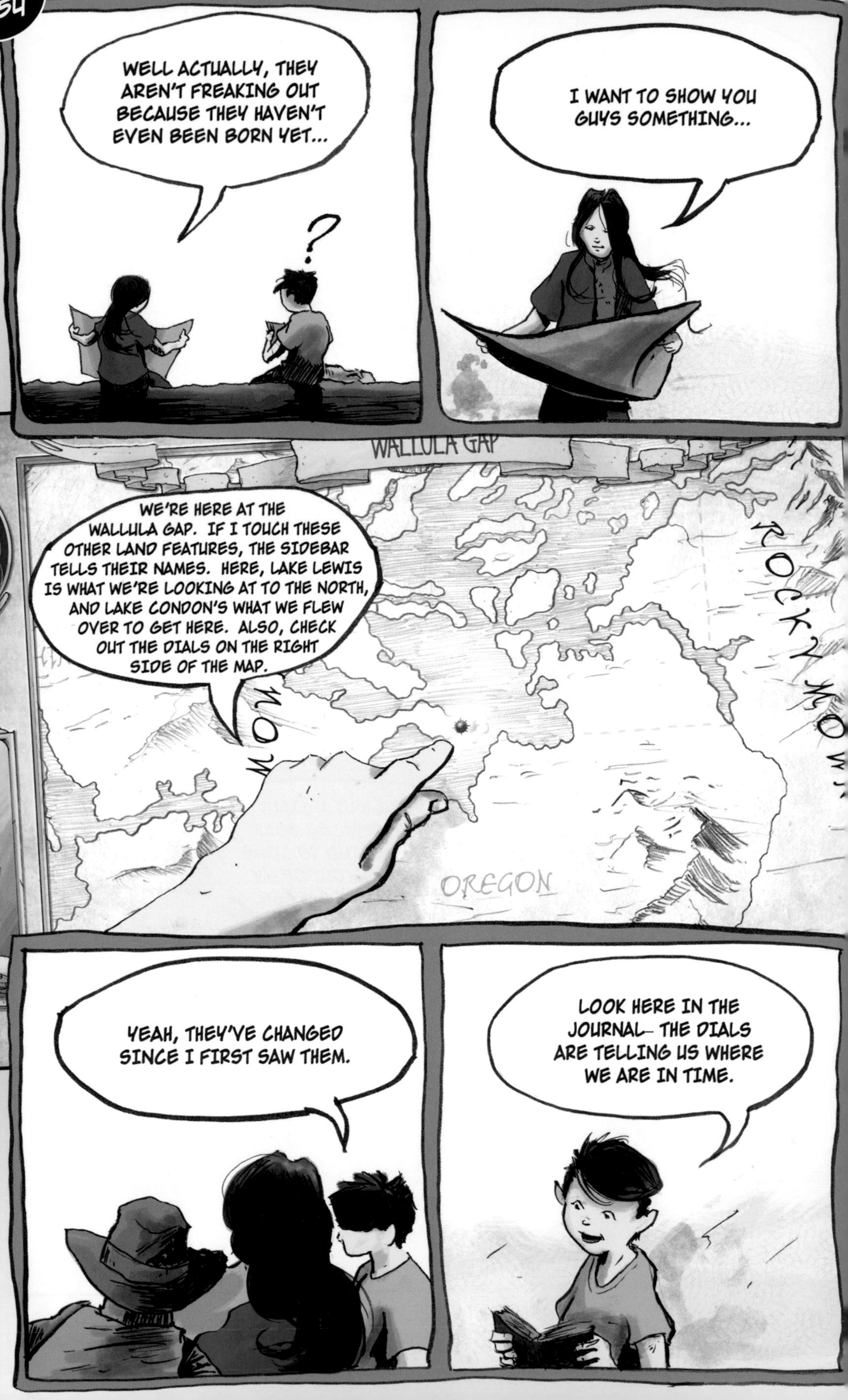
WELL ACTUALLY, THEY AREN'T FREAKING OUT BECAUSE THEY HAVEN'T EVEN BEEN BORN YET...
?
I WANT TO SHOW YOU GUYS SOMETHING...
WALLULA GAP
WE'RE HERE AT THE WALLULA GAP. IF I TOUCH THESE OTHER LAND FEATURES, THE SIDEBAR TELLS THEIR NAMES. HERE, LAKE LEWIS IS WHAT WE'RE LOOKING AT TO THE NORTH, AND LAKE CONDON'S WHAT WE FLEW OVER TO GET HERE. ALSO, CHECK OUT THE DIALS ON THE RIGHT SIDE OF THE MAP.
ROCKY MOUN
OREGON
YEAH, THEY'VE CHANGED SINCE I FIRST SAW THEM.
LOOK HERE IN THE JOURNAL– THE DIALS ARE TELLING US WHERE WE ARE IN TIME.

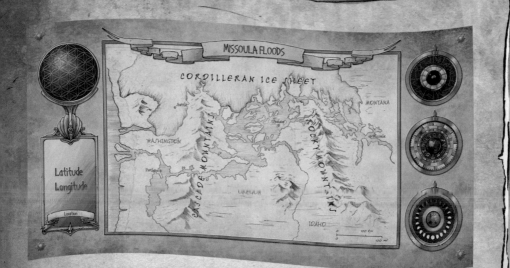

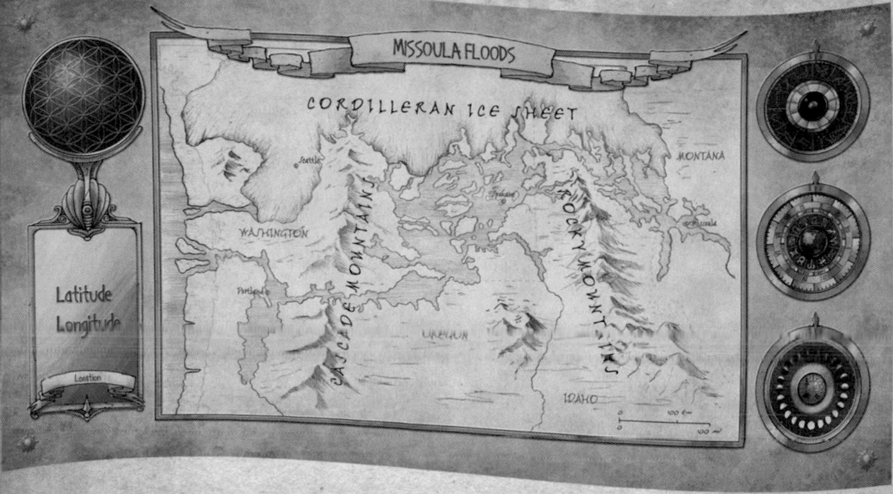
MISSOULA FLOODS
CORDILLERAN ICE SHEET
MONTANA
WASHINGTON
CASCADE MOUNTAINS
ROCKY MOUNTAINS
IDAHO
Latitude
Longitude
Location

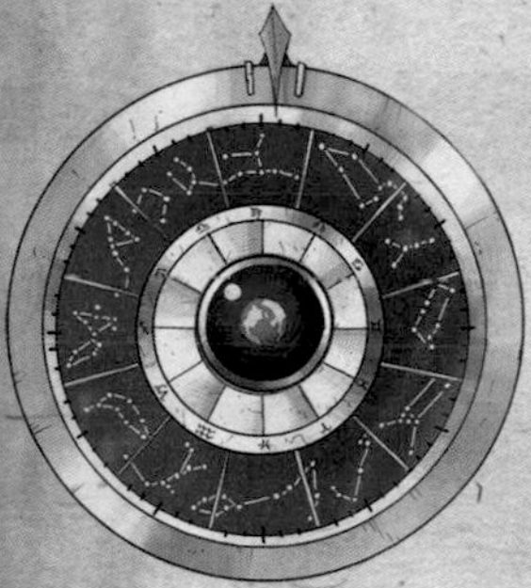

Precessional Dial

Marks time periods of 2,150 years, known as "ages". Each "age" is assigned a constellation from the ecliptic.

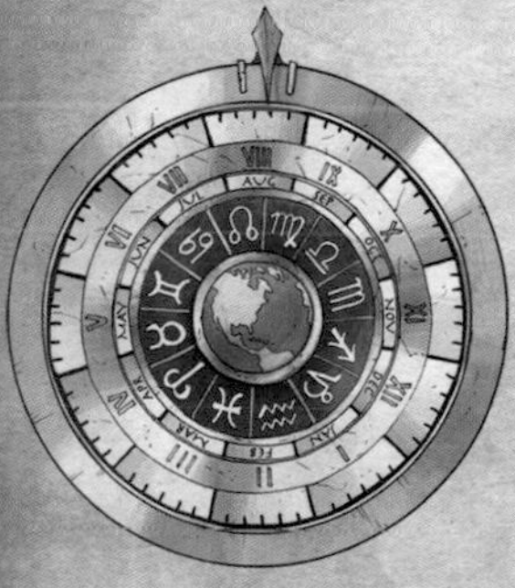

Month Dial

Marks the lunar month periods with signs of the classical zodiac.
Example: Most of the month of August is in the sign of Leo the lion.

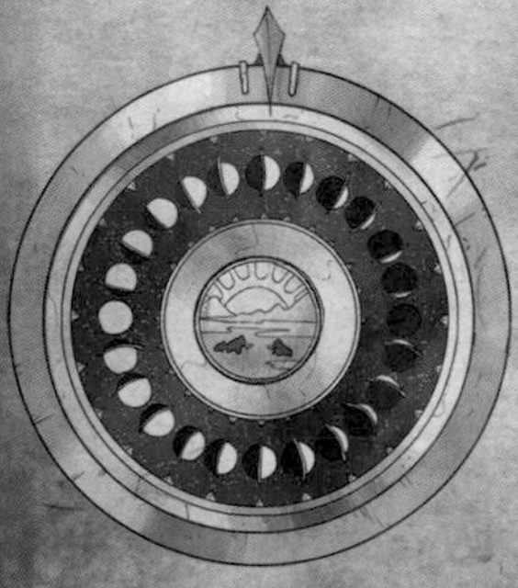

Lunar Dial

Counts the days by the phases of the moon.

Note: It takes about 28 days to complete a lunar cycle.

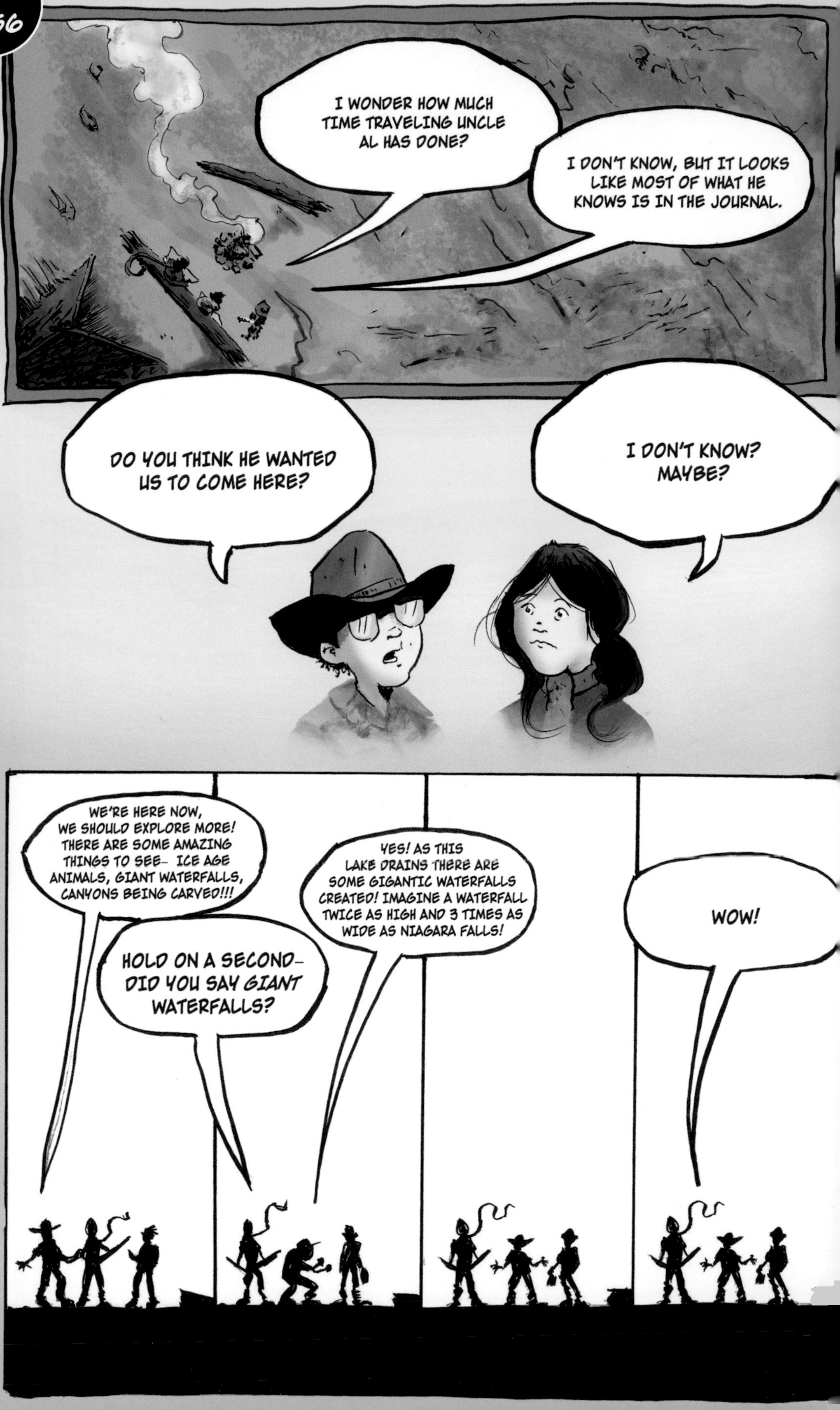
I WONDER HOW MUCH TIME TRAVELING UNCLE AL HAS DONE?
I DON'T KNOW, BUT IT LOOKS LIKE MOST OF WHAT HE KNOWS IS IN THE JOURNAL.
DO YOU THINK HE WANTED US TO COME HERE?
I DON'T KNOW? MAYBE?
WE'RE HERE NOW, WE SHOULD EXPLORE MORE! THERE ARE SOME AMAZING THINGS TO SEE- ICE AGE ANIMALS, GIANT WATERFALLS, CANYONS BEING CARVED!!!
HOLD ON A SECOND- DID YOU SAY GIANT WATERFALLS?
YES! AS THIS LAKE DRAINS THERE ARE SOME GIGANTIC WATERFALLS CREATED! IMAGINE A WATERFALL TWICE AS HIGH AND 3 TIMES AS WIDE AS NIAGARA FALLS!
WOW!

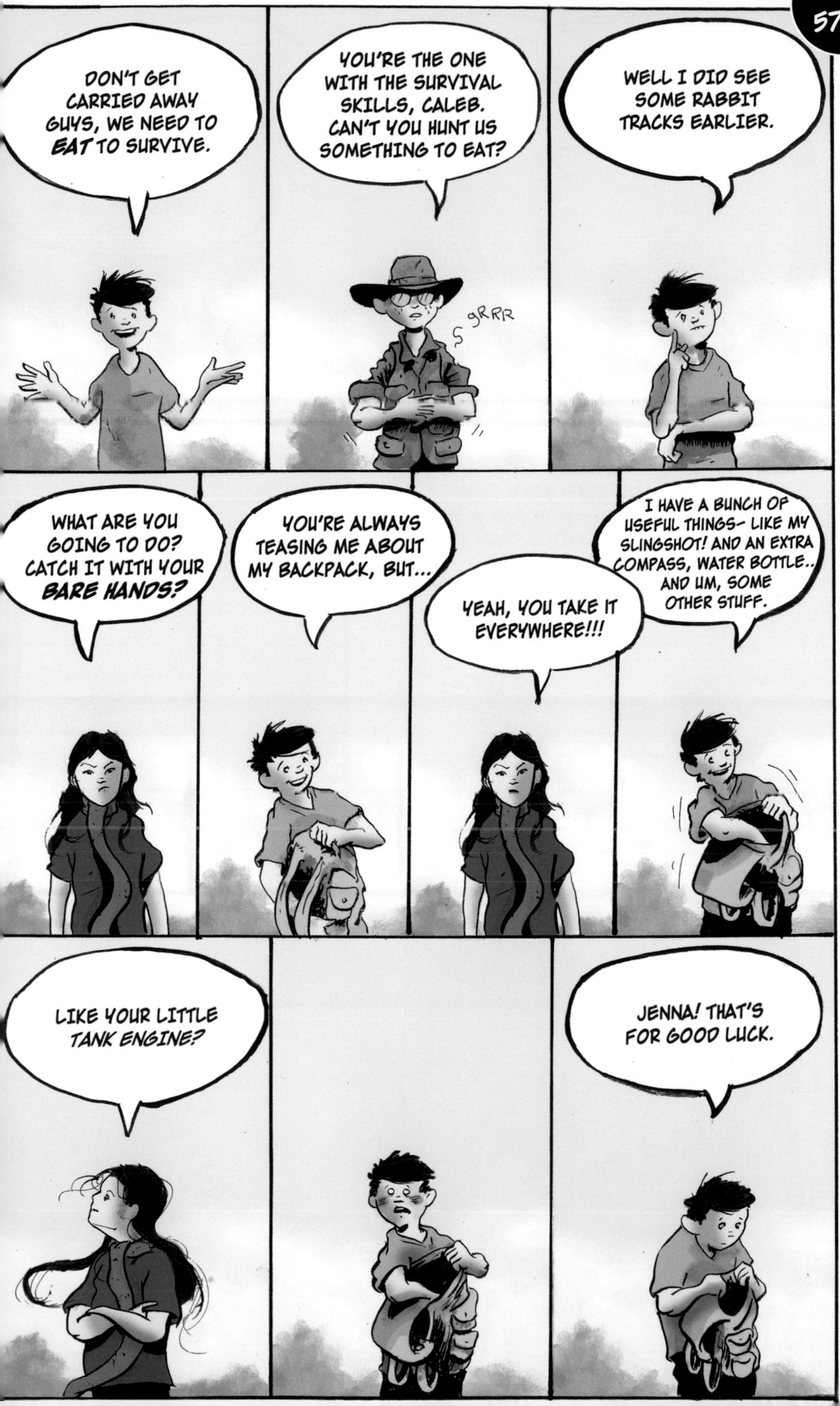
DON'T GET CARRIED AWAY GUYS, WE NEED TO EAT TO SURVIVE.
YOU'RE THE ONE WITH THE SURVIVAL SKILLS, CALEB. CAN'T YOU HUNT US SOMETHING TO EAT?
GRRR
WELL I DID SEE SOME RABBIT TRACKS EARLIER.
WHAT ARE YOU GOING TO DO? CATCH IT WITH YOUR BARE HANDS?
YOU'RE ALWAYS TEASING ME ABOUT MY BACKPACK, BUT...
YEAH, YOU TAKE IT EVERYWHERE!!!
I HAVE A BUNCH OF USEFUL THINGS- LIKE MY SLINGSHOT! AND AN EXTRA COMPASS, WATER BOTTLE.. AND UM, SOME OTHER STUFF.
LIKE YOUR LITTLE TANK ENGINE?
JENNA! THAT'S FOR GOOD LUCK.

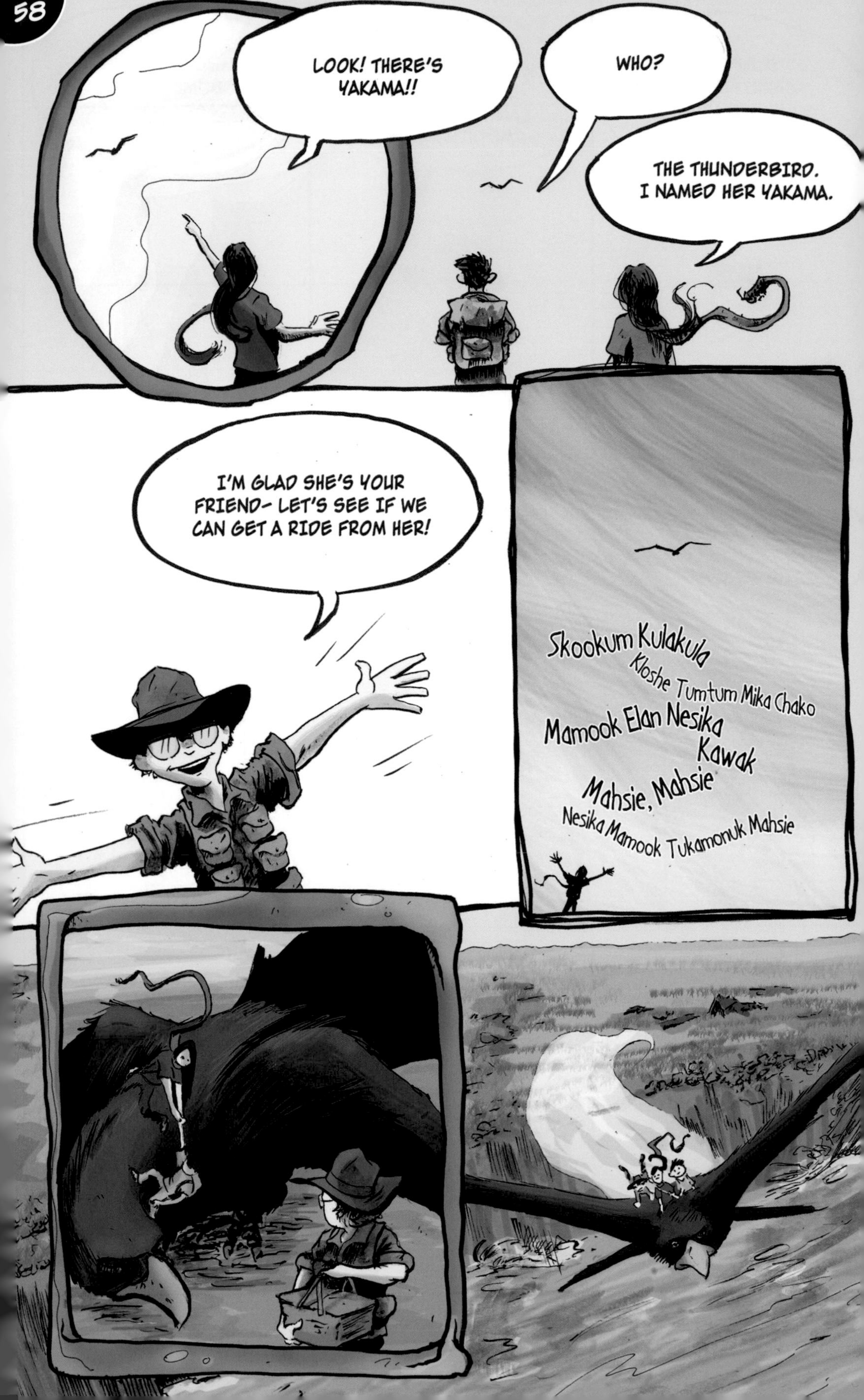
LOOK! THERE'S YAKAMA!!
WHO?
THE THUNDERBIRD. I NAMED HER YAKAMA.
I'M GLAD SHE'S YOUR FRIEND- LET'S SEE IF WE CAN GET A RIDE FROM HER!
Skookum Kulakula
Kloshe Tumtum Mika Chako
Mamook Elan Nesika
Kawak
Mahsie, Mahsie
Nesika Mamook Tukamonuk Mahsie

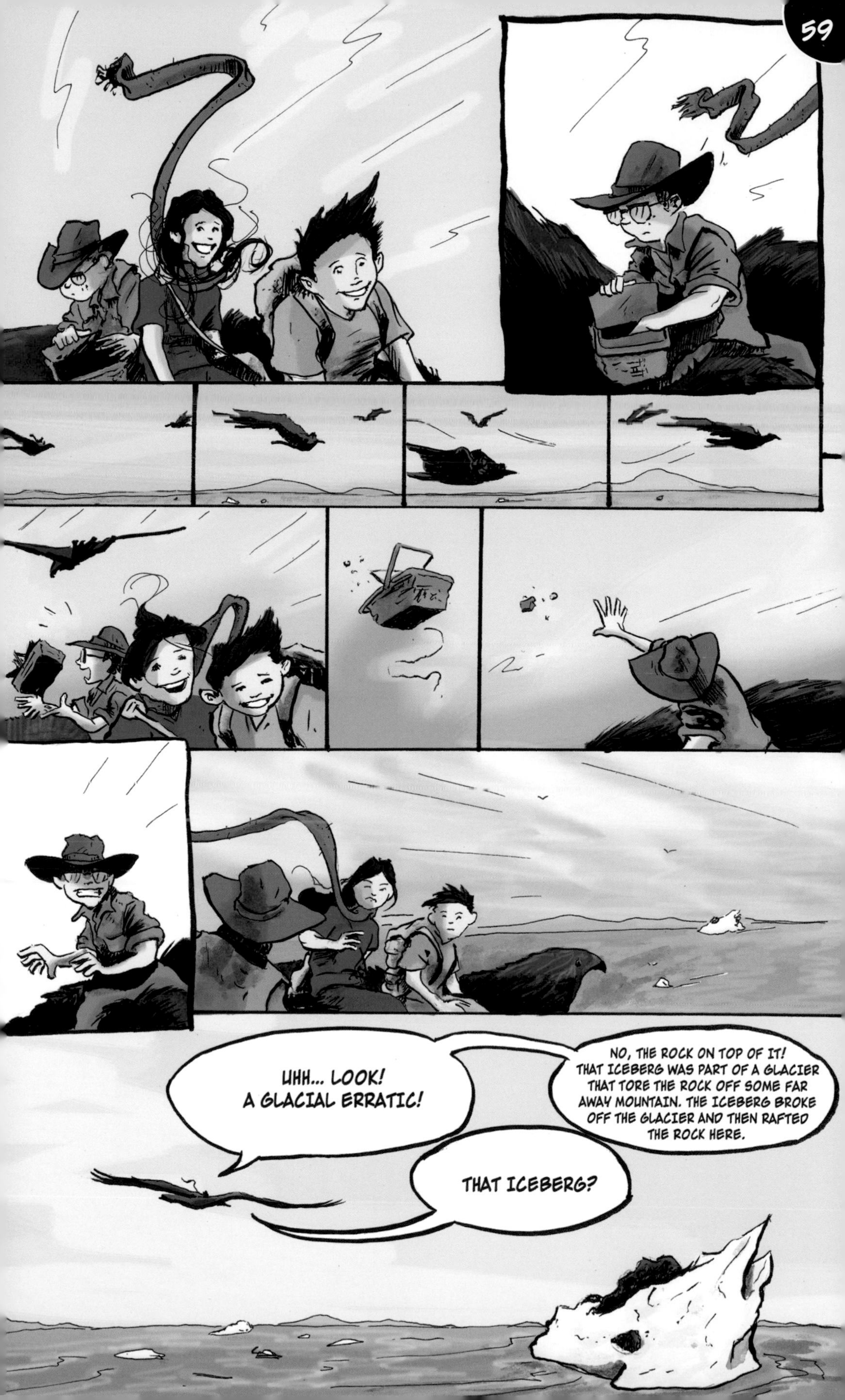
UHH... LOOK!
A GLACIAL ERRATIC!
NO, THE ROCK ON TOP OF IT! THAT ICEBERG WAS PART OF A GLACIER THAT TORE THE ROCK OFF SOME FAR AWAY MOUNTAIN. THE ICEBERG BROKE OFF THE GLACIER AND THEN RAFTED THE ROCK HERE.
THAT ICEBERG?

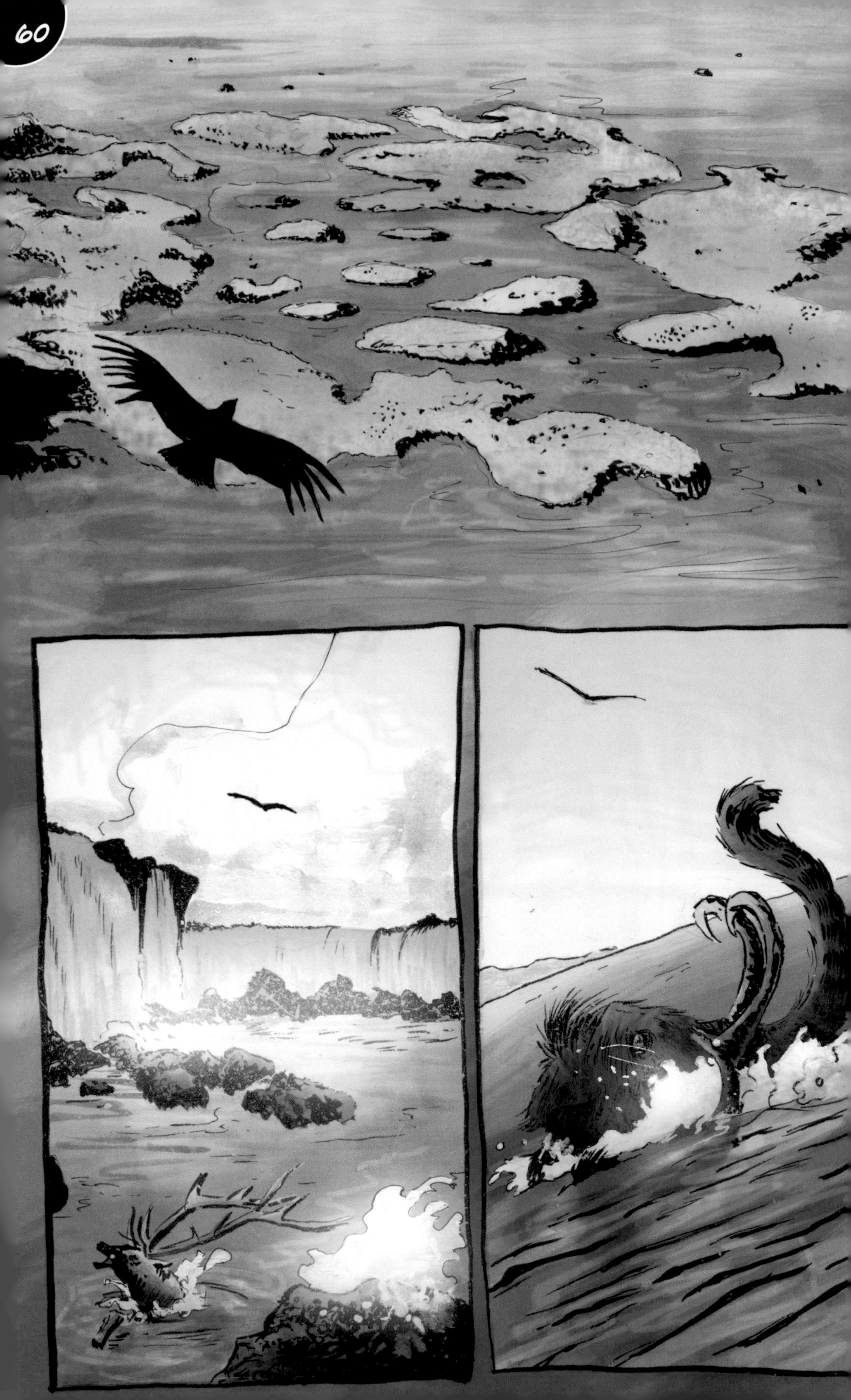

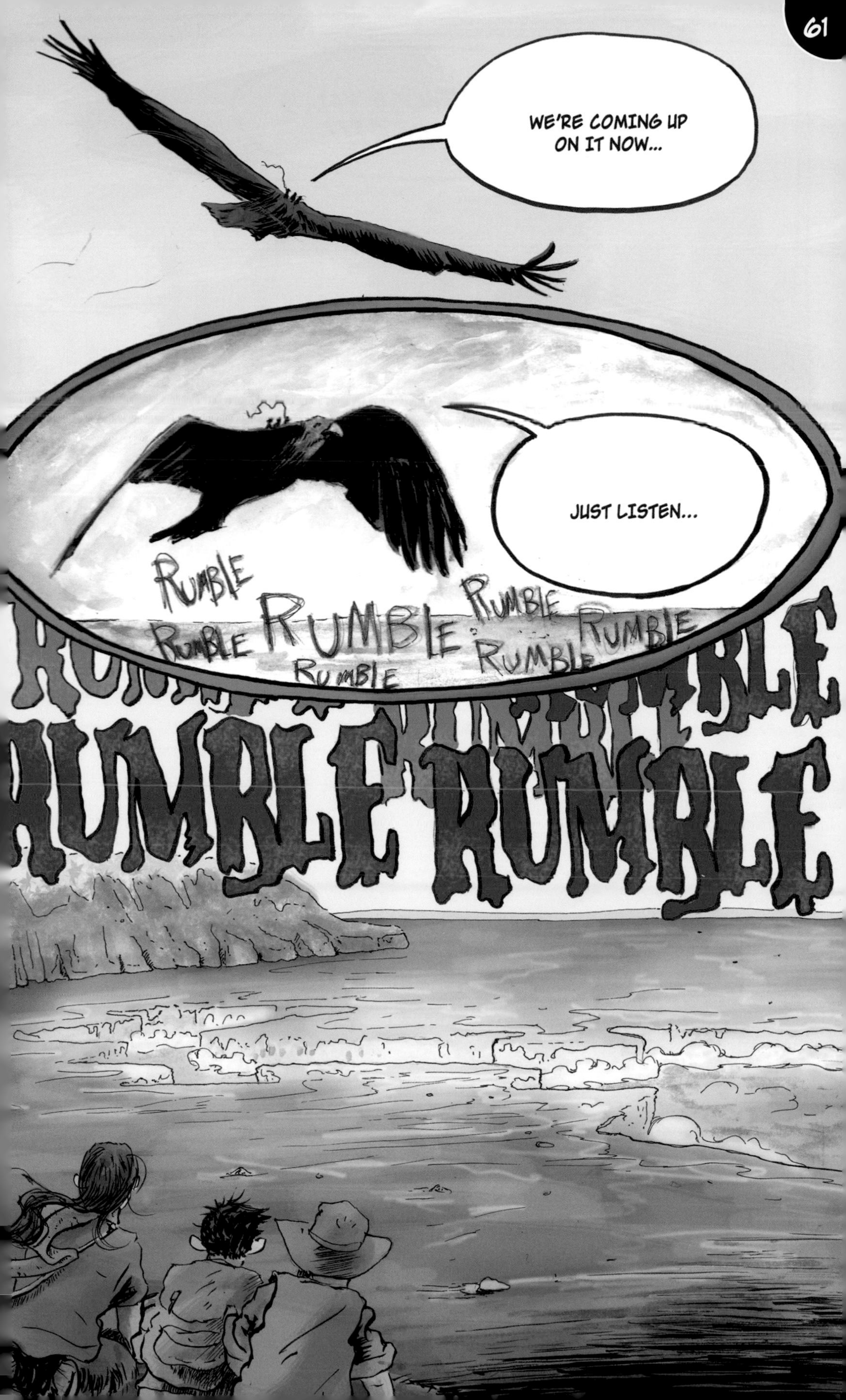
WE'RE COMING UP ON IT NOW...
JUST LISTEN...
RUMBLE
RUMBLE
RUMBLE
RUMBLE
RUMBLE
RUMBLE
RUMBLE
RUMBLE
RUMBLE

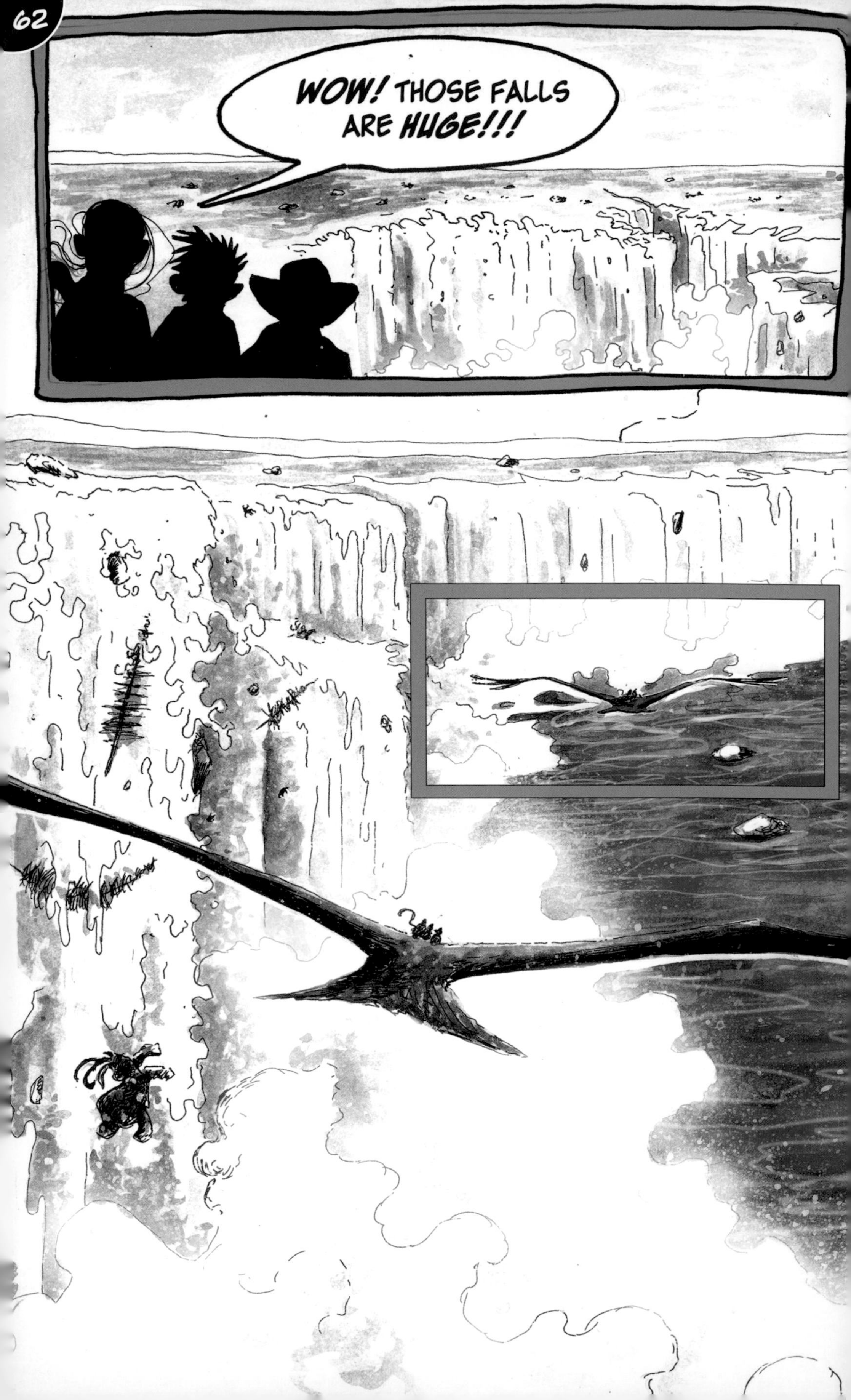
WOW! THOSE FALLS ARE HUGE!!!

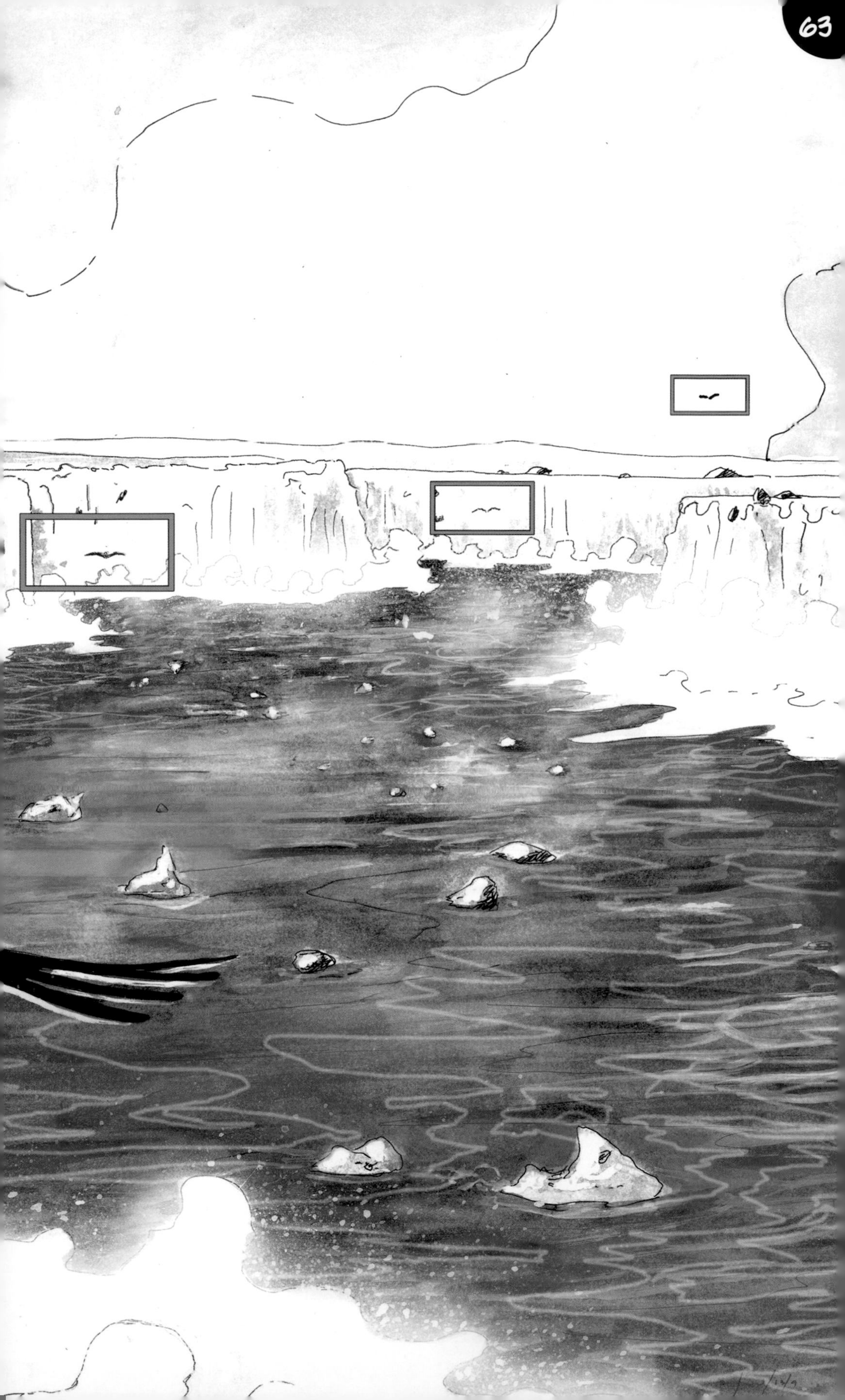

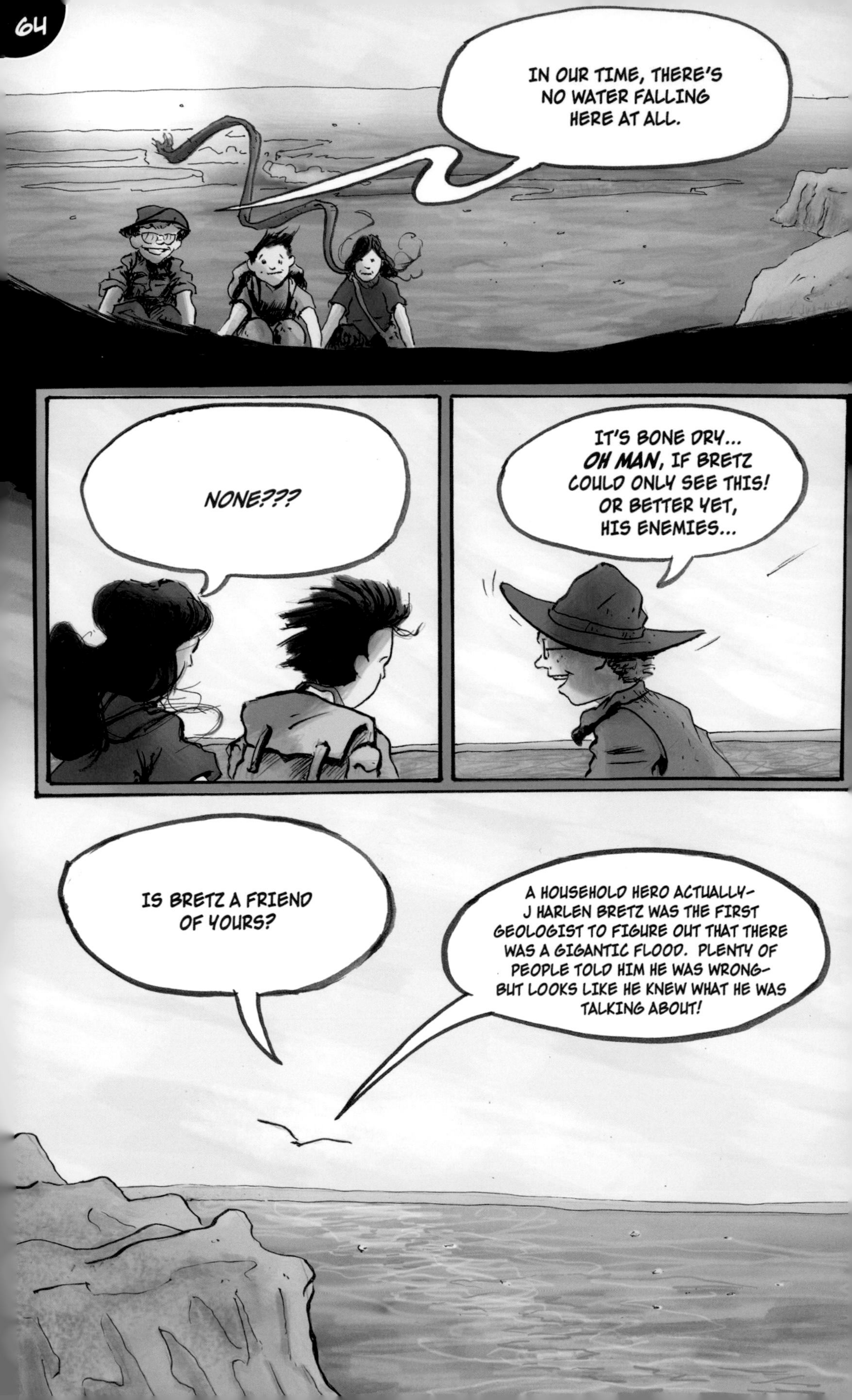
IN OUR TIME, THERE'S NO WATER FALLING HERE AT ALL.
NONE???
IT'S BONE DRY... OH MAN, IF BRETZ COULD ONLY SEE THIS! OR BETTER YET, HIS ENEMIES...
IS BRETZ A FRIEND OF YOURS?
A HOUSEHOLD HERO ACTUALLY- J HARLEN BRETZ WAS THE FIRST GEOLOGIST TO FIGURE OUT THAT THERE WAS A GIGANTIC FLOOD. PLENTY OF PEOPLE TOLD HIM HE WAS WRONG- BUT LOOKS LIKE HE KNEW WHAT HE WAS TALKING ABOUT!

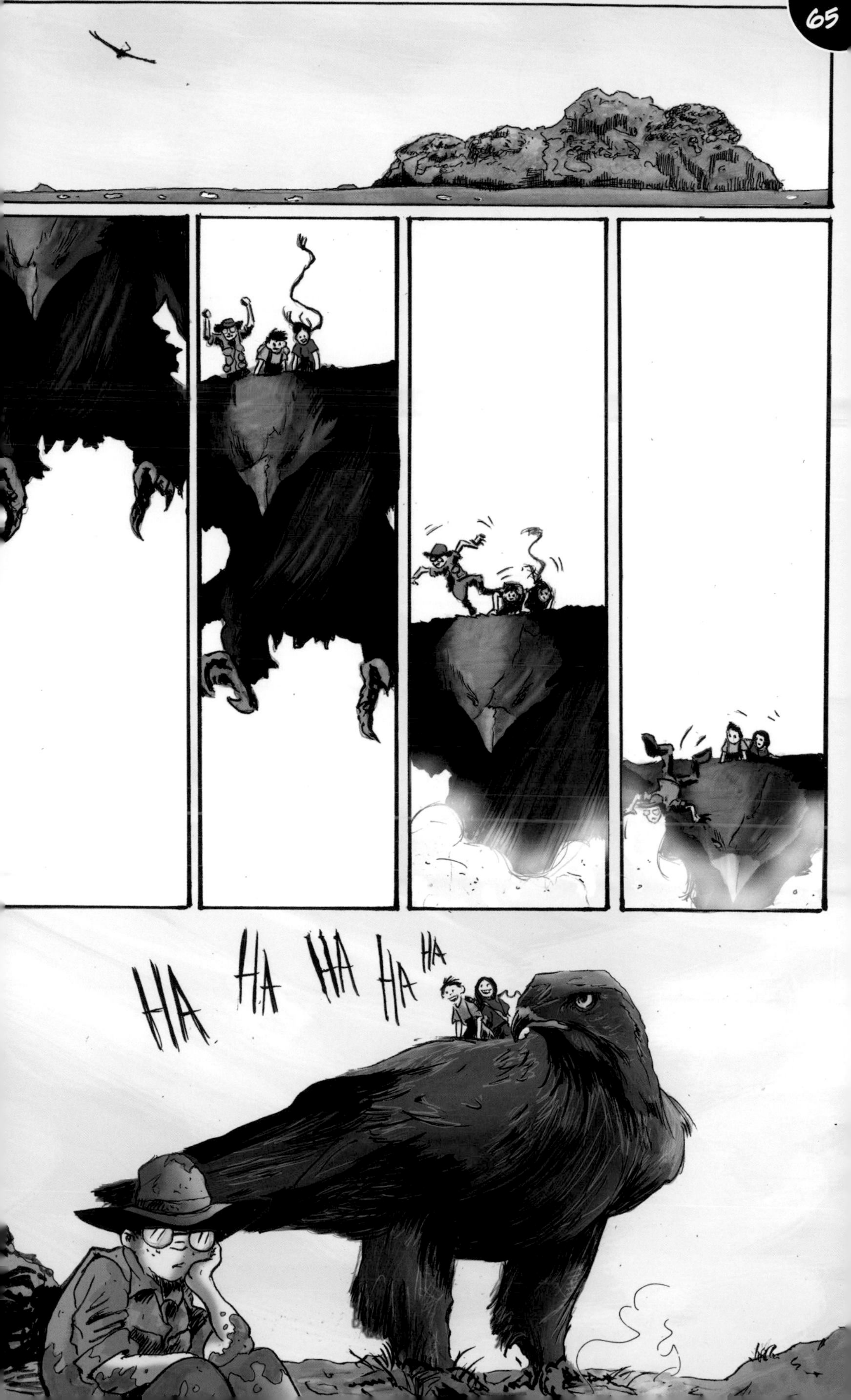
HA HA HA HA HA

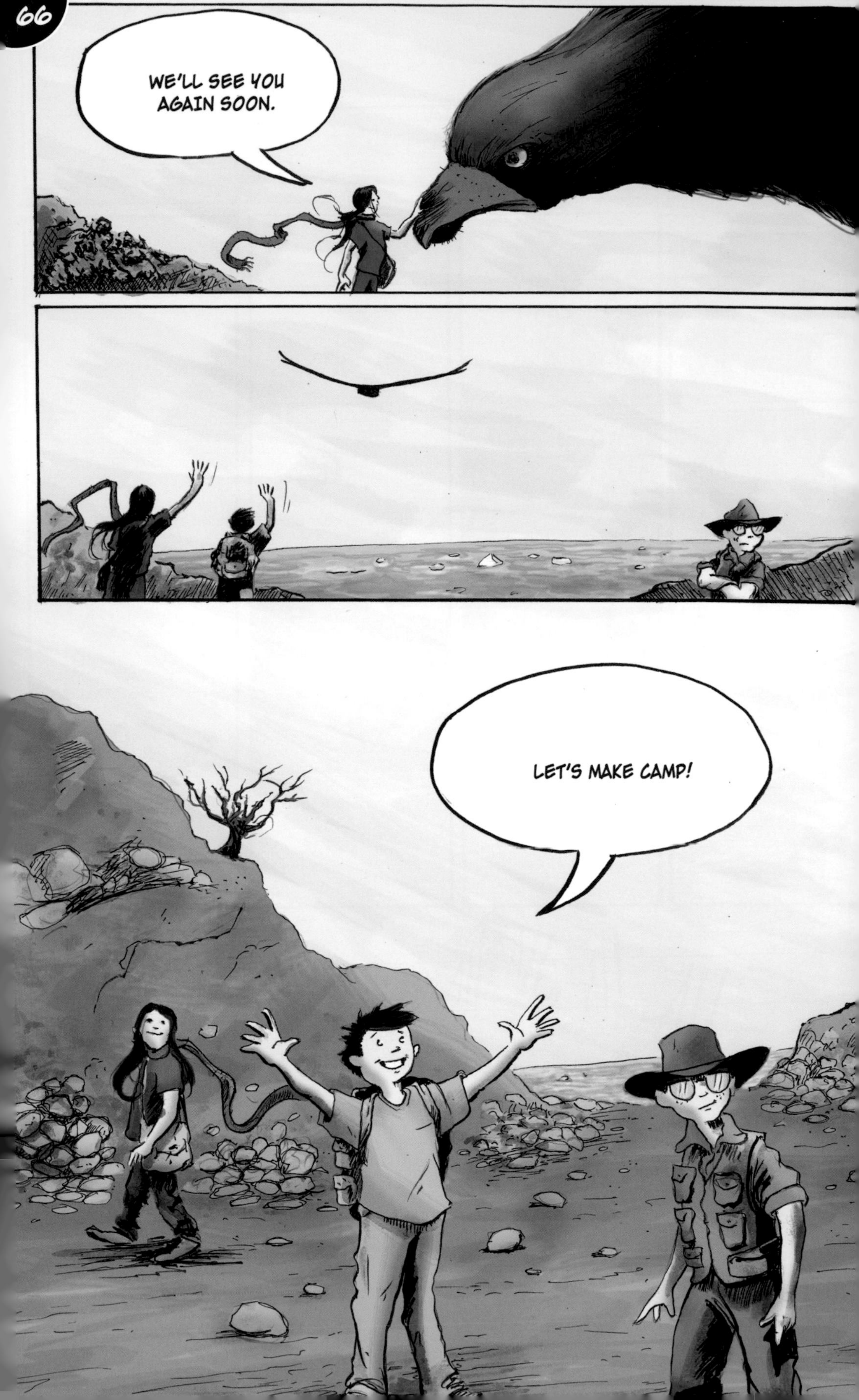
WE'LL SEE YOU AGAIN SOON.
LET'S MAKE CAMP!

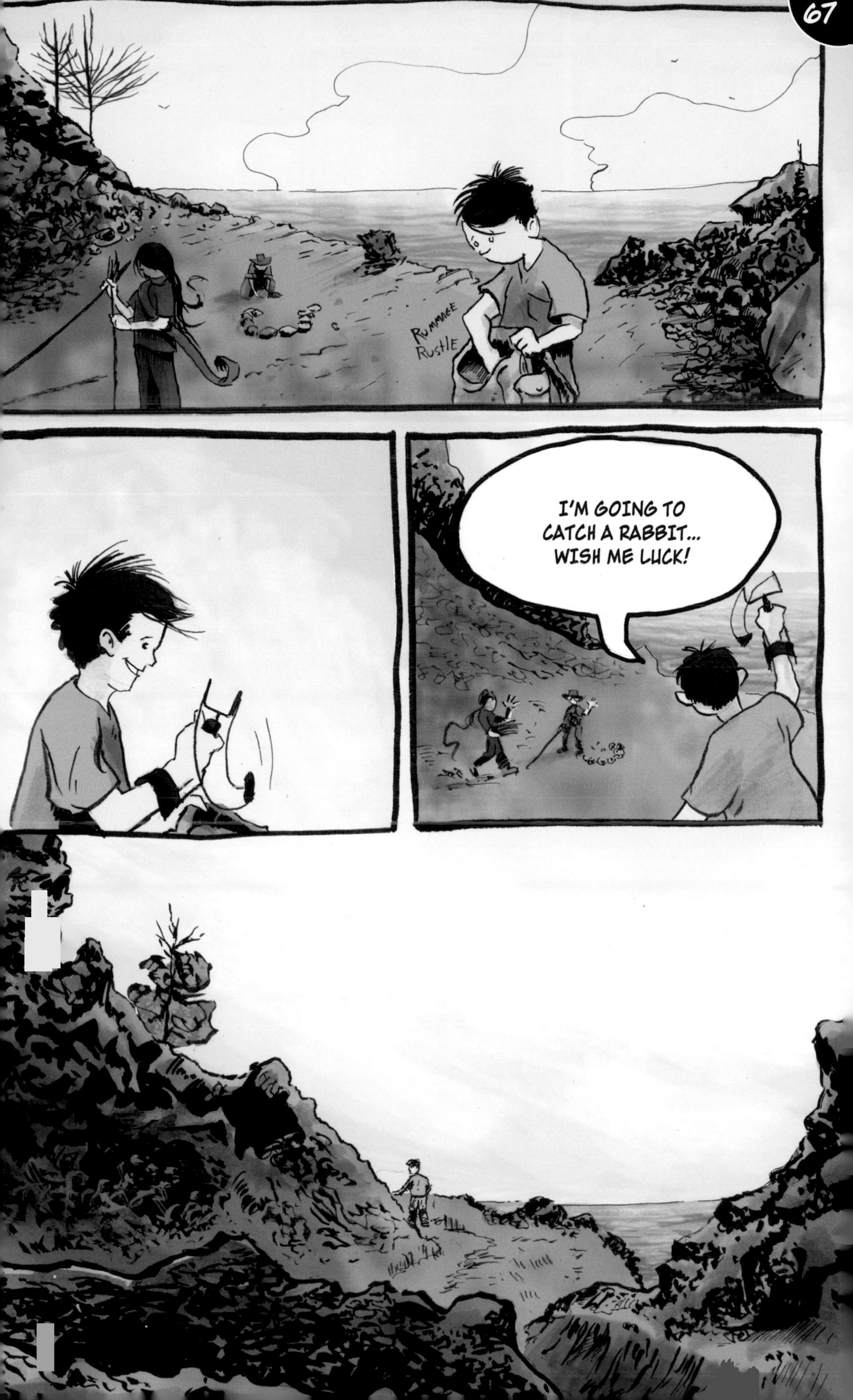
RUMMAGE
RUSTLE
I'M GOING TO CATCH A RABBIT... WISH ME LUCK!

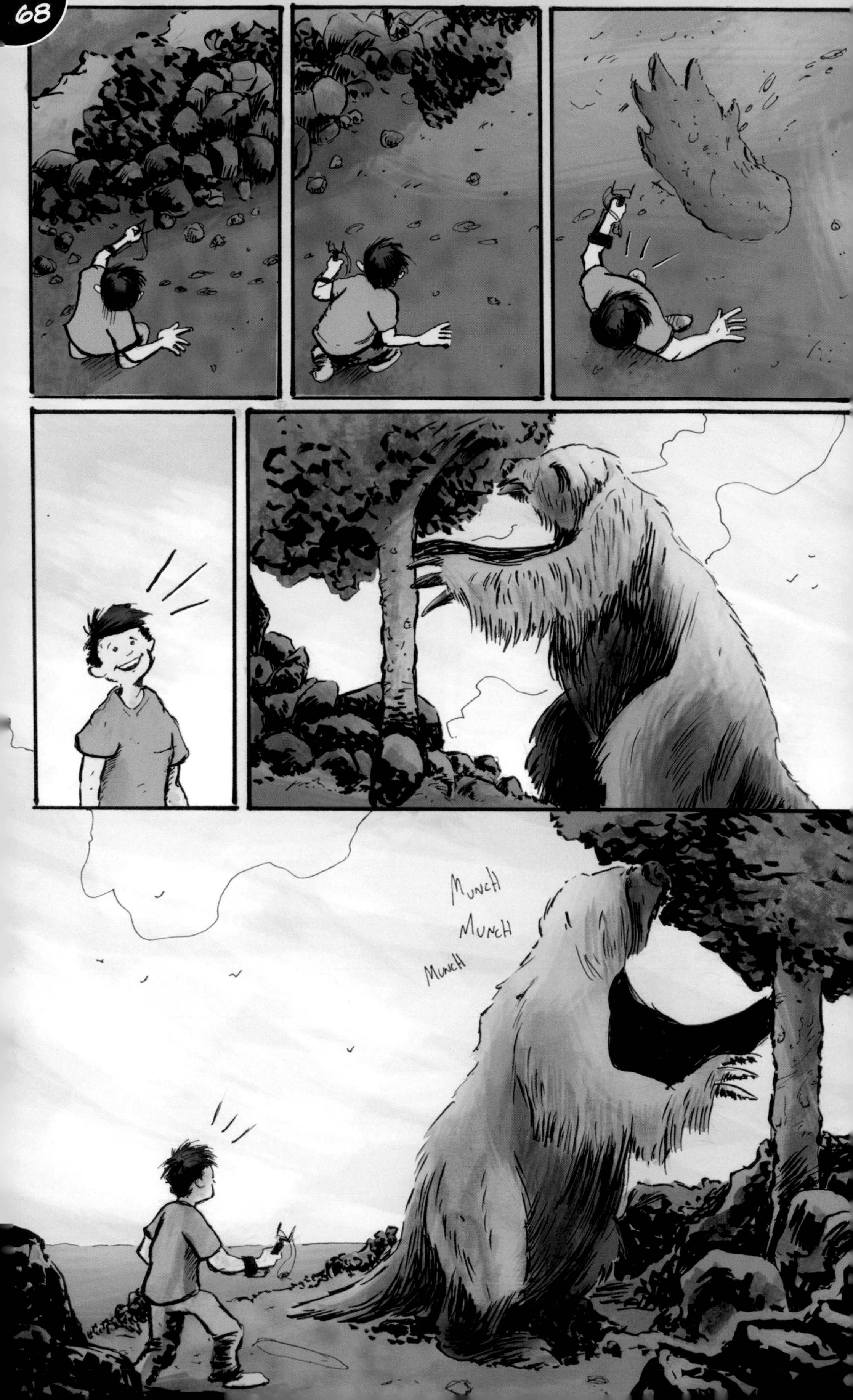
MUNCH
MUNCH
MUNCH

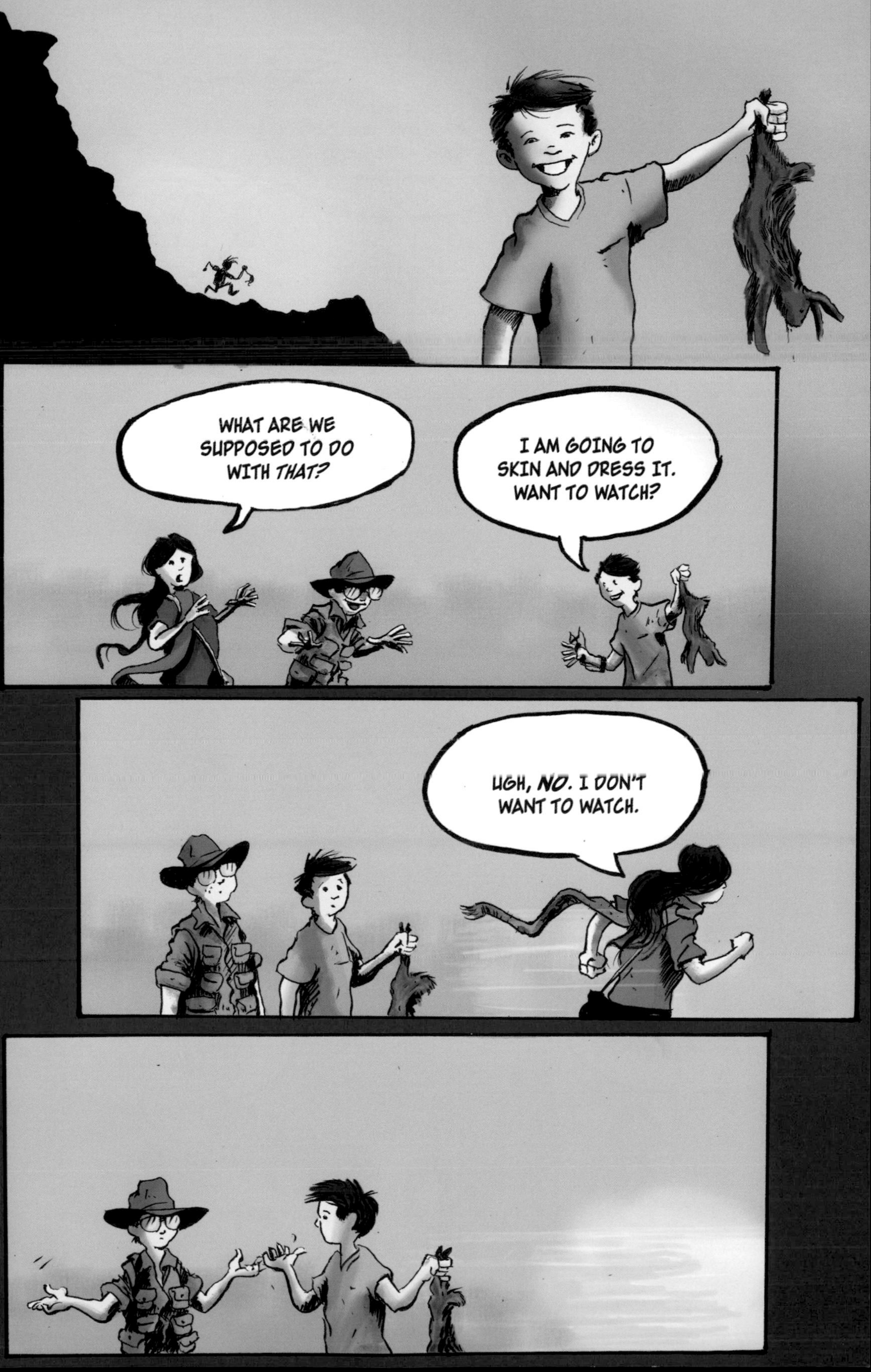
WHAT ARE WE SUPPOSED TO DO WITH *THAT?*
I AM GOING TO SKIN AND DRESS IT. WANT TO WATCH?
UGH, ***NO***. I DON'T WANT TO WATCH.

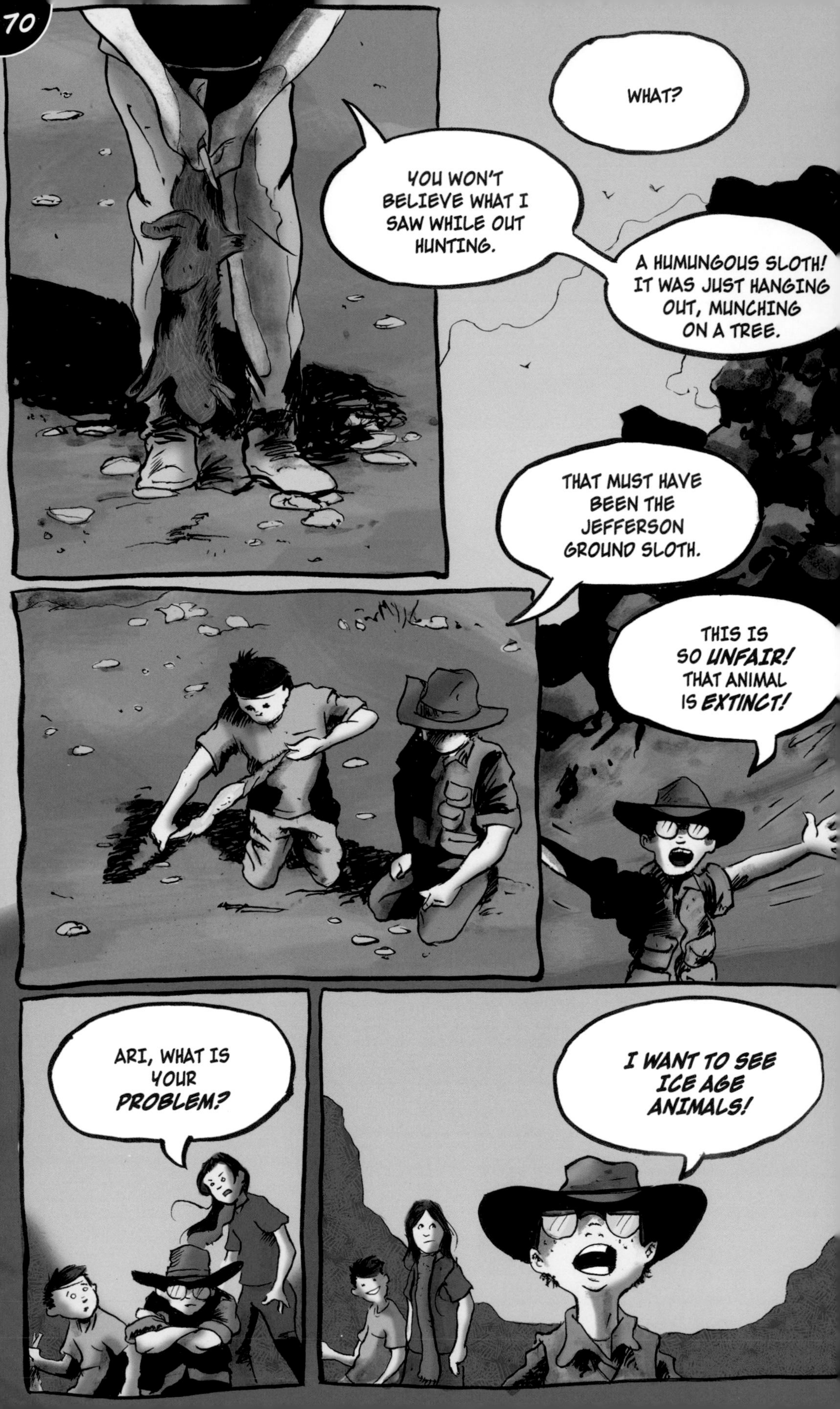
WHAT?
YOU WON'T BELIEVE WHAT I SAW WHILE OUT HUNTING.
A HUMUNGOUS SLOTH! IT WAS JUST HANGING OUT, MUNCHING ON A TREE.
THAT MUST HAVE BEEN THE JEFFERSON GROUND SLOTH.
THIS IS SO *UNFAIR!* THAT ANIMAL IS *EXTINCT!*
ARI, WHAT IS YOUR *PROBLEM?*
I WANT TO SEE ICE AGE ANIMALS!

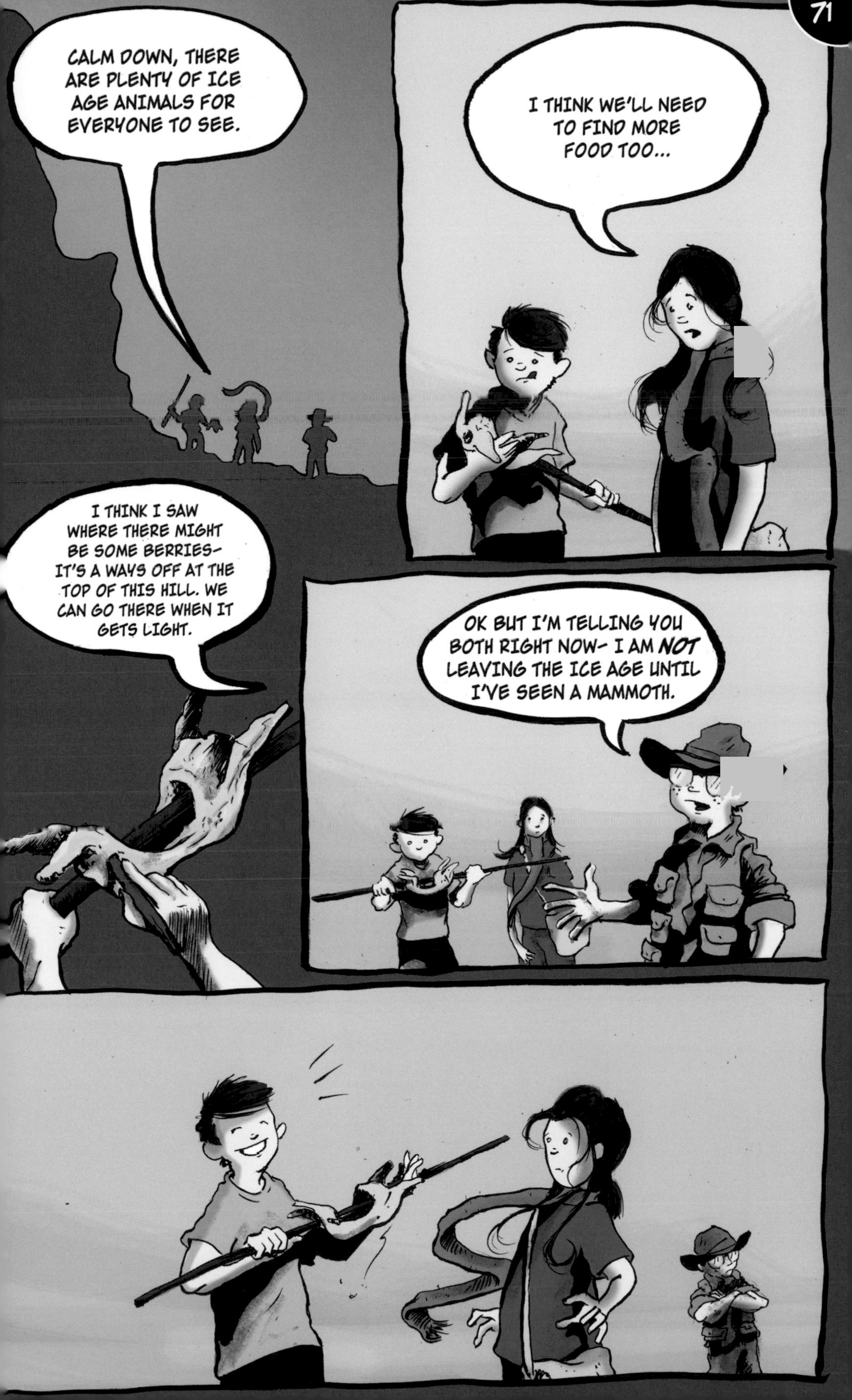
CALM DOWN, THERE ARE PLENTY OF ICE AGE ANIMALS FOR EVERYONE TO SEE.
I THINK WE'LL NEED TO FIND MORE FOOD TOO...
I THINK I SAW WHERE THERE MIGHT BE SOME BERRIES- IT'S A WAYS OFF AT THE TOP OF THIS HILL. WE CAN GO THERE WHEN IT GETS LIGHT.
OK BUT I'M TELLING YOU BOTH RIGHT NOW- I AM *NOT* LEAVING THE ICE AGE UNTIL I'VE SEEN A MAMMOTH.

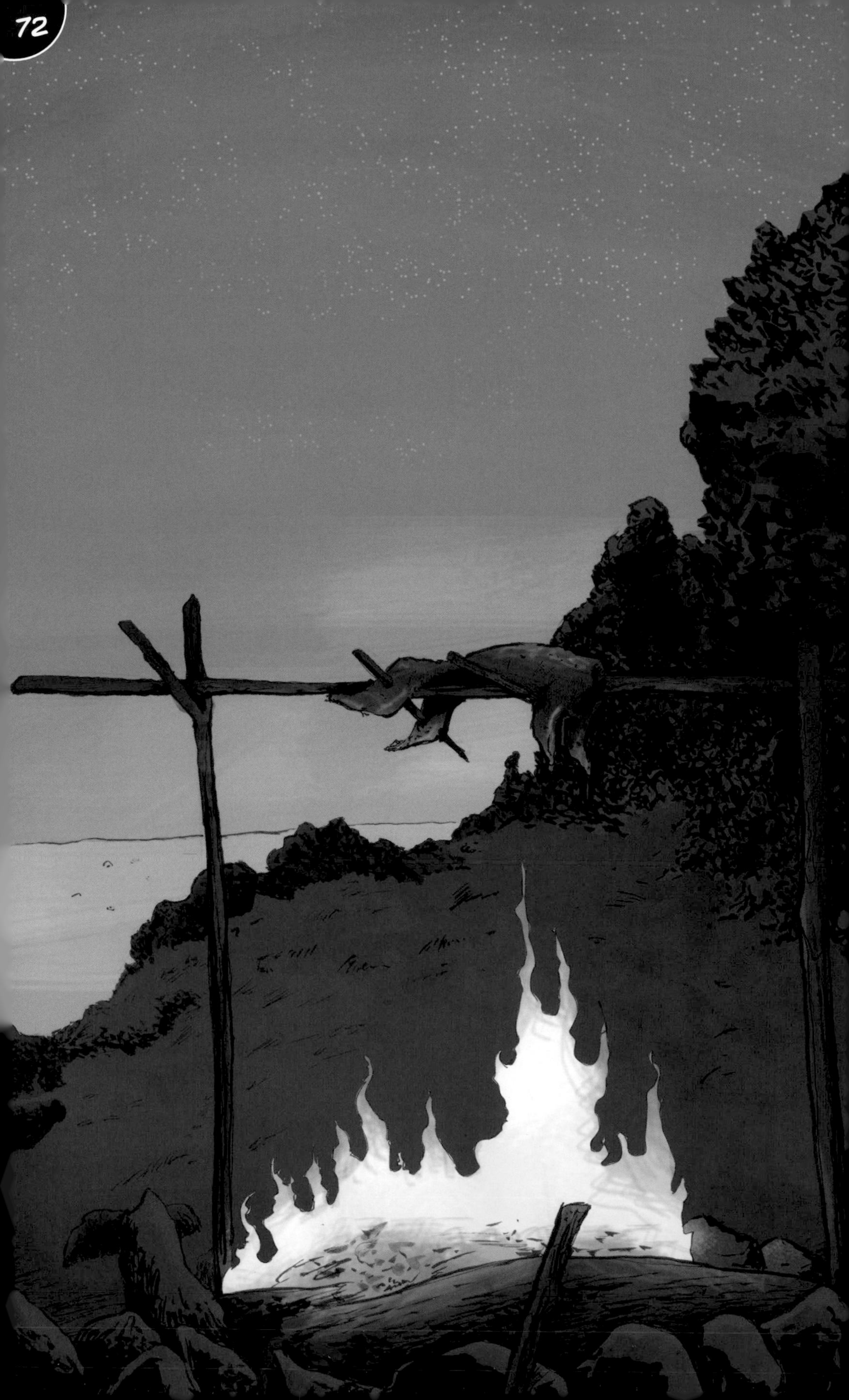

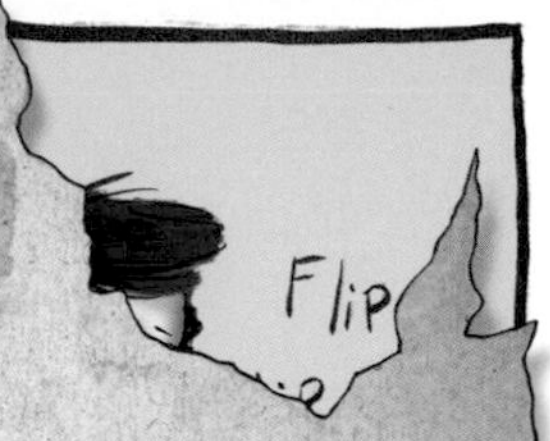
Flip

CHAPTER FIVE

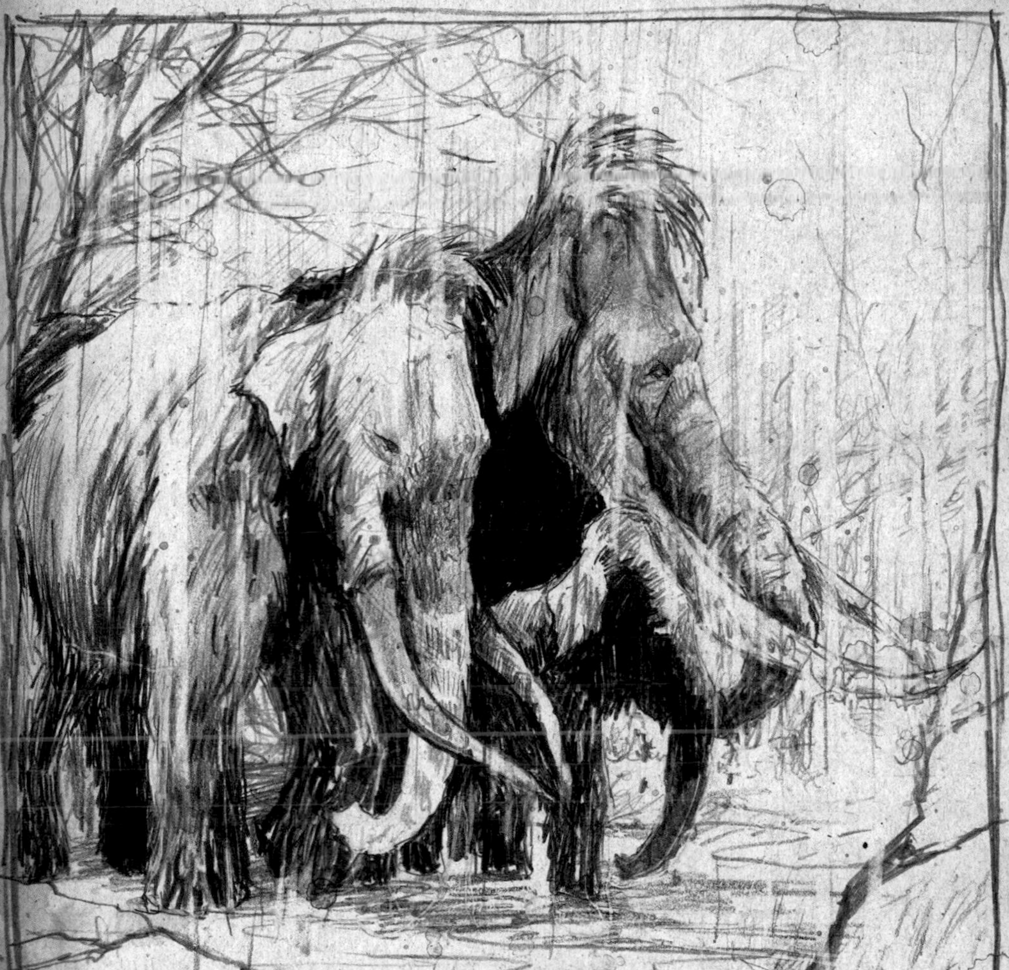

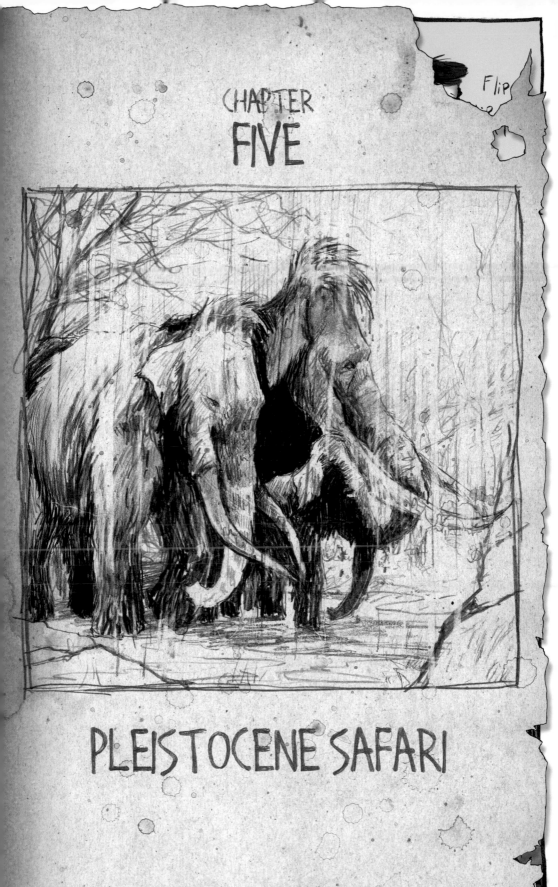

PLEISTOCENE SAFARI

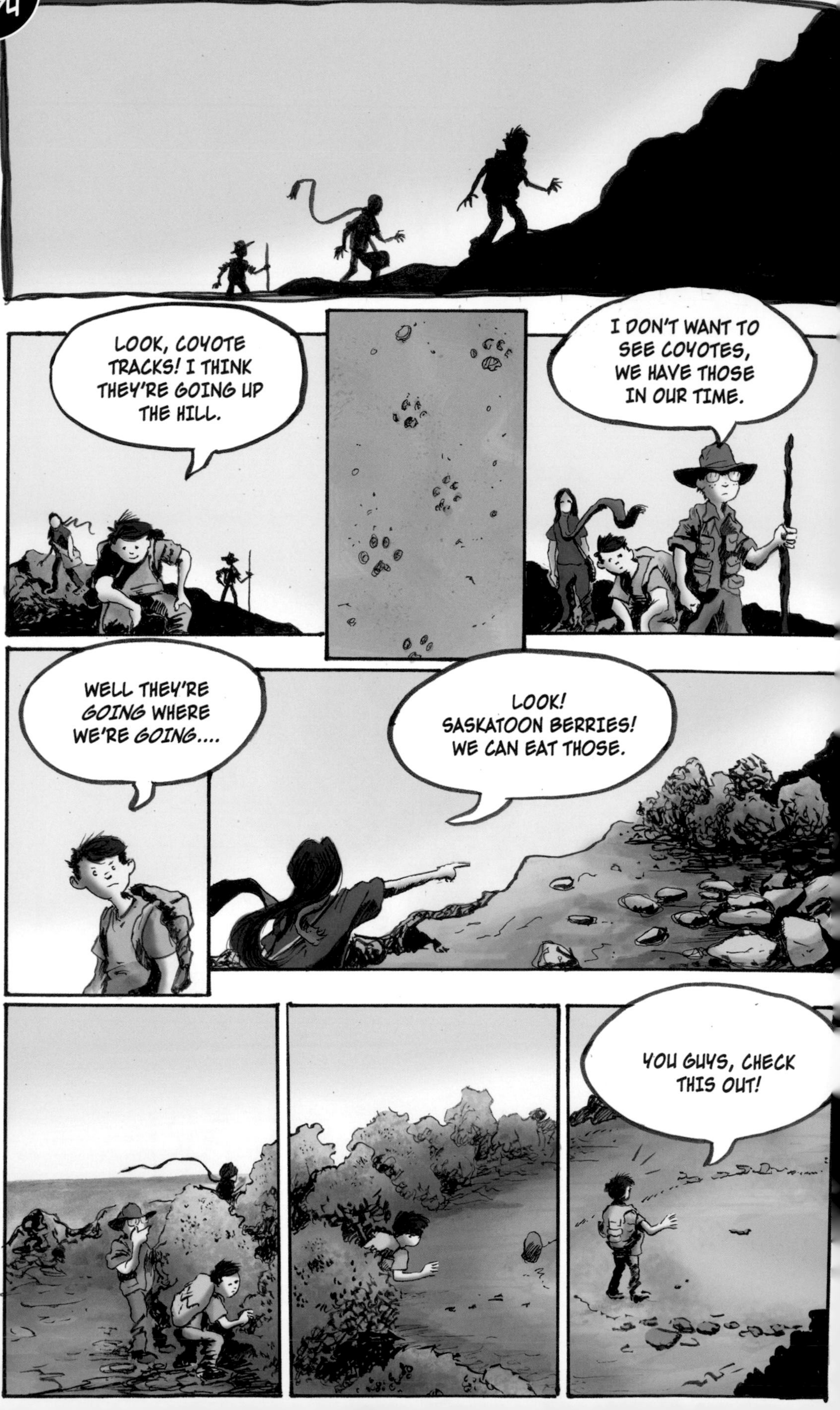
LOOK, COYOTE TRACKS! I THINK THEY'RE GOING UP THE HILL.
I DON'T WANT TO SEE COYOTES, WE HAVE THOSE IN OUR TIME.
WELL THEY'RE GOING WHERE WE'RE GOING....
LOOK! SASKATOON BERRIES! WE CAN EAT THOSE.
YOU GUYS, CHECK THIS OUT!

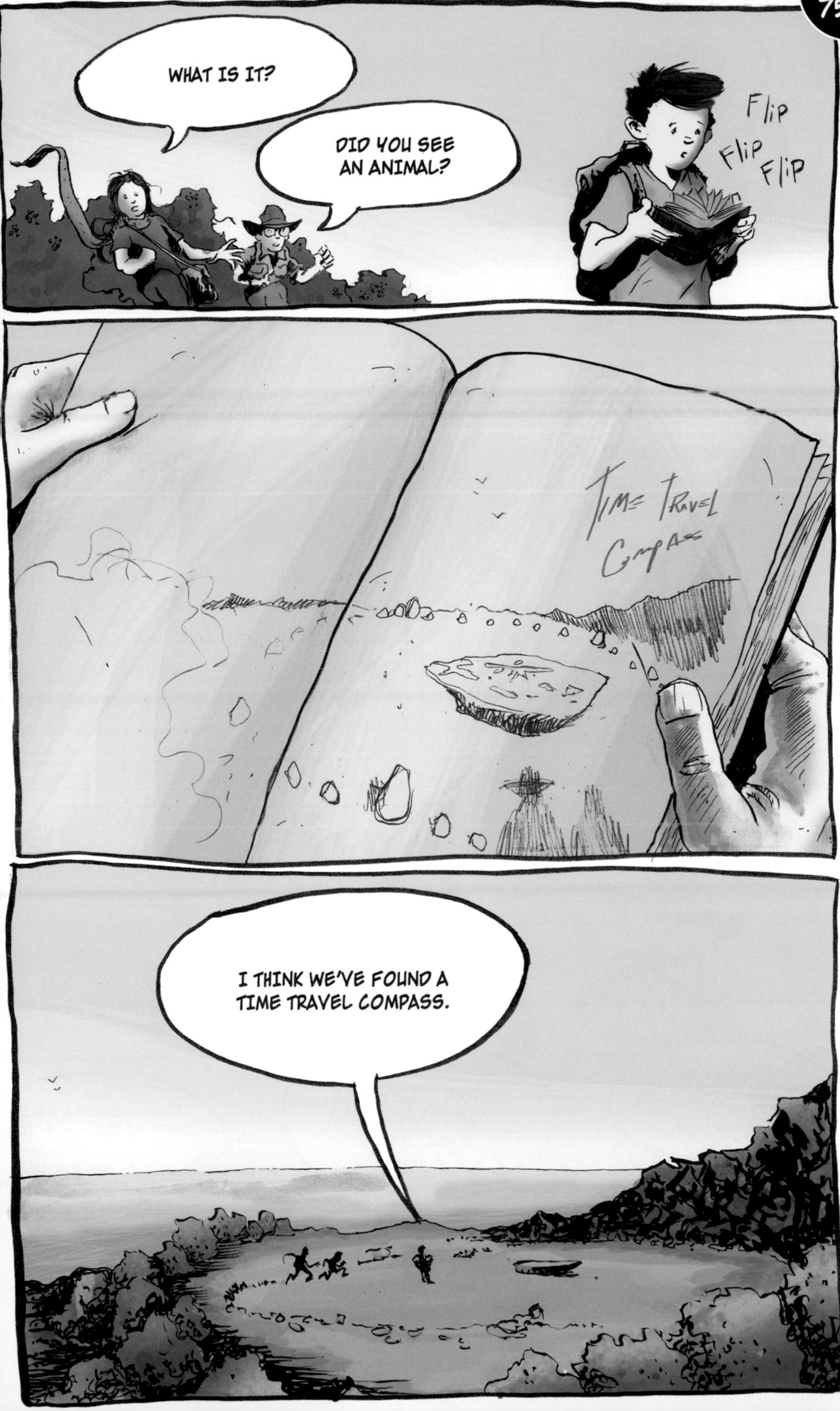
WHAT IS IT?
DID YOU SEE AN ANIMAL?
Flip Flip Flip
TIME TRAVEL COMPASS
I THINK WE'VE FOUND A TIME TRAVEL COMPASS.

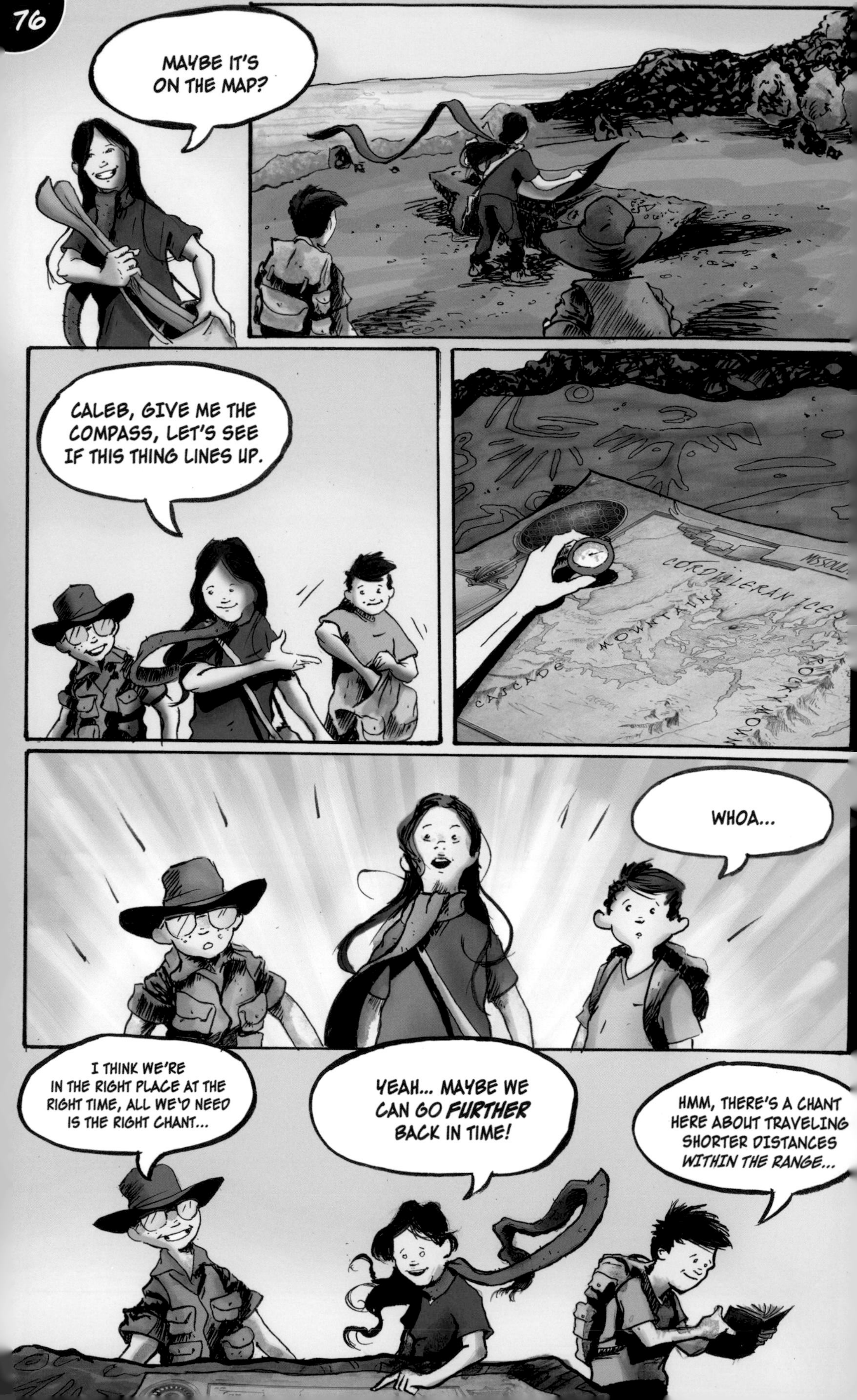
MAYBE IT'S ON THE MAP?
CALEB, GIVE ME THE COMPASS, LET'S SEE IF THIS THING LINES UP.
CORDILLERAN ICE
MOUNTAINS
CASCADE
WHOA...
I THINK WE'RE IN THE RIGHT PLACE AT THE RIGHT TIME, ALL WE'D NEED IS THE RIGHT CHANT...
YEAH... MAYBE WE CAN GO *FURTHER* BACK IN TIME!
HMM, THERE'S A CHANT HERE ABOUT TRAVELING SHORTER DISTANCES *WITHIN THE RANGE*...

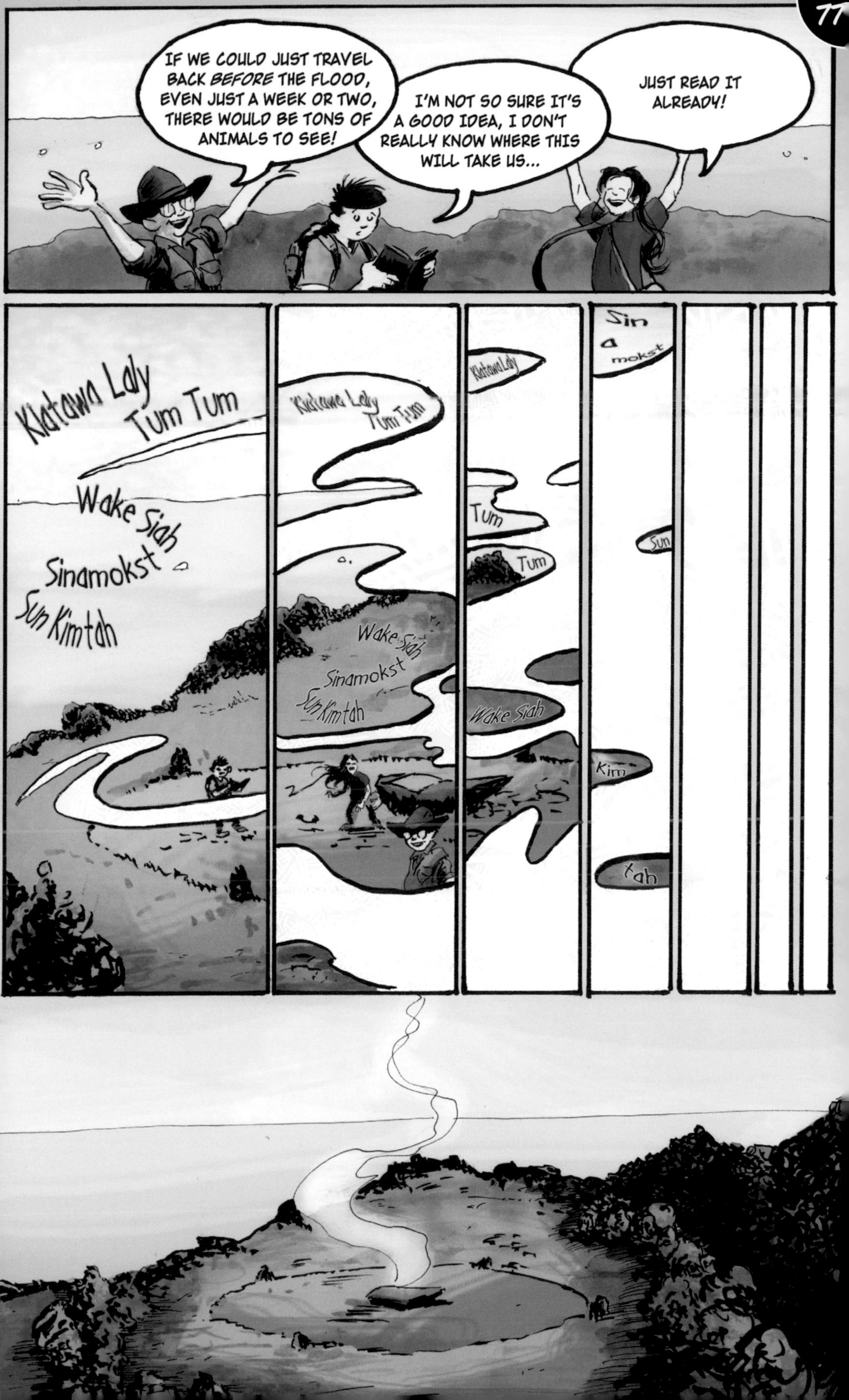
IF WE COULD JUST TRAVEL BACK *BEFORE* THE FLOOD, EVEN JUST A WEEK OR TWO, THERE WOULD BE TONS OF ANIMALS TO SEE!
I'M NOT SO SURE IT'S A GOOD IDEA, I DON'T REALLY KNOW WHERE THIS WILL TAKE US...
JUST READ IT ALREADY!
Klatawa Laly Tum Tum
Wake Siah
Sinamokst
Sun Kimtah
Klatawa Laly Tum Tum
Wake Siah
Sinamokst
Sun Kimtah
Klatawa Laly
Tum
Tum
Wake Siah
Sin a mokst
Sun
Kim
tah

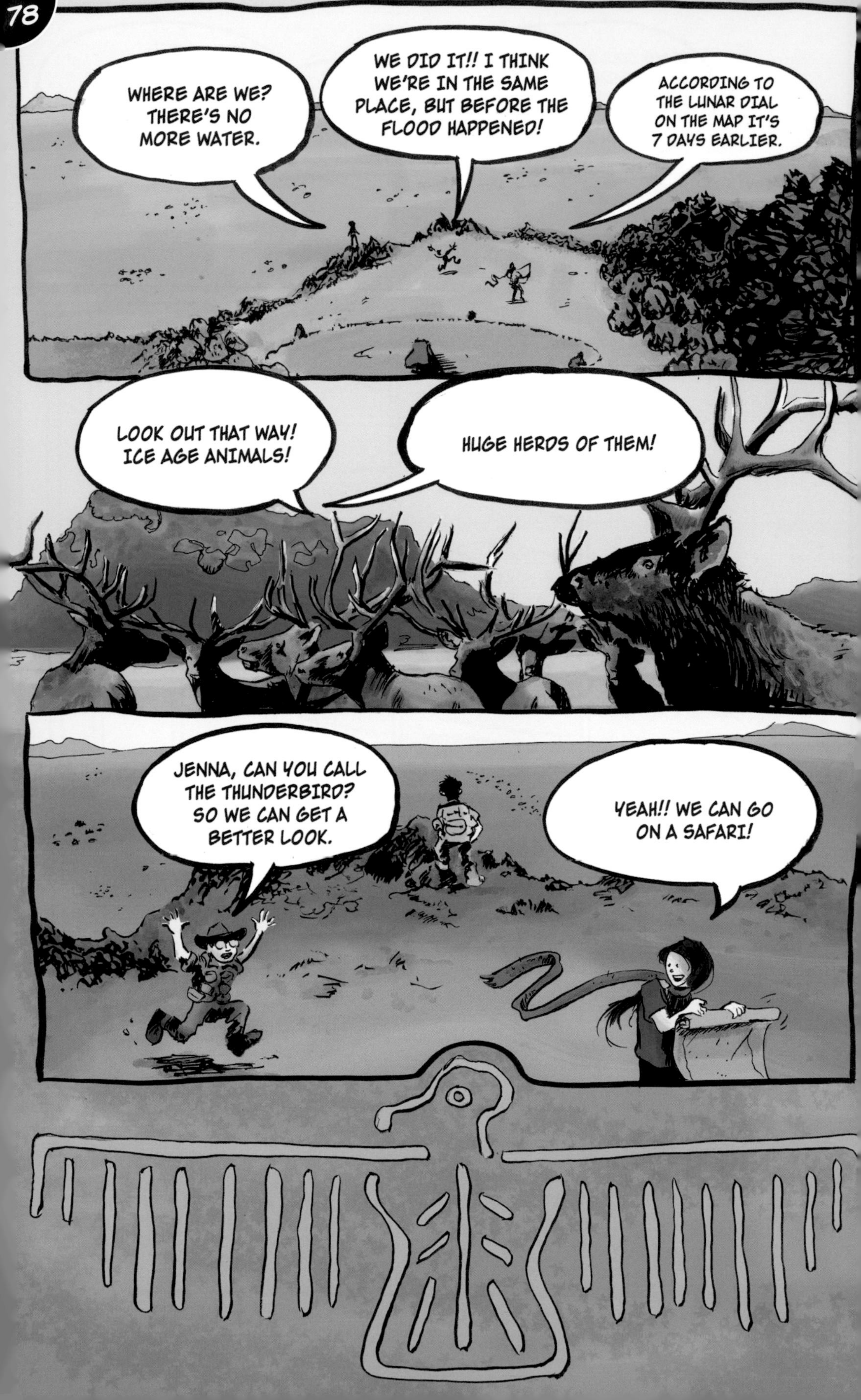
WHERE ARE WE? THERE'S NO MORE WATER.
WE DID IT!! I THINK WE'RE IN THE SAME PLACE, BUT BEFORE THE FLOOD HAPPENED!
ACCORDING TO THE LUNAR DIAL ON THE MAP IT'S 7 DAYS EARLIER.
LOOK OUT THAT WAY! ICE AGE ANIMALS!
HUGE HERDS OF THEM!
JENNA, CAN YOU CALL THE THUNDERBIRD? SO WE CAN GET A BETTER LOOK.
YEAH!! WE CAN GO ON A SAFARI!

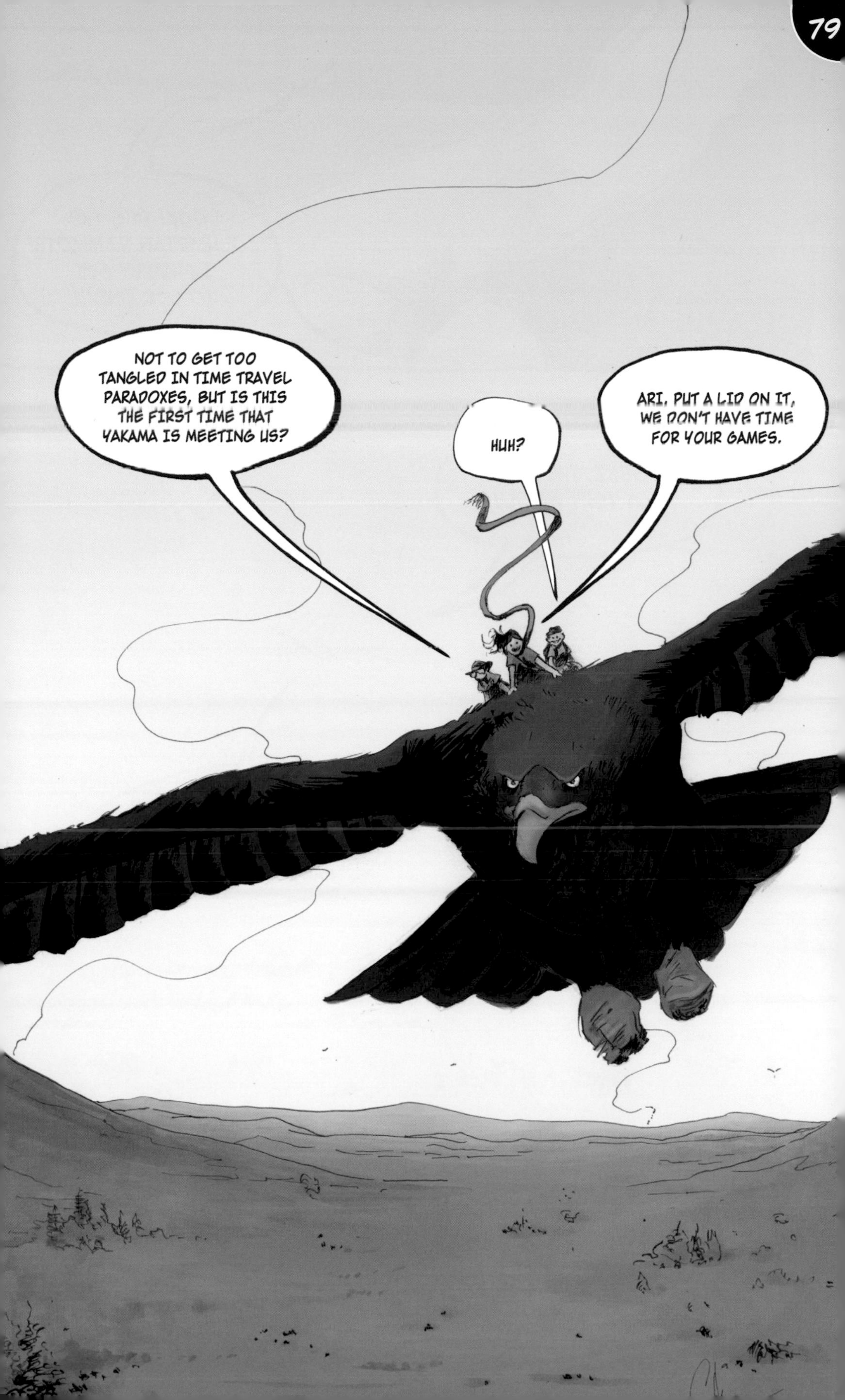
NOT TO GET TOO TANGLED IN TIME TRAVEL PARADOXES, BUT IS THIS THE FIRST TIME THAT YAKAMA IS MEETING US?
HUH?
ARI, PUT A LID ON IT, WE DON'T HAVE TIME FOR YOUR GAMES.

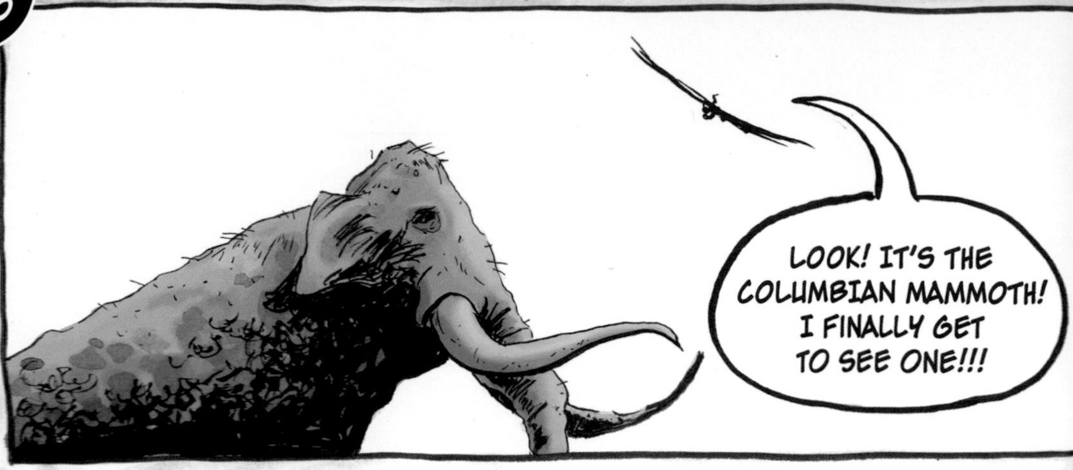
LOOK! IT'S THE COLUMBIAN MAMMOTH! I FINALLY GET TO SEE ONE!!!

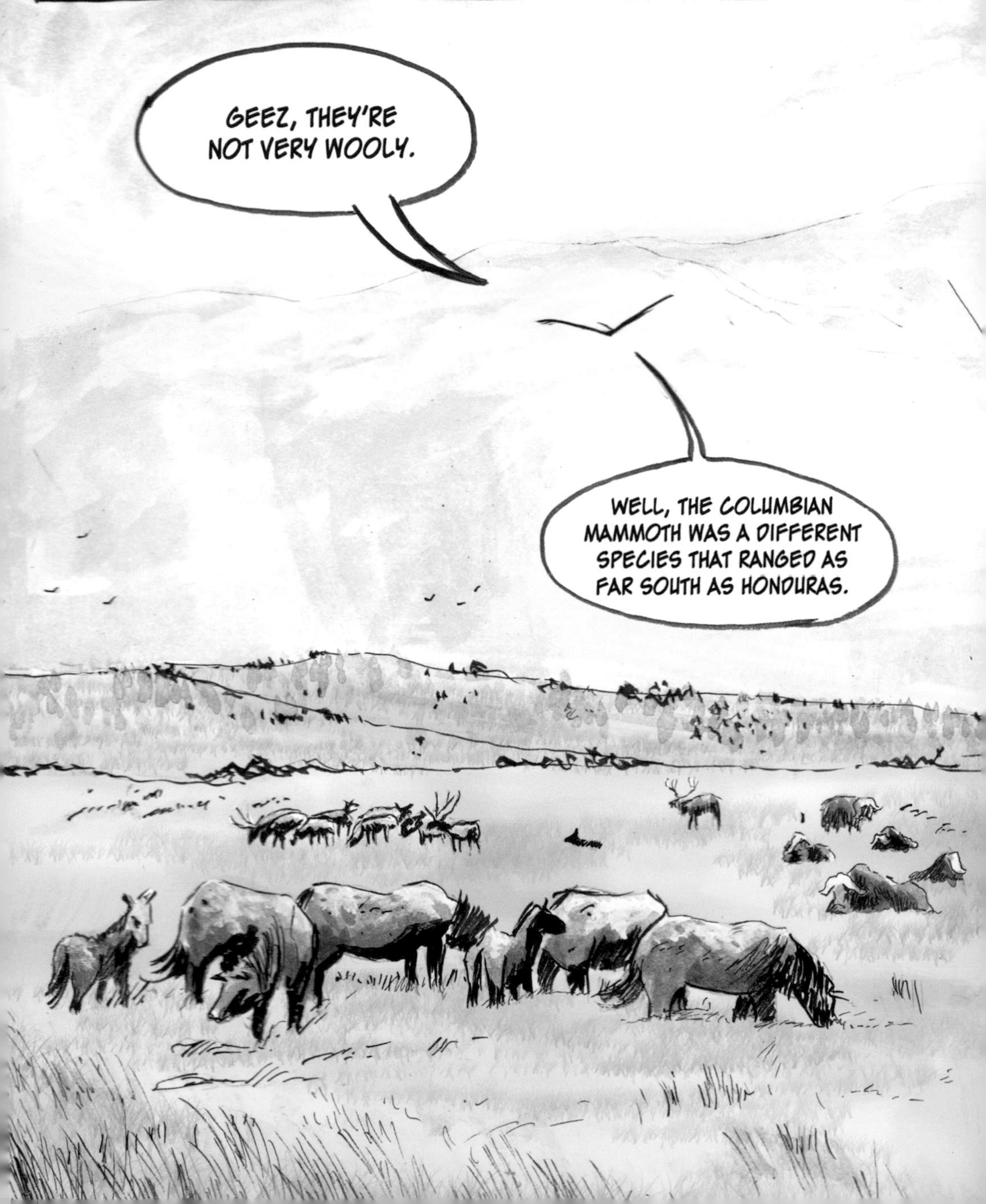
GEEZ, THEY'RE NOT VERY WOOLY.
WELL, THE COLUMBIAN MAMMOTH WAS A DIFFERENT SPECIES THAT RANGED AS FAR SOUTH AS HONDURAS.

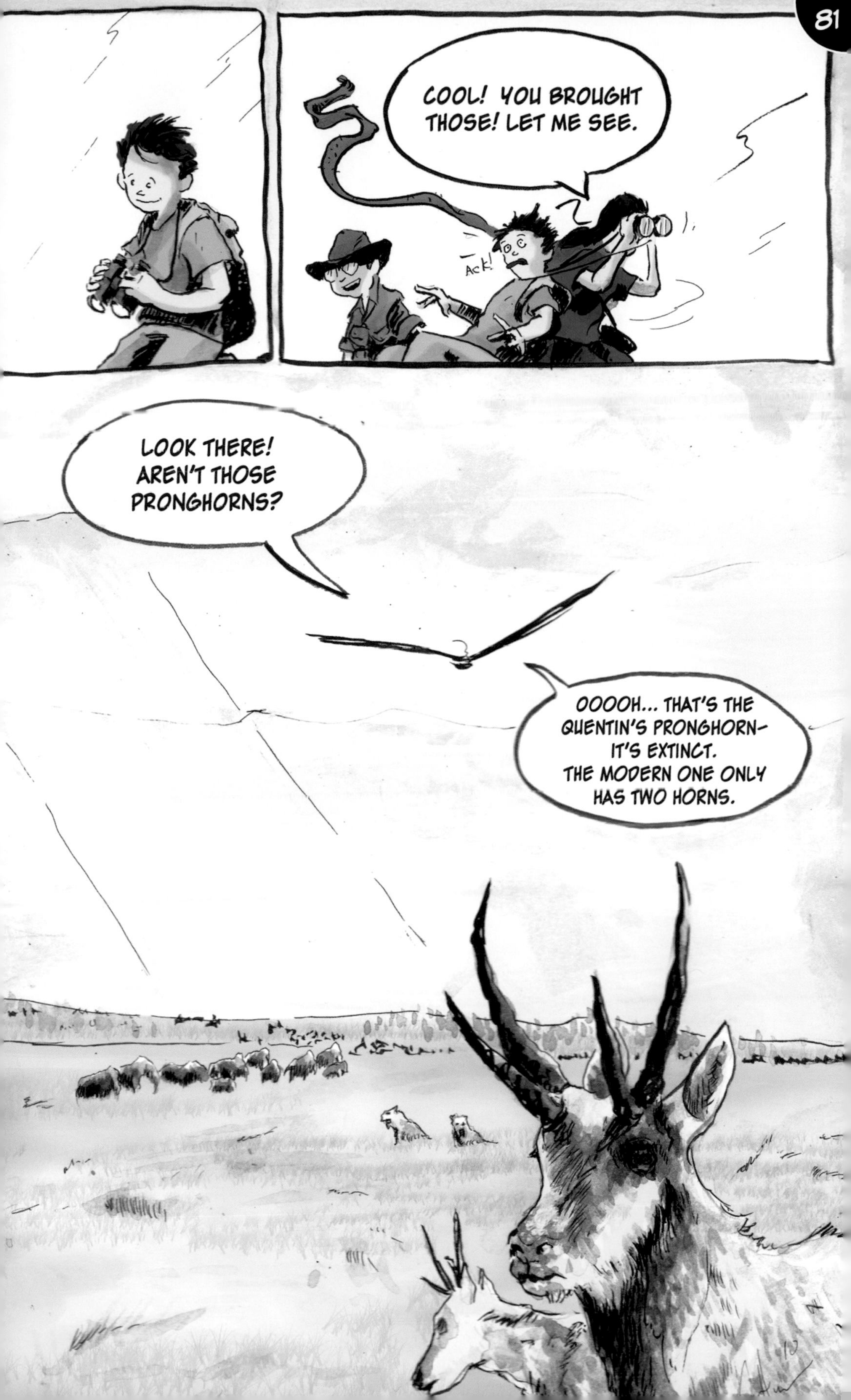
COOL! YOU BROUGHT THOSE! LET ME SEE.
ACK!
LOOK THERE! AREN'T THOSE PRONGHORNS?
OOOOH... THAT'S THE QUENTIN'S PRONGHORN- IT'S EXTINCT. THE MODERN ONE ONLY HAS TWO HORNS.

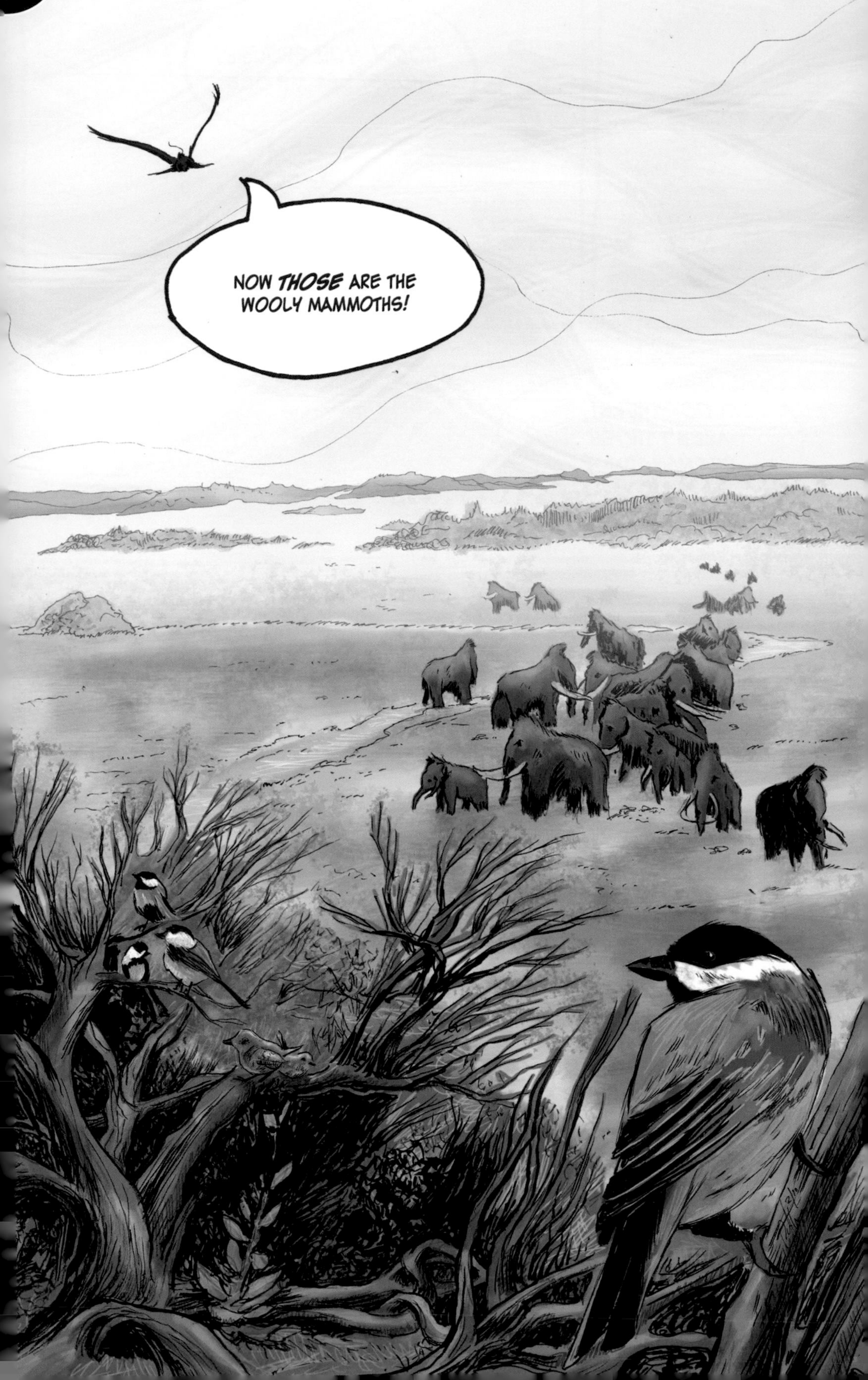
NOW *THOSE* ARE THE WOOLY MAMMOTHS!

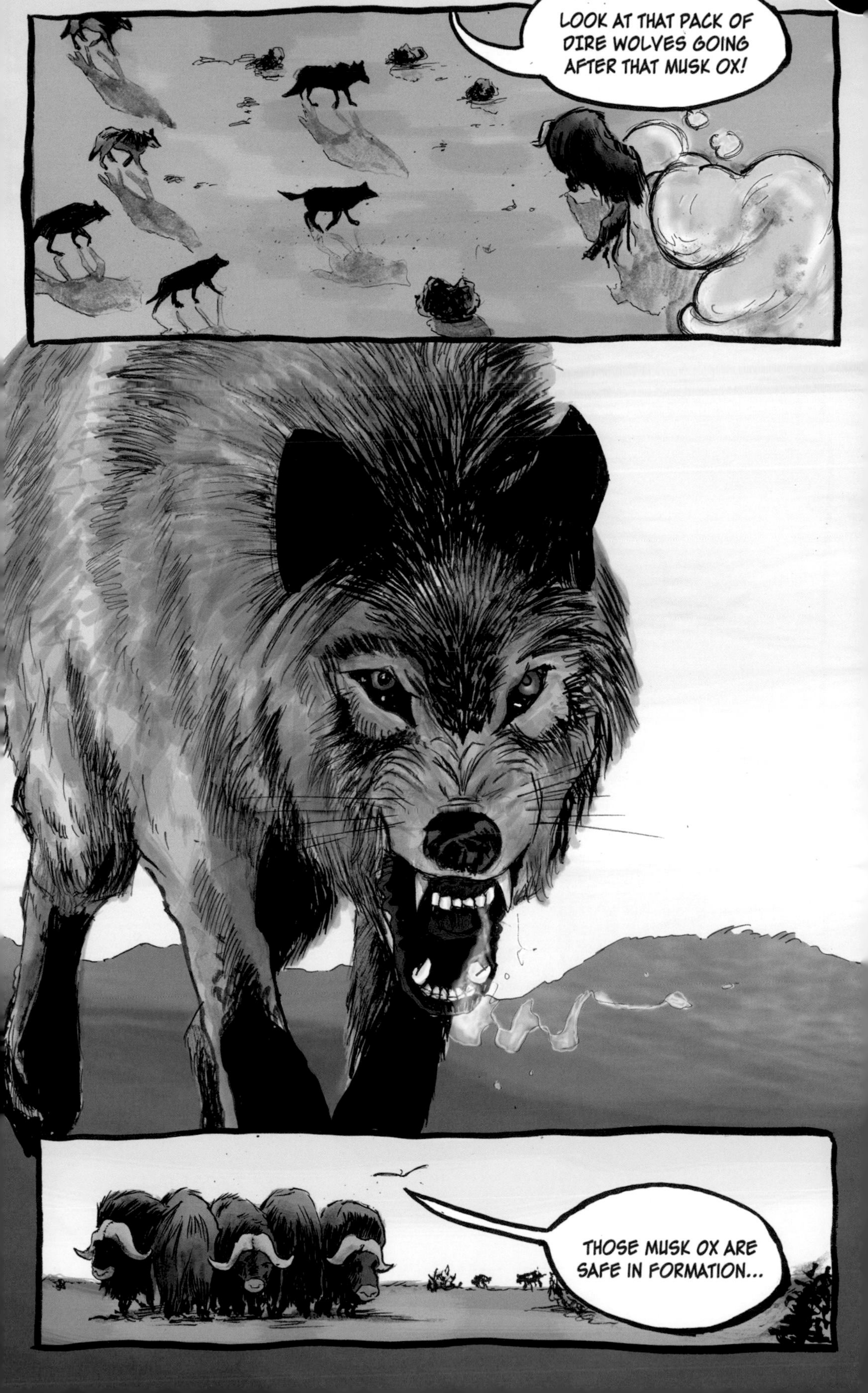
LOOK AT THAT PACK OF DIRE WOLVES GOING AFTER THAT MUSK OX!
THOSE MUSK OX ARE SAFE IN FORMATION...

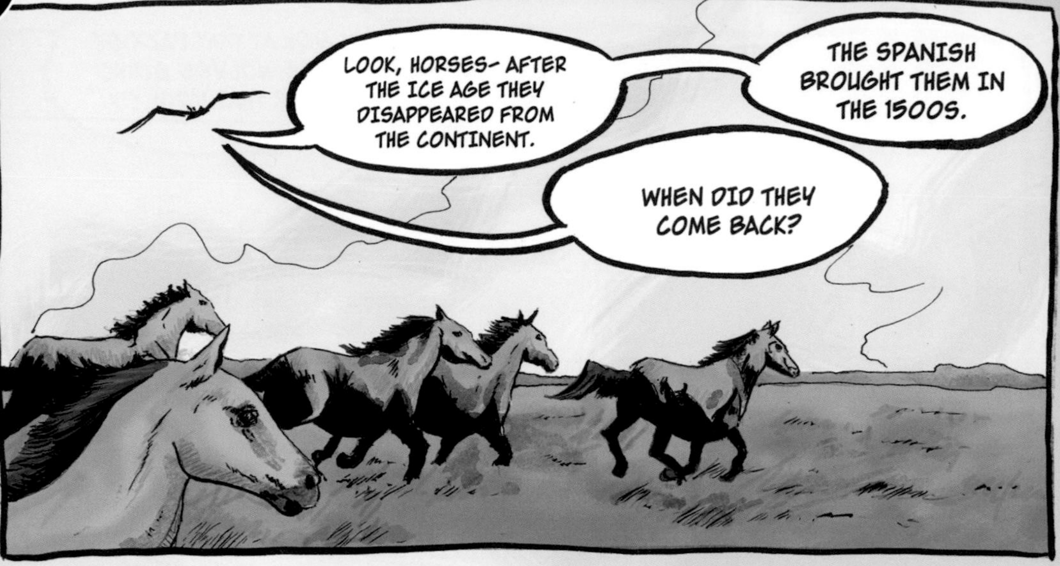
LOOK, HORSES- AFTER THE ICE AGE THEY DISAPPEARED FROM THE CONTINENT.
THE SPANISH BROUGHT THEM IN THE 1500S.
WHEN DID THEY COME BACK?

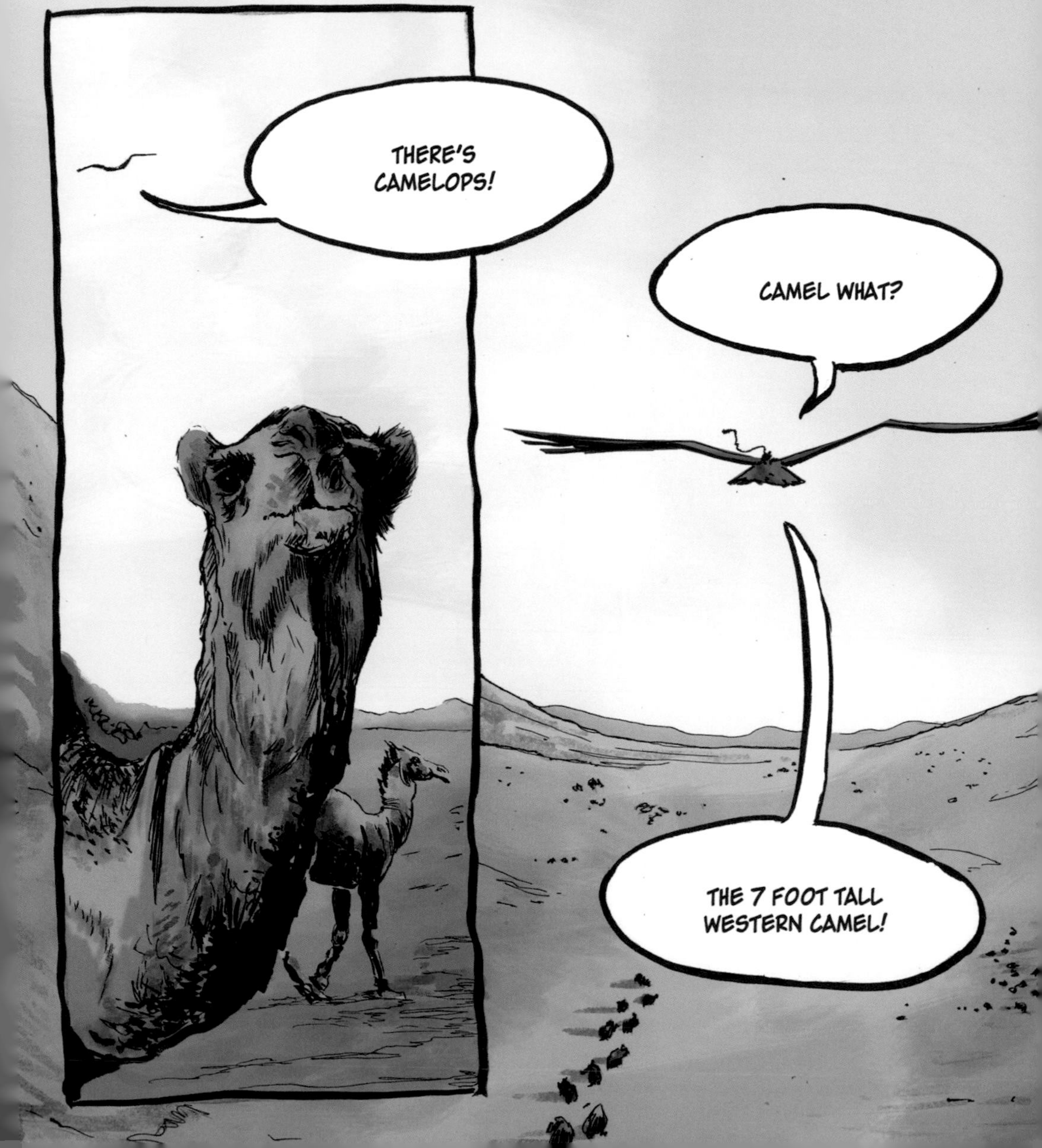
THERE'S CAMELOPS!
CAMEL WHAT?
THE 7 FOOT TALL WESTERN CAMEL!

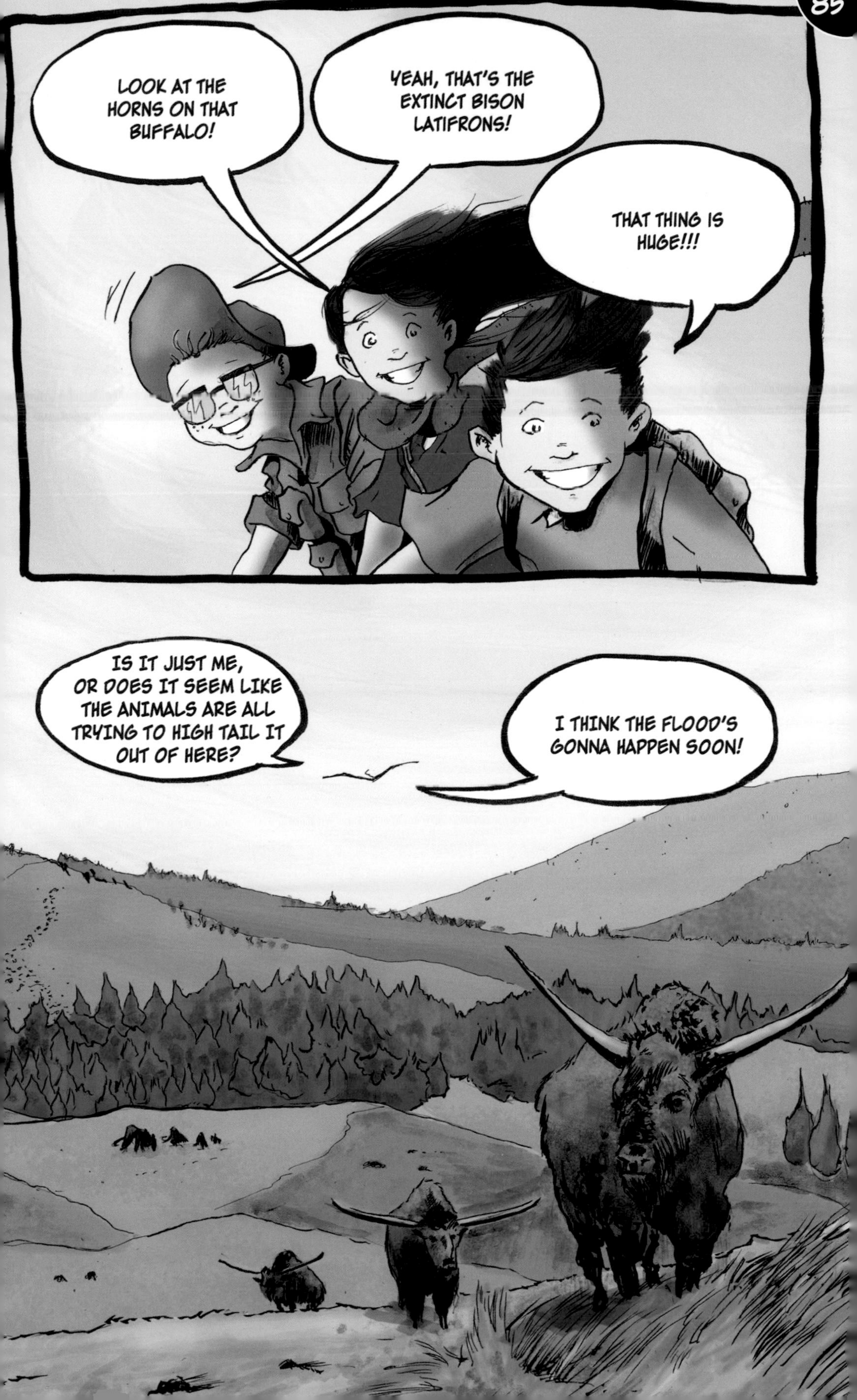
LOOK AT THE HORNS ON THAT BUFFALO!
YEAH, THAT'S THE EXTINCT BISON LATIFRONS!
THAT THING IS HUGE!!!
IS IT JUST ME, OR DOES IT SEEM LIKE THE ANIMALS ARE ALL TRYING TO HIGH TAIL IT OUT OF HERE?
I THINK THE FLOOD'S GONNA HAPPEN SOON!

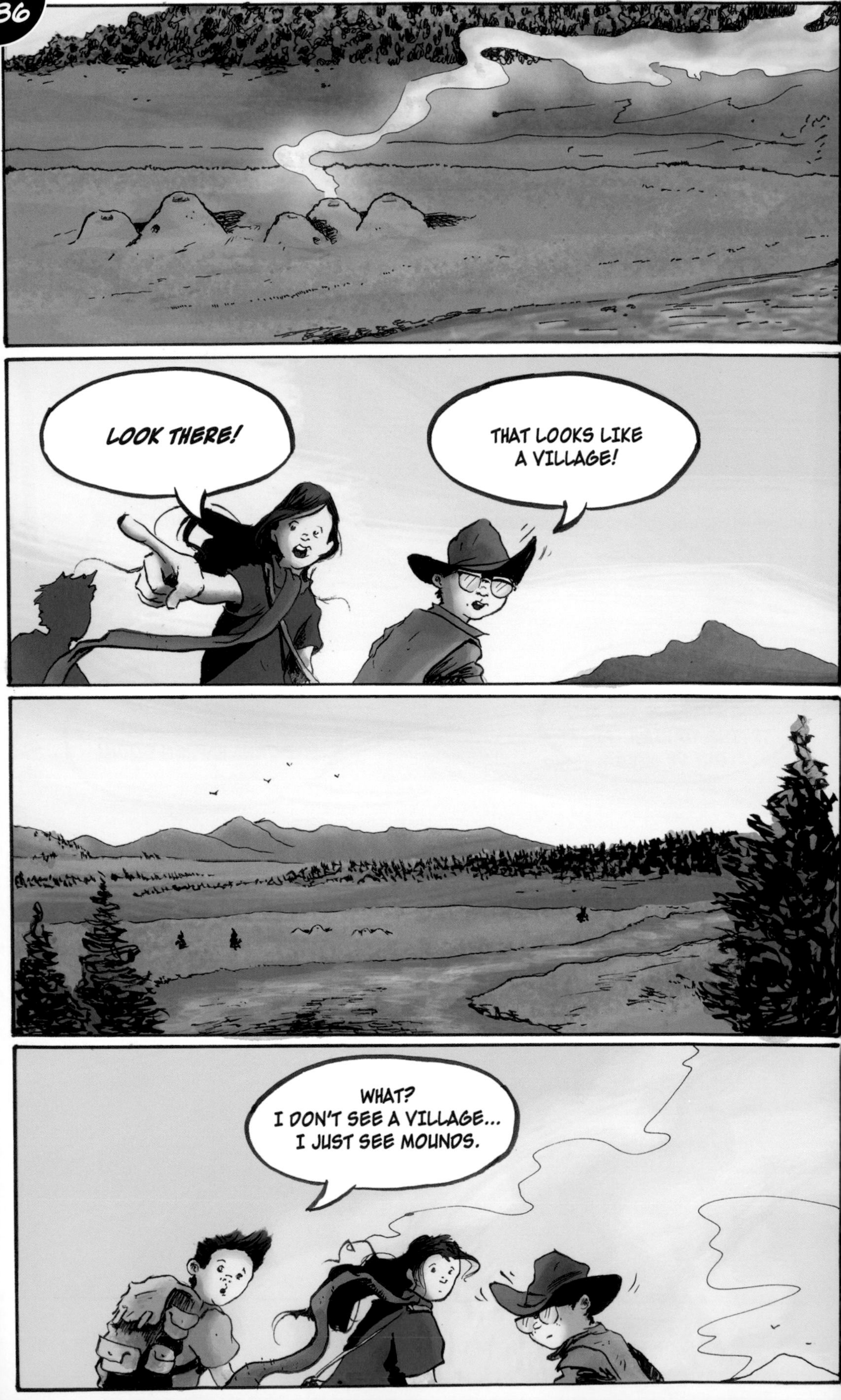
LOOK THERE!
THAT LOOKS LIKE A VILLAGE!
WHAT? I DON'T SEE A VILLAGE... I JUST SEE MOUNDS.

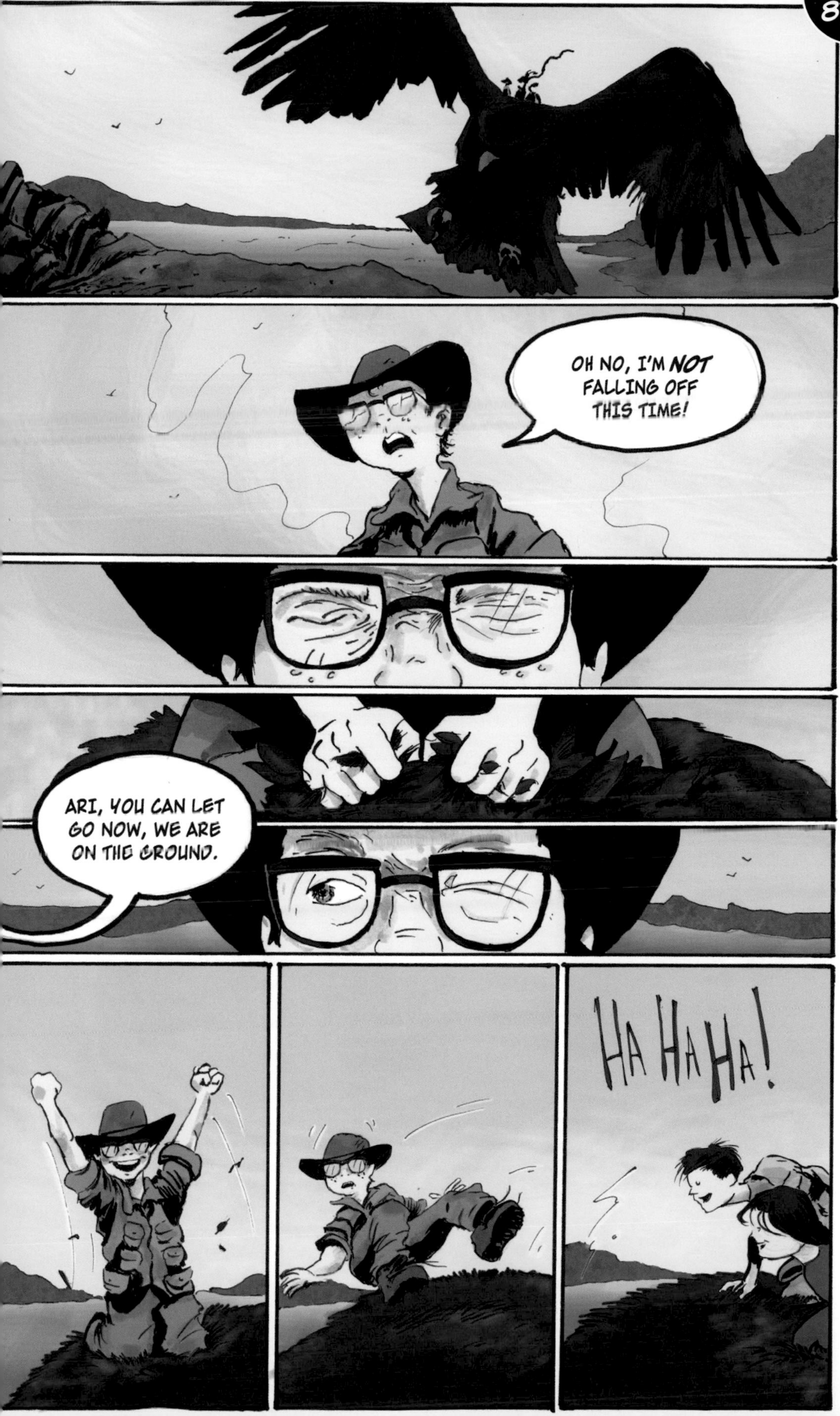
OH NO, I'M ***NOT*** FALLING OFF THIS TIME!
ARI, YOU CAN LET GO NOW, WE ARE ON THE GROUND.
HA HA HA!

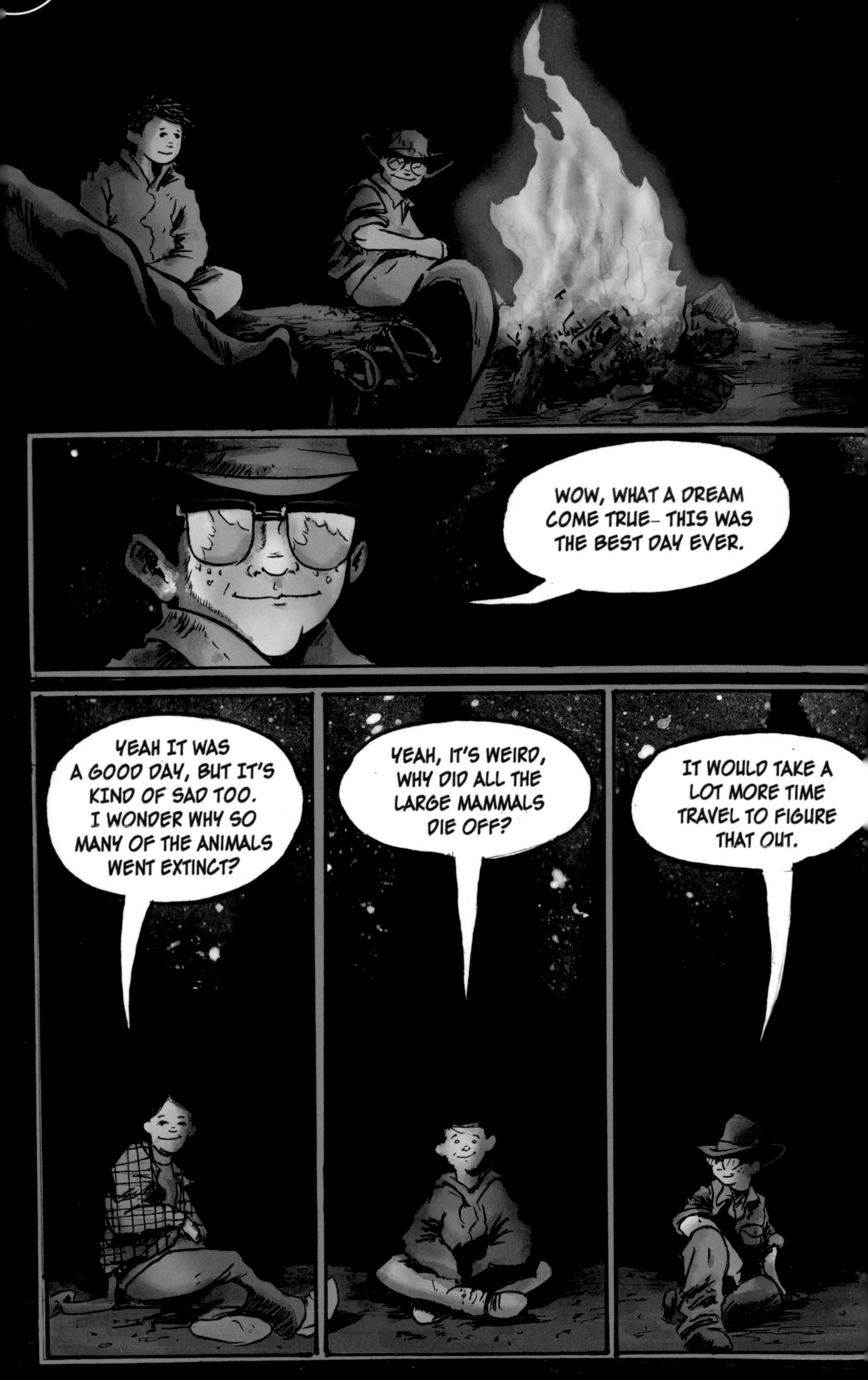
WOW, WHAT A DREAM COME TRUE– THIS WAS THE BEST DAY EVER.
YEAH IT WAS A GOOD DAY, BUT IT'S KIND OF SAD TOO. I WONDER WHY SO MANY OF THE ANIMALS WENT EXTINCT?
YEAH, IT'S WEIRD, WHY DID ALL THE LARGE MAMMALS DIE OFF?
IT WOULD TAKE A LOT MORE TIME TRAVEL TO FIGURE THAT OUT.

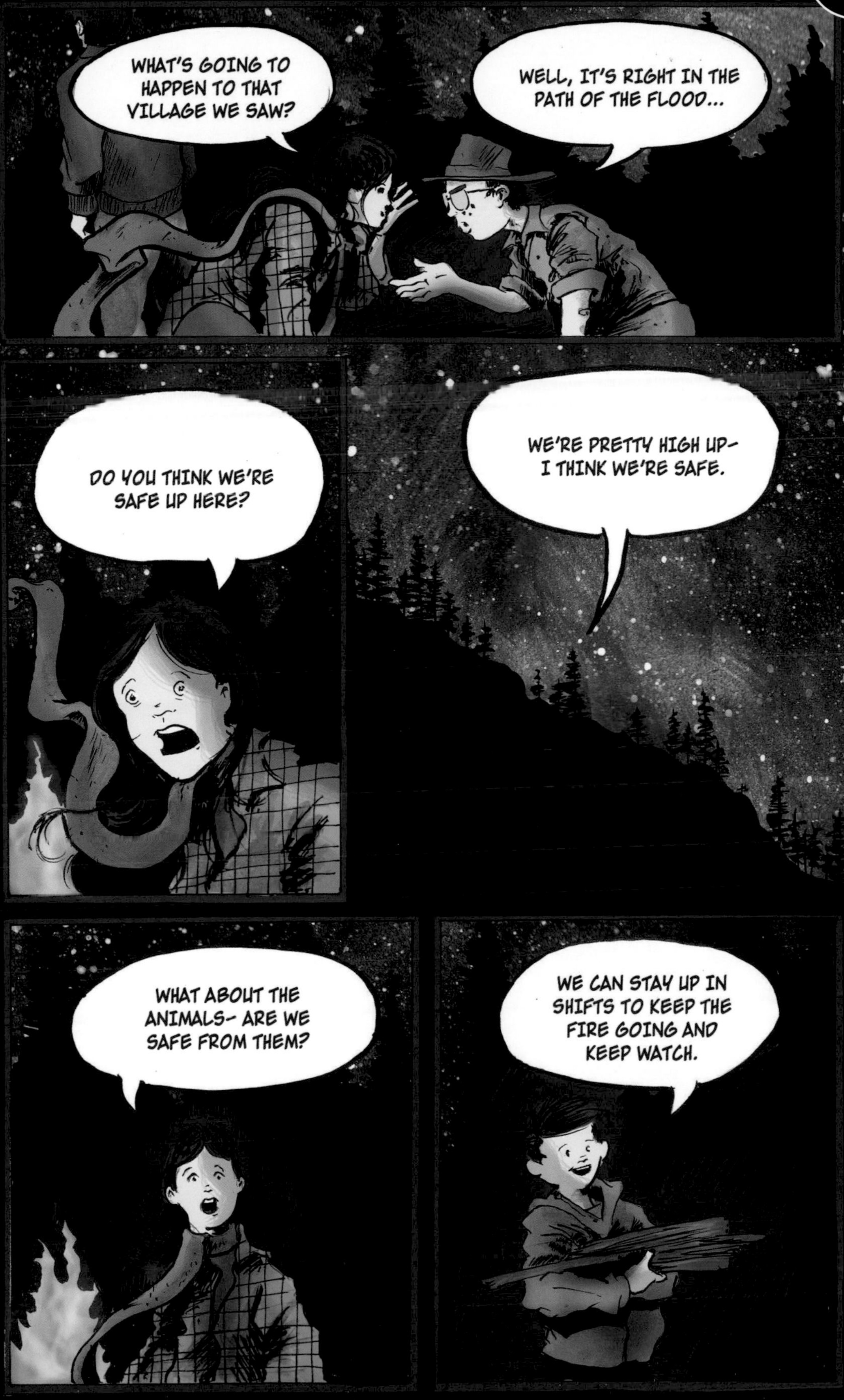
WHAT'S GOING TO HAPPEN TO THAT VILLAGE WE SAW?
WELL, IT'S RIGHT IN THE PATH OF THE FLOOD...
DO YOU THINK WE'RE SAFE UP HERE?
WE'RE PRETTY HIGH UP- I THINK WE'RE SAFE.
WHAT ABOUT THE ANIMALS- ARE WE SAFE FROM THEM?
WE CAN STAY UP IN SHIFTS TO KEEP THE FIRE GOING AND KEEP WATCH.

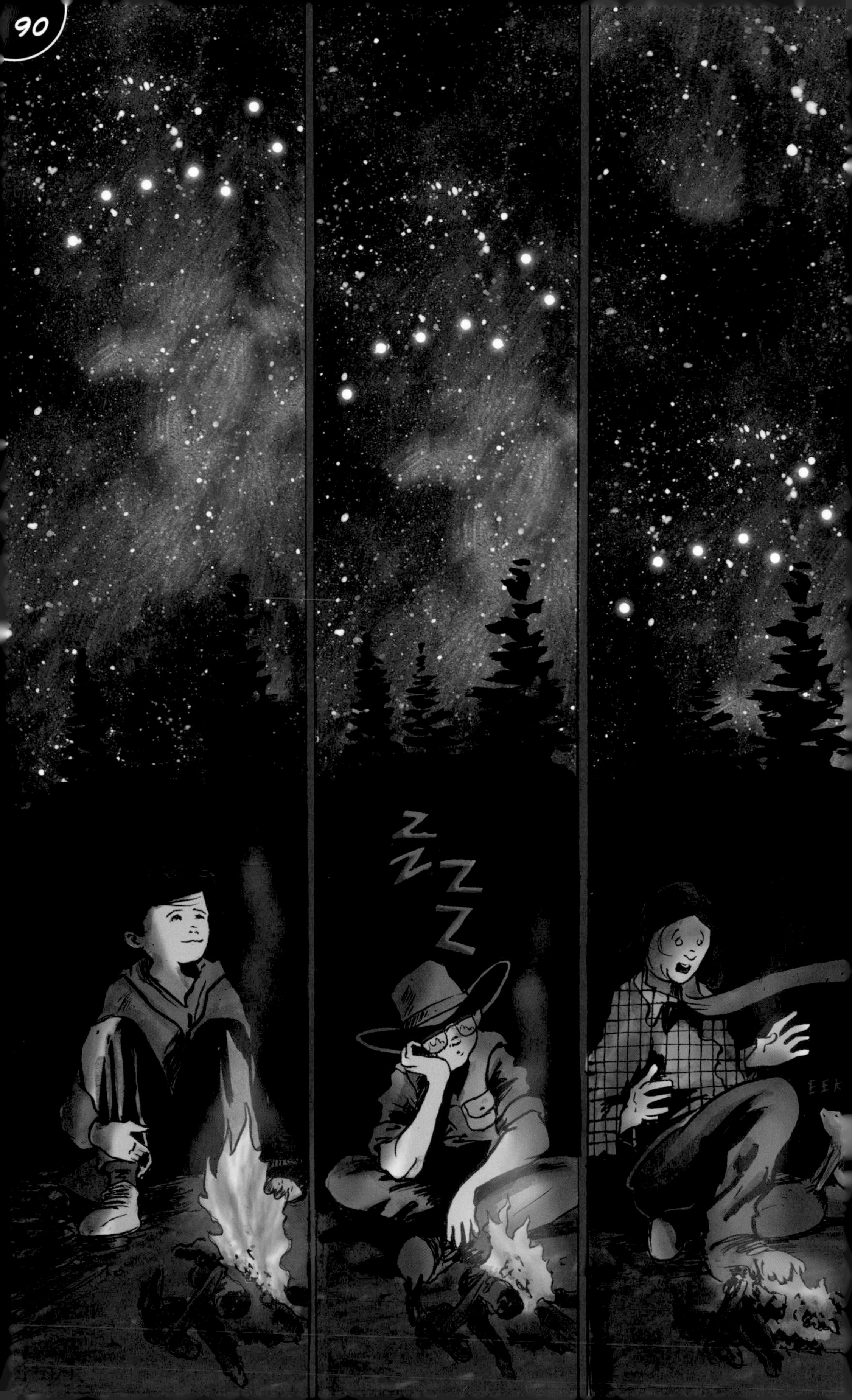
Z Z Z Z
EEK

CHAPTER SIX

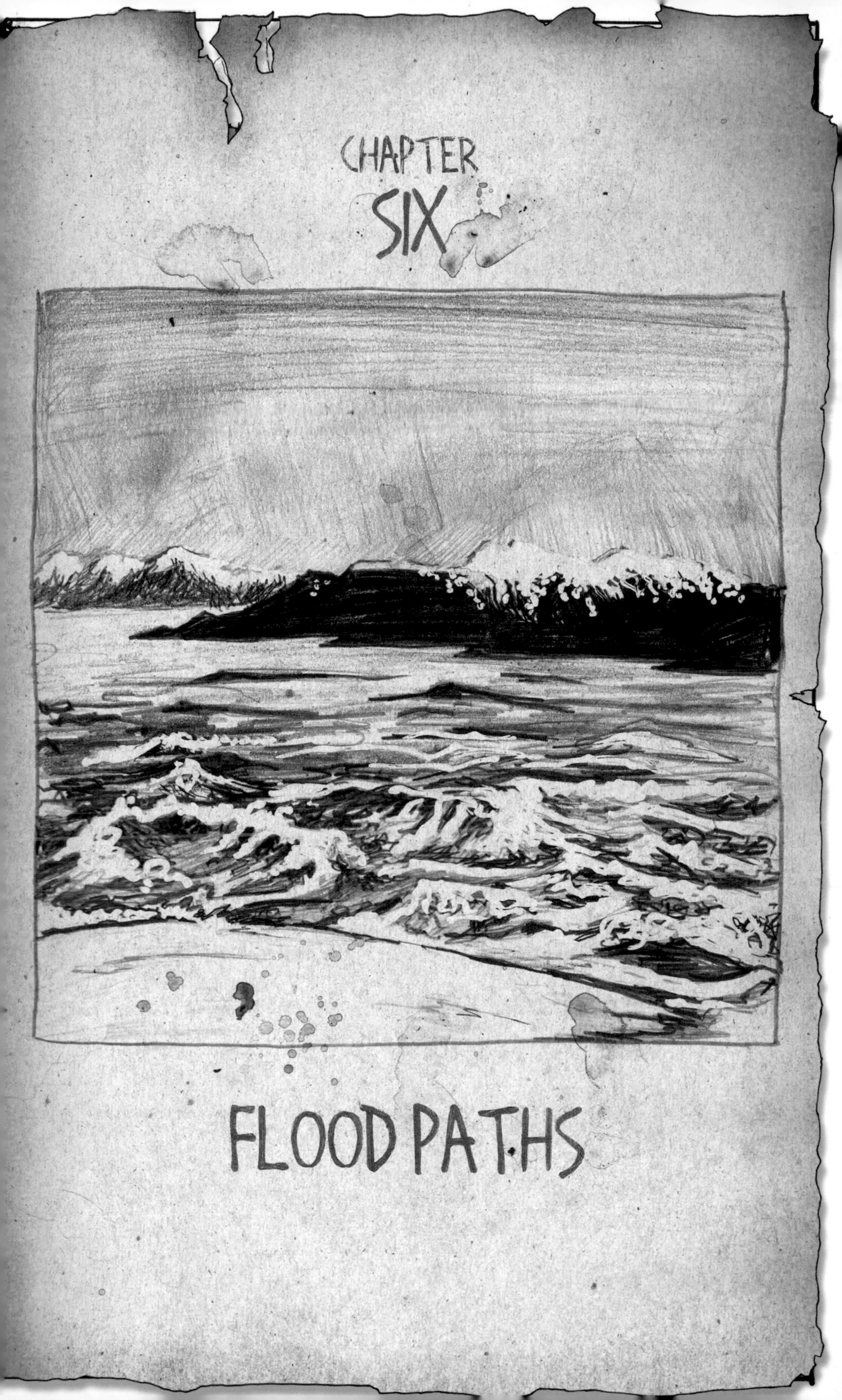

FLOOD PATHS

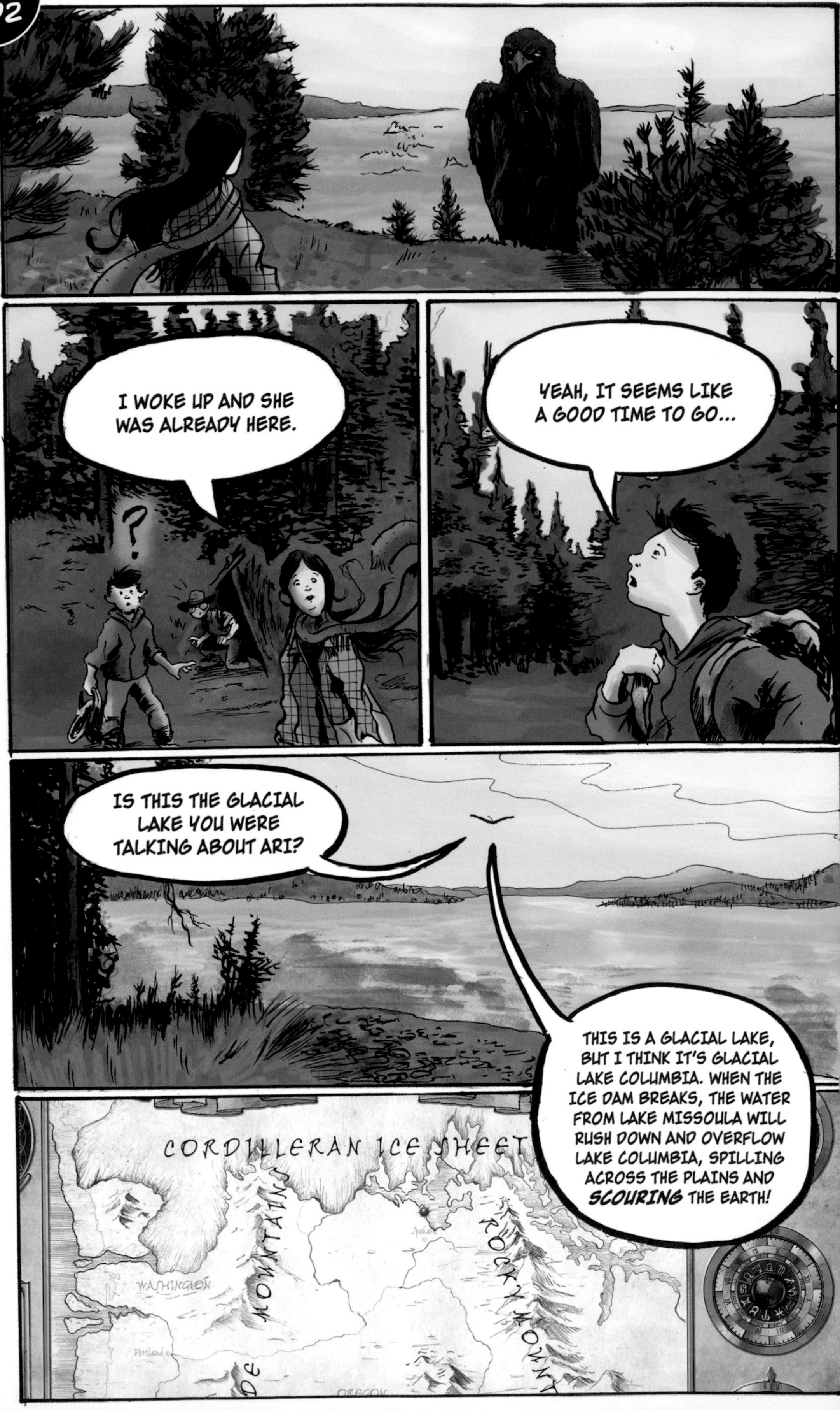
I WOKE UP AND SHE WAS ALREADY HERE.
?
YEAH, IT SEEMS LIKE A GOOD TIME TO GO...
IS THIS THE GLACIAL LAKE YOU WERE TALKING ABOUT ARI?
THIS IS A GLACIAL LAKE, BUT I THINK IT'S GLACIAL LAKE COLUMBIA. WHEN THE ICE DAM BREAKS, THE WATER FROM LAKE MISSOULA WILL RUSH DOWN AND OVERFLOW LAKE COLUMBIA, SPILLING ACROSS THE PLAINS AND *SCOURING* THE EARTH!
CORDILLERAN ICE SHEET
MOUNTAINS
WASHINGTON
Spokane
Portland

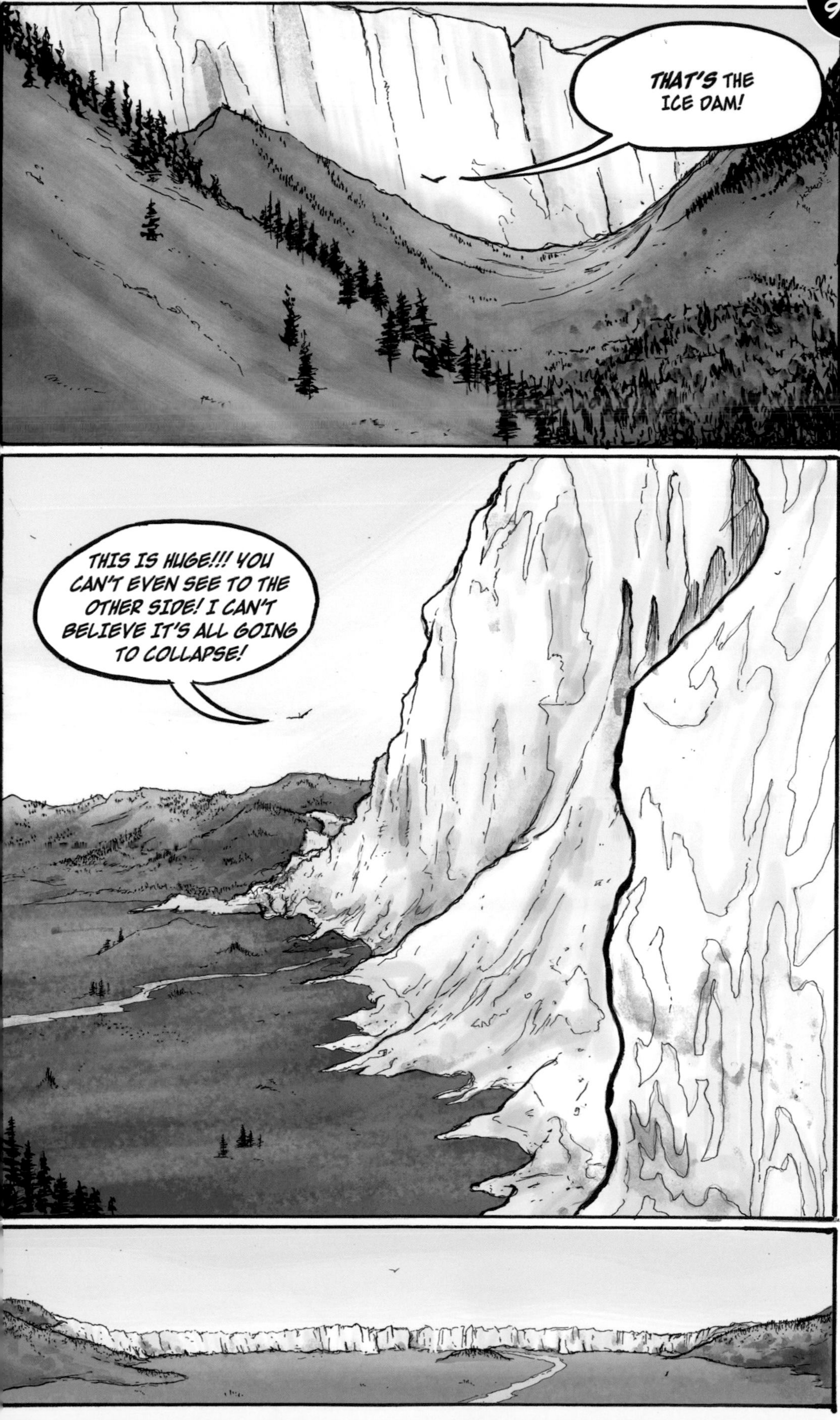
THAT'S THE ICE DAM!
THIS IS HUGE!!! YOU CAN'T EVEN SEE TO THE OTHER SIDE! I CAN'T BELIEVE IT'S ALL GOING TO COLLAPSE!

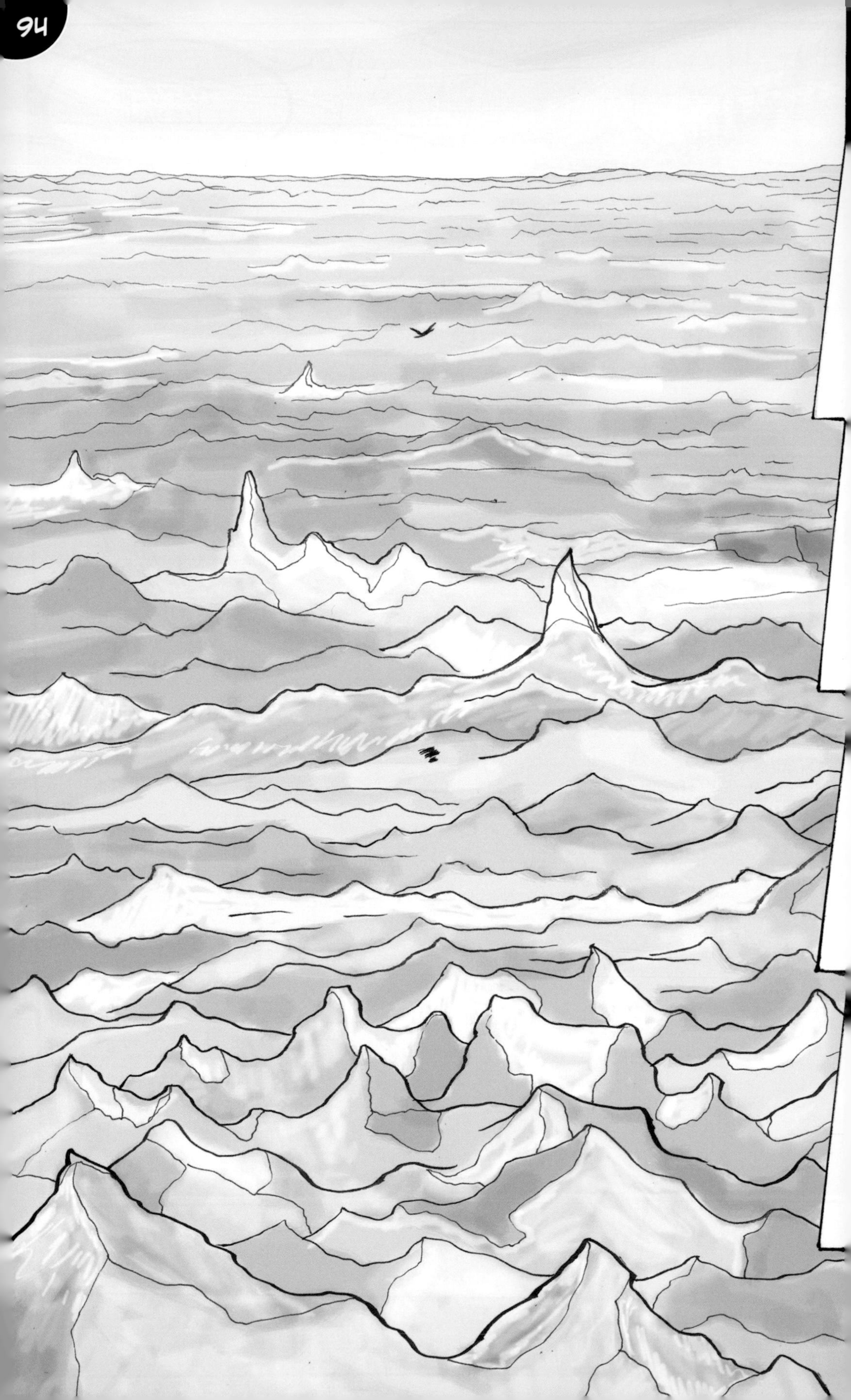

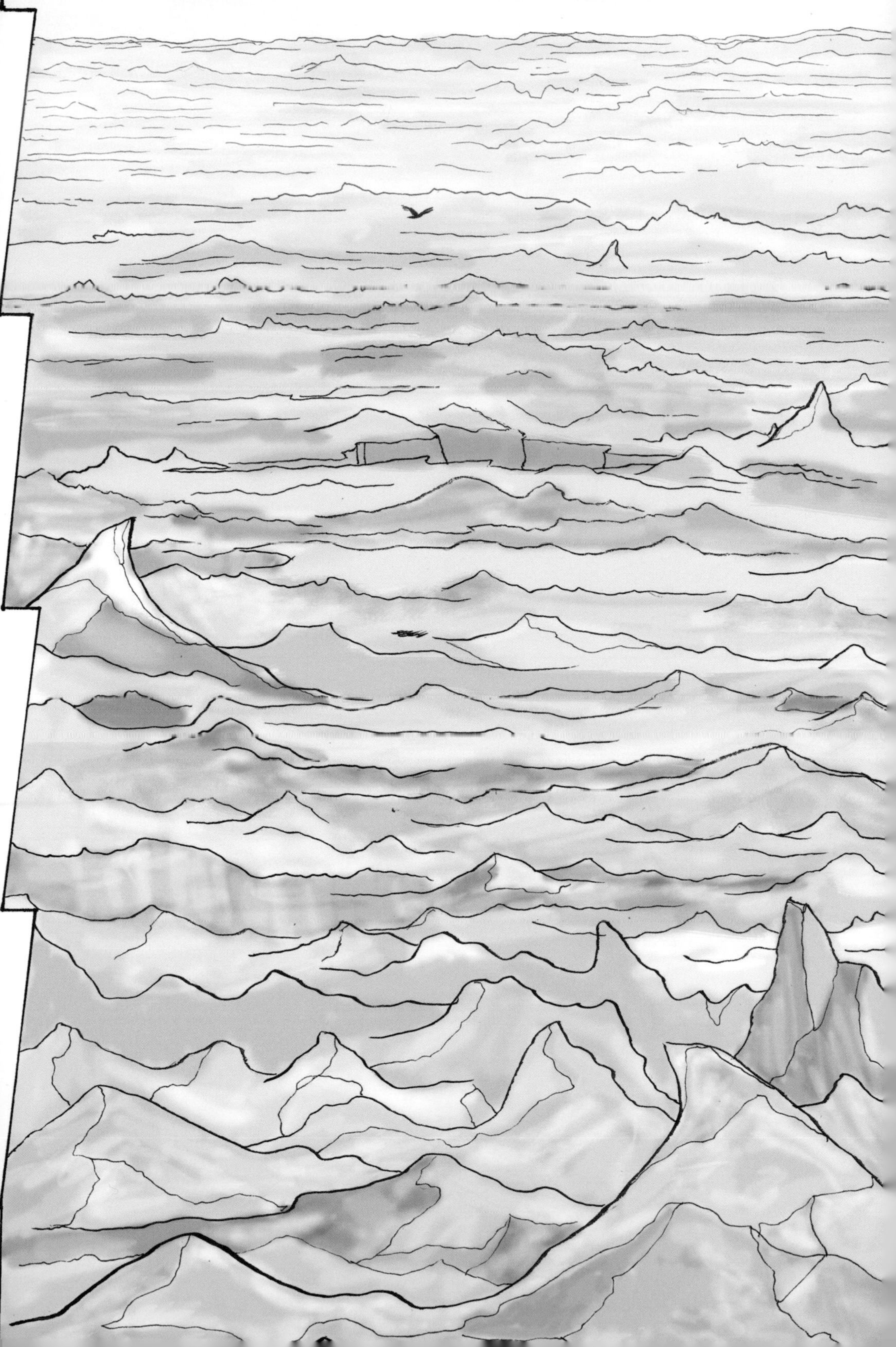

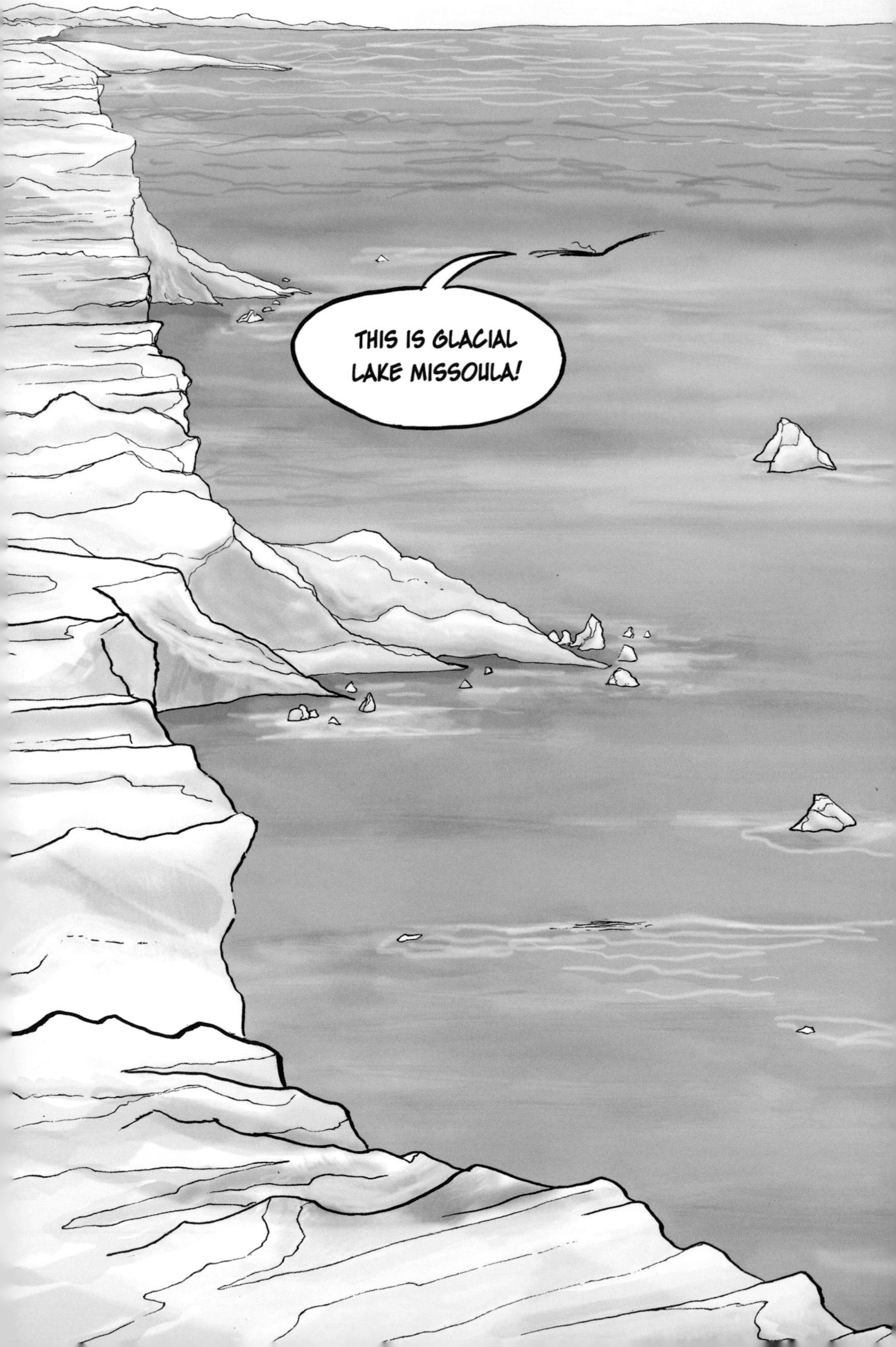
THIS IS GLACIAL LAKE MISSOULA!

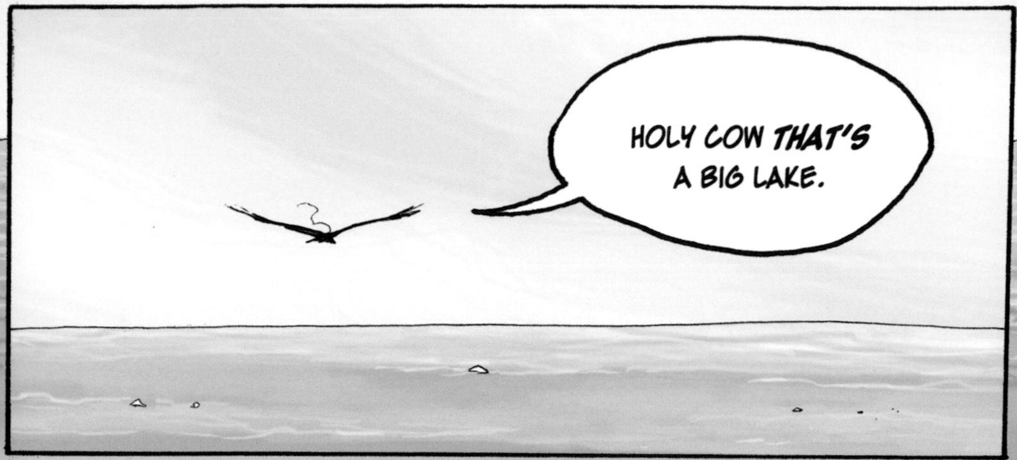
HOLY COW THAT'S A BIG LAKE.

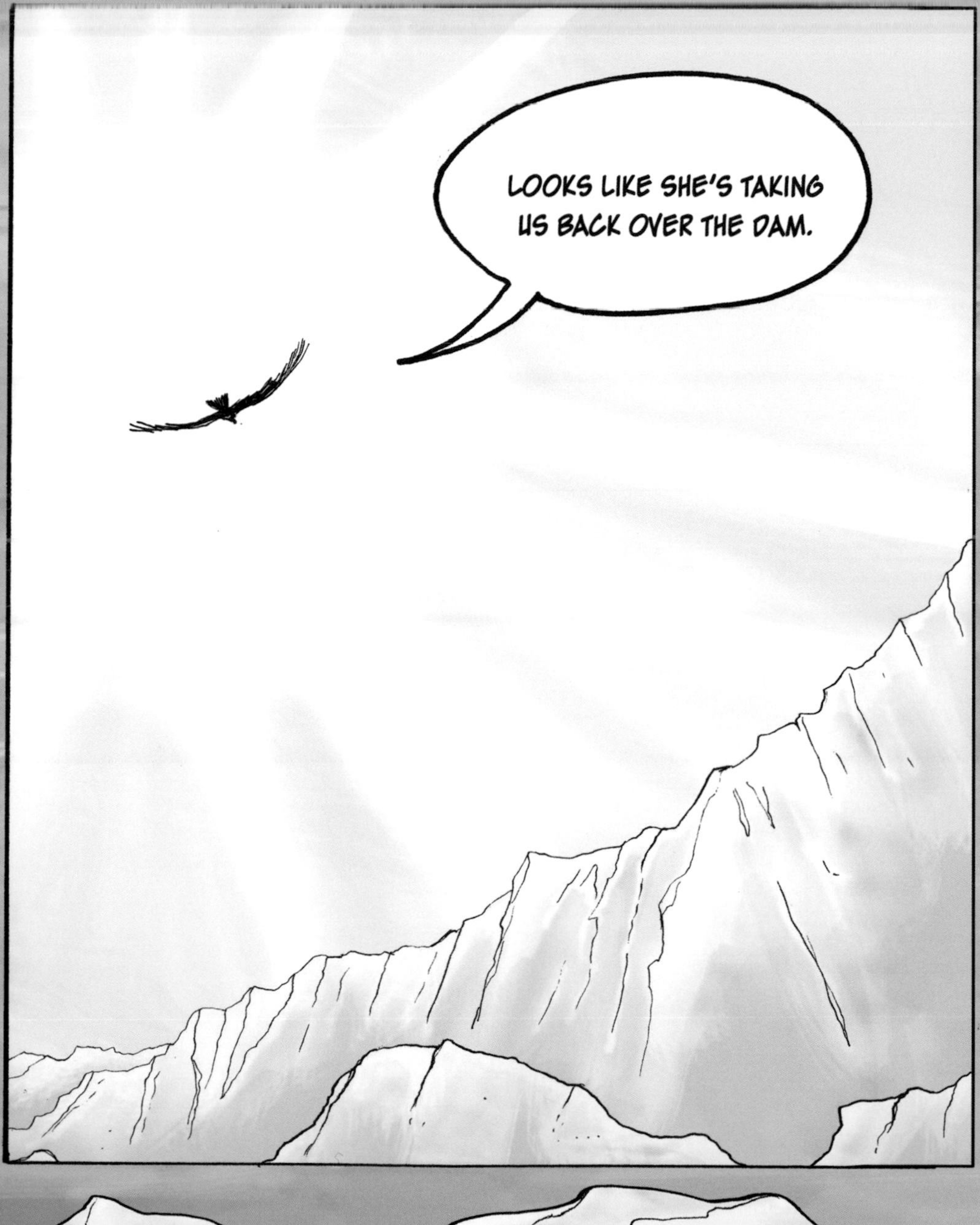
LOOKS LIKE SHE'S TAKING US BACK OVER THE DAM.

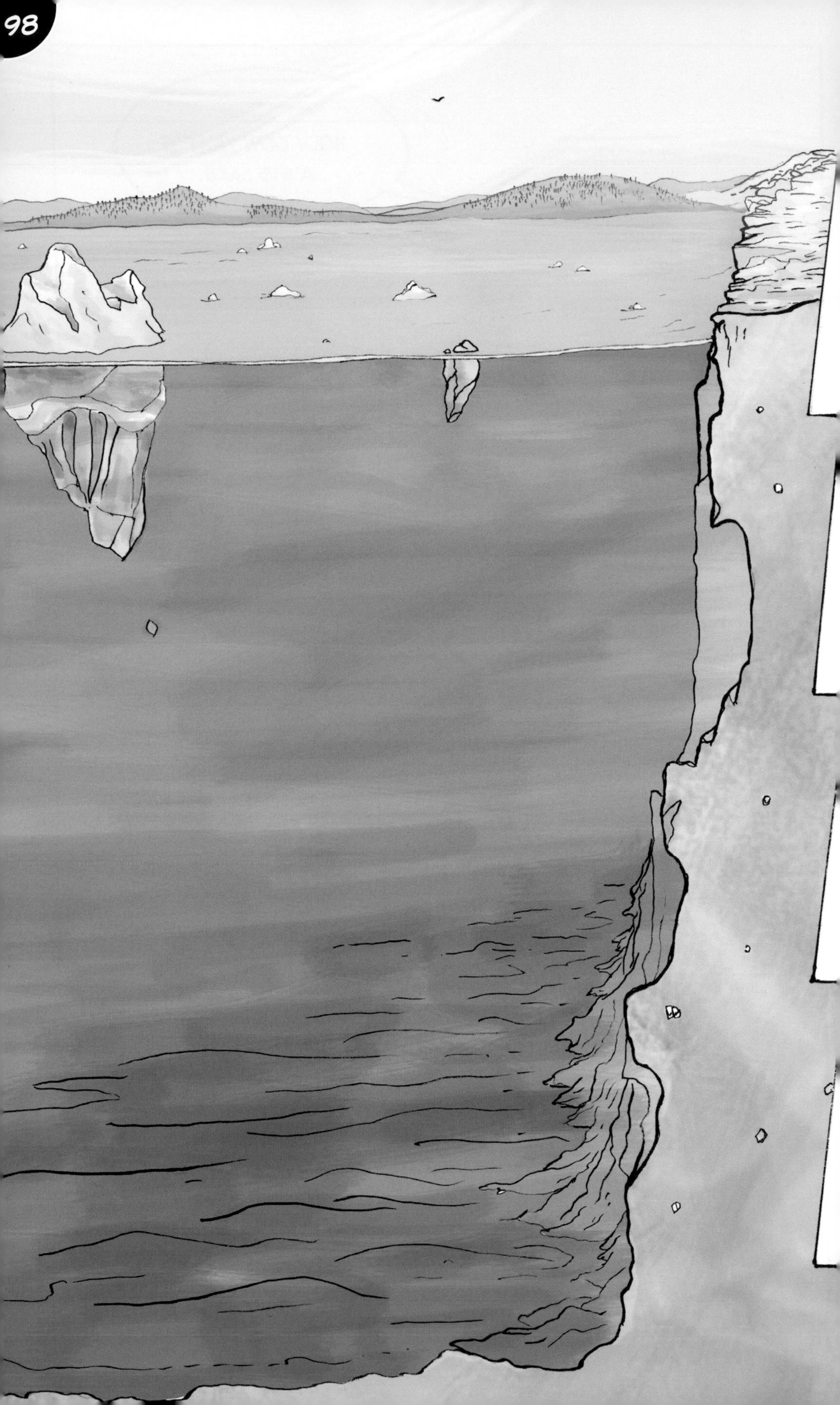

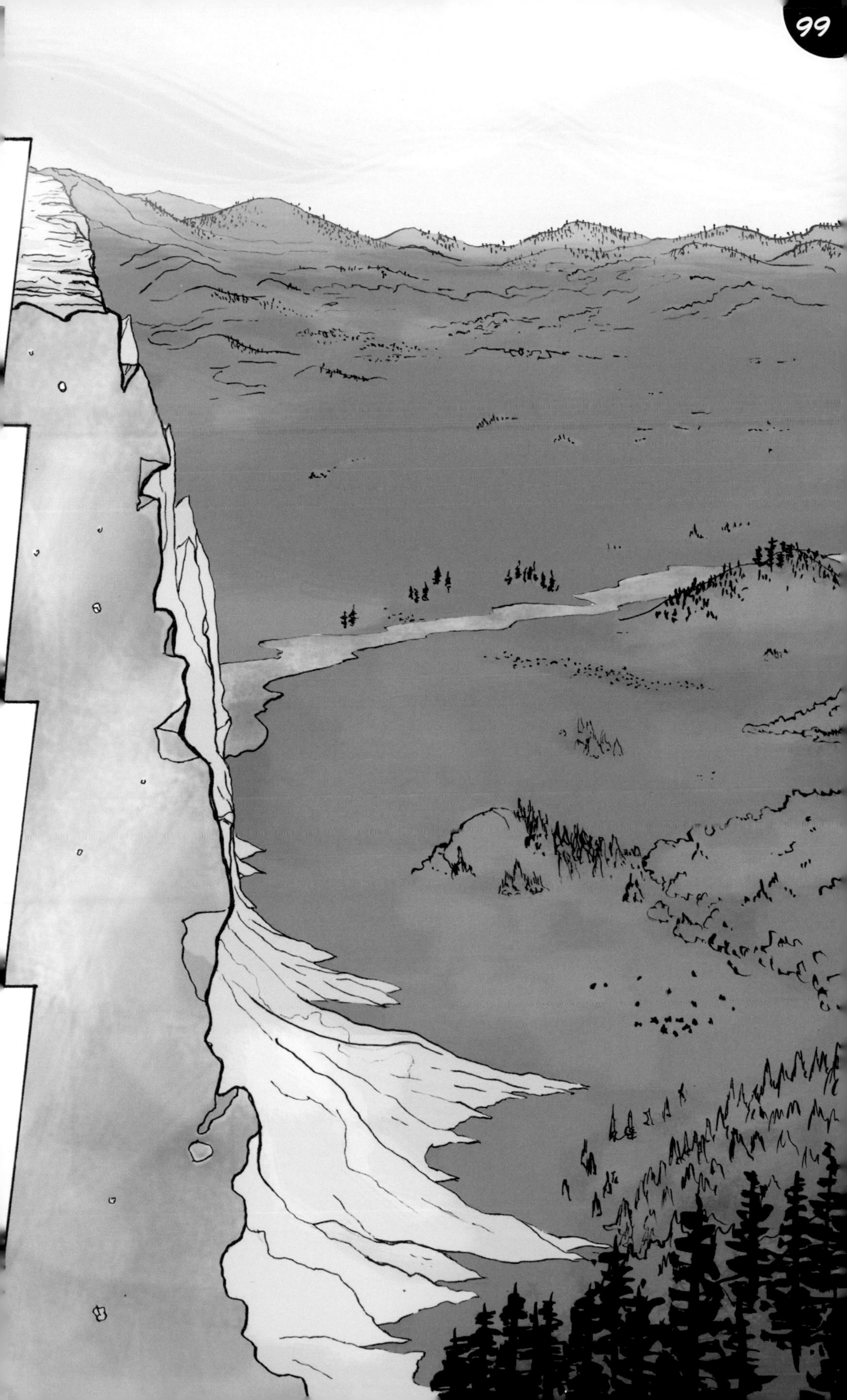

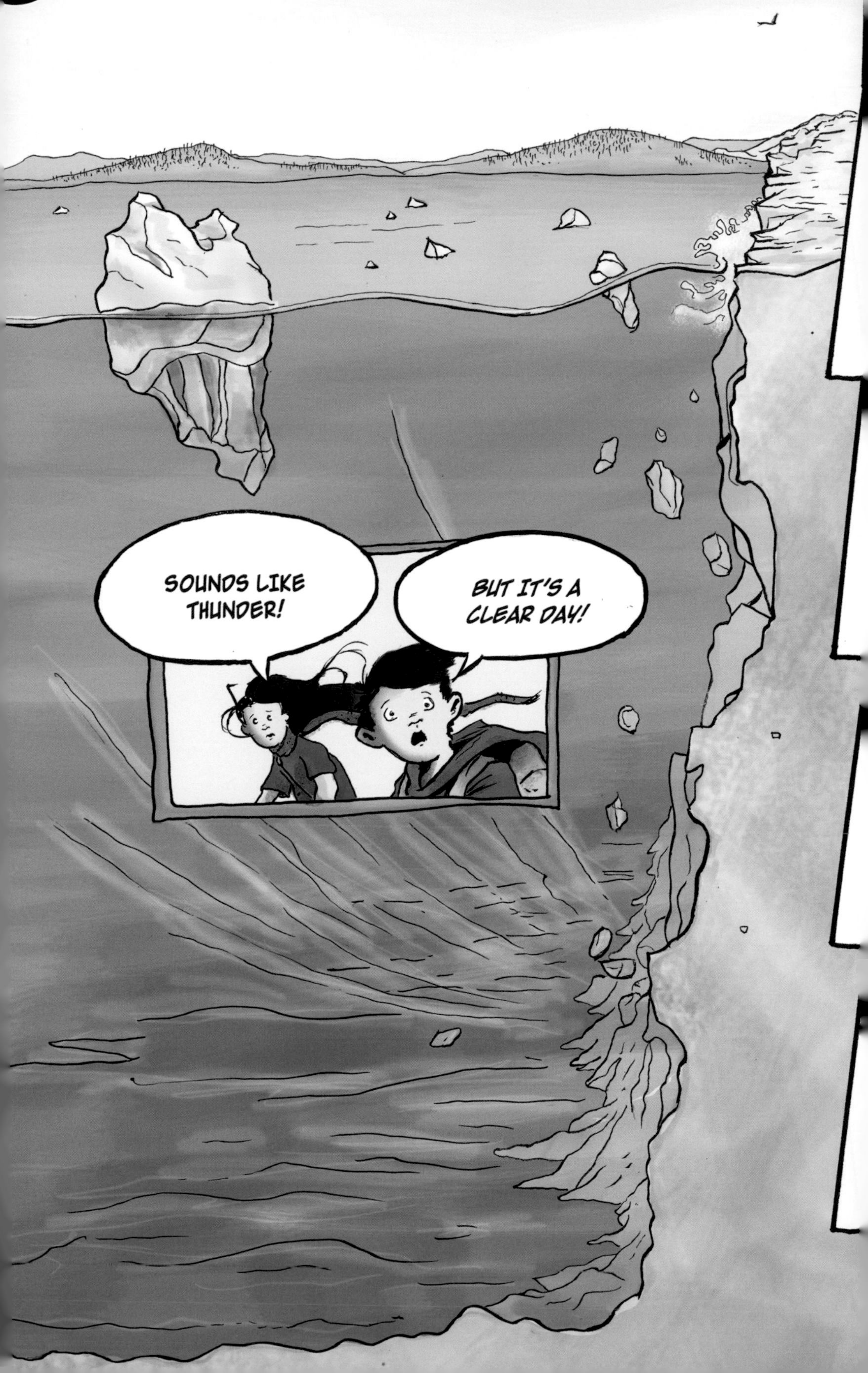
SOUNDS LIKE THUNDER!
BUT IT'S A CLEAR DAY!

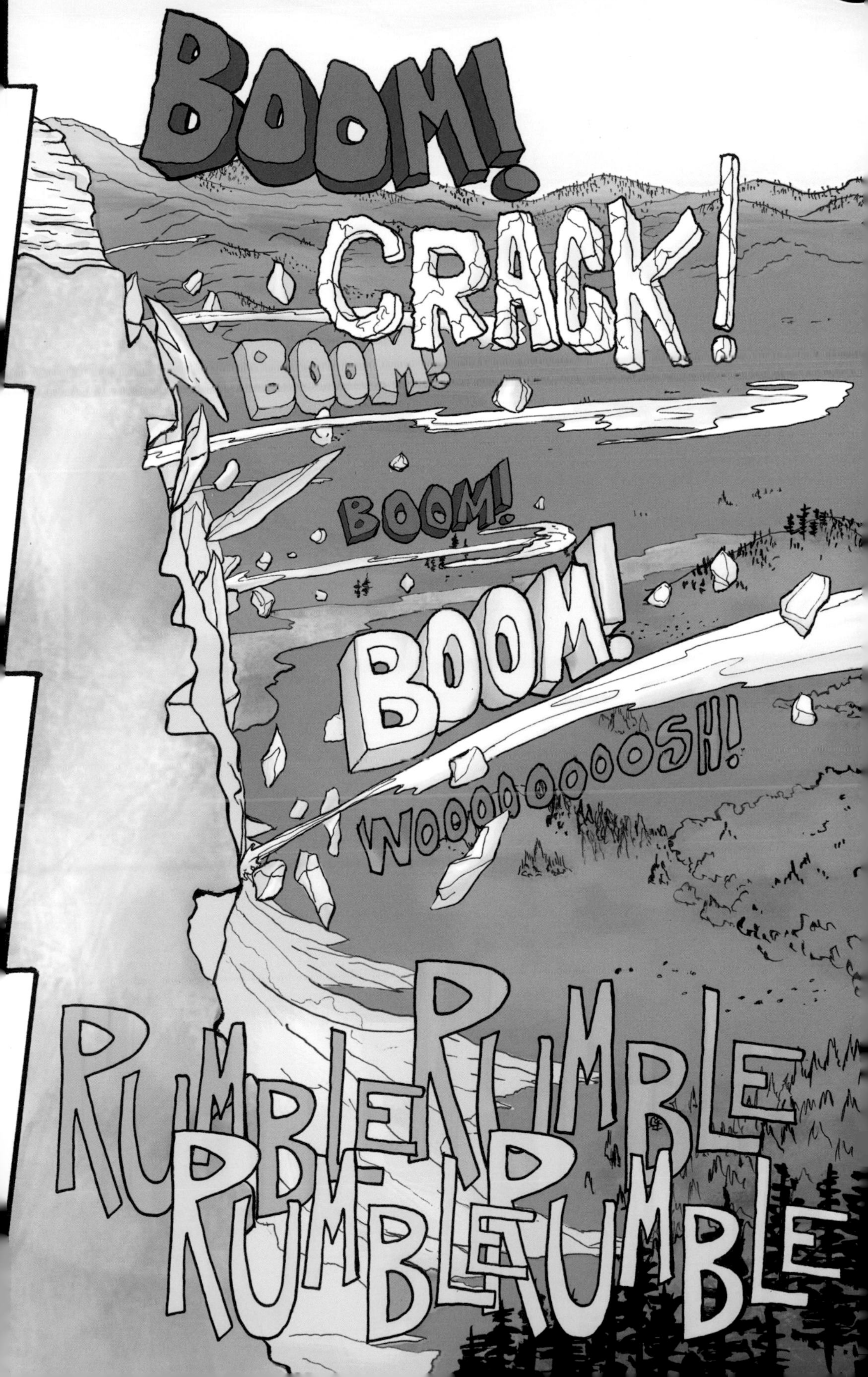
BOOM!
CRACK!
BOOM!
BOOM!
BOOM!
WOOOOOOOOOSH!
RUMBLERUMBLE
RUMBLERUMBLE
RUMBLERUMBLE

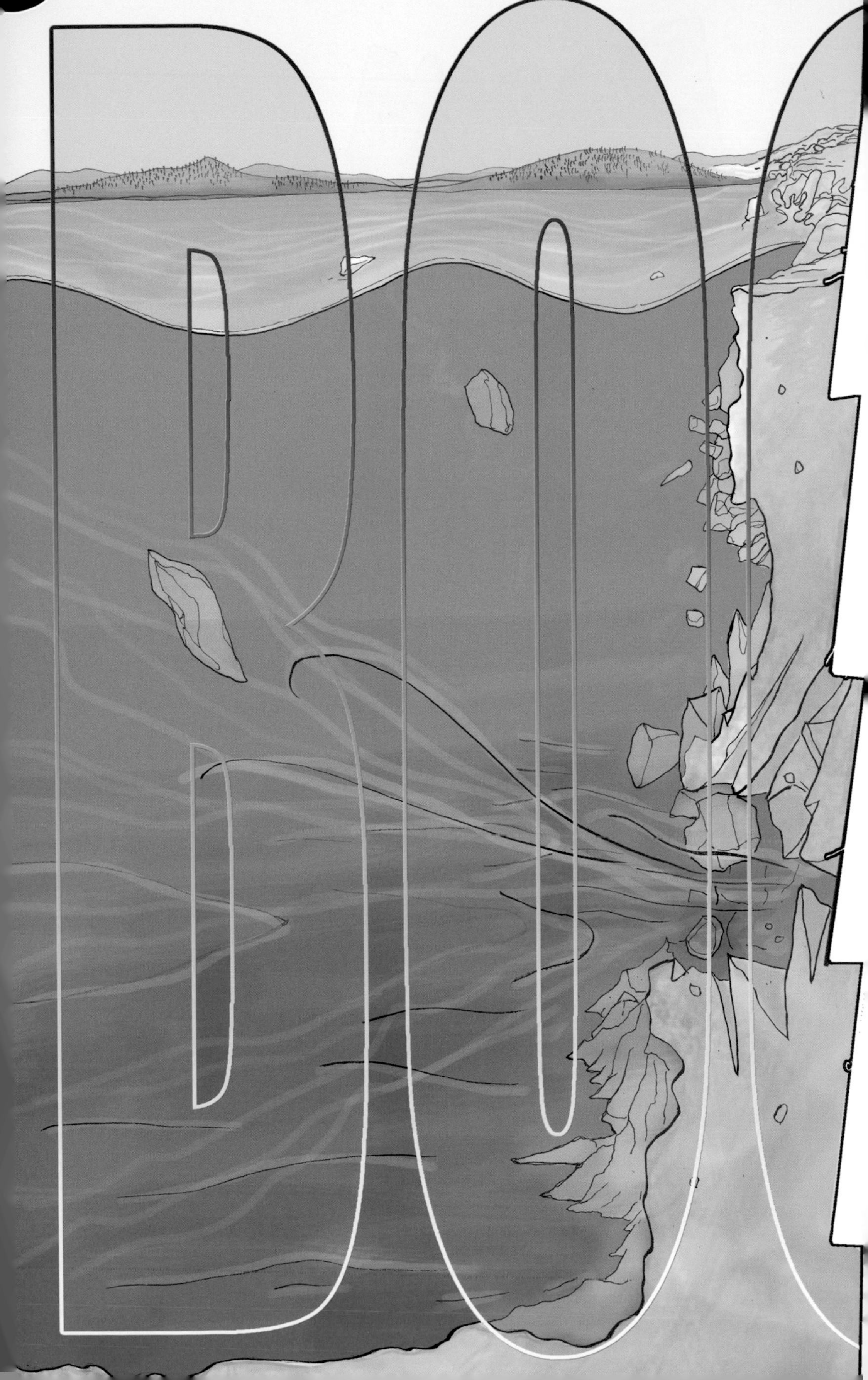
BOO

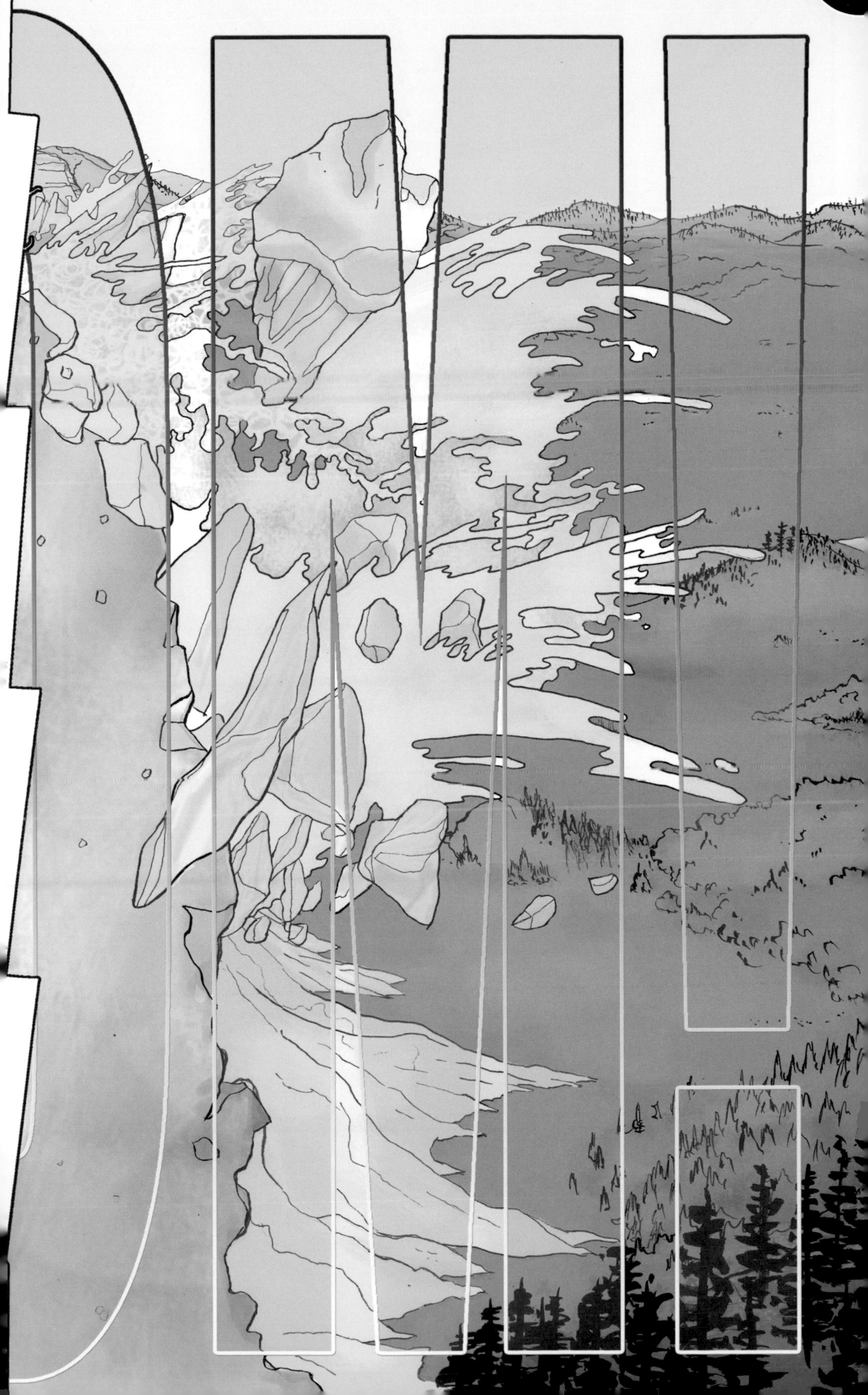

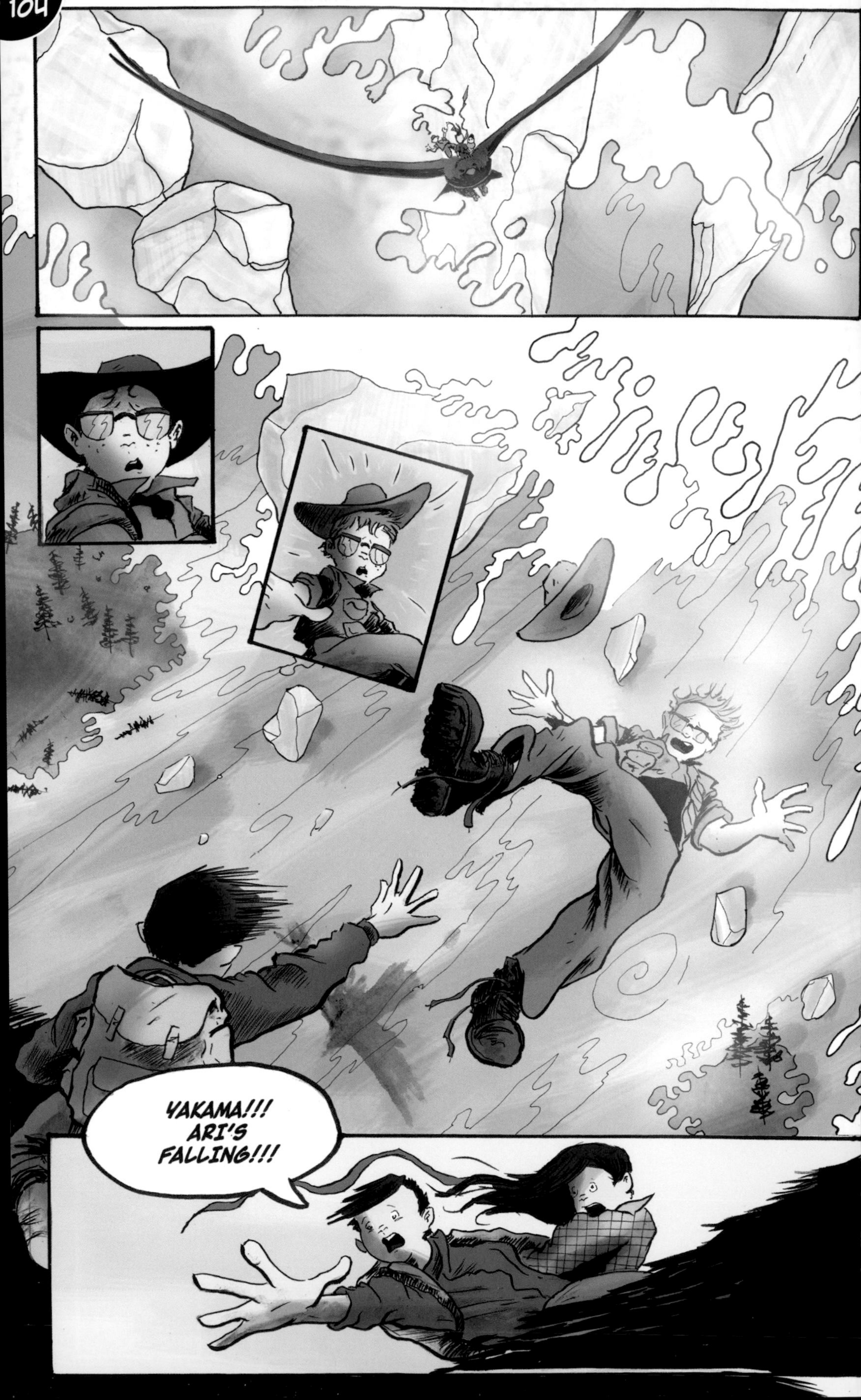
YAKAMA!!! ARI'S FALLING!!!

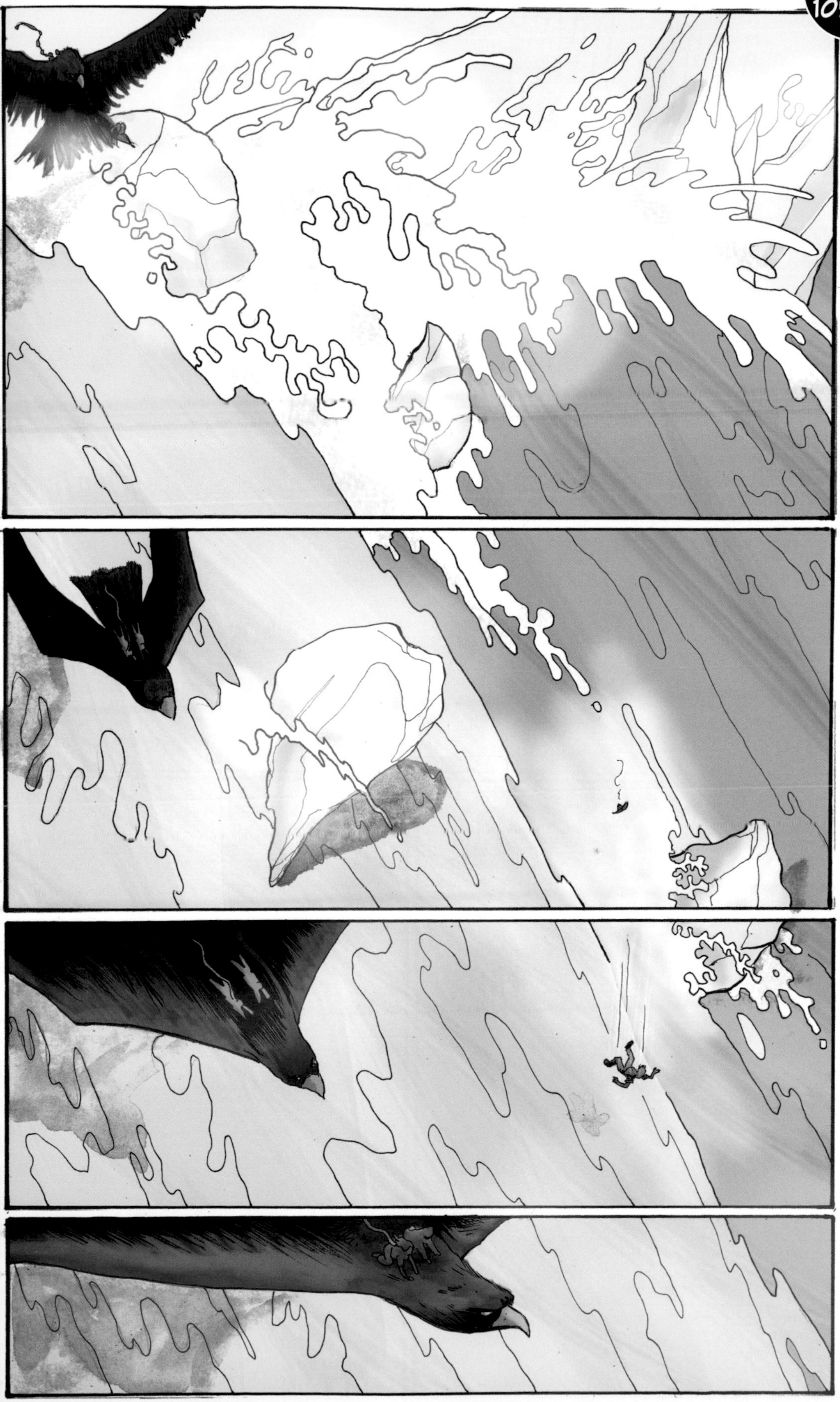

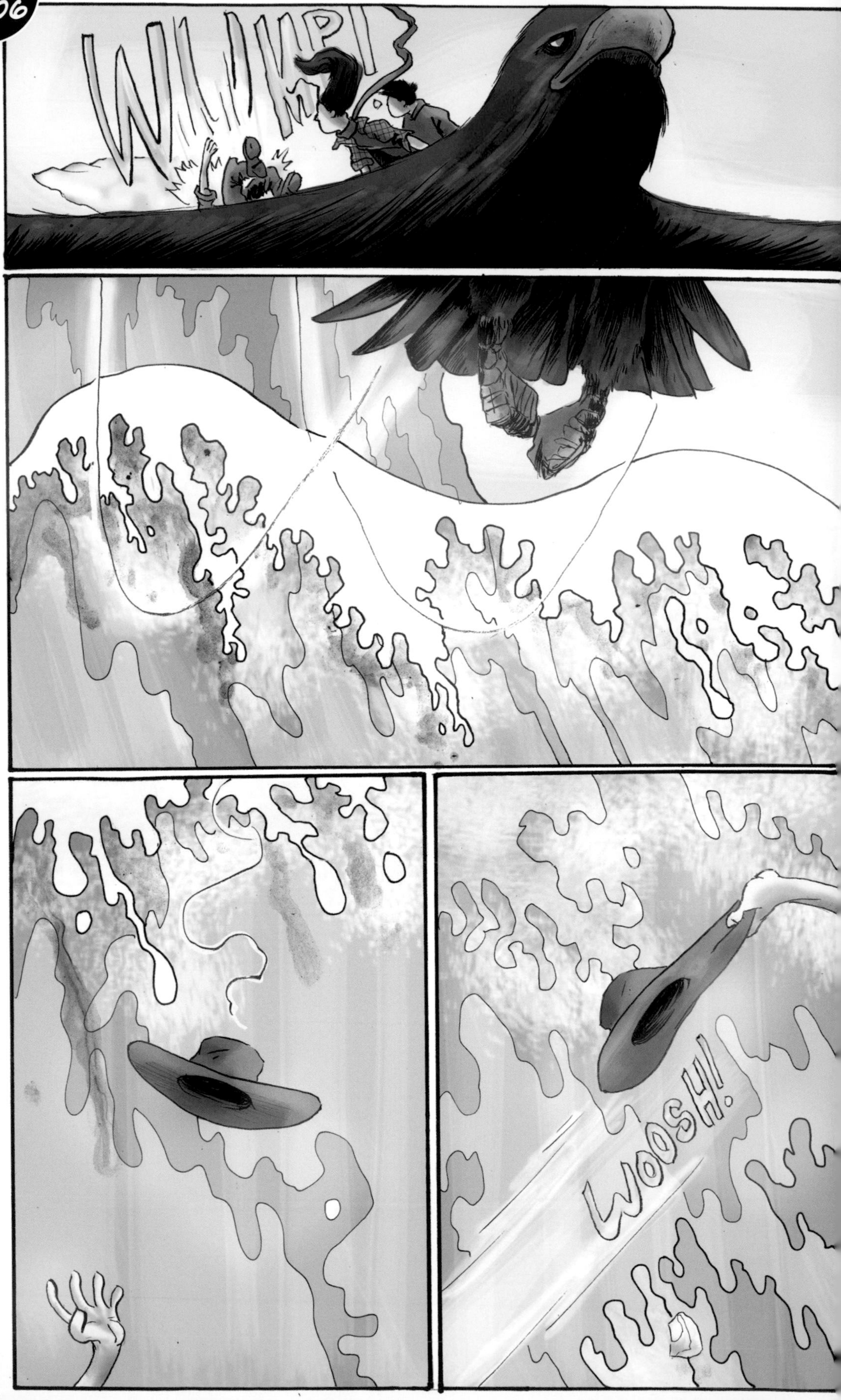
WHUMP!
WOOSH!

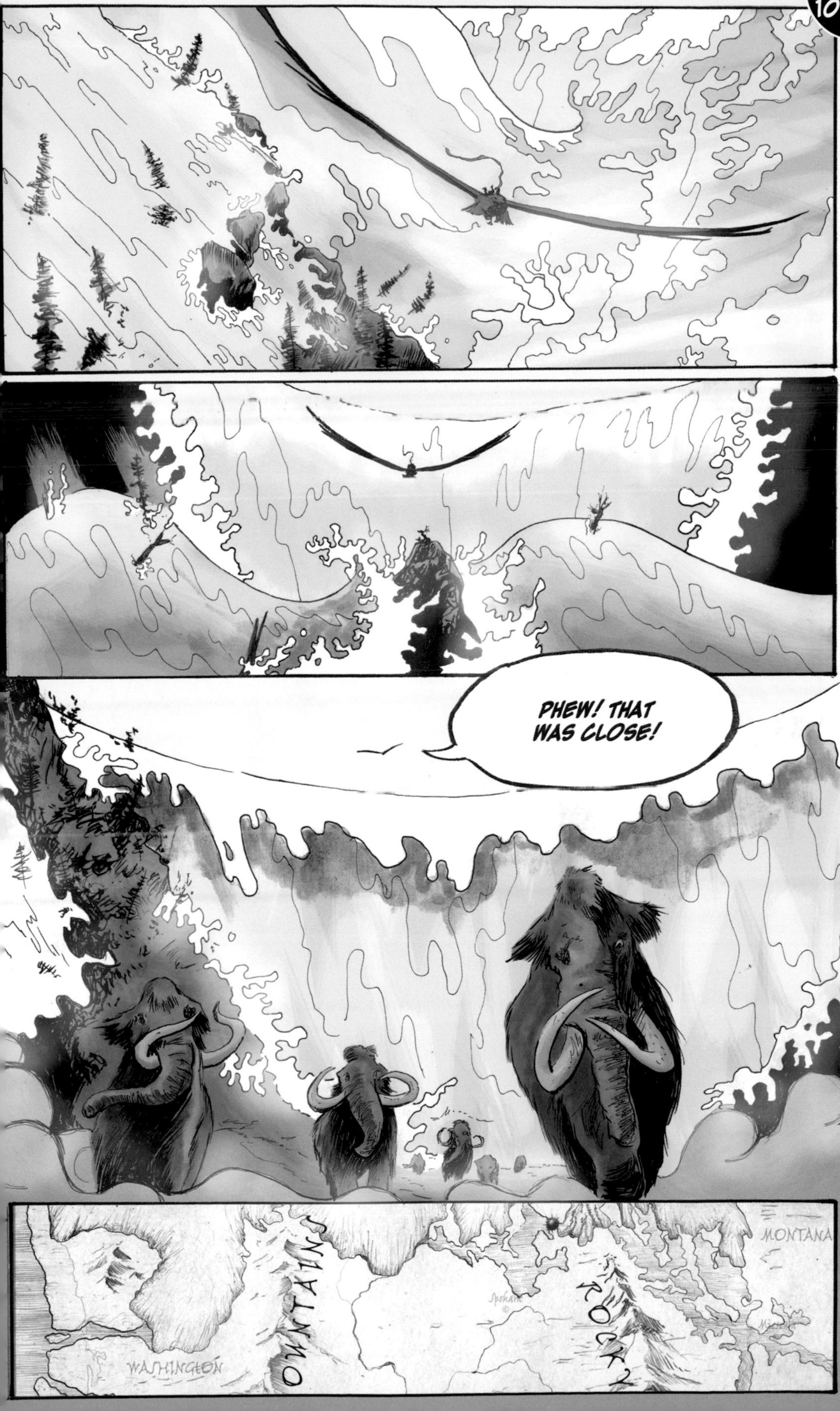
PHEW! THAT WAS CLOSE!
MONTANA
ROCKY
WASHINGTON

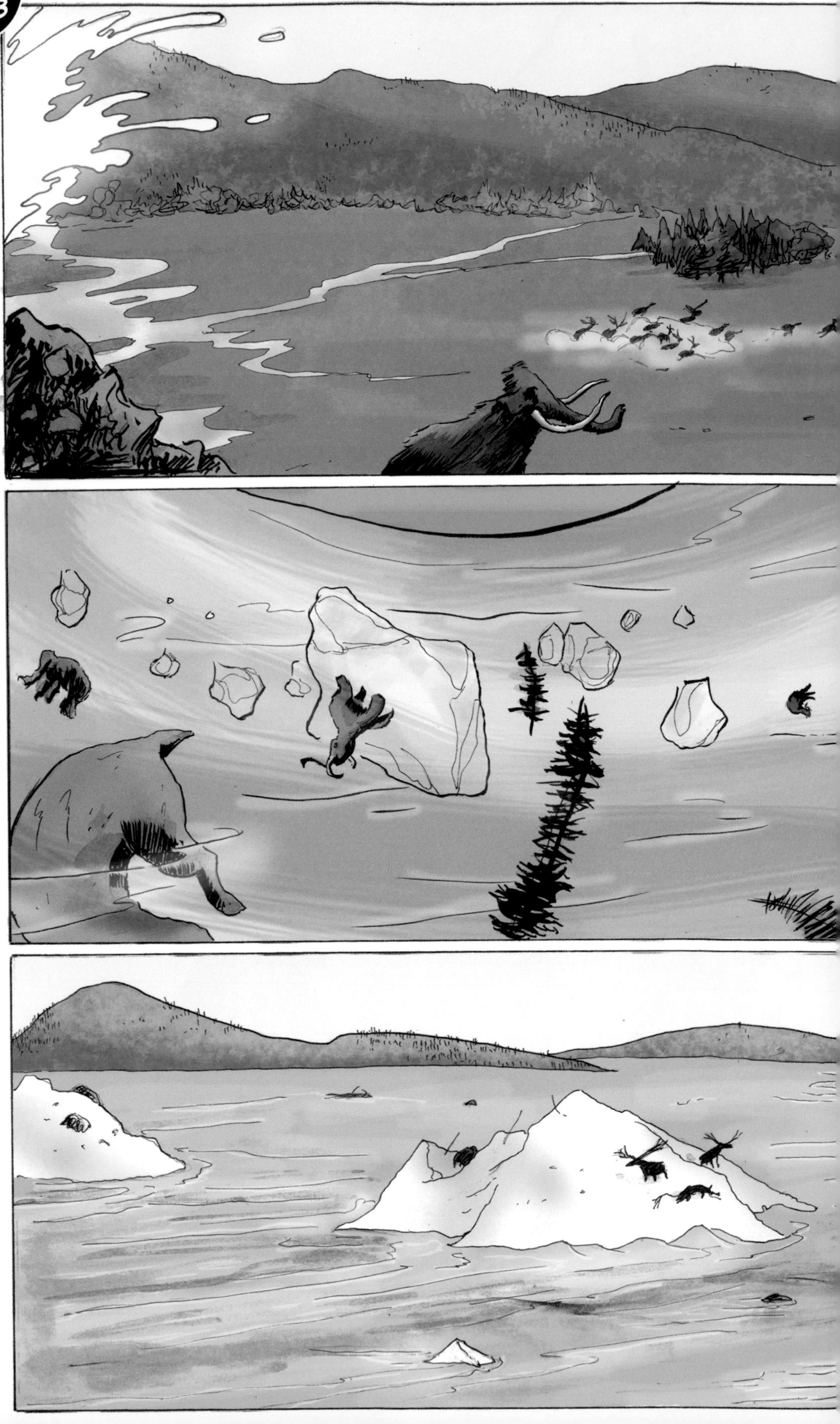

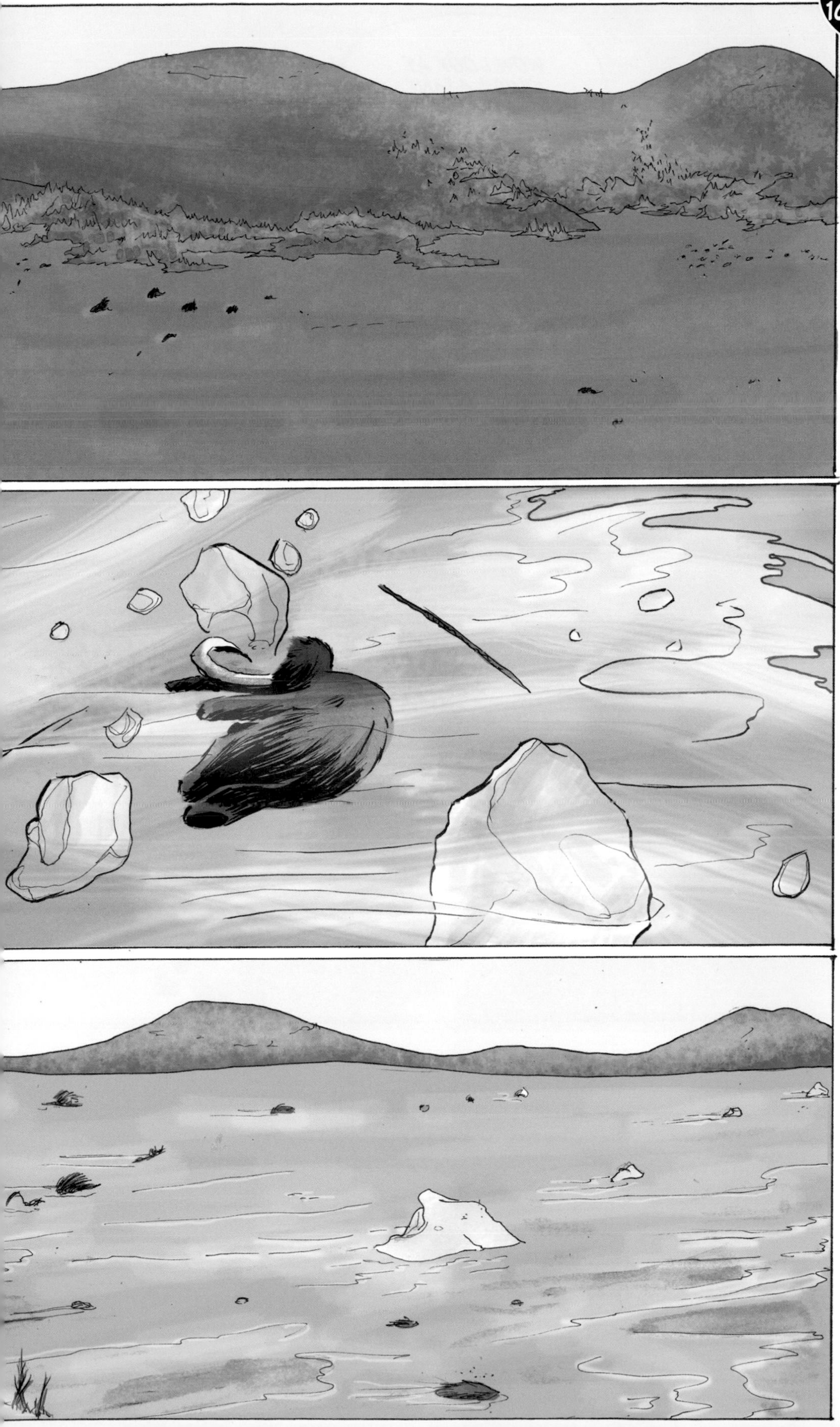

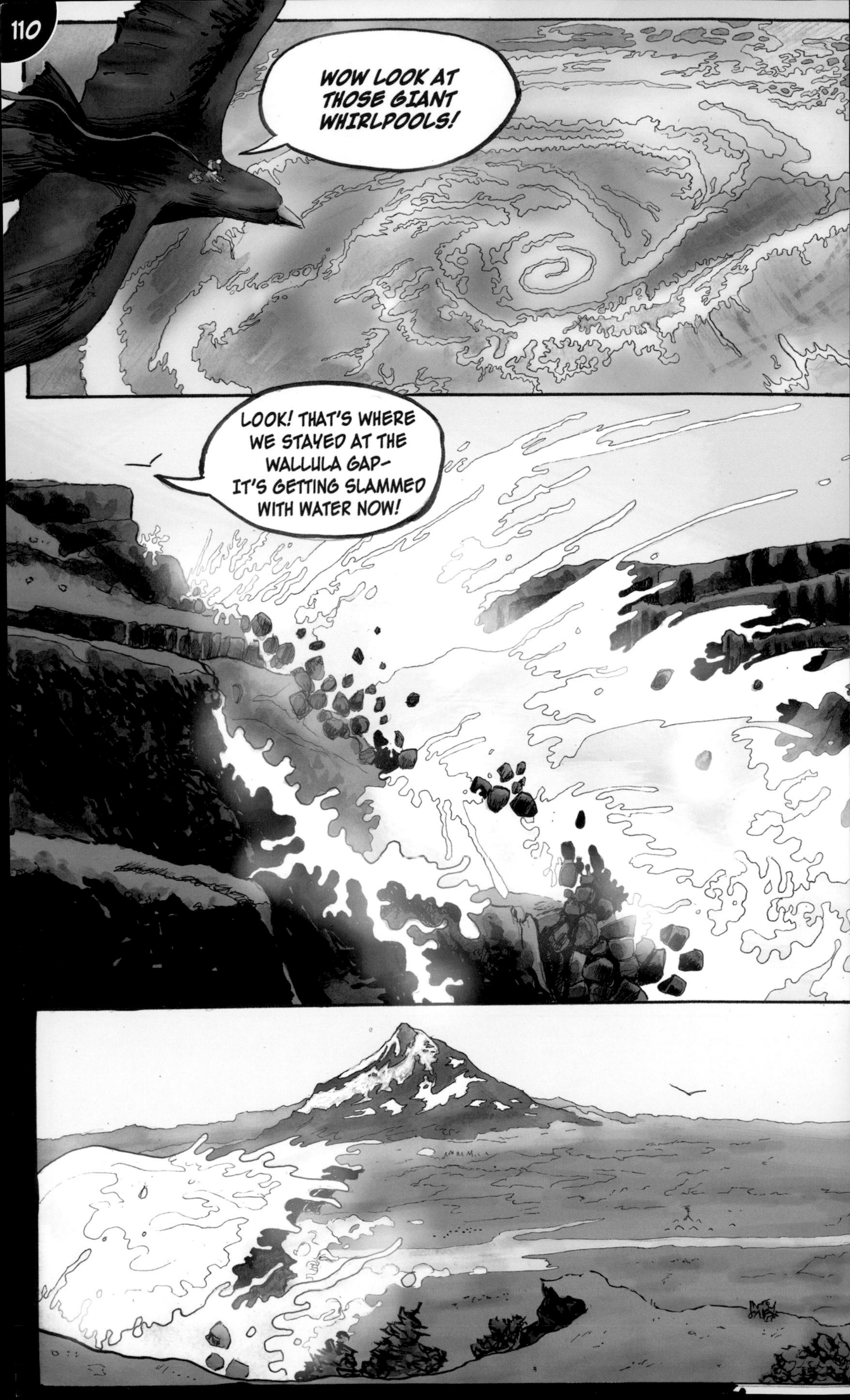
WOW LOOK AT THOSE GIANT WHIRLPOOLS!
LOOK! THAT'S WHERE WE STAYED AT THE WALLULA GAP- IT'S GETTING SLAMMED WITH WATER NOW!

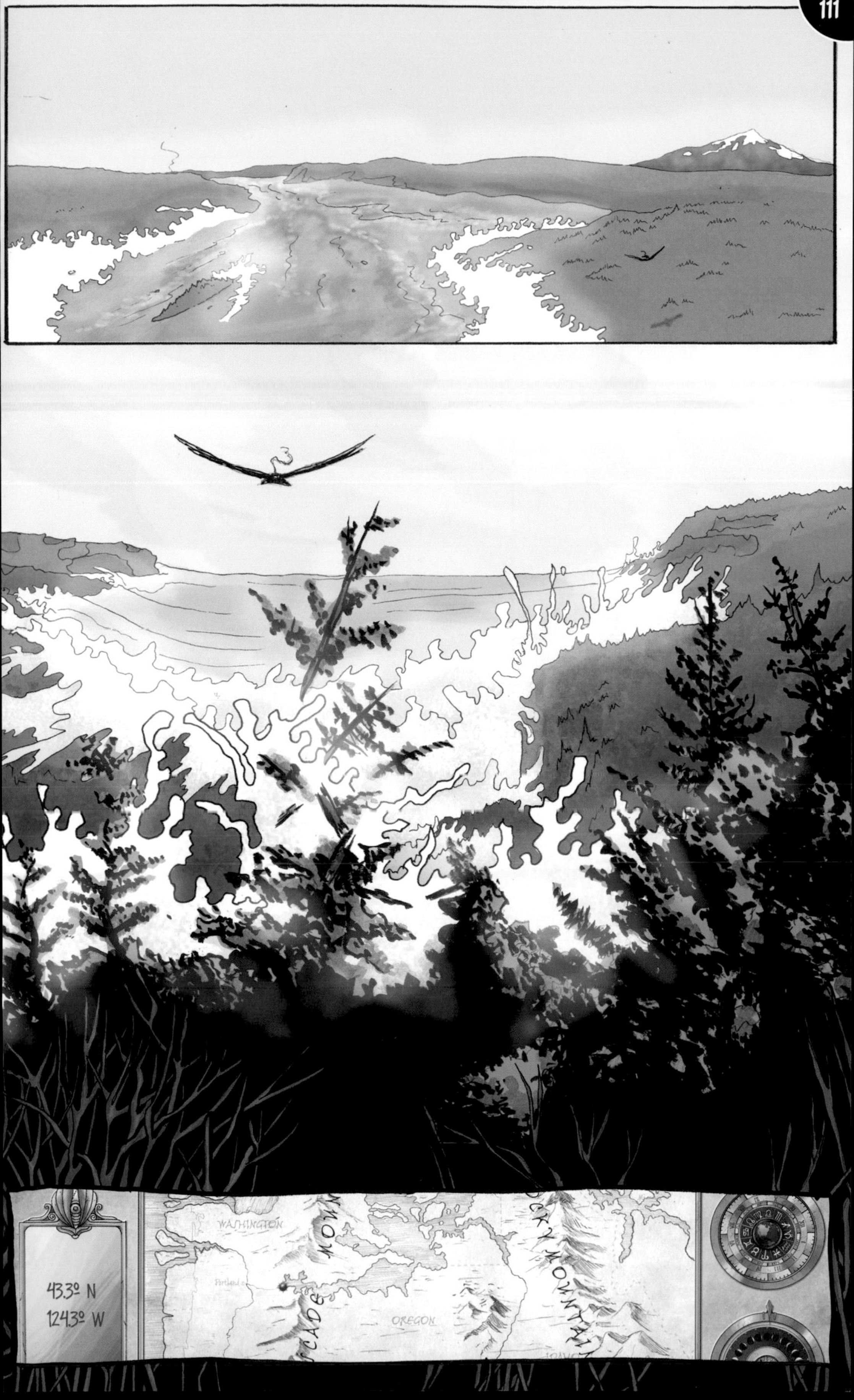
WASHINGTON
OREGON
43.3º N
124.3º W

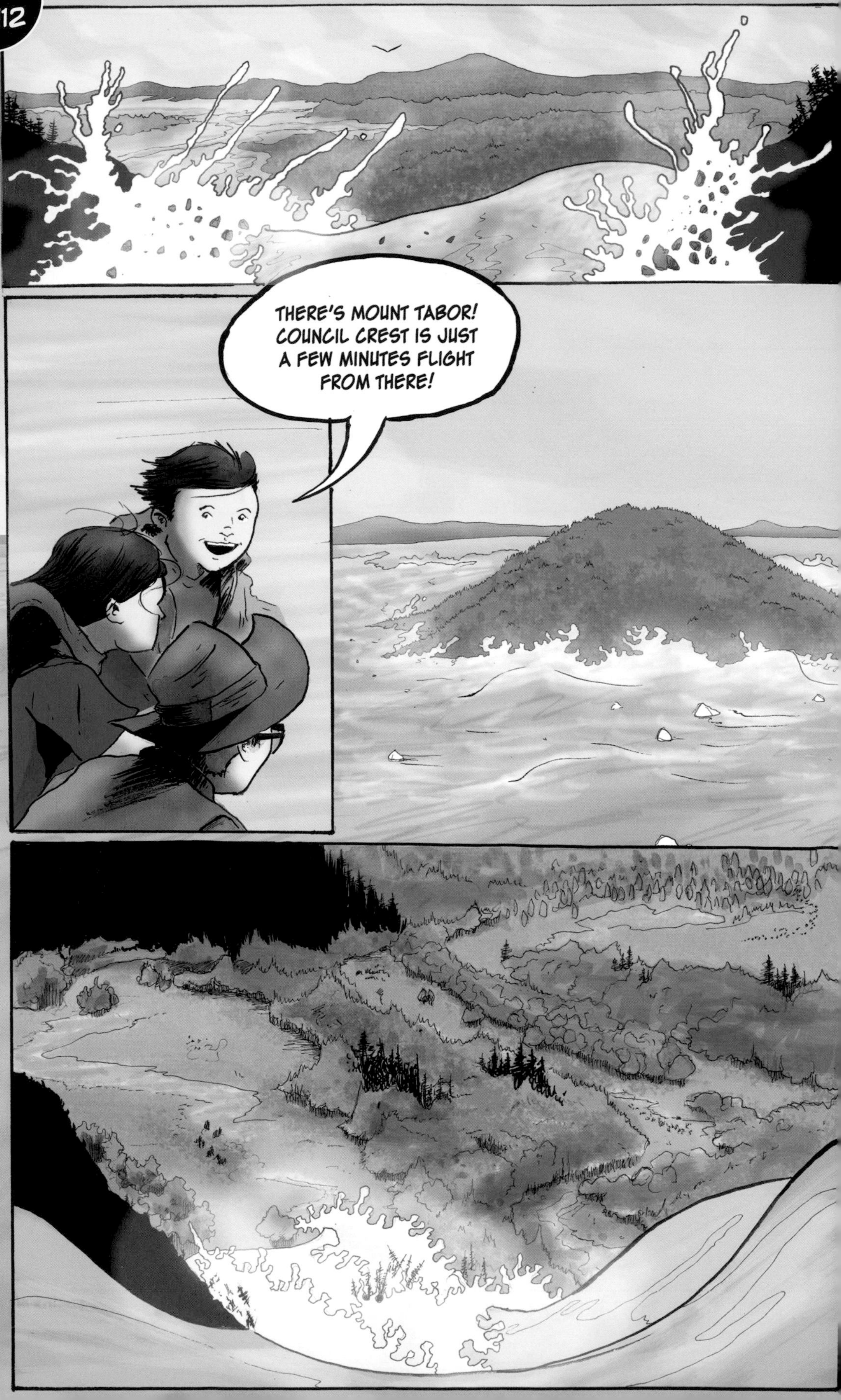
THERE'S MOUNT TABOR! COUNCIL CREST IS JUST A FEW MINUTES FLIGHT FROM THERE!

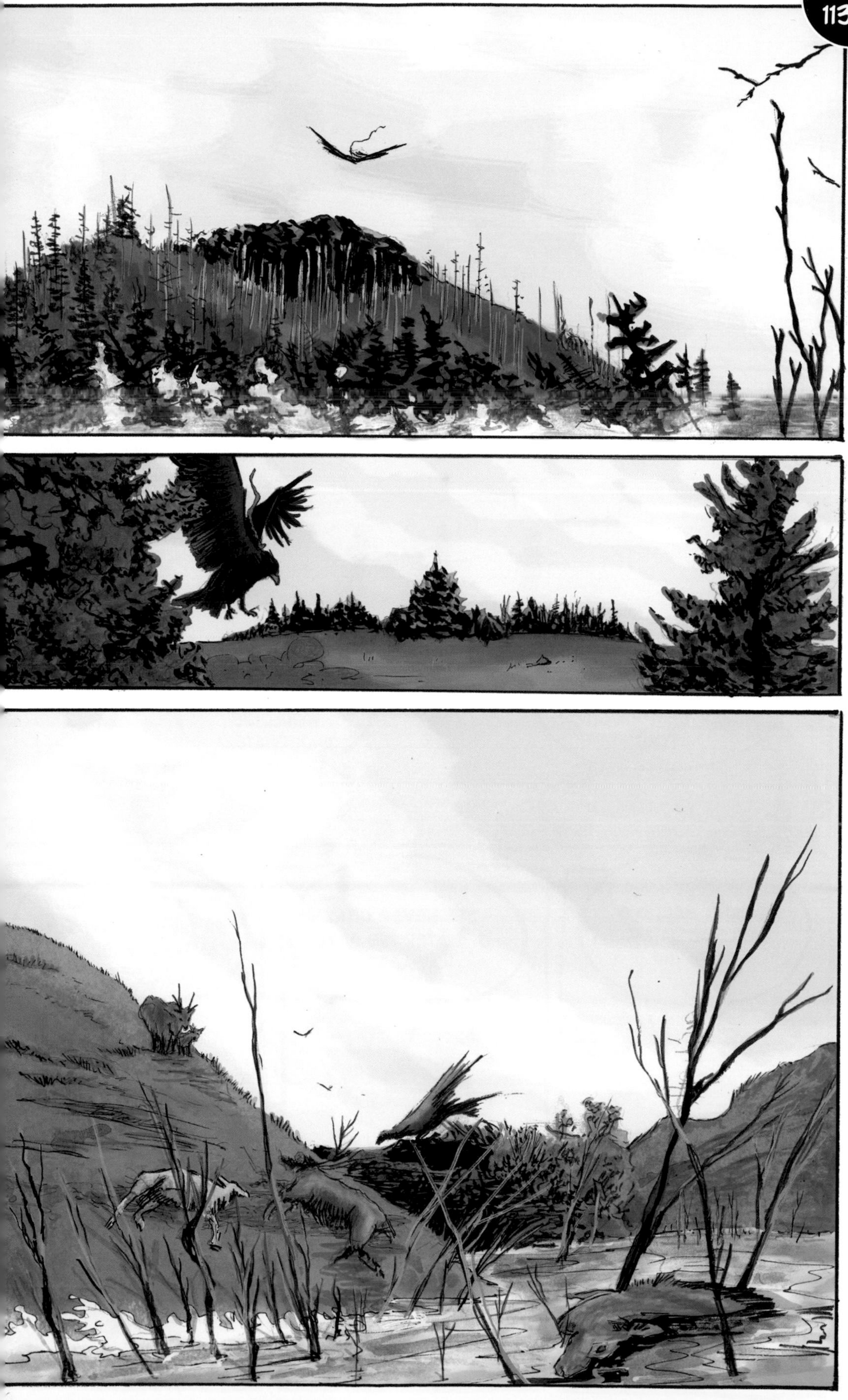

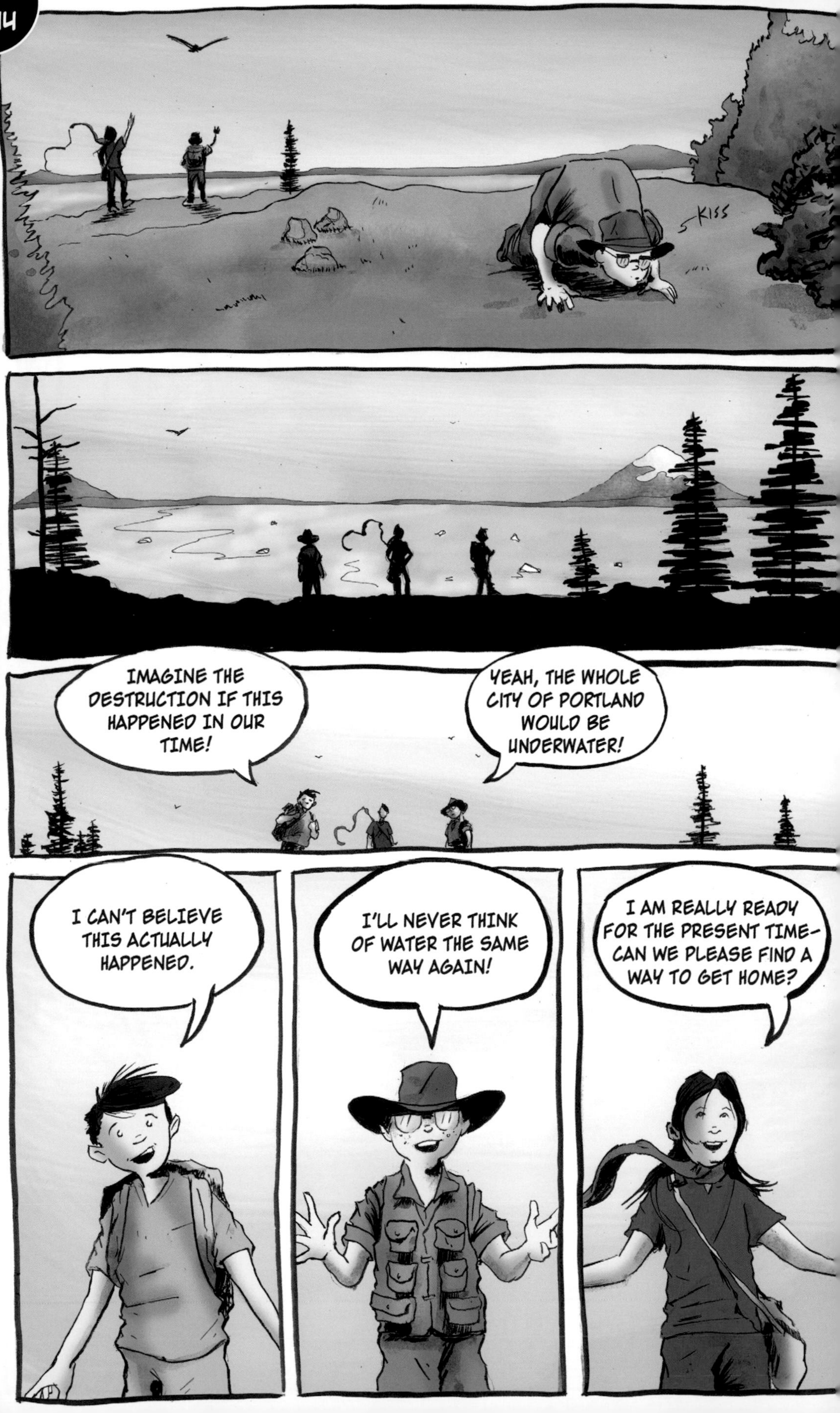
KISS
IMAGINE THE DESTRUCTION IF THIS HAPPENED IN OUR TIME!
YEAH, THE WHOLE CITY OF PORTLAND WOULD BE UNDERWATER!
I CAN'T BELIEVE THIS ACTUALLY HAPPENED.
I'LL NEVER THINK OF WATER THE SAME WAY AGAIN!
I AM REALLY READY FOR THE PRESENT TIME- CAN WE PLEASE FIND A WAY TO GET HOME?

CHAPTER SEVEN

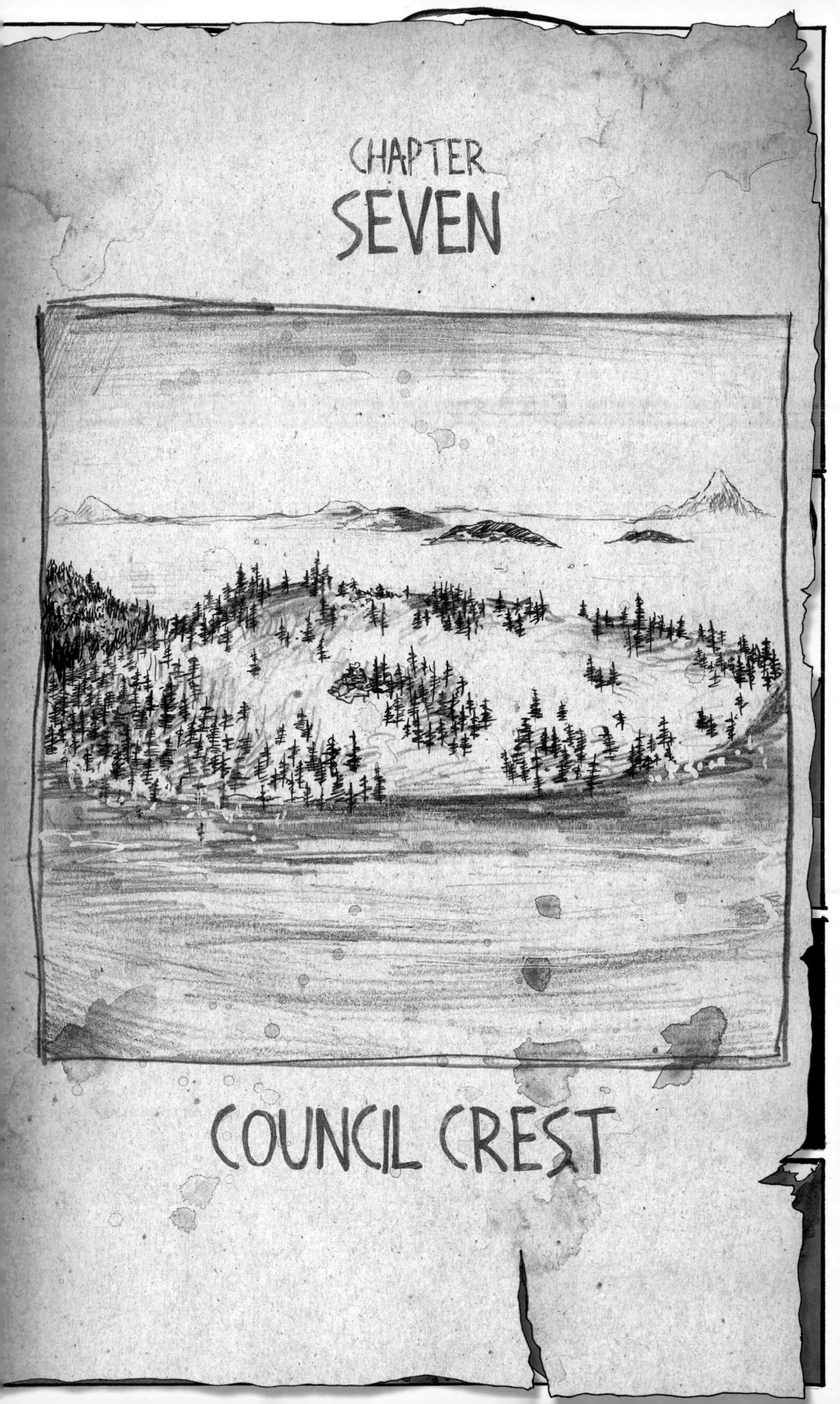

COUNCIL CREST

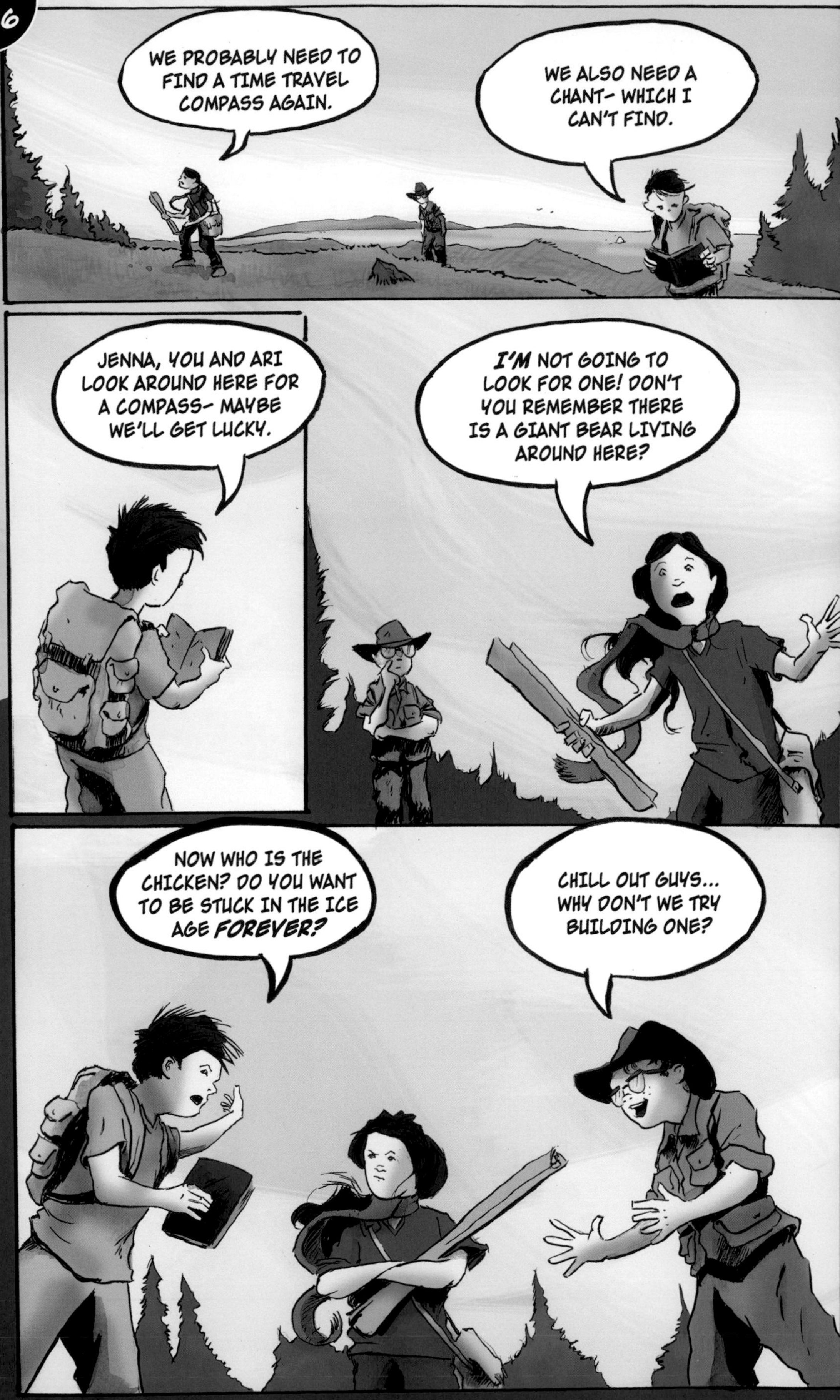
WE PROBABLY NEED TO FIND A TIME TRAVEL COMPASS AGAIN.
WE ALSO NEED A CHANT- WHICH I CAN'T FIND.
JENNA, YOU AND ARI LOOK AROUND HERE FOR A COMPASS- MAYBE WE'LL GET LUCKY.
I'M NOT GOING TO LOOK FOR ONE! DON'T YOU REMEMBER THERE IS A GIANT BEAR LIVING AROUND HERE?
NOW WHO IS THE CHICKEN? DO YOU WANT TO BE STUCK IN THE ICE AGE FOREVER?
CHILL OUT GUYS... WHY DON'T WE TRY BUILDING ONE?

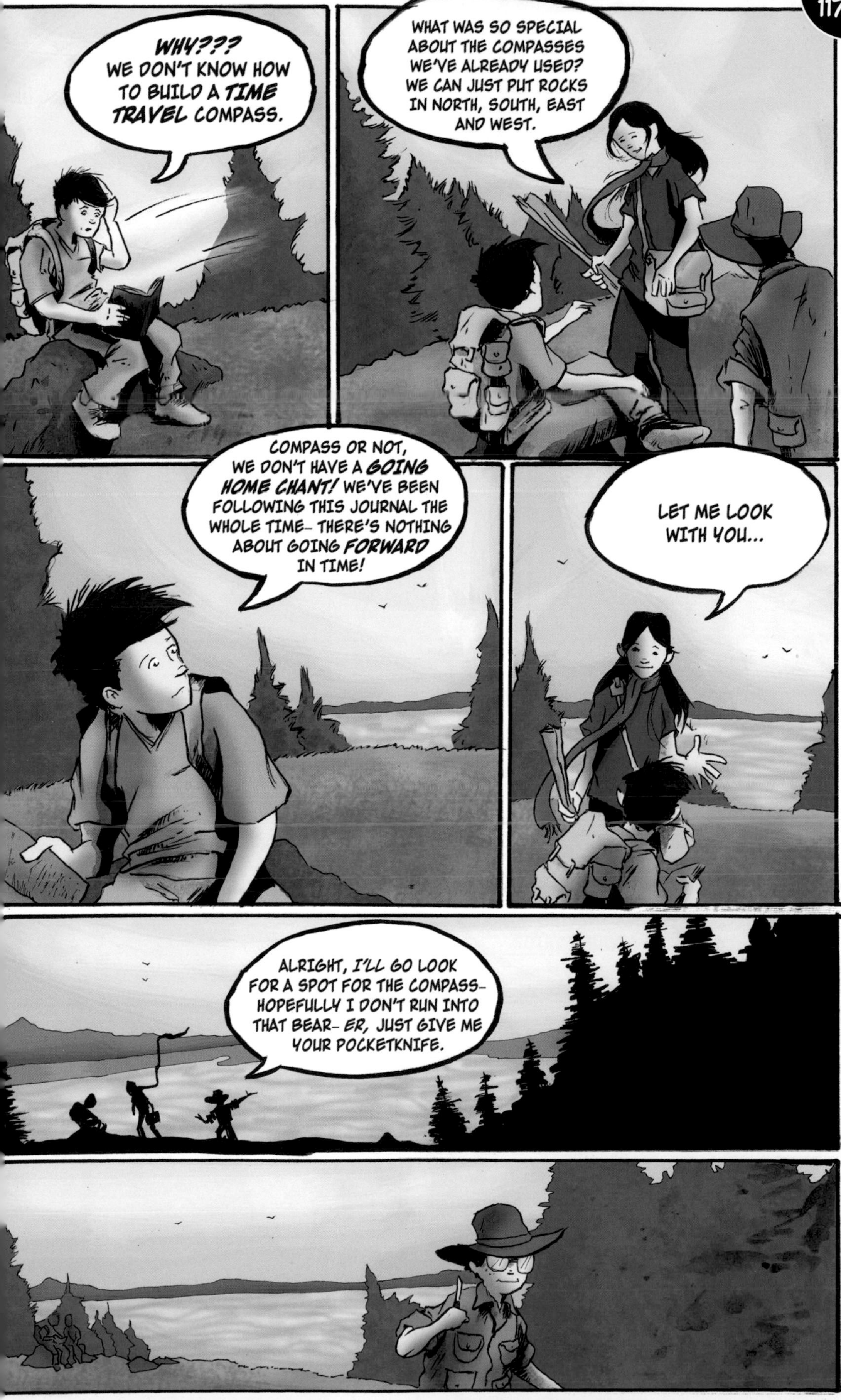
WHY??? WE DON'T KNOW HOW TO BUILD A TIME TRAVEL COMPASS.
WHAT WAS SO SPECIAL ABOUT THE COMPASSES WE'VE ALREADY USED? WE CAN JUST PUT ROCKS IN NORTH, SOUTH, EAST AND WEST.
COMPASS OR NOT, WE DON'T HAVE A GOING HOME CHANT! WE'VE BEEN FOLLOWING THIS JOURNAL THE WHOLE TIME– THERE'S NOTHING ABOUT GOING FORWARD IN TIME!
LET ME LOOK WITH YOU...
ALRIGHT, I'LL GO LOOK FOR A SPOT FOR THE COMPASS– HOPEFULLY I DON'T RUN INTO THAT BEAR– ER, JUST GIVE ME YOUR POCKETKNIFE.

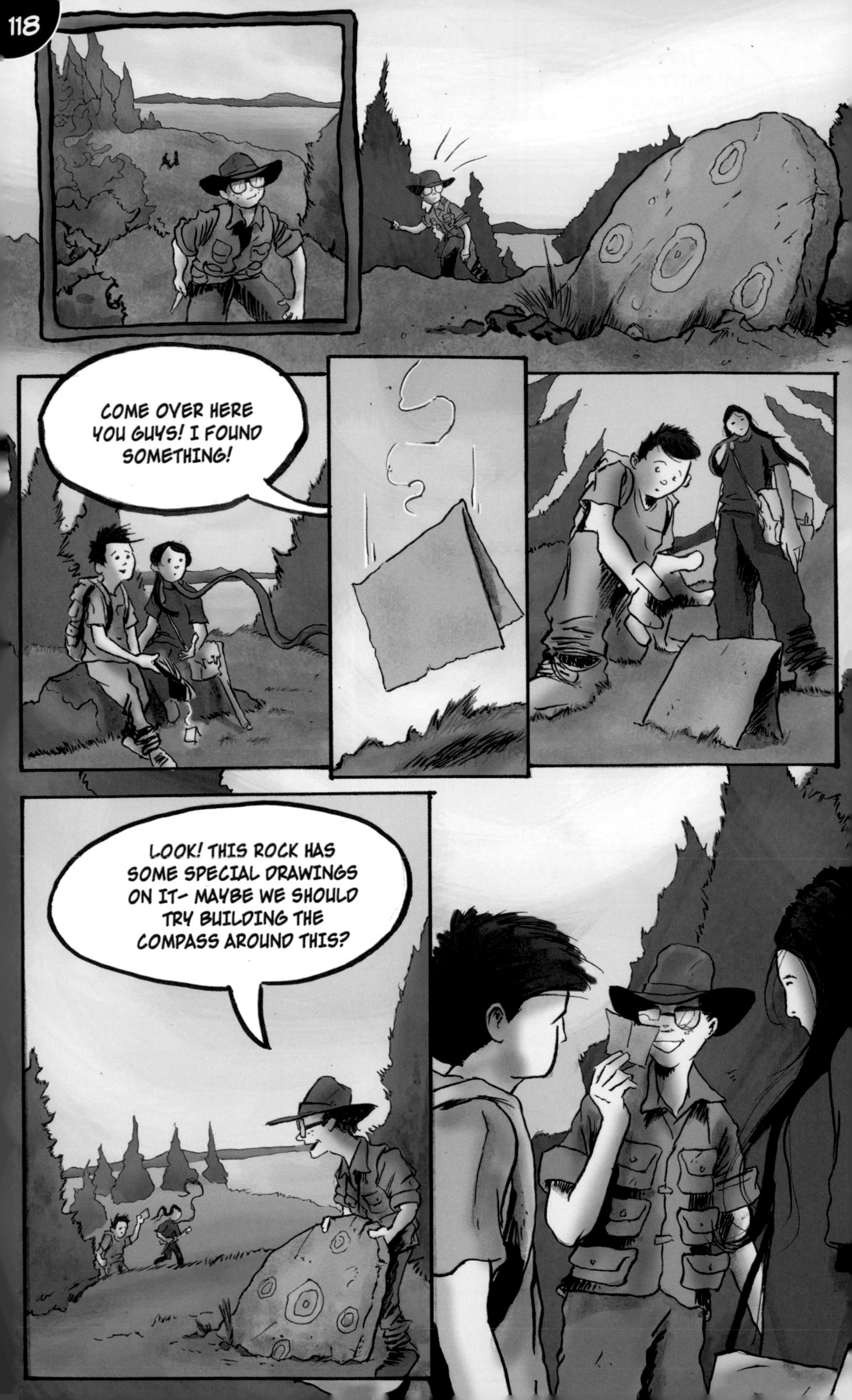
COME OVER HERE YOU GUYS! I FOUND SOMETHING!
LOOK! THIS ROCK HAS SOME SPECIAL DRAWINGS ON IT- MAYBE WE SHOULD TRY BUILDING THE COMPASS AROUND THIS?

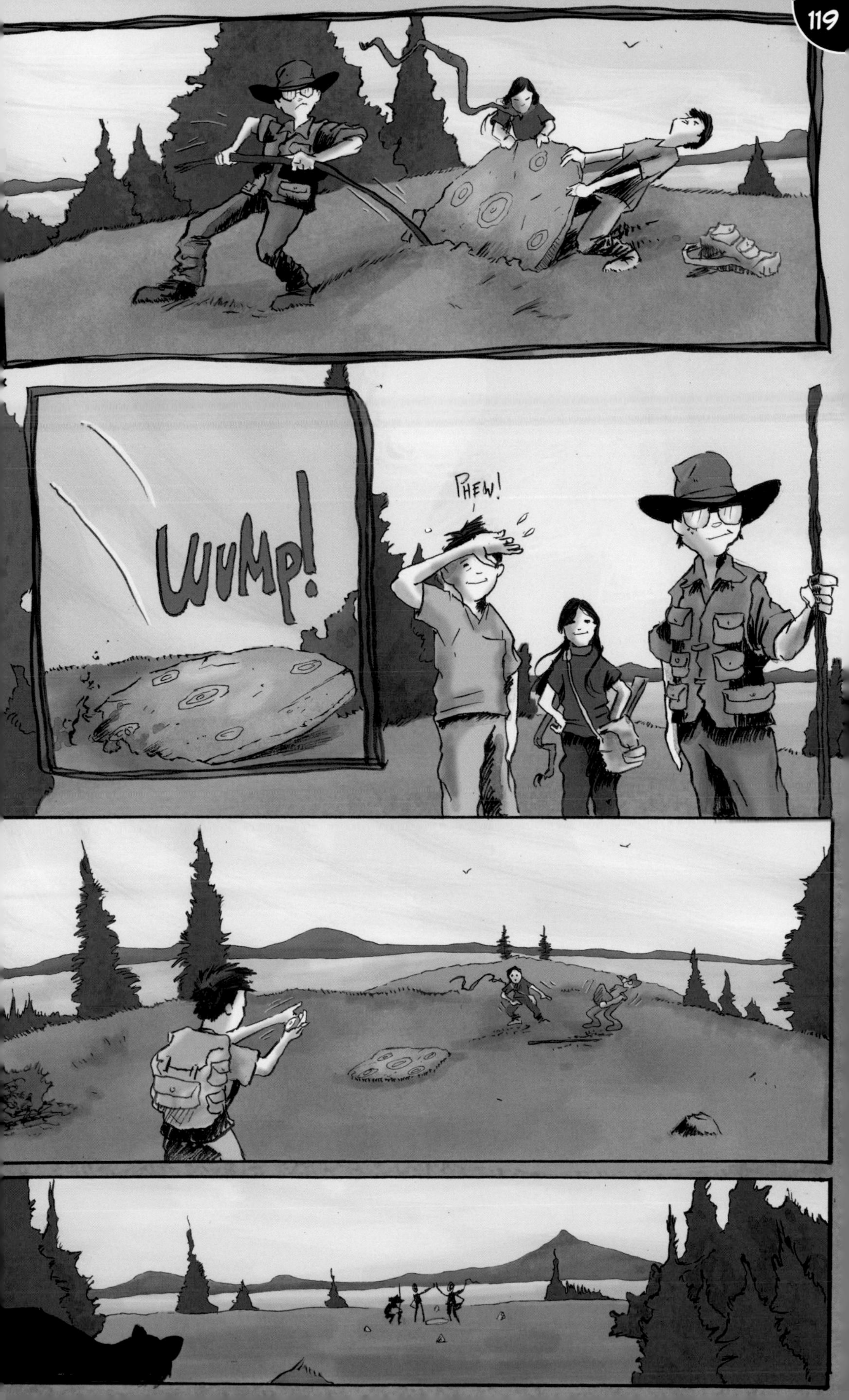
WUMP!
PHEW!

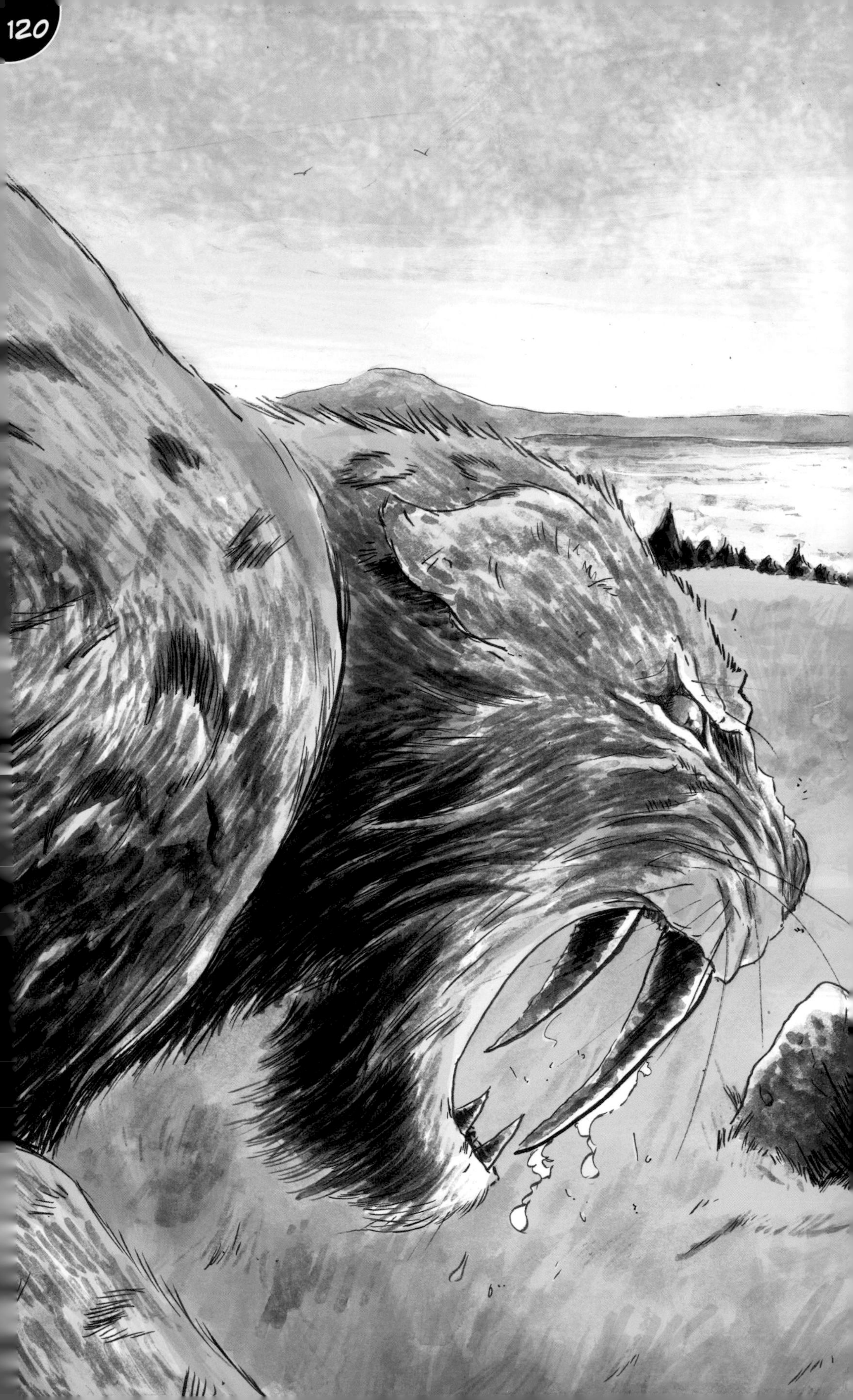

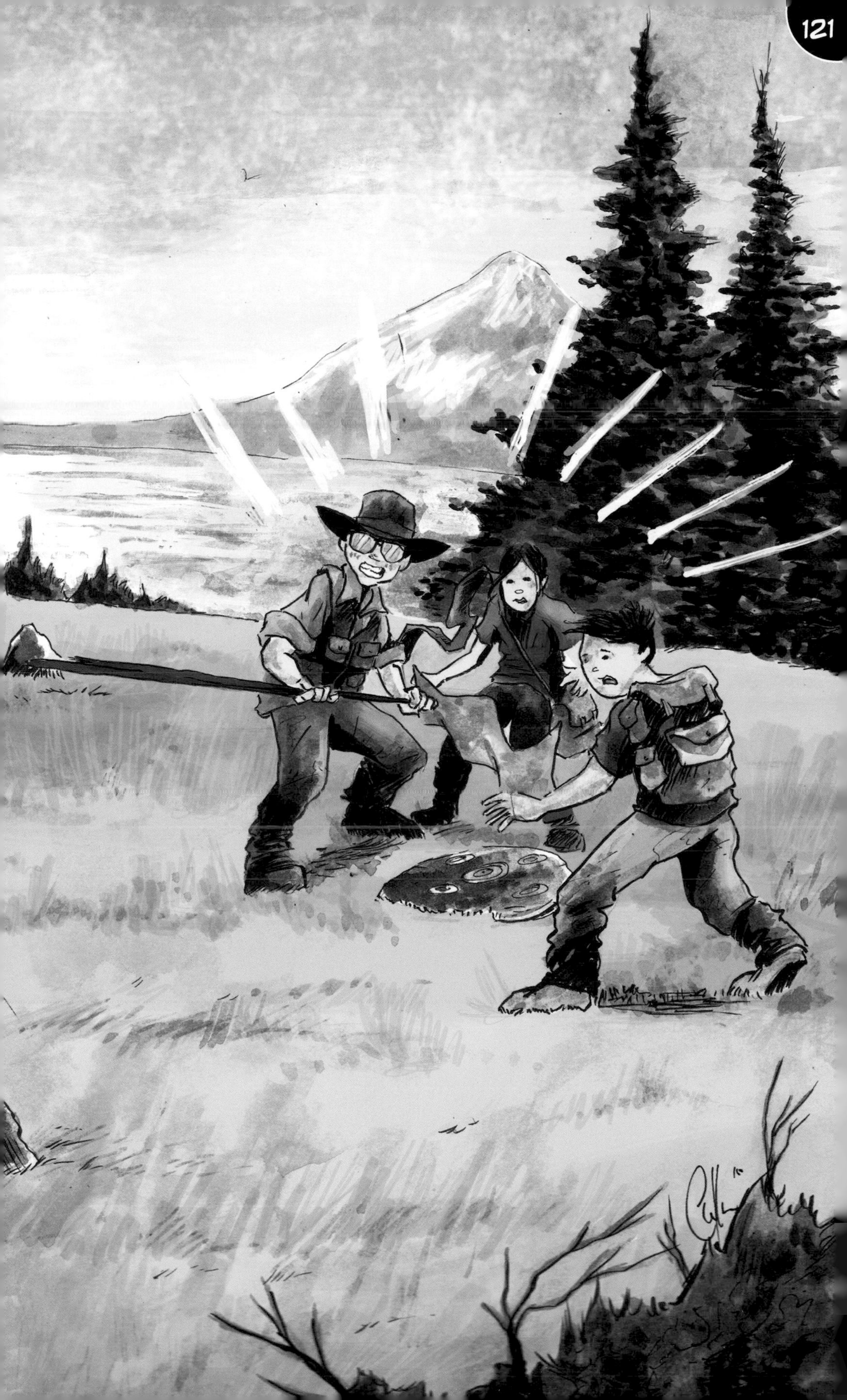

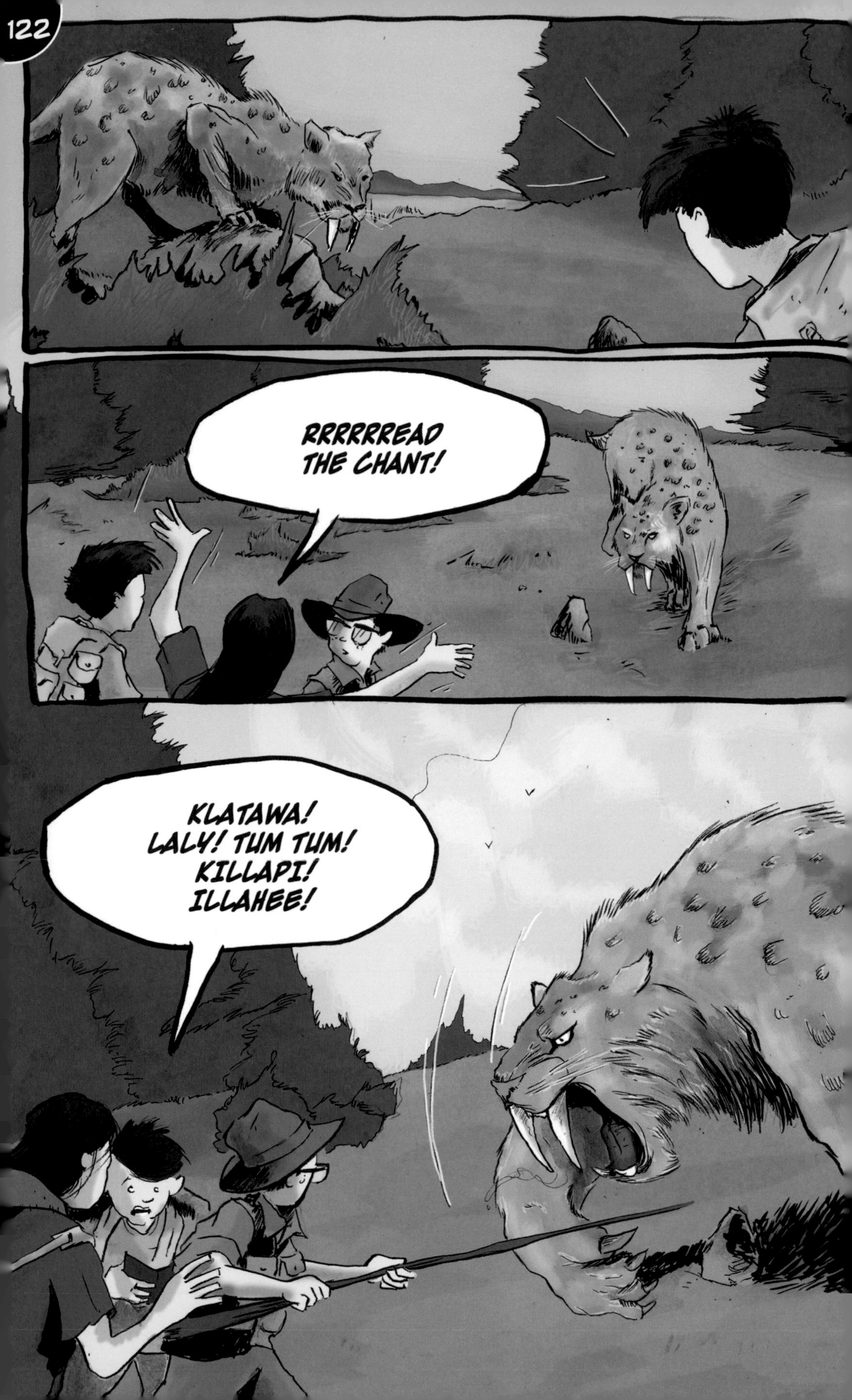
RRRRRREAD THE CHANT!
KLATAWA! LALY! TUM TUM! KILLAPI! ILLAHEE!

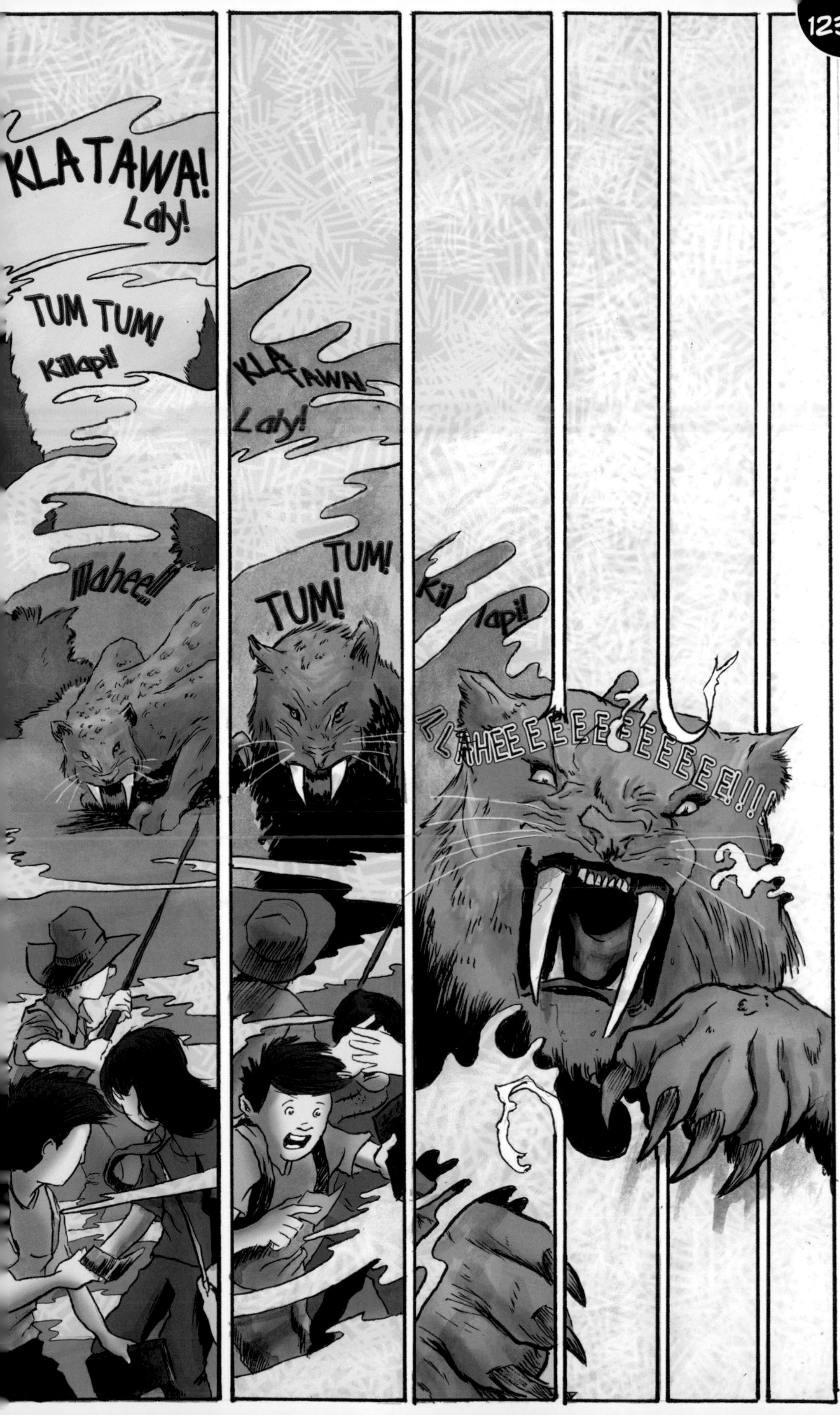
KLATAWA!
Lady!
TUM TUM!
Killapi!
Mahee!!
KLA TAWA!
Lady!
TUM! TUM!
Kil lapi!
MAHEEEEEEEEEEEEE!!!

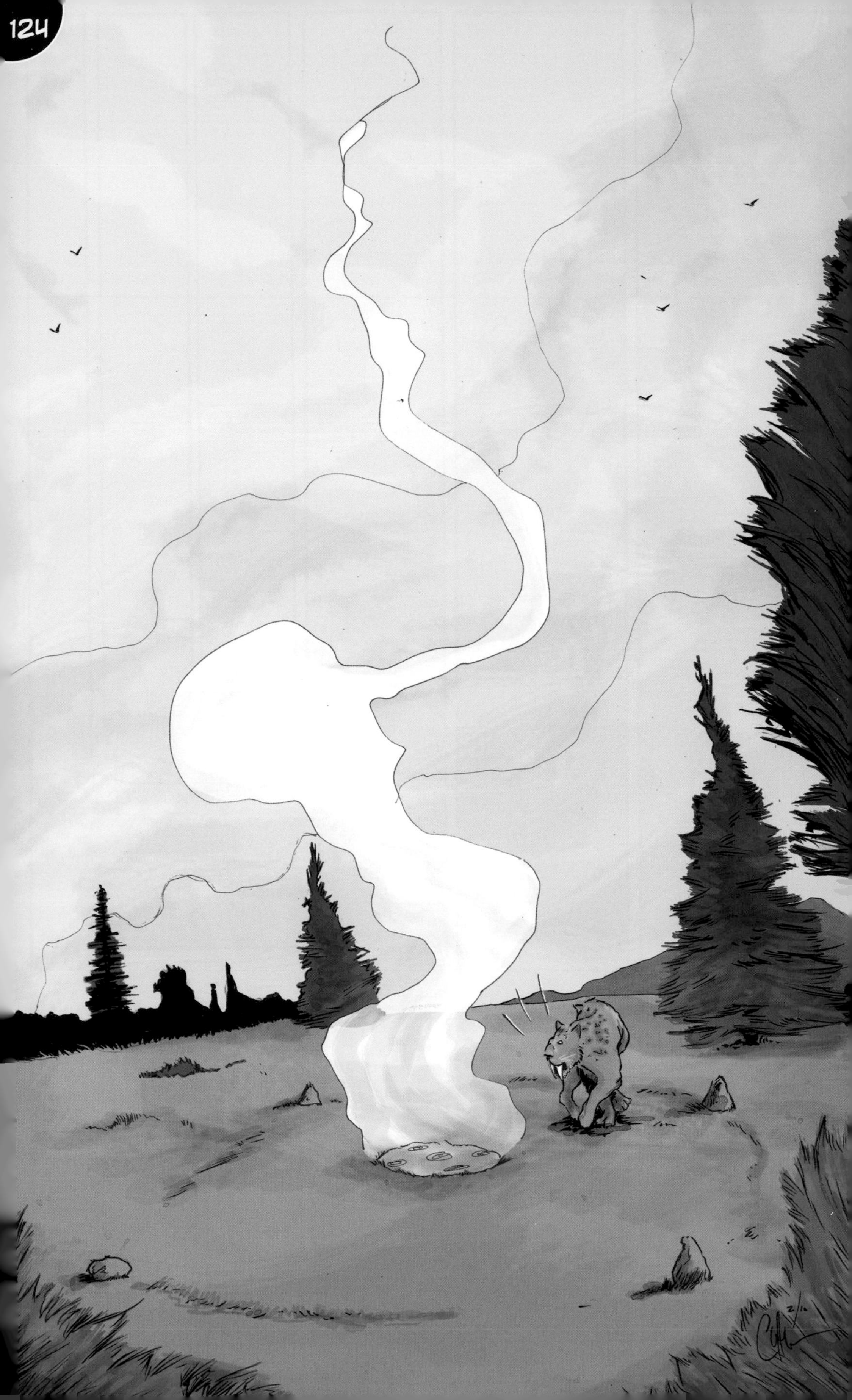

CHAPTER
EIGHT

PORT OF ORIGIN

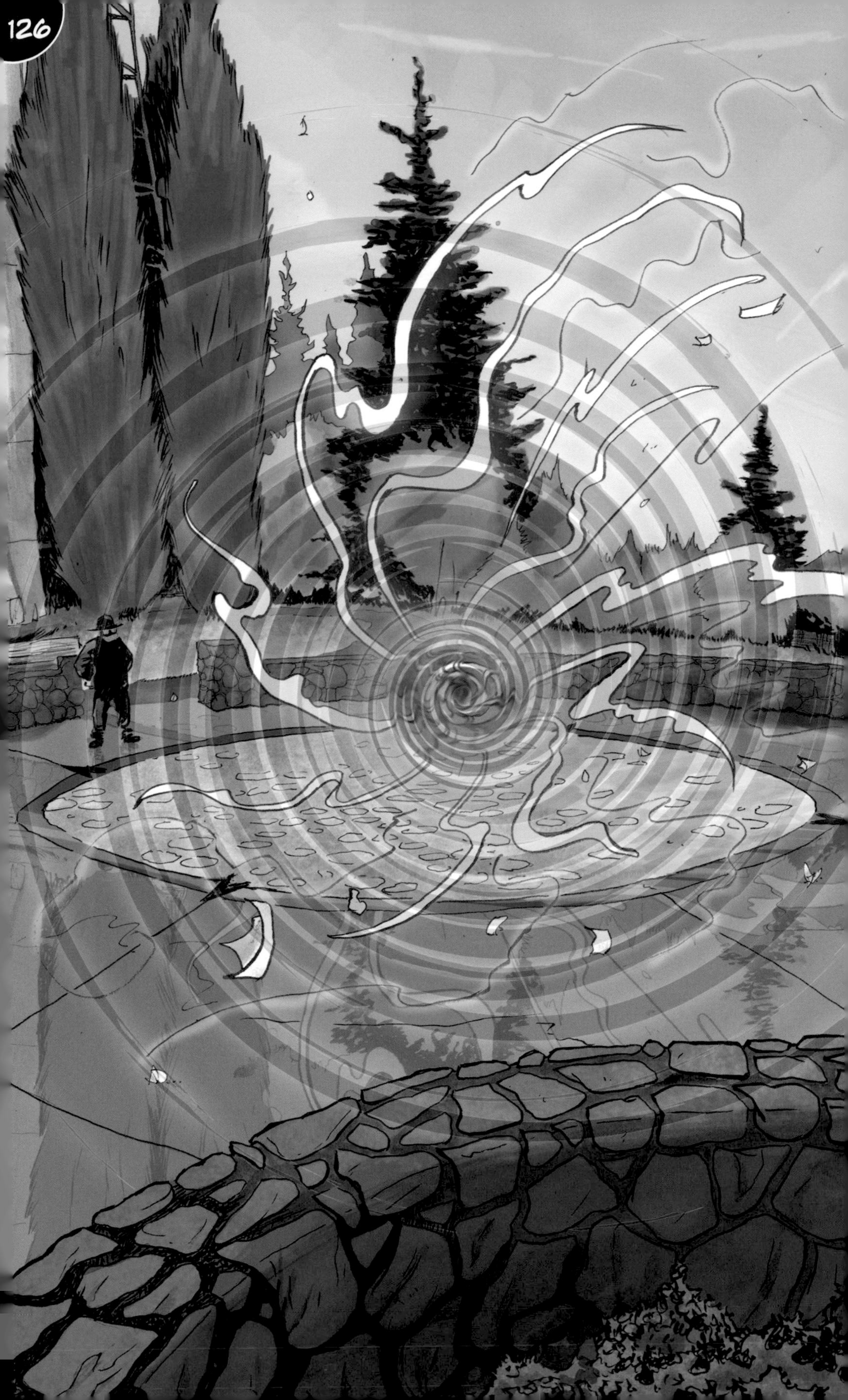

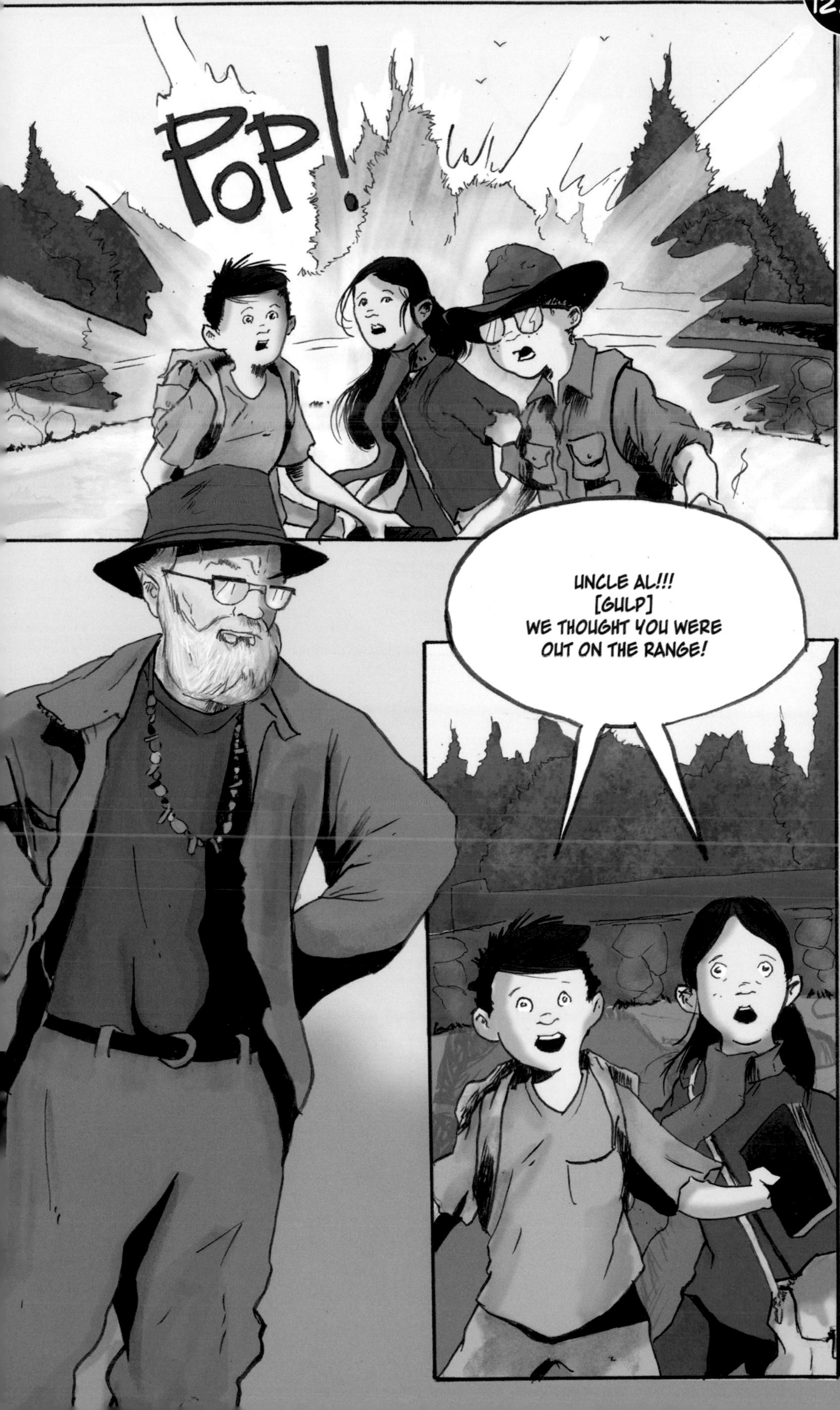
POP!
UNCLE AL!!! [GULP] WE THOUGHT YOU WERE OUT ON THE RANGE!

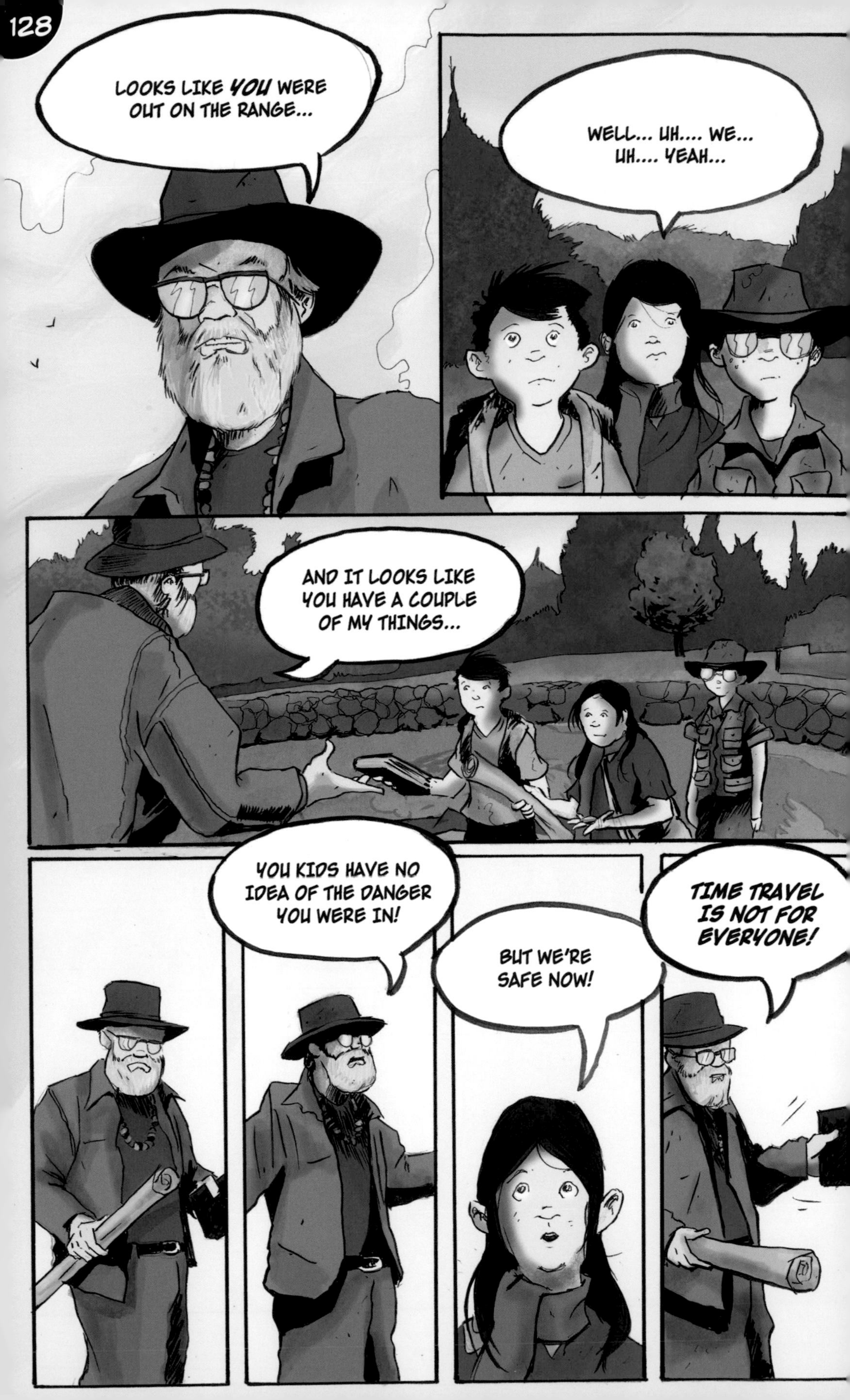
LOOKS LIKE *YOU* WERE OUT ON THE RANGE...
WELL... UH.... WE... UH.... YEAH...
AND IT LOOKS LIKE YOU HAVE A COUPLE OF MY THINGS...
YOU KIDS HAVE NO IDEA OF THE DANGER YOU WERE IN!
BUT WE'RE SAFE NOW!
TIME TRAVEL IS NOT FOR EVERYONE!

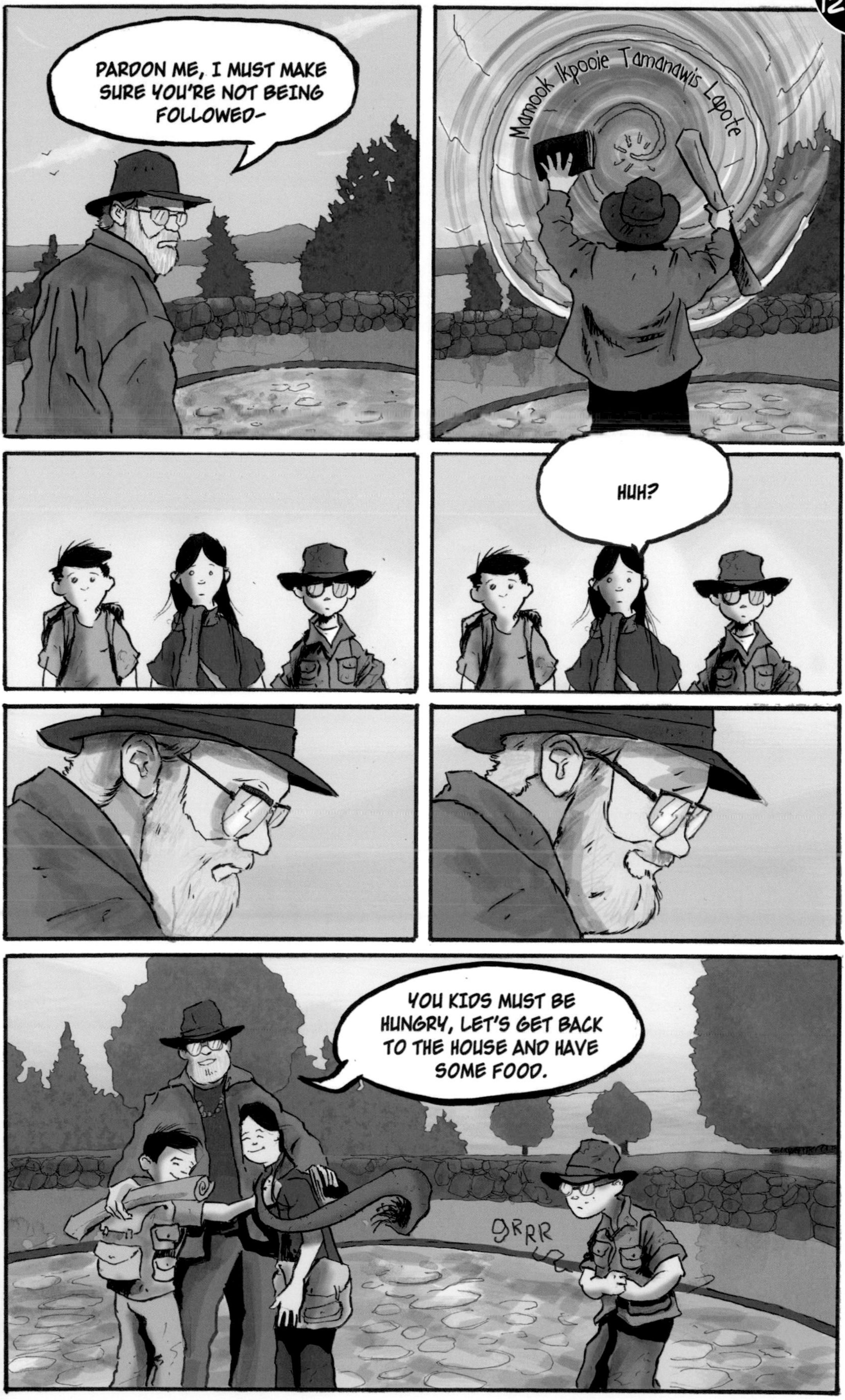
PARDON ME, I MUST MAKE SURE YOU'RE NOT BEING FOLLOWED-
Mamook Ikpooie Tamanawis Lapote
HUH?
YOU KIDS MUST BE HUNGRY, LET'S GET BACK TO THE HOUSE AND HAVE SOME FOOD.
gRRR

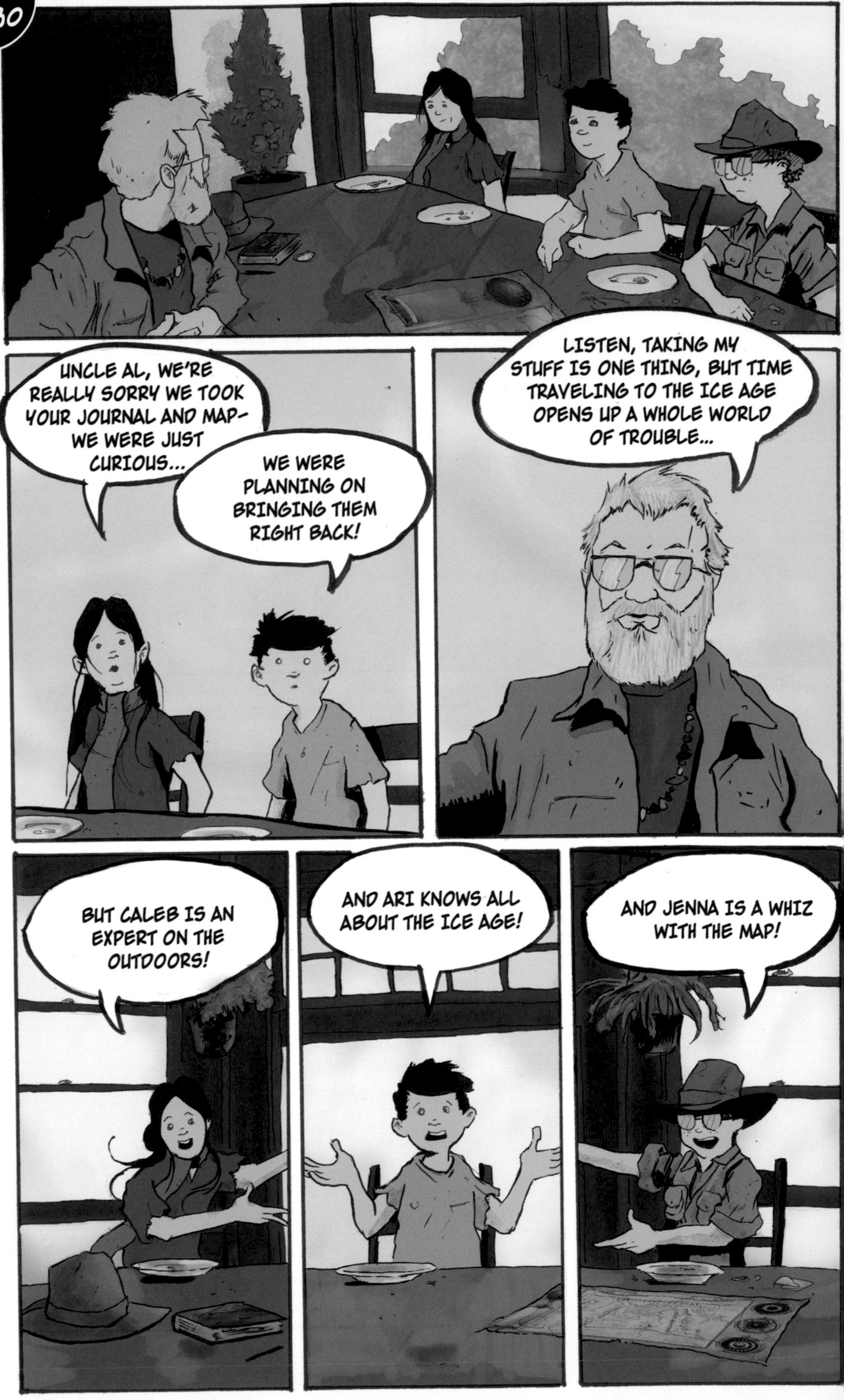
UNCLE AL, WE'RE REALLY SORRY WE TOOK YOUR JOURNAL AND MAP- WE WERE JUST CURIOUS...
WE WERE PLANNING ON BRINGING THEM RIGHT BACK!
LISTEN, TAKING MY STUFF IS ONE THING, BUT TIME TRAVELING TO THE ICE AGE OPENS UP A WHOLE WORLD OF TROUBLE...
BUT CALEB IS AN EXPERT ON THE OUTDOORS!
AND ARI KNOWS ALL ABOUT THE ICE AGE!
AND JENNA IS A WHIZ WITH THE MAP!

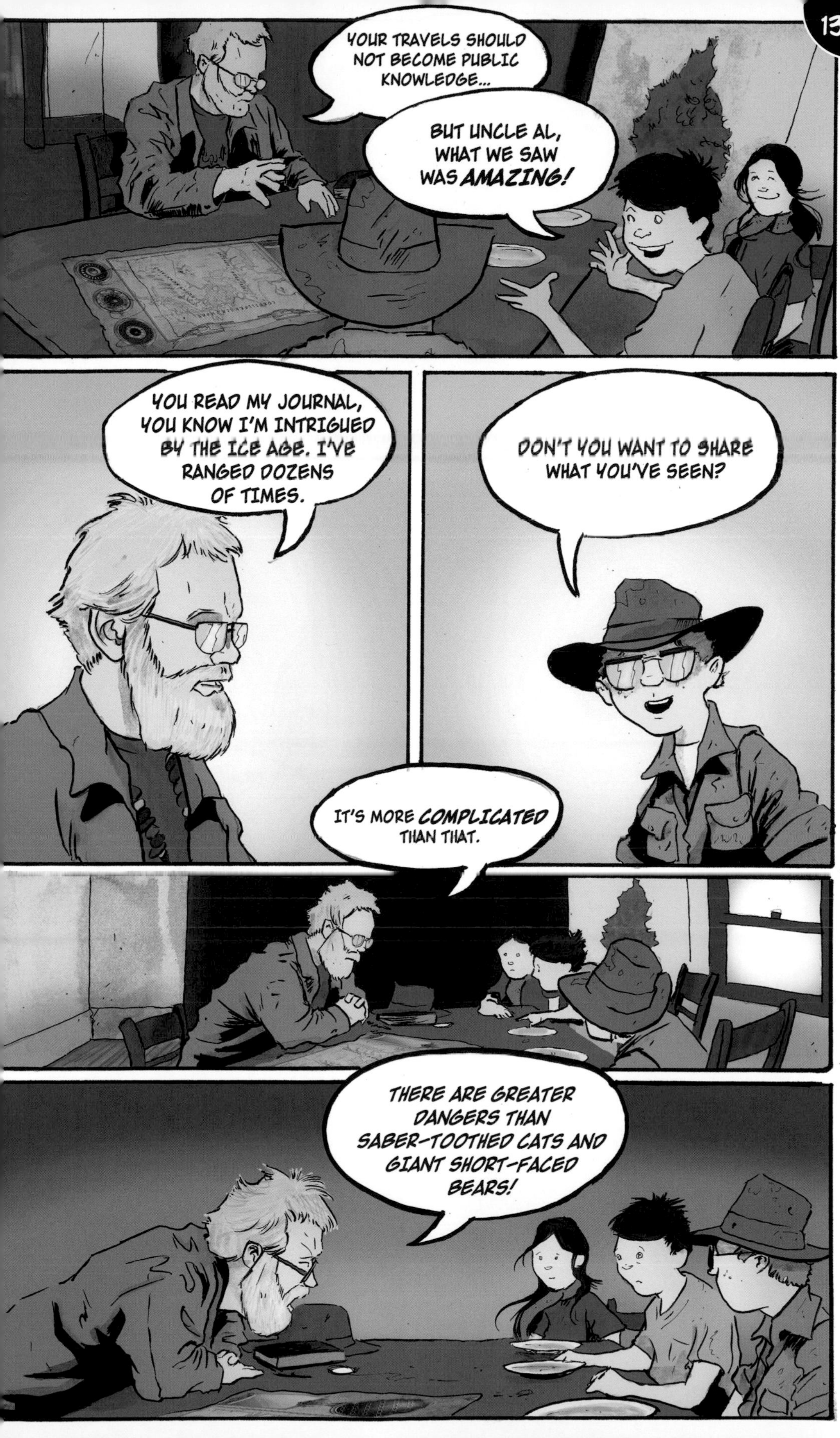
YOUR TRAVELS SHOULD NOT BECOME PUBLIC KNOWLEDGE...
BUT UNCLE AL, WHAT WE SAW WAS AMAZING!
YOU READ MY JOURNAL, YOU KNOW I'M INTRIGUED BY THE ICE AGE. I'VE RANGED DOZENS OF TIMES.
DON'T YOU WANT TO SHARE WHAT YOU'VE SEEN?
IT'S MORE COMPLICATED THAN THAT.
THERE ARE GREATER DANGERS THAN SABER-TOOTHED CATS AND GIANT SHORT-FACED BEARS!

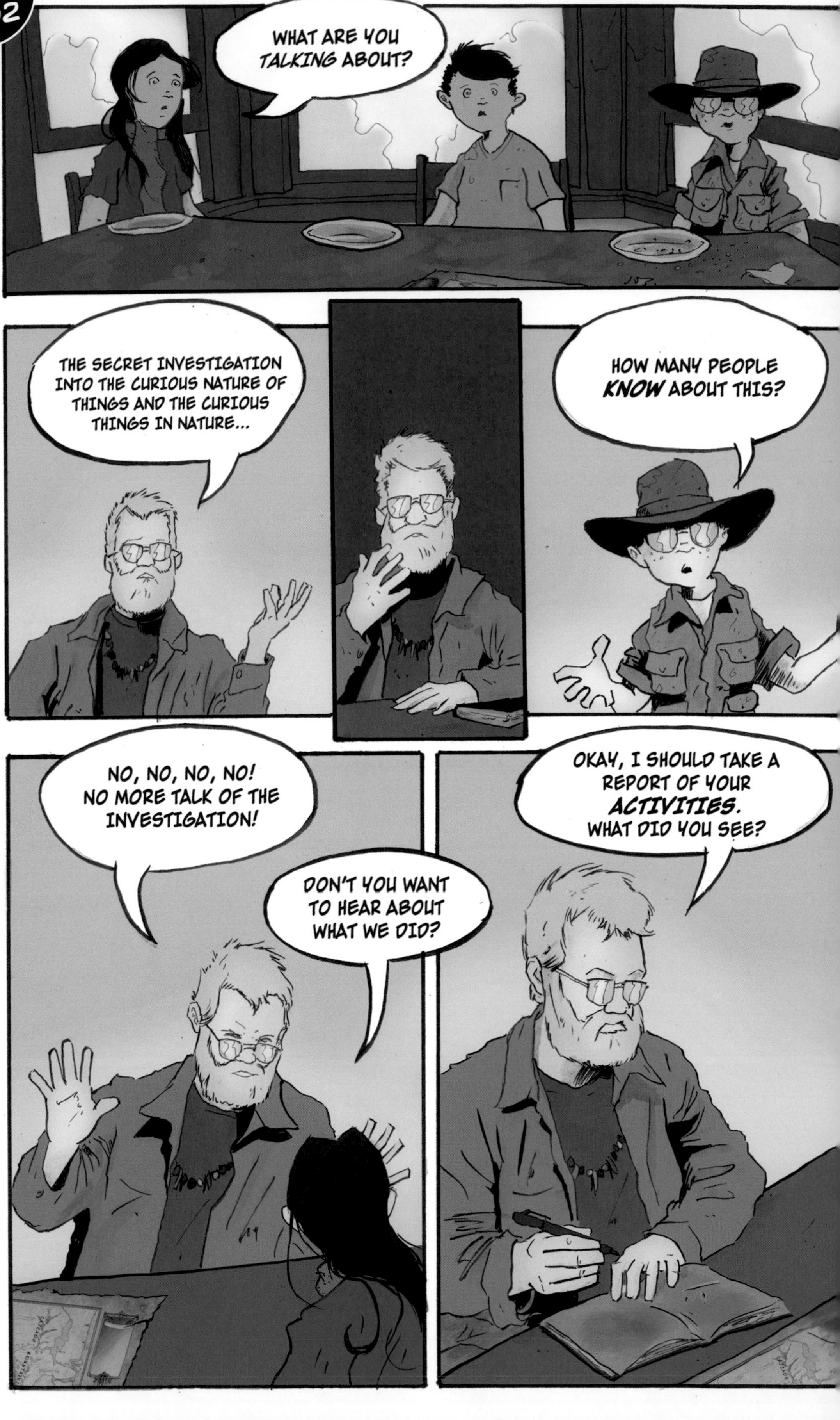
WHAT ARE YOU TALKING ABOUT?
THE SECRET INVESTIGATION INTO THE CURIOUS NATURE OF THINGS AND THE CURIOUS THINGS IN NATURE...
HOW MANY PEOPLE KNOW ABOUT THIS?
NO, NO, NO, NO! NO MORE TALK OF THE INVESTIGATION!
DON'T YOU WANT TO HEAR ABOUT WHAT WE DID?
OKAY, I SHOULD TAKE A REPORT OF YOUR ACTIVITIES. WHAT DID YOU SEE?

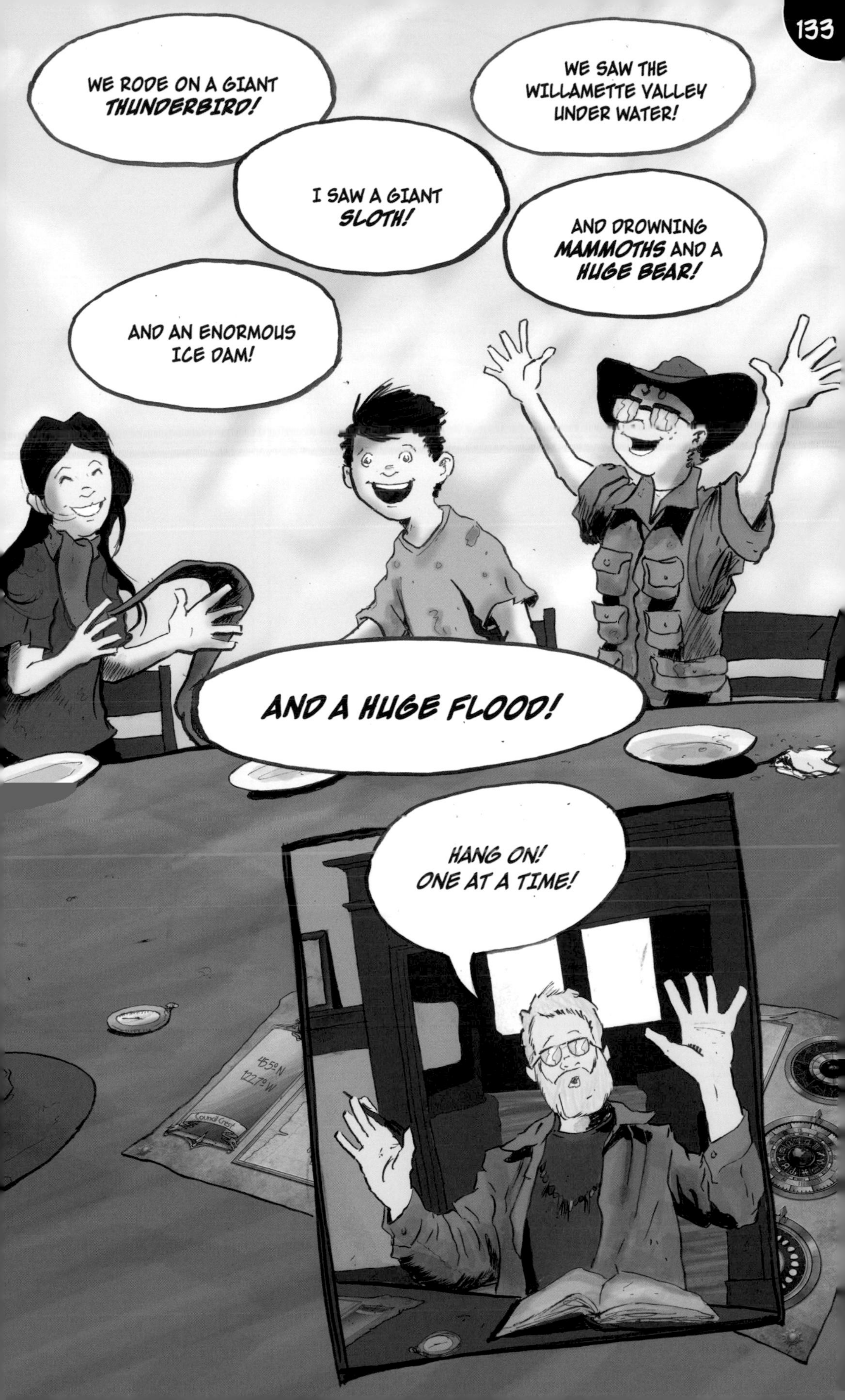
WE RODE ON A GIANT *THUNDERBIRD!*
WE SAW THE WILLAMETTE VALLEY UNDER WATER!
I SAW A GIANT *SLOTH!*
AND DROWNING *MAMMOTHS* AND A *HUGE BEAR!*
AND AN ENORMOUS ICE DAM!
AND A HUGE FLOOD!
HANG ON! ONE AT A TIME!
Council Crest

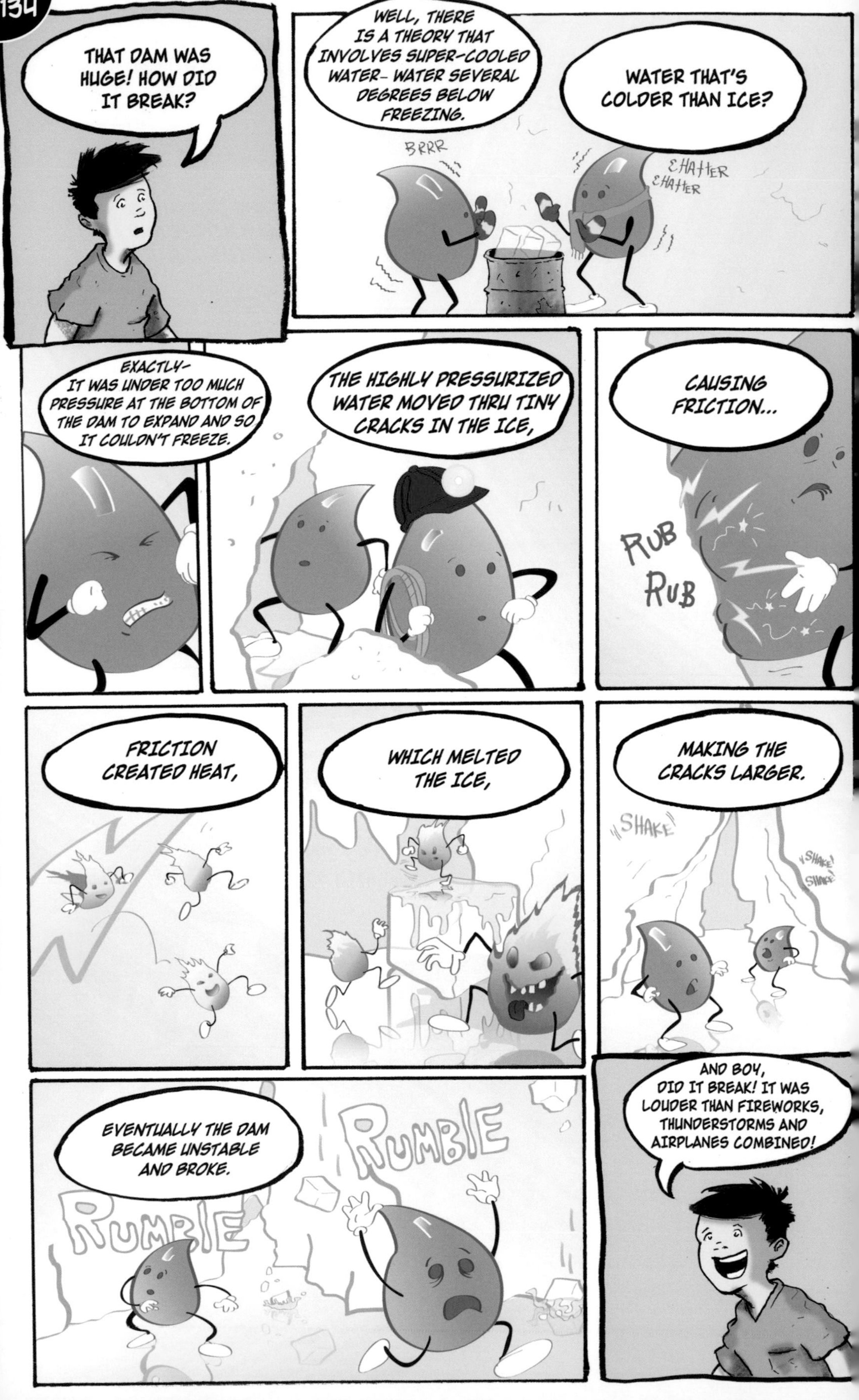
THAT DAM WAS HUGE! HOW DID IT BREAK?
WELL, THERE IS A THEORY THAT INVOLVES SUPER-COOLED WATER- WATER SEVERAL DEGREES BELOW FREEZING.
WATER THAT'S COLDER THAN ICE?
BRRR
CHATTER CHATTER
EXACTLY- IT WAS UNDER TOO MUCH PRESSURE AT THE BOTTOM OF THE DAM TO EXPAND AND SO IT COULDN'T FREEZE.
THE HIGHLY PRESSURIZED WATER MOVED THRU TINY CRACKS IN THE ICE,
CAUSING FRICTION...
RUB RUB
FRICTION CREATED HEAT,
WHICH MELTED THE ICE,
MAKING THE CRACKS LARGER.
SHAKE
SHAKE! SHAKE
EVENTUALLY THE DAM BECAME UNSTABLE AND BROKE.
RUMBLE
RUMBLE
AND BOY, DID IT BREAK! IT WAS LOUDER THAN FIREWORKS, THUNDERSTORMS AND AIRPLANES COMBINED!

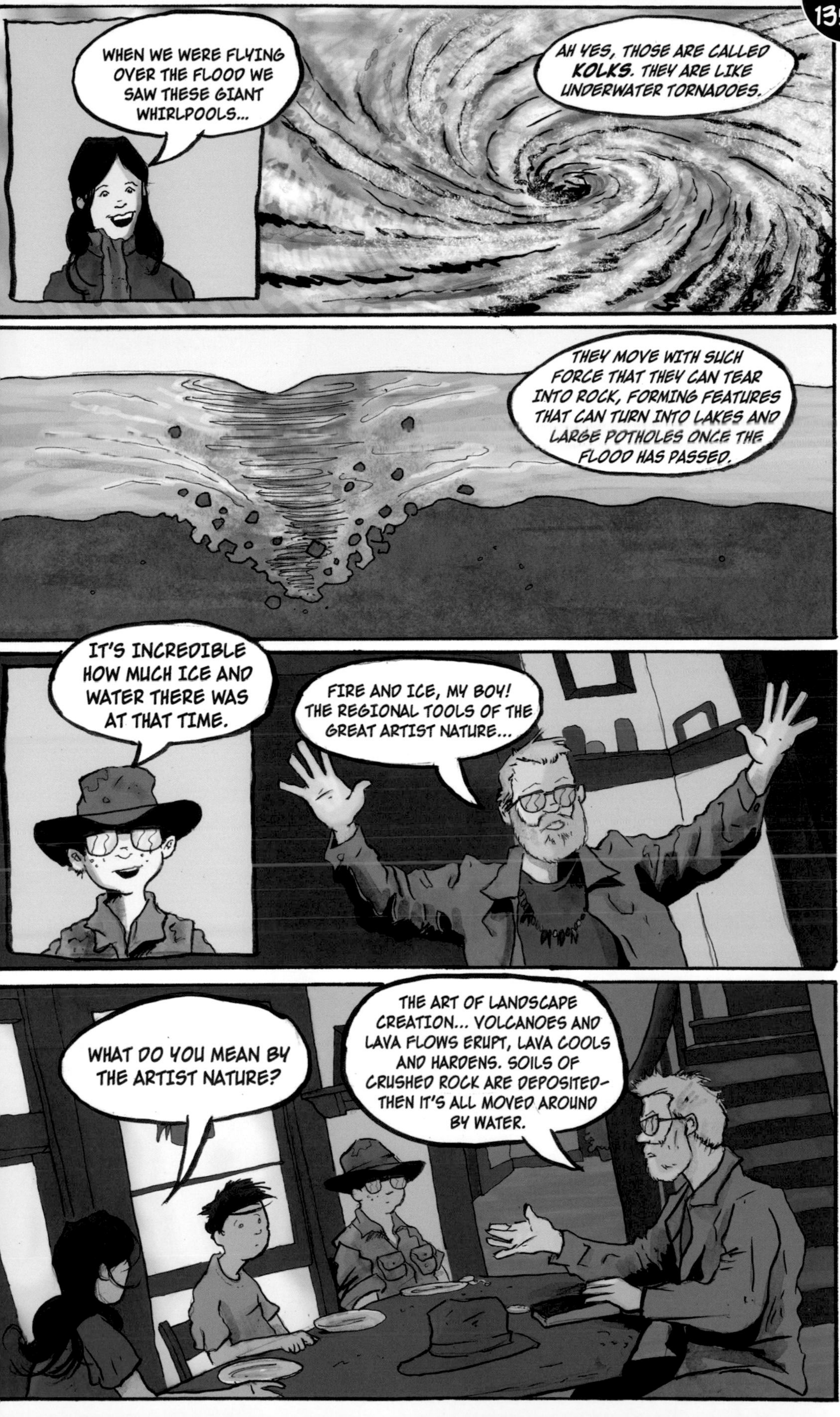
WHEN WE WERE FLYING OVER THE FLOOD WE SAW THESE GIANT WHIRLPOOLS...
AH YES, THOSE ARE CALLED **KOLKS**. THEY ARE LIKE UNDERWATER TORNADOES.
THEY MOVE WITH SUCH FORCE THAT THEY CAN TEAR INTO ROCK, FORMING FEATURES THAT CAN TURN INTO LAKES AND LARGE POTHOLES ONCE THE FLOOD HAS PASSED.
IT'S INCREDIBLE HOW MUCH ICE AND WATER THERE WAS AT THAT TIME.
FIRE AND ICE, MY BOY! THE REGIONAL TOOLS OF THE GREAT ARTIST NATURE...
WHAT DO YOU MEAN BY THE ARTIST NATURE?
THE ART OF LANDSCAPE CREATION... VOLCANOES AND LAVA FLOWS ERUPT, LAVA COOLS AND HARDENS. SOILS OF CRUSHED ROCK ARE DEPOSITED-THEN IT'S ALL MOVED AROUND BY WATER.

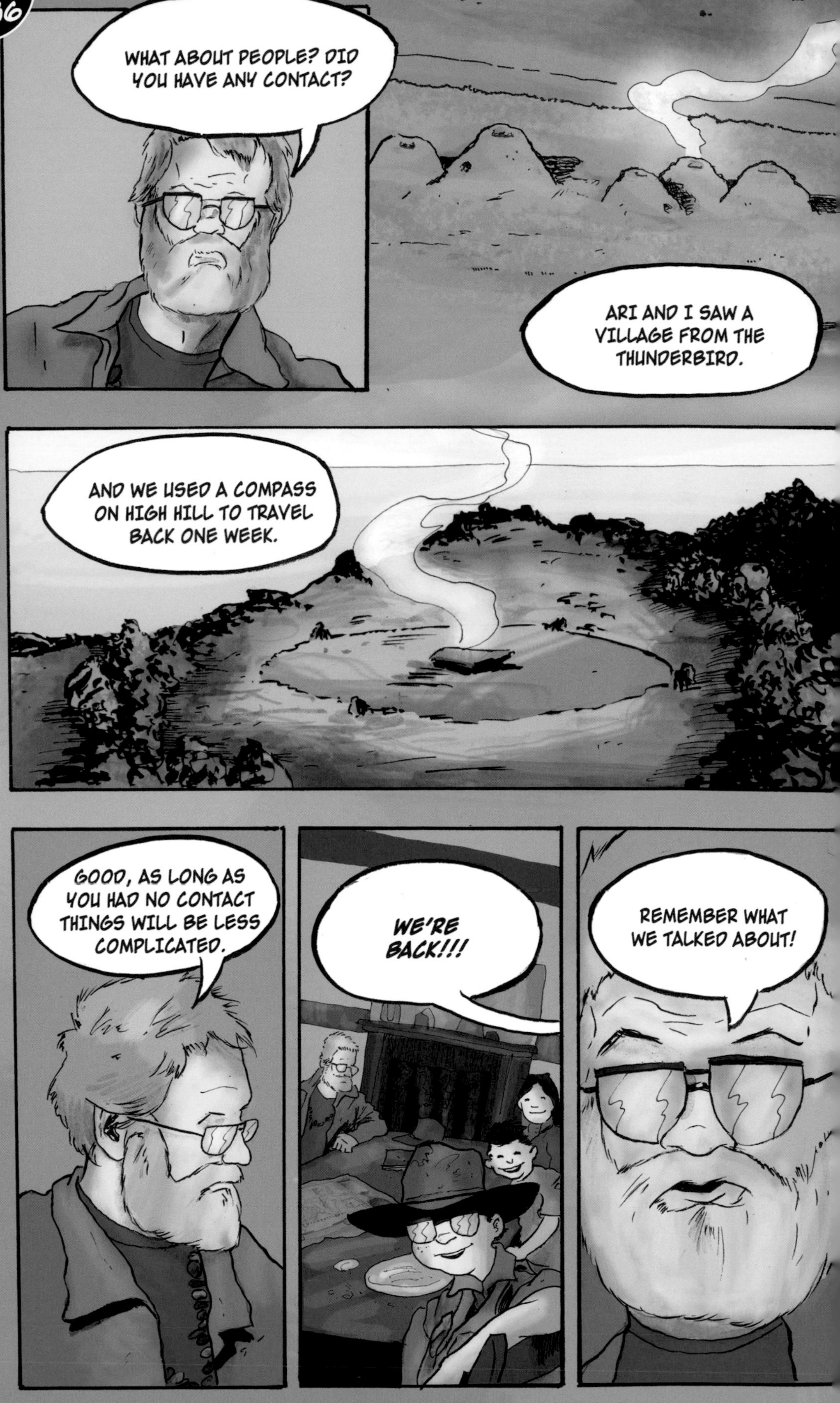
WHAT ABOUT PEOPLE? DID YOU HAVE ANY CONTACT?
ARI AND I SAW A VILLAGE FROM THE THUNDERBIRD.
AND WE USED A COMPASS ON HIGH HILL TO TRAVEL BACK ONE WEEK.
GOOD, AS LONG AS YOU HAD NO CONTACT THINGS WILL BE LESS COMPLICATED.
WE'RE BACK!!!
REMEMBER WHAT WE TALKED ABOUT!

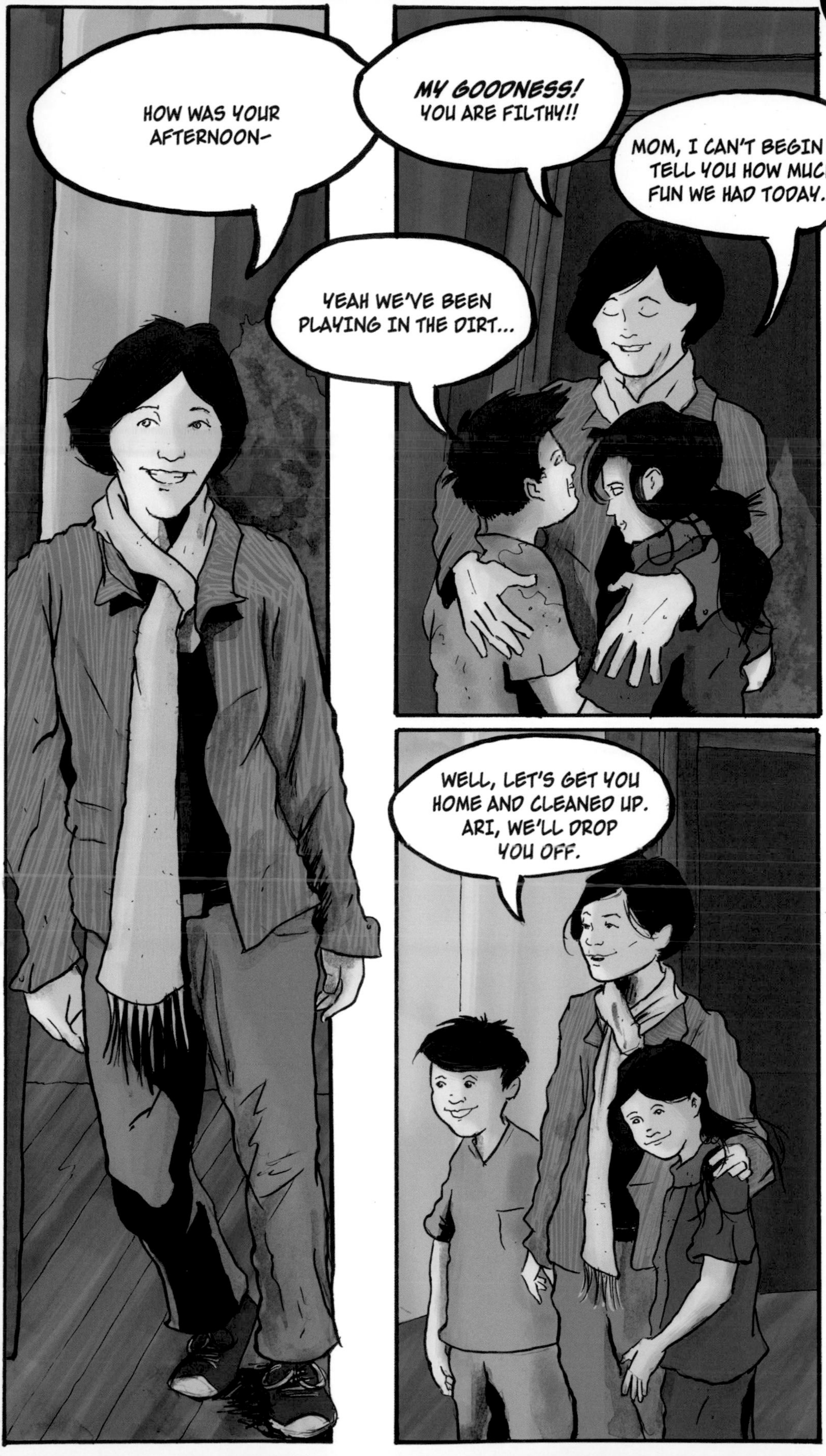
HOW WAS YOUR AFTERNOON-
MY GOODNESS! YOU ARE FILTHY!!
MOM, I CAN'T BEGIN TO TELL YOU HOW MUCH FUN WE HAD TODAY...
YEAH WE'VE BEEN PLAYING IN THE DIRT...
WELL, LET'S GET YOU HOME AND CLEANED UP. ARI, WE'LL DROP YOU OFF.

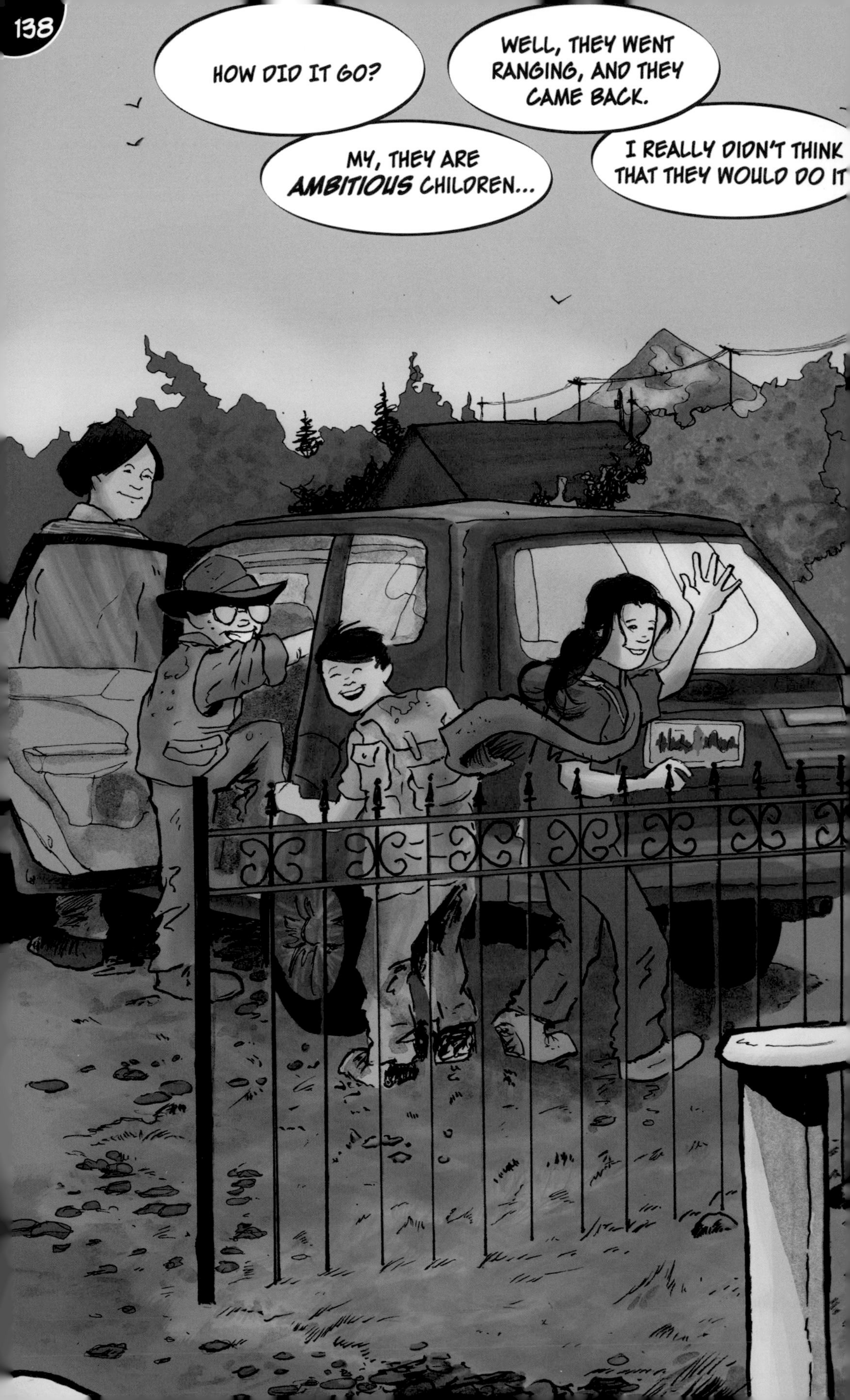
HOW DID IT GO?
WELL, THEY WENT RANGING, AND THEY CAME BACK.
MY, THEY ARE AMBITIOUS CHILDREN...
I REALLY DIDN'T THINK THAT THEY WOULD DO IT

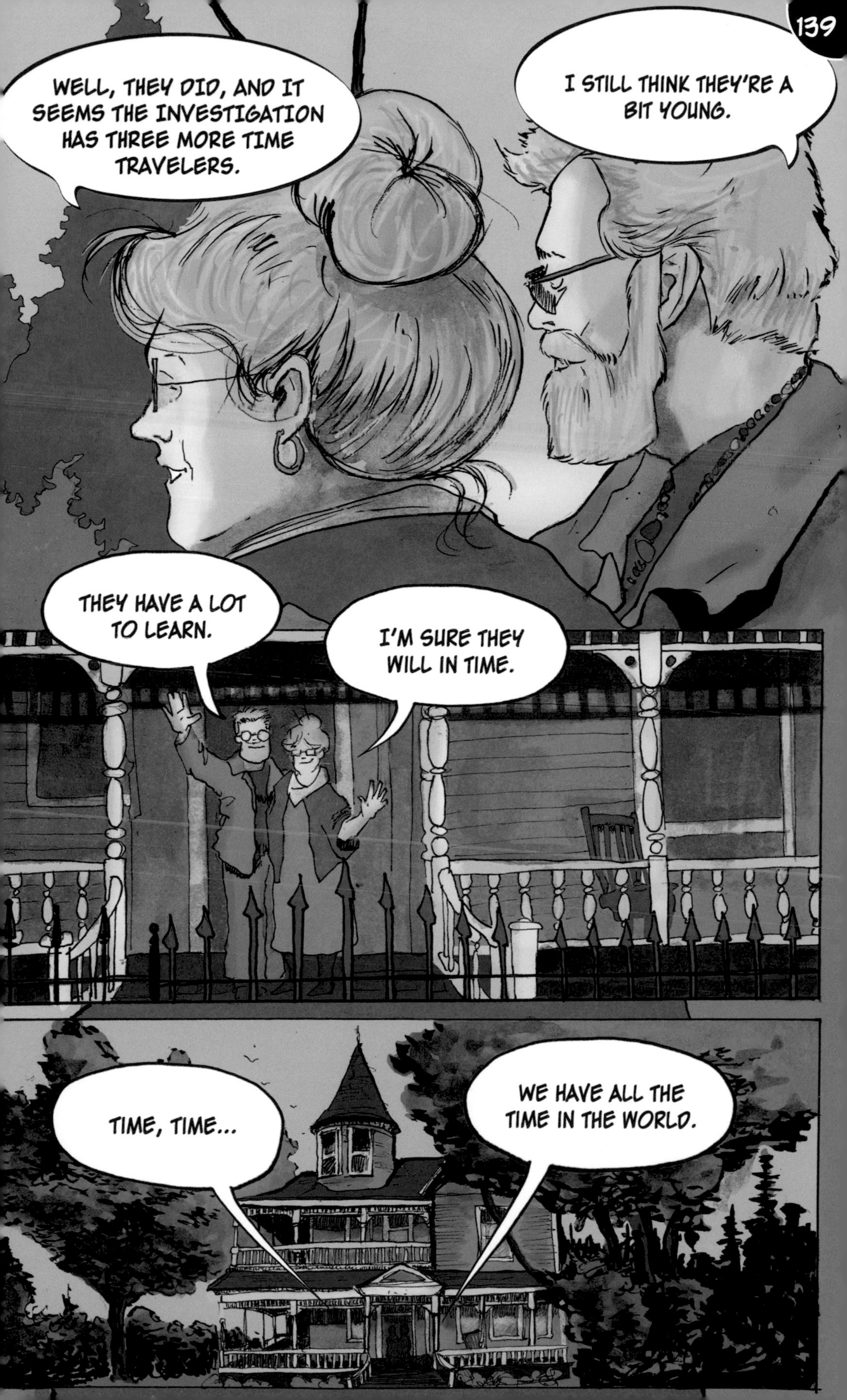
WELL, THEY DID, AND IT SEEMS THE INVESTIGATION HAS THREE MORE TIME TRAVELERS.
I STILL THINK THEY'RE A BIT YOUNG.
THEY HAVE A LOT TO LEARN.
I'M SURE THEY WILL IN TIME.
TIME, TIME...
WE HAVE ALL THE TIME IN THE WORLD.

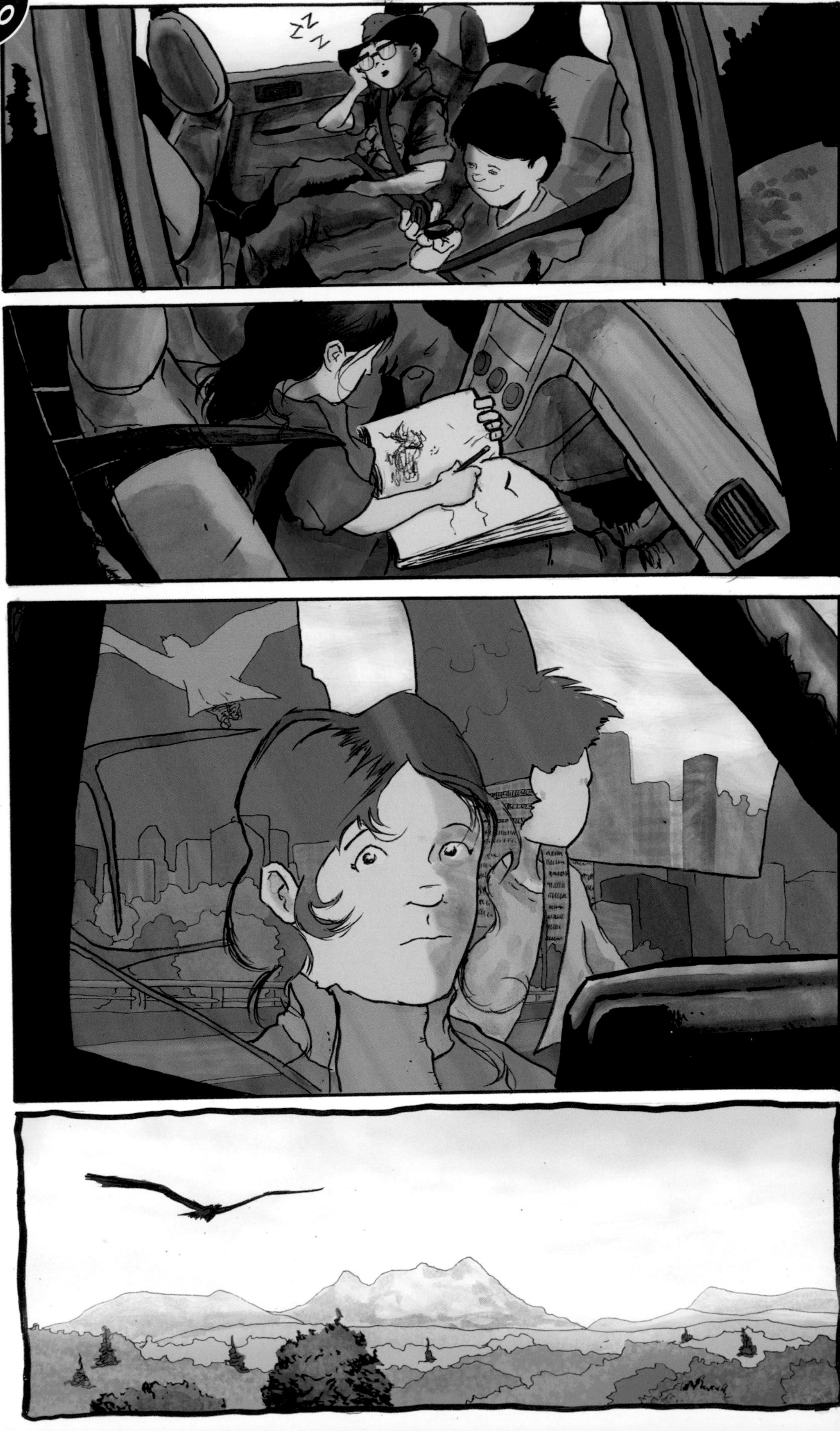
Z Z Z

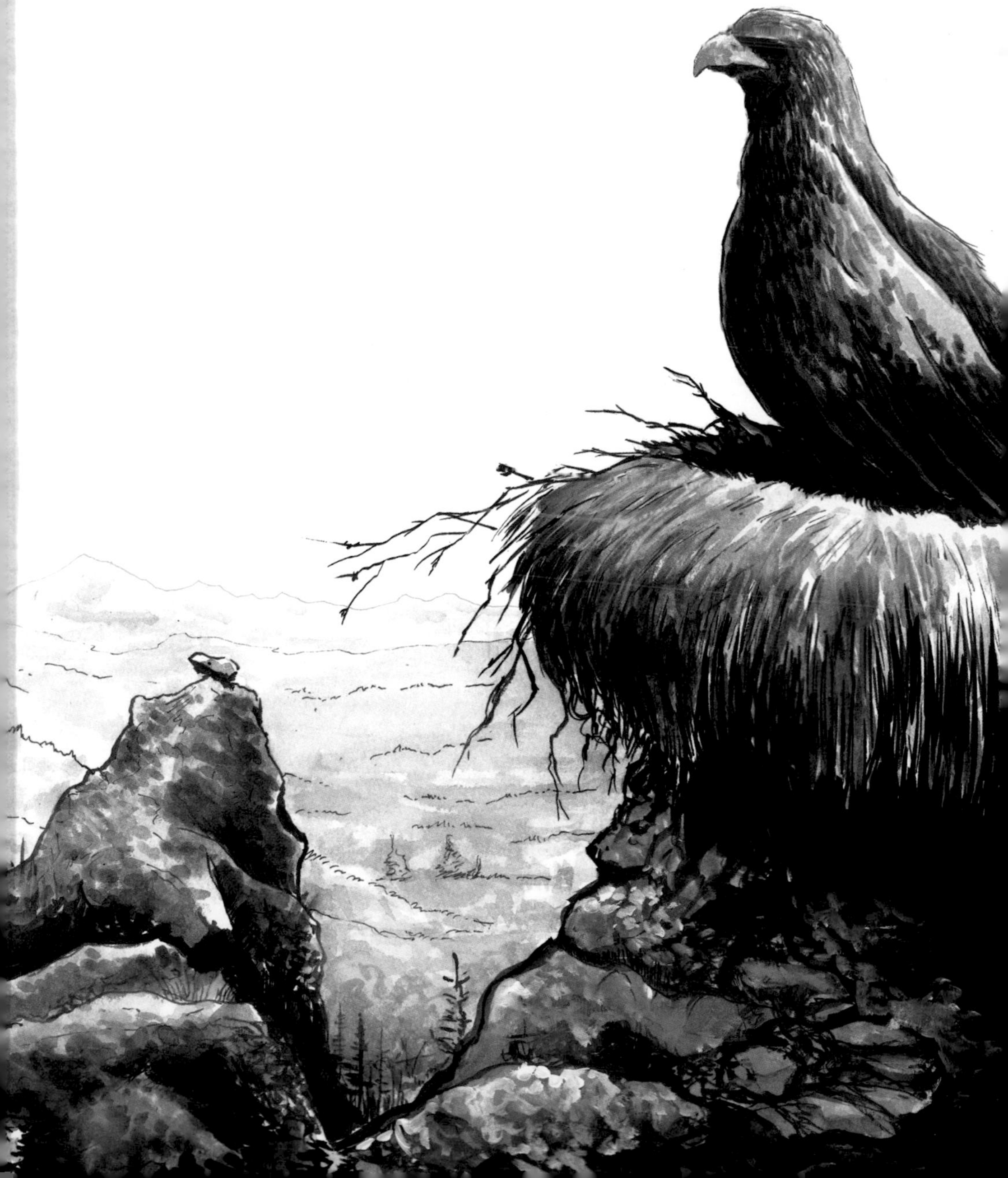

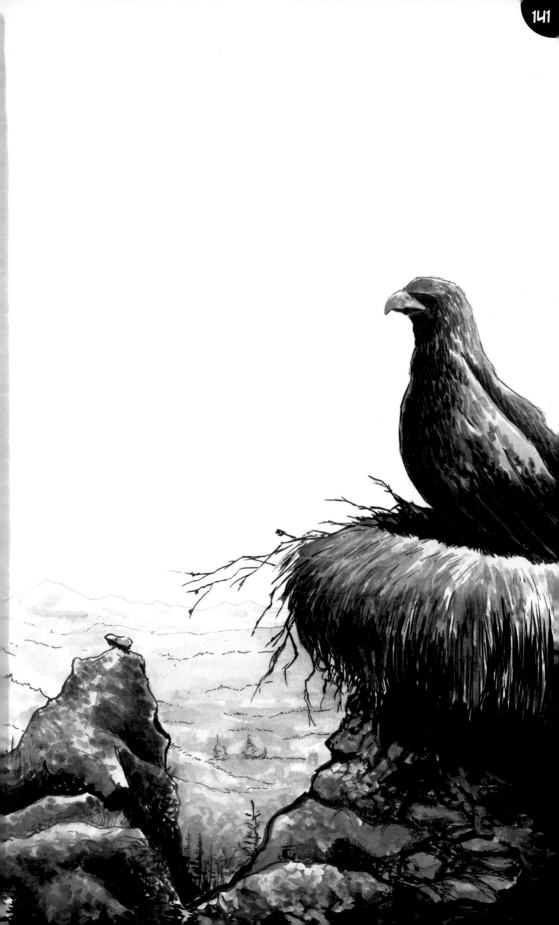